FAKING IT WITH THE SEALs

D. E. BARTLEY

VINCI
BOOKS

By D.E. Bartley

O'Reilly Fight Club

Four Stepbrothers & I
Four Daddies & I
Faking it with the SEALs
Three Stepbrothers Save Christmas
Four Fiancés and I

Vinci Books

vinci-books.com

Published by Vinci Books Ltd in 2025

1

Copyright © D.E. Bartley 2023

A CIP catalogue record for this book is available from the British Library.
Paperback ISBN: 9781036709679

Trigger Warnings

Please know there is help out there.
You and your mental health matter.

Past domestic abuse
Death of a loved one
PTSD
Military experiences

Chapter One

CALVIN

"Alright, traitor!"

I turn to see Terry and Layton walking towards me, smiling and laughing.

"Less of the traitor shit. Remember, I can still kick your ass, pipsqueak," I jest, flipping Layton off before shaking Terry's hand.

"He's just sour because he's got to escort Jaz to get her nails done, and he couldn't get an appointment himself," Terry laughs as Layton glares at him. "So, today's your last official day as a member of the team?" Terry asks, ignoring the rookie. I nod, smiling.

"Yep. I'm officially no longer working for the O'Reillys."

"How does it feel?" Layton asks.

"A little daunting, to be honest. It's been a good five years. They've looked after me as much as I've looked after them. Being my own boss will be strange, but I know it's the right time."

Terry claps me on the shoulder before gripping it.

"I'm proud of you. You struggled returning to civilian

life after leaving the SEALs, but you worked hard and achieved a lot in the time you were with us. I know you will make a great boss and achieve big things with your own business." He squeezes my shoulder one last time before removing his hand. "How are your mates handling the change?"

"Yeah, they've settled into English life as well as can be expected. Everything's been snowballing, and it feels like we haven't stopped," I laugh, rubbing the back of my neck. I check my watch and curse. "I gotta go. Christian wants to see me before I leave."

I shake hands with Terry and Layton as they wish me good luck, and I head towards the main office, where I know Christian O'Reilly's waiting for me.

Seven years ago, I was injured in the line of duty and medically discharged from the SEALs. I moved to the UK with only the clothes and belongings I could fit into a suitcase and holdall. Did I know what I was going to do when I got here? No. I only knew I would stay with an old friend I met when serving. Terry helped me get back on my feet and adapt to life outside the SEALs. He knew I wanted a new way of life and helped me find it here.

Terry got me a job working as security in one of the O'Reilly clubs. He helped me gain my security license, as well as many other work-related courses. He gave me everything I needed, and I will be forever grateful. I wanted a fresh start, and I got it, but I always felt like I was destined for more. I pushed myself to prove my worth, and after defusing a dangerous situation in a club, which involved me nearly taking a bullet for Jason O'Reilly, he promoted me to be his personal guard.

It was a step up from bouncing and a role that often tested

my loyalty to the O'Reillys. But I'm proud of what I've achieved in the five years I've been guarding Jason, and I've kept him alive and relatively unharmed. I don't take any blame for the facial injury he received five months ago. He went off without telling me. It's his own stupid fault. He took a knife to the face and has a scar down the left side. The idiot learnt his lesson and now doesn't go anywhere without backup.

Now the duty of protecting his stubborn ass falls on to the guy I've spent the last two months training. It will take a little time to get used to not seeing him daily, but I've already promised to pop in now and again for a drink. Let's face it: why would I give up the chance to taste the fantastic yet highly priced bourbons these guys drink?

I stop outside Christian's office and knock three times. I hear him talking to someone inside before calling for me to enter.

Inside, I see two O'Reilly brothers and Jasmine, their fiancée. All four brothers are in a reverse harem with Jasmine Connors, who they met when their father married her mother six years ago. Even though they've only been in the poly relationship for approximately eight months, there's no mistaking the soul-bound connection between them all. There's nothing they wouldn't do for each other, which they've shown time and time again.

"Hey, Cal! How does it feel to be a free man?" Jasmine asks, grinning at me from Jason's lap. Jason and Christian laugh as I smile at her.

"You have no idea. At least I don't have to take you to the hairdresser or clothes shopping anymore."

"Hey! You only took me once!" she protests, pouting.

"I was talking to Jason."

Christian and Jasmine both roar, laughing as Jason flips

me off. Jasmine climbs to her feet, still laughing and kisses Jason.

"He's not wrong; you do shop a lot," she teases. Jason threads his fingers into the hair at the back of her head and holds her in place.

"But who do I shop for the most, angel?" he asks, looking deep into her eyes as she grins.

"Me, and I thank you for it in my own way," she teases, kissing him again before standing up and walking away. She stops in front of Christian, who wraps an arm around her waist and kisses her hard on the mouth.

"Be good and try not to get into trouble whilst you are out," he smiles as Jasmine steps out of his arms.

"I'll be on my best behaviour, I promise," she smirks at him as he arches one brow at her. We all know she could get into trouble in her sleep.

Jasmine takes me by surprise by throwing her arms around my neck and giving a big hug. I chuckle as I hug her back.

"Keep safe, and don't be a stranger."

I give her one last squeeze before kissing her cheek and taking a step back.

"I wouldn't dare. I have a very important wedding to attend in six months," I reply with a wink. She pats me on the chest before walking towards the door, no doubt to find Layton, her personal guard.

"See you all later," she calls, leaving the office. I turn back to catch the O'Reillys watching the door, even after it's closed firmly in place. They worry about her every time she leaves their sight, which isn't surprising after all she has been through.

"So that's it? You're done protecting my ass?"

I look to Jason and smile whilst Christian pulls a seat

around for me. I thank him before sitting down as he walks over to the bar.

"Yeah, I guess so. You've got Gordon now; he will do you well."

"If he doesn't, I will hunt you down," he smirks as he takes a glass from Christian, who also passes me one with a measure of bourbon in it. I thank him before taking a sip.

"So, you all set to focus purely on your company?" Christian asks as he sits beside his brother.

"I think so. We have a large workforce, and our client list is growing daily. We also have two big events lined up where we are providing security. It's all looking good," I explain as I take another sip of the liquor, the flavour exploding on my tongue. The O'Reillys really do have the best taste in drinks.

"I have put the word out about you guys and given you glowing references," Jason says, leaning back and placing his ankle on his opposite knee. "If you need anything else, don't hesitate to ask. We are happy to help where we can."

"Thank you. I appreciate that." I don't know why I'm shocked. The O'Reillys are fair employers; if you show them the respect they deserve, they give it back tenfold.

"I would like to give you a little advice if you will hear me out," Christian says as he leans his elbows on his knees.

"I'll take any advice you have." I mean it because what this man doesn't know about business isn't worth knowing.

Christian sits back next to his brother and takes a sip of his drink.

"You need to start networking. I know you already have when you worked a few of our events and fights, but you need to do more. I will put your name down as a guest at a few charity and social events. Use them to get in people's faces and make them want your company. But don't take your mates to these events; take a date. It will look better, and people won't assume you are only there to talk business. If they think that, they will avoid you."

"You got anyone you can take?" Jason asks, and I quickly shake my head. "Thought as much, you haven't done anything but work for the last five years. Have you ever taken a holiday?"

I shrug whilst chuckling.

"What can I say? Keeping your ass alive was a full-time job."

"Well, that's another thing. You want to show people you are serious about your work, but they need to see that you are also human. Don't work as security unless you have no other choice. The three of you must prove that you can manage the company, not work it. Always have people on standby, so you are covered if you need them for an event."

That shouldn't be too hard. So far, we have about twenty-two people, all trained and situated in various locations and roles. We also have fourteen more down to be called in when needed. After seeing how well it worked for this team, I thought ahead with that one.

"The most important thing is to enjoy your work. If you don't enjoy it, there is no point as you won't put your heart and soul into it like you otherwise would."

That's no problem either, as I have always loved protecting others. It's why I joined the SEALs and would still be enrolled if the accident hadn't happened. That's why when Terry said he knew of a security position that would be perfect for me, I jumped on the next plane out of the States and haven't looked back since.

"Whatever happens, if you need a job, you know we are just a phone call away. There are no hard feelings about you leaving; we are all sorry to see you go. Not just Jason, but all of us."

I look to Christian and smile whilst nodding.

"I'm sorry to be leaving if I'm honest. But this will be good for me and the guys. It's been a long time in the making, but I know it will be worth it."

I down the rest of my drink and place my empty glass on the table. The three of us stand up together, and the O'Reillys walk around the coffee table to stand in front of me. Christian takes my hand and grasps it between his own.

"Thank you for everything; you will be missed."

"Thanks, Christian. I wouldn't be where I am now if you hadn't trusted Terry and given me a chance."

He nods once before letting go of my hand, and I turn to Jason. He takes my hand and pulls me into a hug.

"Thanks for everything, brother. You have saved my ass more times than I care to admit, and I will never forget it."

"Your ass was worth saving," I reply, slapping him on the back before stepping back. "Anyway, like I said to Jaz, I will see you all at the wedding and no doubt before," I add with a smile. The two guys look at each other, and I can see how much they are looking forward to making Jasmine an O'Reilly. Even though it's only Christian who is marrying her legally, the five of them are having their relationship blessed afterwards.

I step back from the two brothers and give them one last nod before leaving the office and heading off to my next big adventure.

Chapter Two

"Oh, come on, Chels, surely even you are sick of sitting in your pyjamas every weekend now?"

I look at my friend Penny and smile.

"I'm perfectly happy to spend my free time in my PJs and slippers, thank you very much. Why would I do anything else when I can get cosy on the sofa with Luna and relax?" I ask as we reach our cars in the work car park. I open the back door and throw my bag onto the footwell before opening the driver side door and grabbing the scrunchie from between the seats.

"I don't know, maybe because you are forty-two and haven't had a date in years! *Years*, Chels!" she throws her hands up dramatically to emphasise the fact. I roll my eyes whilst pulling my blonde hair into a high ponytail, glad to finally get it off my neck.

"I tried dating, even got married; look how that ended," I point out with an arched brow.

"Not all men are like that nut job!"

"I don't want another man in my life, Penny. I have

8

Luna, that's all I need." I turn to look at my friend, who is leaning on the roof of her car and looking over at me. I know she means well, but I can't date.

"I'm not going to argue with you; I get it, I do. But you have every right to enjoy your life and don't give me that crap that you are, because I know you're lying. A part of you is lonely, and you know it." Penny climbs into her car as her passenger window opens, and she leans towards it from the driver's seat.

"I will see you Monday, and we'll make plans for next weekend. Luna can have a sleepover at mine with Ayva watching them. No arguing." Before I can say anything else, she backs out of her parking space and yells. "I'll call you tomorrow!" before driving out of sight as I wave.

I laugh to myself as I climb into my car and connect my phone to the console. I quickly check my surroundings, back out of my parking spot and start the short journey to my daughter's school.

I know Penny means well, but I've worked hard and endured a lot to be as at peace as I am now. I don't want to risk anything changing that. So what if I wish now and again I could come home to someone else having done the housework or cooked dinner? That doesn't mean I'm lonely; I'm just a little sick of doing everything myself.

I pull up outside Luna's school and let out a deep sigh. I hate it when people assume I need a man in my life just because of my age. I worked hard to get us where we are today. I will never put myself in a position where I have to answer to anyone but myself again. No one, and I mean *no one*, means as much to me as my little girl. She is my everything, and there's nothing I'm not willing to do to keep her happy and safe, even if that means accepting that it's just me, myself and I.

Who am I trying to kid? Of course, there are nights I find myself sitting on the sofa with nothing but a blanket to comfort me, wishing someone would hug me. Maybe now and again, it would be nice to have an adult conversation in the evening or someone to hold me when nightmares plague me. I certainly wouldn't say no to the occasional meal out, but the fear of history repeating itself is enough to stop me from ever dating again.

I sigh as I climb out of my car and head up the path towards where I need to collect Luna from the after school club. Maybe one day, a knight in shining armour will sweep in and rescue me from this lonely life and make me his everything. I stop myself from laughing out loud at the sheer thought of it.

Knight in shining armour? Please, knowing my luck, I'd get a twat in tin foil with a toy horse's head on a stick.

No, I'm better off on my own. I know that everything else would be a fantasy, and I know it will never happen. Dreams don't come true for single mums in their forties; they don't for this one, anyway.

Chapter Three

DREW

I look around the bar, and it all still seems so unreal.

If you had asked me three years ago where I saw myself now, I would have said in the SEALs, fighting for my country and doing all I could for the America I love. I never thought I would move to England to start my own security company because I was medically discharged from the only job I have ever known.

All my life, I knew I wanted to join the SEALs, and nothing was going to get in my way. From the age of fifteen, I worked out every day to make sure my body was in peak condition. I studied my ass off to ensure I got the grades and constantly checked in with recruitment to see if I was on the right track.

The day of my passing out parade was the proudest moment of my life. I had sacrificed everything to get to where I was, and it was worth every single drop of tears, blood and sweat that went into it. Even my old man was proud of me that day, and that's saying something as he has had no problem telling me I was wasting my time and would never make it; I soon proved him wrong.

"Earth to Bambi, you in there, buddy?"

"What?" I turn to see my friend and fellow ex-SEAL Logan standing beside me. He pushes a bottle of beer towards me, which I pick up and take a swig of as he sits on the other side of the table. At least it's not the warm piss they serve in other bars.

"You were a million miles away then. Everything okay?" he asks before taking a sip of his drink. I nod, looking down at the bottle in my hand.

"Just thinking how this still feels so unreal. We have been in the country for five months, and I still expect to wake up back home." I turn to look at Logan and find him looking at me. "Do you know what I mean?"

Logan nods as he takes another sip of his beer.

"Yeah, I do. This is the last place I ever thought I would be at thirty-nine. But here we are, and we might as well get used to it. England's been good to Cal; otherwise, he wouldn't have suggested us joining him. We need to trust the process, or whatever they say these days."

I know he's right, and I'm sure everything will click into place. We've worked hard for what we've accomplished so far. It wasn't easy, mainly when we still lived in the States, but we made it work. We conducted interviews via apps like Zoom when we couldn't come over and do them in person. It's been tough, but now everything has finally fallen into place.

"Hey, there you are. I was starting to think you weren't turning up," Logan calls next to me.

I look up to see Calvin walking into view, his hands shoved in his trouser pockets and a grin on his face.

"Yeah, sorry. I got held up talking to the O'Reillys,"

Calvin explains as he sits at the table and takes the beer bottle Logan pushes towards him.

"How did your last day go?" I ask. I know he's been apprehensive about today. As excited as he is to run our company full-time, he has enjoyed working with his old team and will leave some good friends behind.

"It was good, they were all giving me the typical shit, so I know there's no hard feelings about me leaving. But as much as I'm going to miss them, I'm looking forward to being able to concentrate on our growing team. I certainly won't miss working two jobs. I'm past exhausted." He looks at the two of us and smiles. "So this is it. No going back now. I can now concentrate purely on expanding our company." He holds his beer out, and we both tap ours against it.

"Cheers, guys. Let the fun times roll," Logan chimes in next to me before grabbing the menu. "But first food, I'm starving."

———————

"So, who's this guy you're meeting with tomorrow?" I ask Calvin as I sit back in the booth and stretch out a little after our meal. I'll give the English one thing: they can cook some fantastic grub.

"His name is Geralt Young; I met him through the O'Reillys. He recently had to change all his security after a trusted friend was anything but. Taylor had supplied all of Young's security, and when he showed his true colours, Young fired them all. But that left him open to attack, which means he's been hiring off other people. He needs some of his own guys, and I dropped a hint or two, as did Jason when he saw him."

"What's he into? Everything legit?" I ask, picking up my bottle of beer and finishing it.

"Mostly. He has a side hustle with illegal fighters and some legit ones. Other than that, it's all real estate and land ownership. He's just made his money's worth, and there are always vultures ready to take what they can." Calvin finishes his beer and places it on the table before running his fingers through his hair.

"What time are you going? Want either of us with you?" Logan asks from his seat. Calvin looks at him and nods.

"I've got to be there for ten. I was thinking you could come with me," he turns his attention to me, and I nod, glad to have something productive to do. "Afterwards, we could go and meet with the team and let them know what they will be doing there." He turns back to Logan and smiles. "You okay to go and open up the office and check the emails first thing? We should be done by eleven, so we can meet you for lunch before the meeting with the team at one."

Logan nods as he is more than happy to sit behind the scenes and keep the paperwork up to date and the contracts typed up. Logan may be comfortable around the two of us and those who are expected to follow his orders. But he isn't great with people he's just met. He's more likely to come off as unapproachable, which is why it's better if Calvin and I do the talking.

"There was one thing Christian said to me that we may need to think about seriously," Calvin says from his seat as he leans forward and rests his arms on the table. Both Logan and I sit up and pay attention.

"He's put our names down for various events and fundraisers. He has suggested that when we attend, we take a date. Apparently, it's a way to make it easier for people to approach us or some shit. But the first one's in just over a week, and I have no idea who I'm going to take," he admits, running a hand over his face.

"Are you telling me you don't have any women around here just waiting for your call?" Logan teases as I laugh out loud. Calvin never had a problem finding a girl whenever he was on leave. He would have a list as long as his arm of ladies waiting for him to return from deployment. But now I think about it, I don't remember him mentioning a woman once since he moved here. Maybe there isn't the usual line of them waiting for him.

"I don't. I have thrown all my time into work and building our contacts. Women just weren't a priority. I've had a couple of one-night stands, and that's it."

"There has to be a way to meet women around here. Singles night? Speed dating?" Logan asks, looking around.

"There's always Tinder? It seemed to work okay in the States. I'm sure the English also use it," I point out.

"It's worth a try. Have either of you used it in the past couple of years?" Calvin asks, looking from Logan to me. Logan shakes his head, which doesn't surprise me in the slightest. I roll my eyes and pull my phone out of my pocket.

"Do I have to do everything around here? Give me your phones, and I'll set up your profiles. I'm sure I can make you seem at least a little appealing to the ladies." Both guys roll their eyes at me as they push their phones across the table, and I start uploading the app before helping them to fill out their profiles. I have no idea how this is going to work, but anything is worth a try. It's not like we have time to go out there and find a girl the old-fashioned way. We don't have months on our hands. We have a matter of a week.

I turn to Logan, knowing he will be the most reluctant

of us. He doesn't date; he hasn't for years, and I'm not sure how he'll feel about this. I know he will be willing to do it for the sake of the business, but how far is he ready to go to help us get the word out about what services we offer? Surely, we can find a woman who can help with that and even pretend to like one of us as we do it.

Chapter Four

CHELSEA

It's Monday morning, and I feel relaxed and refreshed after a lazy weekend with my little girl. We baked cookies, watched her favourite film every day whilst eating popcorn and just enjoyed not having to get up for work or school.

"Chelsea, can you come in here for a moment please?"

I look up from my desk to see Mr Young retreating into his office. Not giving me a chance to gauge what mood he's in.

"Of course, sir," I call back, grabbing a notepad, pen, and the tablet his schedule's on and hurrying after him.

"Close the door, please, Chelsea. Then take a seat."

"Yes, sir," I reply anxiously. I'm not usually his personal assistant; I'm only his PA's assistant. But Harper's been off for the last three weeks, and I've been filling in for her. I thought I'd done well, but looking at Mr Young now, I can see he looks stressed as he rubs his face and leans his elbows on the desk in front of him. I quickly rack my brains for anything I might have missed, but nothing comes to mind.

"I have just gotten off the phone with Harper. As you

know, her mother had a fall and broke her hip, which is why she's been off. Unfortunately, her mother will need around-the-clock care for the foreseeable future, which Harper has decided to do herself. This means she has resigned with immediate notice."

"I'm sorry to hear that, sir. She has always enjoyed working for you, and you rely heavily on her."

Mr Young nods as he sits back in his desk chair and lets out a deep sigh.

"She has been my PA for many years and is part of the family. She speaks to my wife and children, Abigail and Gethin, more than I do most days. Many will miss her, but I understand why she is leaving. Family is important, and we must always look after our own."

I nod in agreement whilst opening my notepad and clicking my pen.

"Would you like me to start advertising for a new PA for you, sir? I can get the notice out in the next couple of hours." I start scribbling the role details and expected working hours on the paper.

"No, I want you to start advertising for my PA's assistant role."

My heart and pen stop abruptly.

Am I being fired? Did I do that bad a job whilst in charge?

"Did I do something wrong, sir?" I ask quietly whilst blinking back the tears. I can't lose this job. How can I afford the bills without an income? My hands start to shake, and I can't bring myself to look at Mr Young for fear of bursting into tears.

"Quite the contrary, you have done an amazing job filling in for Harper. I've been very impressed."

I slowly look up to see Mr Young watching me with a smile.

"Then I don't understand. Why am I being let go?" my voice starts to break as the smile on Mr Young's face drops.

"You're not being let go, Chelsea. You're being promoted."

"What?" My heart restarts only to race at a million miles per hour. Did he say what I think he said?

"Chelsea, you have done a fantastic job whilst Harper has been away. She's just sung your praises on the phone. She told me several times she called to ask you to do something, but it had already been done. You haven't let me miss a single appointment and have exceeded my expectations of you. My life has never been so organised; I don't think you realise how good you are at your job or how much I have relied on you the last few weeks."

"I don't know what to say; I thought you were getting rid of me."

I watch Mr Young laugh as I try to process it all.

"I think Harper would hunt me down if I got rid of you. No, Chelsea, I think you have proven time and time again that you are more than capable of fulfilling the role." Mr Young stands from his chair and heads over to the pot of coffee I brought up half an hour ago. I watch him pour two black coffees, adding two sugars into one and none into the other.

Walking back over, he stands before me and hands over a mug before leaning back against his desk.

"Now, how about we discuss pay and what I will expect of you before you go about your day." He takes a sip of his coffee as I take the time to sip on my own, trying to hide how excited I am for things to be heading in the right direction.

"So let me get this straight. Not only do you get the promotion, but a huge pay rise, and your own assistant, too?" Penny asks as we sit in the break room on her floor. I finish making my coffee and turn to her, nodding.

"Yeah. I still can't believe it. I'm half expecting him to tell me it's all a joke," I admit as I sip my drink.

"Why would he? You deserve this, Chels. You work harder than anyone I know and are bloody good at your job."

I know she's right; I always go above and beyond, but that doesn't mean I deserve to have everything handed to me like this. I thought I'd have to at least interview for the job, but apparently not. Mr Young has said that today is my first day in the role and that I'm to list anything I may need. He also explained that Harper would be coming to see me in the next few days to go over a few things and collect her belongings. I really hope I'm doing the right thing here and that I won't find myself in over my head or that Mr Young will start regretting his decision to promote me.

"Earth to Chelsea. Are you in there?"

I look at Penny, surprised that I've completely blocked her out.

"Did you say something?"

"When do you start advertising for someone to fill your role?" Penny asks, rolling her eyes at me.

"This afternoon. I have already started putting together the job description. I'll finish it after a meeting. Mr Young wants me to sit in with the new security firm."

"Oh, hot security men, can I sit in too?" She wiggles her eyebrows as I roll my eyes.

"It's the owners of the company. They are probably old

men who hire people to do the work they used to do thirty years ago." I look at the clock on the wall and curse under my breath. "I need to go. I'll see you at lunch." Turning on my heels, I head for the door, needing to return to my desk in five minutes.

"You better, as we need to work out a way to celebrate! I'm thinking of a pizza party at yours tonight!" Penny calls behind me as I close the door and rush towards the elevator. Luckily, as I reach it, the doors open for someone to exit. I go to step inside but almost trip over my feet when I see the two hot guys standing inside. I quickly remember myself and step into the elevator before the doors close.

Lifting my hand to press the button for my floor I notice it has already been pressed. I glance at the mirror beside me and see the two men looking straight ahead at the doors. No other buttons on the panel are lit up, and it dawns on me that these are probably the guys from the security company. Penny would have a field day if she saw them. I think every woman in a five-mile radius would kill for a moment with these two, especially if they were to detain and cuff them. I quickly push that thought out of my mind as the last thing I need right now is to have inappropriate thoughts whilst in the meeting.

Both men are over six feet tall, with brown hair, and look younger than me. Are they old enough to have any real experience of providing security? One of them looks like he's just left school. Okay, he doesn't look quite that young, but he has a definite baby face.

I force myself to look away from the mirror and back to the panel showing our slow journey to the top floor. The elevator stops abruptly, and the doors open, revealing a large filing cabinet. The maintenance guy, Grant, doesn't look before pushing the filing cabinet into the cramped space, and I only just manage to jump out of the way in time. I start to lose my balance on my high heels and would have fallen if two hands hadn't grabbed my arms from behind, steadying me.

"Hey! Watch where you're pushing that thing, buddy!" a thick American accent calls from behind me. I stand back up and look to my right, where the older looking of the two is watching me, his hands still on my arms from where he caught me.

"Are you okay, ma'am?" he asks, his voice a little deeper than the one who shouted at Grant, but his American accent is just as thick.

"Yes. Thanks," I stutter before stepping away from him. His grip on my arms loosens, but he seems to take a step with me as if to check I'm truly stable on my feet. "Thanks for catching me," I add, not knowing what else to say. He smiles, his head tipped slightly to the side.

"You're welcome."

Our eyes met, and I can't tear myself away from them. They are a gorgeous shade of brown that reminds me of the hazel desk my father used to have in his office. They may be the most beautiful eyes I've ever seen.

"You alright, Chels?"

I look at Grant and give him a reassuring smile.

"I'm fine. But be more careful next time, please."

"I will. I'm so sorry, Chels."

I place a hand on his arm before giving it a reassuring squeeze.

"No harm done, so don't worry about it."

The doors close, and we continue our journey. I try not to notice how much closer I am to the American who caught me, but I can feel his presence behind me like a solid wall. The smell of his cologne overpowers my senses and leaves me wanting to smell it up close and personal.

What the hell?

Thankfully, the elevator opens, and Grant leaves with the filing cabinet. I quickly follow behind him, desperate to distance myself from the hot Americans. I hear Grant asking where I want the cabinet, and I remember I'd asked him to bring it up before I went on my coffee break. What the hell has gotten into me in the last few minutes? It's like my mind stopped working when I saw those hot men.

Needing to clear my head before I'm forced to endure being near those two hot Americans, I show Grant into the office at the far end of the floor. After showing him where to place the cabinet, I thank him again before returning to my desk. As soon as it comes into view, I see the two Americans standing, talking to Mr Young, who turns his attention to me and smiles.

"Ah, here she is. Chelsea, come and meet the owners of the new security company who will be taking over the contract."

I stand beside Mr Young and smile at the two gentlemen before me, reminding myself to be as professional as possible.

"Chelsea, this is Calvin Anderson. Calvin, this is my PA, Chelsea Hughes," Mr Young announces as Calvin holds out a hand, which I give a quick shake. He's the one who caught me in the elevator.

"It's a pleasure," I say, trying to keep my tone as professional as possible, but my heart is racing a hundred miles an hour. He doesn't reply; he just smiles and nods as Mr Young draws my attention to the younger guy beside him.

"And this is one of his business partners, Drew Cambell."

"It's lovely to meet you, Mr Cambell," I smile. He has a dazzling smile that lights up his baby face. God, how young is this guy?

"You too, Mrs Hughes. But please call me Drew," he says, shaking my hand. I nod once, returning the smile as I look between the two men.

"It's Miss, and please call me Chelsea." Why did I feel the need to point out I'm not married? *Get a grip, woman.*

"Why don't we all go into the office and discuss a few things before I give you a tour of the premises," Mr Young announces beside me, and I quickly make my way to his office door and hold it open for the three men to walk through. Calvin comes to a stop beside me first and takes the door.

"After you, Chelsea," he says in a voice that I bet sounds amazing if he were to whisper in my ear. *Oh my god, sort it out, Chels!*

"Thank you," I reply quickly before walking into the office, hoping to get some control of my body and inappropriate thoughts before I make a complete fool of myself.

Chapter Five

CALVIN

"This is the main office for security. All the CCTV and staff panic buttons are monitored from this hub. There are two on each floor and in each toilet in case of emergency," Chelsea explains as she leads us into a reasonably small office filled with CCTV screens and computers. "There is also a small room though here which you can interview people in, should you need to. But you can also just detain them until the police arrive, whichever your guys think best."

I look around and see that some of the equipment here is old and could probably be upgraded. I can't imagine Young would know the slightest thing about what this stuff should really do.

"Has anyone else used this stuff since Taylor's men?" I ask, clicking on a screen to check if the cameras move.

"Only agency. The O'Reillys offered a few guys to help, but Mr Young refused. Said he didn't want to put on them when they have had such a rough time."

Sounds about right. Geralt Young took it personally when Jasmine was kidnapped three months ago. He had told the O'Reillys they could trust the man who turned out to be the one who kidnapped her in the first place.

"How long have you been Geralt's PA?" I ask, checking through the data on the screen.

"About two hours."

I spin around to stare at her as Drew laughs beside me.

"I've been filling in for his previous PA for the last few weeks whilst she handled a family emergency, but she called this morning to say she wouldn't be able to return, so Mr Young hired me." Judging by her face, she still doesn't quite know how to process the change in circumstances.

"Well, congratulations on the promotion," Drew says with that charming smile he saves for the women he likes. I have to stop myself from rolling my eyes at him. He is such a flirt when he wants to be. There again, who can blame him for flirting with the attractive woman in front of us? She's beautiful. Not only does she have the petite body of a supermodel, but her shoulder-length blonde hair and blue eyes shine as she smiles at us and makes me weak at the knees. I've already checked her hand for a wedding ring and see nothing, but I know that doesn't mean she's single. I remind myself that she works for a client, which puts her out of bounds, which is just bloody typical. What are the odds we sign up for a dating app and a woman lands right in front of me?

"Yes, congratulations," I add, quickly flashing her a smile.

"Thank you, both." I watch as her cheeks flush and stop myself from moaning out loud. Fuck, this woman is going to crack me wide open with how adorable she is. What the hell? I haven't been interested in the opposite sex for so long that I thought I had lost my touch. But here I am with a semi, over a woman I can't even have.

We sat in Young's office for an hour reviewing the quote we gave him for his needs. He seems to be happy with everything and has just left us to look around and check out everything he has in place already. I know he will want to speak to me privately about the other things he will need security for, but I imagine Chelsea knows very little of the other side of Geralt Young.

"Will you both be working here occasionally? Or do you hire people in?" Chelsea asks as she leans against one of the desks whilst crossing her ankles in front of her.

She looks every part the PA, in her pencil skirt, high heels and blouse. She's wearing minimal makeup, which is still more than she needs. She has a natural beauty you don't see in women often these days. She's one of the most beautiful women I have ever seen.

"No, we have people who work for us. We employ and train them to ensure they are suitable for the job; we manage, not work," Drew explains beside me.

I watch Drew and Chelsea as they start talking about the different services we offer and how we train our employees. Both seem comfortable around each other, which is why I wanted to bring Drew today rather than Logan. Drew is great with people, and you can't help befriending him in comparison to Logan, who is a little less approachable. If he can speak to people face to face or via text and email, the electrical version wins every time. He has already told me he would rather focus on the training side of the business, which I'm more than happy to agree with.

What Logan doesn't have in communication skills, he more than makes up for in his fighting skills. No one can fight better than Logan. I have seen the man take down four or five of the enemy on the ground with nothing but his fists on more than one occasion. He is a machine when he gets going and trains harder than anyone I know.

The office door opens, and Geralt walks in smiling. Chelsea quickly straightens up and looks slightly less relaxed than she did a moment ago. I can't imagine Young being a demanding boss, but if she is still new to the role, then she's probably still trying to impress as much as possible.

"Sorry for the delay. My daughter called, so I had to speak to her quickly." He stops beside me and looks at the computer screen. "What do you think of the equipment? Is it up to scratch? Taylor said it was fine, but …" his voice trails off as he thinks of the guy he thought was a lifelong friend. I place a hand on his shoulder and squeeze it, hoping to show that I understand. He gives me a slight nod, and I remove my hand before focusing back on the screens.

"I'll be honest. It could do with an upgrade, but I'll get our tech guy to pop in and look into that to be certain. From what I see, I think it's okay, but he will be able to tell you more."

Taylor nods and turns to Chelsea.

"Can you work out a date and time that he could have a look at it all?"

"I'll send you my email address and direct number so you can arrange it and let me know," she says, looking between me and Drew, obviously unsure of who to address. Drew pulls out a business card from his pocket and hands it to her with a smile.

"This is the best email to get us all on. The office number is there, too. It is always directed to one of our mobiles after of hours."

She takes it with a nod and scribbles something onto a

notebook she's had in her hand all morning, which she writes little notes.

"I'll send over everything later this morning once I get all your details on the system. Can you send me the licence numbers and documentation for the team working in the building? I can then get them onto the system, with login details and so on."

I pull out my phone and open my planner.

"I will get it all to you as soon as I get back to the office," I reply, adding it to my to-do list for the day. Chelsea gives me a list of other things she will need, photos for their passes, etc. I add it all to the list while trying to act as professional as possible and not stare at her lips and how they move when she speaks. I'm also struggling with the way her perfume floats in the air around us. Every time she moves just slightly, the scent gets stronger, pulling my focus back on her and nothing but her.

Fuck, I need to get out of here.

"I think that we have covered everything. Let me show you both out," Geralt smiles before turning to Chelsea. "Would you mind going to that café around the corner and getting me the usual BLT sub, please?"

"Of course," she replies before looking at Drew and me. "It was a pleasure to meet you. I'm sure we will speak again soon." She holds out her hand, and we both shake it.

"It was a pleasure to meet you too, Chelsea," we reply simultaneously. She gives us one last smile before leaving the room.

As soon as the door is closed behind her, I turn my attention to Geralt, watching the screens as Chelsea walks away from the office and towards the elevators.

"How much does she know?" I ask, leaning against the desk behind me.

"Everything legal, nothing that's not," he answers before looking from the screen to me and Drew. "I want to keep it that way."

I nod, understanding completely. I've been in this game long enough to know the importance of keeping my mouth shut.

"Just so you know, I will always respect the O'Reillys, but that does not mean I will discuss anything with them I'm not meant to."

Geralt nods, giving me a small smile.

"I wouldn't expect it any other way. The O'Reillys trust you completely, and that is enough for me." Geralt makes sure to look at Drew as well as me, letting us both know he trusts us but not to do anything to jeopardise that.

Deciding now is probably the best time to end the meeting, I stand up straight and shake Geralt's hand; Drew quickly follows suit.

"I look forward to your tech guy coming in and having a look at the system. I want to know it hasn't been compromised." He's been on edge since the whole Taylor incident, and I can't blame him.

Geralt walks us to the front of the building and bids us farewell before heading back inside, no doubt up to his office. Drew and I head to the parking lot where we parked earlier, discussing everything we must do for the rest of the day. It doesn't take long for the conversation to turn to Chelsea.

"So, his PA is a bit yummy," Drew smirks next to me. I roll my eyes as I unlock the driver side door.

"Hands off, we don't date people we work for," I point out whilst sliding in behind the wheel.

"But technically, we don't work for her. We work for her boss," Drew points out, still smiling.

"She's still off limits," I tell him, as much as myself. Damn it, why does she need to be off-limits? She is intelligent, funny, professional, beautiful, and everything I'm looking for in a date for these events.

Typical, I meet someone, and I can't date them.

Fuck my life.

Chapter Six

CHELSEA

I walk into the lounge where Penny sits with her legs underneath herself and an empty wine glass in her hand.

"I hope you realise we're staying tonight," she declares with a wink. I roll my eyes whilst filling up her glass.

"I figured that when you walked through the door with two bottles of wine and a bag."

"Well, we had to celebrate your promotion somehow, and since we have been promising the girls a sleepover for weeks, I figured it was the perfect time."

"Even if it is a school night?" I point out, but Penny shrugs.

My daughter Luna and Penny's daughter Kylie are in the same class in school and are close friends. They love nothing more than spending time together and having sleepovers, which is fine by us as it gives us a reason to have a night of wine and put the world to rights.

I first met Penny three months before I started the job as Mr Young's PA's assistant. Penny had seen the position become available and persuaded me to apply. I thought I had no chance of being successful, but somehow, I got the job.

I'm older than most of the staff who work for Mr Young. At forty-two years of age, I figured my chances of being in top roles were low as they were looking for people who weren't single, middle-aged mums. But here I am, getting a fantastic promotion.

"How did your day go as Mr Young's new PA?" Penny asks, taking a sip of her wine and grinning at me.

"I've been acting as his PA for three weeks, so it wasn't a completely new experience," I sigh, tucking my legs underneath me as I make myself comfortable.

"But it was the first time you've officially been in the role." Penny leans forward, smirking, and I know what's coming next. "How was the meeting with the new security company?"

"Fine," I reply, sipping my wine.

"Oh, I heard they were *fine*. Pretty damn fine, in fact," she smirks and wiggles her eyebrows at me for emphasis.

"Really? I didn't notice." That's a lie; they were two of the most attractive men I have ever met. They were funny and professional and a sight to behold.

"You are such a liar. Everyone who saw them swooned. You can't say you felt nothing!"

I take a sip of my wine before letting out a deep breath.

"Fine, they were gorgeous. Is that what you want to hear? I nearly died when I realised who they were and that it wasn't two older men. They are built and looked like gods, and I sat there wondering if an old girl like me would ever turn their heads."

"You aren't old!" Penny protests loudly. I look at my friend with an arched brow.

"I'm officially classed as middle age; I'm old. Plus, there

is no way these guys are older than thirty-five. One of them was so baby-faced I had difficulty believing he was in his thirties," I explain whilst picturing how they both smiled at me and how I felt it deep in my stomach.

I haven't been able to stop thinking of them since, which made me consider whether Penny has been right and it's time I looked into dating again.

There are times that I'm lonely, and the thought of having someone now and again to hold me after a long day or show me just the slightest bit of affection would be nice. Someone who can give me an orgasm that doesn't come with batteries or charging wire would be good, too. There again, I haven't had the best experience with sexual partners. Very few have given me an orgasm, let alone one better than I can give myself with a toy. But it would be nice just once for someone to try and top them, at least.

I look at Penny and find her grinning at me with a knowing look. She knows exactly where my mind just went and is waiting for me to say it out loud. Bitch can read me like a book.

"I think I want to try dating again."

Penny squeals, almost spilling her wine in the excitement. She quickly puts it on the small table beside her sofa and reaches for her phone.

"I've been waiting so long for this!" she giggles happily. Oh shit, what have I done? I'm going to regret this; I know it.

I watch as she types away on her phone before jumping in her seat so she is facing me more, causing me to nearly spill my wine. She ignores my protests whilst tapping away on her phone.

"Okay, there is a speed dating event next Friday in town."

"I'm not going speed dating! Do you remember the last one you dragged me to? I left after some guy offered to meet me out back!"

Penny roars, laughing as I roll my eyes.

"But that was just one guy."

I give her a side eye, and she rolls hers dramatically.

"Fine, dating app it is." She reaches over and grabs my phone from the arm of the chair next to me. "Right, let's find the right one for you."

I climb into bed just after midnight. The girls are finally asleep, and Penny is passed out on the bed beside me. The third bottle of wine seemed like a good idea at the time. It was not. I'm so drunk and have no idea what I let her talk me into. If I remember rightly, she also pulled the old tequila out of the cupboard at some point. My head will not thank me in the morning when I have to work, that's for sure.

I pick up my phone and look at it through one eye as I attempt to focus. Nope. I can't see a thing through the blur. I know it's on the Tinder app that Penny insisted on down-loading onto my phone. I remember at one point, she went on a swiping mission and decided for me which way to swipe. Probably because I can't remember if it's right or left for like.

Did I see Calvin and Drew on there earlier? No, I couldn't have. There's no way they're single. If they are, then they're gay. Are they together? Why does that sound appealing? Shit, now I know I'm drunk if I'm getting turned on by the thought of those two hunks together.

I put my phone back on the side and lie down, throwing

my arms over my face. I might as well get to sleep because I know for a fact, I'm going to spend tomorrow regretting every decision I have made today, like letting Penelope sign me up to that bloody app.

Chapter Seven

DREW

I sit back on the couch and continue to flick through my phone. I don't even know what I'm looking at anymore. I've been flicking through Tinder for half an hour, and no one is catching my attention. All I can think about is a particular blonde-haired PA with hips I want to grab and hold on to as I fuck her over that huge desk. Fuck, she's gotten under my skin, and I can't think of anything else.

"Dude, if you reposition your cock one more time, I will cut the fucker off."

I look down at my hand and realise I have a firm grip on my semi-hard dick. No wonder Logan's growling at me.

"Shit. Sorry, buddy," I mutter as I put my arm on the back of the sofa. Keeping it as far away from my crotch as possible.

"What's got you so highly strung?" I hear Calvin ask from the dinner table, where he's going over some paperwork with Logan.

"Nothing," I answer, not wanting to give him the satisfaction of telling me again that Chelsea's off-limits.

"By nothing, he means a certain PA he met today," Logan teases. I glare at him whilst flipping him the bird.

"Chelsea is -"

"Off-limits. I know. I heard you," I sigh, leaning my head against the back of the couch. "But let's just say she wasn't," I start, but one look from Calvin stops me in my tracks.

"You know why we can't date someone linked to us professionally."

I roll my eyes and go back to looking through the pictures on Tinder. I'm casually swiping left when a familiar face appears on my screen. I smile to myself as I look at the picture of her. So, she's forty-two? I never would have guessed she was four years older than me. She looks so good for her age. Her blue eyes are sparkling in the picture as she sits in a bar with a cocktail in her hand. Was this picture taken tonight? Is she out celebrating her promotion?

"Is that her?"

"Fuck." I turn my head so fast to look over my shoulder at Logan; I don't know how I don't get whiplash.

"What have I told you about sneaking up on me, fuck-face!" Fuck I hate it when he does that. He's always been stealthy, which was why we would send him in first when out on the field.

"She's pretty. I see why you're stuck on her," he says, walking over to his chair. I look back at the screen and consider swiping right to see what happens. Let's face it: she isn't interested in a younger guy like me, especially when I look younger than I am. Most are happy to look ten years younger, but the others in the SEALs loved making my life hell for it. It earned me several nicknames, the foremost being "Bambi". I fucking hated it to start with, but once you get a nickname in any of the forces, it's with you for life. I soon got used to it, though. Now it feels weird if the guys call me anything else.

"She's come up on mine too," Logan says as he shows me his phone. I hadn't even realised he'd started using the app. Since I signed him up, all he's done is complain that he doesn't want to take anyone to these events. But here he is, looking at Chelsea, and I feel somewhat jealous.

"And mine."

I turn to look back to the table where Calvin is now looking at his phone rather than the paperwork.

"There's no way that woman is forty-two! She looks the same age as you guys!" Logan announces. Calvin and I are the same age at thirty-eight. Calvin's always looked a couple of years older than he is, so people assume he's more Logan's age. Logan's the eldest of the three of us at thirty-nine. He will be forty just before Christmas.

"Why don't we all swipe right and see if she matches with any of us?" Calvin asks, looking at the two of us.

"Oh, you've changed your tone, mister *'she's off-limits'*. You want to see if *you* match with her, don't you? What are you going to do if she does? Will she be off-limits if she is interested in you too?" I demand as my eyebrows disappear into my hairline. I hear Logan chuckling from his seat and turn to look at him. "And you, *'I don't need a date'*, are going to join in too, aren't you?"

Logan shrugs whilst looking at his phone.

"I'm not bothered either way. It's just fun watching you squirm," he teases as I flip him off again. I look back at my screen and consider swiping right to see if we do, in fact, match. If we do, then surely, I should be able to take her on one date at least to see if we get along. It would be rude not to, right?

"Well, now I just want to match with her to annoy the

hell out of you," Logan teases from his seat. He starts laughing as I throw a cushion at him, yelling "asshat!". He and Calvin laugh harder as I look down at my phone again.

"Fuck it," I snap, swiping right and looking up to see the other two grinning at me before showing they also have.

"What happens if she likes both of you?" Logan asks, chuckling.

"She won't like any of us," Calvin laughs as he puts his phone on the table and returns to the paperwork in front of him. Logan places his phone on the coffee table in the middle of the room and picks up the TV remote. I quickly lock my phone, as I'm too anxious to see if we get matched or not.

Why the hell do I care if I do or not? She's one woman. Yes, she may be beautiful, intelligent, and funny, but so are many women I have met. What makes Chelsea so special? Probably the fact that Calvin has said she's out of bounds. Like everything else in my life, if I get told I can't do something, I make it my mission to achieve it. Are my feelings for Chelsea another example of that? Do I want to prove to Calvin that I don't need his permission and can date who I want?

"Oh fucking hell!" Logan bursts out laughing. I look over at him to see him looking at his phone. He turns it around to show the screen. "She must like what she sees," he laughs as Calvin laughs from the table.

"Snap, I matched with her too," he laughs. I grab my phone and look at the app.

"Fuck."

"Don't worry, Bambi. She obviously likes the older-looking men," Logan teases. I shake my head and hold up my phone.

"Obviously not, as she matched with me as well," I

reply smugly. The two look at each other, and we all burst out laughing.

"I can't believe she has matched with all three of us. What are the odds?"

"Well, she hasn't met Houdini over there, so she doesn't know about his winning personality," I reply, nodding towards Logan, who just rolls his eyes at me.

"I don't need a winning personality, as I have no interest in getting to know her. I'm going to find a woman to take to these functions; that's it. I might even go on my own and claim I'm asexual yet." I know he's seriously considering doing just that. It's been years since he last went on a date.

I walk over to our makeshift bar, pouring three whiskeys and handing them out to the guys before sitting back on the couch.

"Anyway, back to something that doesn't involve Bambi's dick. What do you make of the security system that's in place at Young's?" Calvin asks, looking at Logan over his glass.

The two of them start throwing around ideas on how the system could have been compromised and what changes need to be made. Calvin suggests getting the guys starting tomorrow to do a report of where the cameras are and if they are all in working condition. That way, Logan isn't going in blind on Wednesday when he goes in to do a full assessment.

The whole time, I try to concentrate on the conversation and throw in my own two cents now and again, but my mind keeps wandering back to my phone and the fact I matched with Chelsea. I'm not blind; I notice that Calvin also keeps glancing at his phone. I saw how he looked at her today when he thought no one was looking. I haven't seen him interested in anyone for a long time, but then Chelsea walked into the elevator and he couldn't take his eyes off her. I know because I couldn't either.

As the evening progresses, so does the amount of whiskey we drink. It's not long before I start feeling the effects of the alcohol.

"You know, us all matching with the same woman may be a good thing."

I look from the TV programme we're all watching to see Calvin looking at his phone.

"Why do you say that?" Logan asks.

"Well, think about it; she says in her profile that she isn't looking for a long-term relationship. What if she was to accompany us all to events and dinners? We wouldn't all have to deal with women getting clingy whilst trying to deal with business stuff. She knows how the business world works and what to expect at these events."

"Are you suggesting we all use her to get ahead?" I ask, shocked that he would think of doing such a thing, especially to someone as lovely as Chelsea.

"Of course not. We would tell her what we wanted, she would have to agree to it, and we would stay as honest with her as possible."

I never thought he could be so heartless. Yes, he's brutal when out on the field, and there isn't much he wouldn't do to get our company off the ground and as successful as we hope it will become. But to use Chelsea in that way seems wrong on so many levels. Would I feel differently if it was a random person I had never met?

"So, we would tell her we want someone to pretend to be dating us? Explain we are not in a position to dedicate time to a real relationship," Logan says, and I realise he seems also to be contemplating it.

"Why the hell would she agree to that? What's in it for her?" I demand.

"She gets taken out for meals and 'dates' and isn't expected to put out. She gets the company she craves, and we get the dates for when we need one," Calvin explains. I look to Logan and find him nodding as if it makes perfect sense.

"If we are honest from day one, then she won't expect anything else, which means she won't get hurt."

"I don't like this. It feels wrong and manipulative," I point out. Logan looks at me and shrugs.

"If we are honest, then we're not manipulating her. She can always say no. We aren't forcing her to do anything she wouldn't want to."

He has a point, but it still doesn't sit right with me.

"So, we are all going to do it then? We'll see if she's interested in fake dating us and take it from there?" Calvin asks. Logan nods before they both turn their attention to me.

"Do I even have a choice?" I ask.

"Of course you do. You know I would never force you to do something you aren't comfortable with," Calvin says from his seat. I look down at my glass, which only has a small amount in it. I lift it to my mouth and let the rest of the liquid pour down my throat.

"Fine, but if she gets hurt, I'm killing you both myself!"

Chapter Eight

LOGAN

"Hi, I'm here to upgrade the security system."

The brunette at the reception desk looks up from her computer and does a double take before a large smile spreads across her face, and she starts fluttering her eyelashes at me.

"Hi, of course. What's your name please?"

"Logan Wilson."

"And your marital status?"

I blink once, convinced I must have misheard, but I know I didn't when she continues to grin at me.

"Not interested," I reply flatly whilst looking anywhere but at her. I hear her muttering something under her breath, but I continue to refuse to look in her direction.

"Here is your pass, Mr Wilson." She says my name with disgust. I look at her with one cocked brow. "I'm to call Mr Young's assistant to let her know you are here," she informs me before picking up the phone and turning in her chair so her back is to me.

I roll my eyes before going back to looking at the large

foyer. Why am I always the bad guy when I refuse a woman's advances? Yet they have every right to refuse mine. Either way, I'm the bad guy, and it's just pathetic.

"Miss Hughes will be with you in a moment," the receptionist announces before walking away from her desk.

"Thank you for the warm welcome," I call after her. She doesn't bother acknowledging me; she just keeps walking away as I chuckle to myself.

I pick the lanyard with a visitor's pass on it and loop it around my neck. I hate wearing these things; it gives people a reason to look at me. I'm not a people person; I much prefer my own company and that of computers. At least they don't judge you or ask personal questions.

I go back to looking around at the cameras I can see. Hugo, one of the guys who started here yesterday, sent the report as Calvin suggested. It wasn't good in any shape or form. Half the cameras are dirty, so the picture is horrendous; five cameras don't work at all, and the system is so slow that a person could steal anything they wanted and get away with it. I spent the night reviewing the report and blueprints to see where I would put the cameras and where they were a waste of space. I have a new system I would like to install, but it's not cheap, and I don't know how much Young wants to spend.

"Excuse me, Mr Wilson?"

Her voice snaps me back to reality as I turn to see Chelsea Hughes smiling up at me.

"You are Mr Wilson, are you not?" she asks as she holds her hand out.

"Yes, sorry, I was in work mode," I apologise as I shake her hand. I remind myself I need to be nice to this one. The guys are hoping she will agree to accompany us to future events. "Miss Hughes, I assume?" Chelsea nods as I let go of her hand. "Why do you look so familiar?" I ask. Calvin had instructed me on the politest way to mention I've matched with her on the app. Apparently, I'm not to be as blunt as I am with others. The asshole is getting a kick out of this, I swear.

"I was just wondering the same thing," she replies, frowning. Before I can ask if it's Tinder, she smiles, slipping back to being the professional the guys told me she is.

"Please follow me to the security hub. I know your guys are already in there unless they've been needed elsewhere." She turns away, leaving me with no option but to follow. Oh well, the guys can't say I haven't tried.

"I will need access to anywhere there's a camera or alarm, as well as the server room," I instruct as I fall into step beside her. At six-foot-five, I tower over her petite frame. She can't be any more than five one, maybe five two at an absolute push.

Chelsea flashes me a smile whilst nodding.

"Of course. I know a few meetings are happening today, so I will give you the times when those conference rooms will be inaccessible. That way, you don't have to wait around longer than you need to."

It sounds good to me, in and out; it's just how I like it.

I follow her to a door at the back of the entrance foyer with a "SECURITY" plaque. Well, I guess there is no mistaking what's in there. Chelsea lifts her pass around her neck and holds it to the lockbox. I hear the click as it unlocks, and she can open the door.

"How many people have access to this room?" I ask as we enter. Two guys turn in their seats to look at the door before jumping to their feet. "At ease, go back to what you were doing," I instruct instantly as they sit back and monitor the CCTV screens.

"To be honest, I'm not sure. I've only been in the position for less than a week, and my predecessor never told me. It will all be on the system, though. Everyone's profile shows where they have access to." She steps forward and lifts my visitor pass. "This one will only have visitor access, which is elevators only. If you want to access the offices or conference rooms, you will need a staff member with you who has access to those areas."

I have no doubt she sees how my eyebrows disappear into my hairline, especially judging by the smirk on her face.

"As I said, I will need access to everywhere."

Chelsea continues to smile up at me with a devious smile. Is she playing with me?

"Then it's a good job your staff have access to all areas and the computer system so they can alter that." Crafty bitch was trying to get a reaction out of me; it nearly fucking worked too. Something tells me she doesn't like me questioning how secure the building her boss runs is.

She turns on her heels and heads towards the door. "I trust they will be able to show you around and help you with anything you need. If you require extra assistance, my extension number is 482," she calls before leaving the room. I look back to the two employees watching me rather than the screen.

"A lot of good she is."

"Chels is alright; she's just straight to the point and doesn't waste her time on things she doesn't need to worry about," Hugo answers, grinning. "She's a bit like you, boss," he adds, winking at me.

I take off my lanyard and toss it in his direction. He catches it before it can hit him in the face.

"Sort that out whilst I make a plan of action." I point to Derryn beside him. "You are with me today unless there is an issue. Hugo, you're on your own." I hear both answering respectfully, "Yes, sir," as I sit at a table and pull my laptop and tablet out of my bag, eager to get to work so I can finish here and return to the office, where I would much rather be.

Five hours later, I ride the elevator to the top floor. I'm tired and dirty from looking into ceilings to check wiring and other issues I found while inspecting the cameras and their system. I have pages of notes in my hand, and I know Young will want to see this stuff sooner rather than later. I will write it all up professionally tonight and email it to him in a day or two.

The doors open, and the first thing I see is Chelsea sitting behind a large reception-style desk. There are papers stacked all over the place in obviously organised chaos, and she's typing away on the keyboard in what I can only describe as aggressive determination. Her nails sound as they strike the keys, telling me she is as quick at typing as I am, which is fast; I'm almost impressed. Not that I would let her know that.

She looks up from the screen and greets me with a friendly smile.

"Mr Young knows you are on your way. He is finishing a meeting, and then he will see you." She stands from her chair and walks over to a coffee machine.

"Would you like a tea or coffee while you wait?" she asks with her back to me.

"Coffee, please. Black, no sugar." While waiting, I sit by the door and unlock my tablet to look through my findings.

"Did you have any issues gaining access to anywhere?" Chelsea asks whilst she makes my drink.

"No, all was fine," I answer, not looking up from the screen. My phone pings in my pocket, and I pull it out, knowing it will be a message from Drew or Calvin.

Calvin: I got your message. It doesn't sound good. Want me to be there when you tell Young?

Logan: Nah, I've got it.

Calvin: Have you had a chat with Chelsea yet?

I've been waiting for him to message me all day about her. I'm surprised neither of them has found a reason to come in so they could see her. Do I believe they aren't eager to spend time with her for their own selfish reasons? Not in the slightest. There is a reason they have both been staring at her profile constantly and are looking for any reason to spend time with her. It's pathetic, and I dread the arguments it will cause when they finally accept they are both falling for the same woman.

Logan: With her now, give me a chance.

Calvin: Don't bottle it. You know we need her.

No, *you* need her, there's a difference. I don't bother replying. Instead, I lock my phone and drop it into my laptop case at my feet, partially hoping it will break, and then he has no way of contacting me until I get home.

"Here you go."

I look up to see Chelsea smiling at me as she holds out a mug of coffee. I thank her and take it. She turns to walk back to her desk, and I know I need to say something to keep her talking.

"So, I figured out where I know you from," I say in a tone that makes me cringe. I hate sounding anything but confident, but right now, I sound like a nervous teenager. I hate small talk, especially when it's of no real benefit to me.

Chelsea turns to look at me as she sits back in her chair. She smiles nervously, and I know she's also worked it out.

"Yeah, me too. Small world." She starts to chew on her thumbnail, instantly giving away her tell. She's nervous and probably realises that she has matched with the three of us. She tries to come off as confident, but when faced with the possibility that the three of us have discussed our Tinder accounts and matches, we might realise what's happened. If only she knew the truth.

"So, I was going to message tonight and see if you fancied a drink one night this week?" I ask, trying to ignore my nerves. Not because I want her to say yes; it doesn't bother me either way. I'm more concerned about what she thinks she will get from me. I am not the flowers and choco-lates type of guy, and I'm certainly not looking for a rela-tionship.

"I'm not sure if that's such a good idea," she starts, continuing to chew on her nail.

"Why not? Because you have matched with my business partners, too?"

Her head snaps up as she stares at me. I shrug my shoul-ders as I try to hide that I didn't mean to say it quite like that.

"You all know?"

I nod, trying to look neutral.

"Yeah, um, sorry about that." Fuck, the guys are going to kill me.

50

"So, what is it? You are all going to see who can seal the deal first?" She snaps, standing with her hands on her hips.

"What? Fuck no!" I say a little louder than I meant to. We both look to the door of Young's office and wait to see if they heard. Luckily, no one comes out, so I stand and move closer to her desk so we can talk and keep the noise down.

"Look, we might be arseholes to each other, but we are not to others that don't deserve it. We all matched with you for a reason. We all have things in common and liked what we saw; you can't say you didn't, as you knew who the other two were when you liked their profile, but you didn't know me."

I run my fingers through my hair to calm my racing mind. This is why I don't talk to people; I have no communication skills except when I'm in command. I'm great at giving orders, but shit when it comes to speaking to those who aren't under my command or when I have to consider their emotions. That's why the SEALs worked for me; you have to leave all emotions at the door. Out on the field, they just distract you and get you and those who have your back killed.

"What I'm trying to say is, give us all a chance if you want. We might be business partners and as close as brothers, but we are also respectful men who may just be looking for the same thing as you. How will you know if you don't give us a chance?"

Chelsea looks at me momentarily and opens her mouth to speak when Young's office door opens, and two guys walk out laughing. I head back to my seat to retrieve my coffee and place my tablet in my bag. The two guys shake hands before one enters the elevator. The guy who remains turns to me with a smile on his face. He's older than I imagined, maybe in his late fifties or early sixties, with short grey hair and no facial hair. His body may be slightly rounder than it probably was a few years back. But there is still the body of a fighter there. I can see why he manages a few of them. Those who can't, teach, or so Calvin keeps telling me.

"Mr Wilson, it's good to put a face to the name. Calvin speaks very highly of you," Young says as he holds out his hand.

"That's because he knows better than to bad mouth me," I chuckle, taking his hand and shaking it.

"I can imagine he does. Do you fight, Mr Wilson?" Young asks. Typical manager, always looking for the next big thing.

"Not unless I have to," I answer with a smile. "And please, call me Logan."

Young nods as he holds out his hand, signalling for me to go ahead of him as we enter his office.

"Chelsea, could you please bring in a tray of drinks." I hear her respond with a "yes" as I walk into the office to find two chairs in front of a desk. "Please take a seat," Young says behind me as he takes the chair behind the desk. I glance behind me and see that the door remains open.

"Will your assistant be joining us? Or do you want me to start with what I've found?" I ask, not wanting to wait around too long. Luckily, Chelsea walks in with a cup of coffee for Young and two water bottles.

"I wasn't sure what you would want as you've just had a coffee, so I brought you water," she says, placing a bottle in front of me.

"Thank you," I reply, smiling at her. She quickly places both in front of Young.

"Chelsea, can you stay, please? I have a feeling things will need to be put in place afterwards, so it will save me from repeating everything."

"Of course," she replies before taking a seat at the side of the desk and picking up a notepad and pen. I'm impressed with how organised this woman is. It's as if she is prepared for every situation. Has she served in the military?

"So, Logan, what did you find?" Young asks, sitting back in his chair. He looks relaxed, but I know he won't be when I'm finished with him.

"I'm afraid to say your security has been seriously compromised."

Young's eyes close as he rubs the bridge of his nose. I'm sure I even hear him curse under his breath.

"Taylor?"

"It wouldn't be possible for me to know for certain. I don't know enough about him and how he worked. But it's a real possibility as the system was compromised a few years ago." I pull my tablet back out of my bag and tap on the screen a few times. With the blueprints on the screen, I turn it so Young and Chelsea can see.

"The red crosses are cameras that have no feed coming from them. The blue crosses are cameras that have been left to get dirty, altering how much is viewable from them. On closer inspection, I think the marks and dirt on them are old and deliberate."

"And the green crosses?" Chelsea asks, looking at the screen.

"They are cameras that are in working order. The purple circles are blind spots. As you can see, there are quite a few of them."

She nods once and starts writing on her pad.

"So that's four red, four blue and sixteen green for the cameras?" she asks, looking at the screen again. I nod in agreement.

"Do you know why those cameras would have been

compromised?" I ask Young, who looks like he has aged about ten years in the space of two minutes.

"They are either on the floor Taylor used for his own business or in the basement." Young leans forward and points to a blue cross. "That room is where he would hold meetings right up until he died."

"I don't know much about this Taylor, only what Calvin has told me. But how clued up was he regarding electronics and how to work around CCTV? Did he hire people to do the work for him? Or would he have been able to control and manipulate it himself?" I ask. Young shrugs, looking defeated.

"The only thing I truly know about that man is how deceitful he was. It seems he manipulated all around him, so nothing would surprise me anymore." He lets out a deep sigh and leans back in his chair again, rubbing his forehead as if chasing off a headache.

"I knew the guy for years, and I always thought of him as an ally until everything came to light."

I can see how devastated the guy is and know what I have to say next isn't going to help.

"That isn't the only issue you have."

Young looks up at me with a look that tells me he knew it wouldn't be. I turn to look at Chelsea, who's looking concerned.

"I asked you how many people had access to security and other areas in the building, and you were unable to answer. So, I did some digging, and it seems that a large number of people here seem to have access to more rooms than they should. I don't know why, but over three-quarters of the workforce has access to the whole building, and I mean the *whole* building. That includes this floor and this office. I tried to work out any consistencies with who has access to all areas and who worked here when Taylor was alive, but I couldn't pinpoint any. I also attempted to track where Taylor's team was going, especially. It seems the most common area was a room in the basement. I went in there, but I couldn't see anything."

Young pales as he looks at the room I'm pointing at.

"It's the one room that has never had cameras."

I watch Young and can tell he knows exactly what's been happening there.

"Leave it with me; I will speak to a few other associates and see what they know." Young stands from his chair and walks to the window to look out. "As for everything else, can I trust your company to right everything and upgrade all the cameras and systems?"

"Of course, anything you need," I promise, knowing he has no reason to believe me.

"Good. I also want all personnel's access restricted to their floors. From now on, if anyone else needs access to other areas, they must report to me first. If they don't have my permission, they cannot have access granted without a security team member accompanying them." He walks away from the window and leans on the back of the seat.

"How long would it take for you to make up all new security passes?"

"I need to put a whole new system into place where things are done electronically and are harder to hack into. But that will take time. The system you have in place now will require all cards to be altered manually. I could change people's access tonight using their current cards if that's any help. I would need a hand, though, as it's a long process."

He turns to Chelsea, who looks at him.

"I could ask Penny to have Luna tonight, and I will work late. It's no problem," she says without having to be asked.

"Are you sure? It's a lot to ask of you. I know you have your daughter at home."

"No, honestly, it's fine. I will get security to take people's cards from them as they leave, and we can get as many as possible. There may be a handful of people who have already left or are on a day off. But I can get them to see security on their first day back." Chelsea stands from her chair and looks at Young. "I'll send an email out now telling everyone to surrender their cards on the way out and to come in slightly early tomorrow to receive their cards back." She turns her attention to me and smiles. "I will be available to help within the hour."

"Thank you. I'll get the word to my team, and they'll start collecting the passes."

She nods and walks out of the door, closing it behind her.

"It looks like you are in for a long night. Please know I will pay whatever you ask. I need to know my employees and colleagues are safe."

I stand from my seat and step in front of him.

"Leave it to my team. We will get this sorted. I know it's asking a lot, but you can trust us." I hold out my hand, and he looks at it momentarily before shaking it.

"I hope I can because I will be putting a lot in your hands."

Chapter Nine

CALVIN

I pull up outside of our office building and turn the engine off. I've been trying to get hold of Drew for the last hour, but he isn't answering any calls or messages. I know there is only one place he could be because there is no signal in that particular room. We designed it that way for a reason.

Climbing out of the car, I pull my coat tighter around myself. The autumn chill is starting to feel more like winter, and I hate being cold. Muttering to myself about how much I miss the Alabama sun, I unlock the door to the office and head to the basement.

Down here, we have four soundproof rooms with thick metal doors and no natural light. Three of them are holding cells, all above board, except they will hold people I know who could kill us as fast as we could.

The fourth room is where I expect Drew is working. This is the room where we keep our weapons and files containing strictly confidential documentation. We aren't talking about the average personnel folders an employer will have of their employees. No, this is the type of information that only us three currently know about.

To most people, we run a security company that offers bodyguards and security to the rich and powerful, but that is just the public persona we uphold. No, behind very secure closed doors, we deal with some of the deadliest people around. We may no longer be SEALs, but we strive to keep the world safe from terrorists of all kinds. We aren't just talking about ISIS. We are talking about the people who terrorise the innocent. A secret organisation uses people like us who are highly trained in dangerous fields to stop criminals that the police don't even know about. For our department, we specialise in high-end drug dealers and weapon manufacturers. That may seem hypocritical, considering who I used to work for, but there are various types of people who manufacture and sell weapons. The O'Reillys sell theirs to organisations like us, ones they know are being used to protect the innocent, not used against them. Trust me, even in the UK, thousands of people are willing to put weapons in the wrong hands to ensure they get a fat paycheck in the end.

The guys and I have taken it upon ourselves to use the training we got from our time in the SEALs and use it to our advantage. We can enter a building, retrieve information and be out again without a single soul knowing we were ever there. Logan can hack any computer and find things in the darkest part of the dark web, giving us leads that the police couldn't find if it was right under their noses.

The organisation that sends us details is not only found in the UK; it's all over the world. You name a country, and we have people in it. All ex-military and all scarier predators than any murderer because we know how to make them pay for their crimes, and we won't lose a moment's sleep over it.

I reach the door at the bottom of the corridor and unlock it with my key and fingerprint. It doesn't sound like much, but if Logan wants to keep someone out of a room, he can do it without breaking a sweat.

Once inside, I close the door and walk over to the far wall where there is another door. This one requires a retinal scanner as well as handprint and voice match. As I said, Logan is that good. If anyone were to try and follow me, they wouldn't get far.

"Bambi!" I call as I enter the area that consists of three separate rooms.

"I'm here!" he calls back. As I expected, he is in front of the whiteboard he has been working on, tracking a massive shipment of drugs that we think is heading this way.

"I need you to come with me. Houdini found a major security breach at Young's place. We need to pull an all-nighter sorting it out."

"Shit," Drew curses as he turns away from the board. "How bad are we talking?"

"Taylor was doing some dodgy shit in there, and Houdini wants to find out what. But in the meantime, we need to reset all the access cards by the morning and start making up new ones for the employees."

"Fuck," he curses again as he walks over to the desk chair and grabs his jacket, which is on the back of it. "How many employees again?"

"Two hundred plus."

Drew spins around and stares at me.

"Over two hundred? How the fuck are we going to do all of that in one night?" He has a point: we could never get that done.

"We have help. Four guys from the security team we placed there, plus one other person."

"Who?" he asks, frowning, as a smile spreads across my face.

"This one will put a smile on your face and make your late night more worthwhile."

"Well, hello again, Chelsea. Imagine seeing you here," Drew coos as he walks into the conference room where Logan has set up shop.

"What are the odds?" Chelsea sighs sarcastically from her spot where security passes and Post-It notes surround her. She looks up and offers us a small smile. "Have you come to help or just stalk me?"

"I have no idea what you mean. How have we been stalking you?" Drew asks, placing a hand on his heart.

"Oh, I don't know through Tinder, maybe?" she sighs, looking back down to the cards in front of her. Drew and I both look at Logan, who shrugs, still refusing to look up from whatever he is doing.

"She knows we know."

As neither seems overly bothered, I shrug off my jacket and hang it on the back of a chair.

"Where are we up to with all of this?"

Logan waves us over and fills us in on all he has learnt about the system being corrupted and that he thinks it was all Taylor's doing. I tell him I'll call the O'Reillys and see if they know anything about his side business. In the mean-time, Logan tells us that he has two guys going floor to floor, rewiring and cleaning the cameras. They plan on them all being in working order by five a.m. when the cleaners arrive. Two more are working in the hub, checking through footage and seeing how many blind spots the cameras leave once they are all working.

So that leaves the four of us here with the two hundred and forty-eight cards they could collect. Now, we have the job of wiping and reprogramming all the cards to ensure no one has access to anywhere they shouldn't. Each card takes about three minutes for me to wipe the access codes and for Logan to put the correct information in place. We have to do them individually to ensure there are no mistakes. The last thing we need is for some that don't programme properly to have access to areas they aren't meant to, it won't look good for the company.

For the next hour, Chelsea and Drew work through the staff list. They tick off the cards they have and highlight the ones they don't. At the same time, they are checking for anyone who may have requested a replacement card, so we know they may still have access to other areas. It's a slow task, but we get into a flow between the four of us and start to see progress.

"Are we going to order food? I'm starving," Drew sighs, leaning back in his chair.

"When aren't you hungry?" Logan sighs from the computer.

"When I'm eating," Drew replies with a grin. Chelsea chuckles from her seat and picks up her phone.

"I could eat. What does everyone fancy?" she asks, tapping on her phone. She frowns at it for a moment before standing up from the table. "I'll be right back."

I watch as she walks out the door, the phone to her ear.

"So, what do you think Taylor had going on in the basement?" I ask Logan while keeping an eye on the door to ensure Chelsea doesn't return.

"I have no idea, but I think Young does. As soon as I

mentioned the room he was going into, all colour drained from his face. I plan to go there later to see what I can find."

"I'll come with you," Drew says from his seat as he stands and stretches.

"You and Chelsea seem very relaxed around each other there," I point out as I sit back in my chair. Drew shrugs whilst pouting.

"We were just talking; she has our sense of humour." He picks up a screwed-up piece of paper and launches it at Logan, who catches it without looking away from his computer.

"Any reason you are throwing rubbish at me?" he asks, throwing the paper into the waste bin by the door, getting it in the first time.

"Why the fuck did you tell her we were all aware she matched with each of us. She was dead embarrassed at first," Drew snaps through gritted teeth. Logan shrugs, still refusing to look away from his screen.

"It slipped out; accidents happen," he mutters, which earns him an eye roll from Drew.

"For a Special OPs specialist, you're shit when it comes to keeping something quiet." Drew sits back in his chair and rolls his neck before rubbing the back of it. "I'm going to order Chinese. Make a list, and I'll order it in. Young can foot the bill."

"He left Chels with the instructions to put a takeaway on his card and anything else we need," Logan says as he lets out a deep breath and leans back in his chair. He looks at the clock on the wall and then the screen. We've been at it for three hours and managed to get fifty-three cards done. It's eight at night, and we have eight hours to finish the other one-hundred and ninety-five. We should be able to do it, as long as we don't lose too much time taking breaks or stopping for food.

Chelsea walks back into the room and places her phone on the table. She's quieter than she has been all evening, and I can see whoever was on the phone has upset her.

"Everything okay?" I ask, leaning on the table, watching her as she takes her seat.

"Yeah, my daughter is having issues at school and has been upset. She's okay now I've spoken to her."

"How old's your daughter?" I ask as I slip the card I just wiped out of the cardholder and hand it to Logan before selecting the next one.

"Six. She has such a kind soul, but it makes her an easy target for bullies," Chelsea sighs as she wipes her cheek, and I can see how hard it is for her to be away from her daughter whilst she's upset.

"If you need to go, Chels," Drew starts as I place a hand on her arm. She looks at him and forces a smile.

"Honestly, it's fine. She's going to sleep now anyway, so it won't make any difference if I'm there or not." She must notice we are all watching her as she flashes a big smile and grabs her phone. "Who wants what for dinner? Mr Young is paying."

Chapter Ten

CHELSEA

"Bambi! Will you shut the fuck up for once in your life!" Logan shouts as he throws a screwed-up paper napkin at Drew.

"Okay, enough, I need to ask. What's with the nicknames?" I laugh as Drew flips the bird at Logan. I don't think I have heard them refer to each other by their real names tonight other than when discussing each other with their employees.

"It's a military thing," Calvin laughs as he sips his water.

"I know that; my dad was in the Navy. But I want to know why you have *your* nicknames," I laugh.

"Drews is Bambi because, well, look at him. He couldn't have more of a baby face if he tried," Logan laughs.

"Logan is Houdini because there is no lock, physical or encoded, that he can't crack," Drew announces. "And Calvin is Pippin."

"As in Pippin Took, from The Lord of The Rings?" I ask, grinning. Calvin rolls his eyes as the others roar, laughing.

"The very same."

"So, how did you earn yourself that nickname?" I ask grinning.

"When I was on one of my first training courses, we had to be stealthy and sneak past our commanders without being seen," Calvin starts.

"Except this dumbass drops his rifle against some rocks and sets off the blanks in it, letting everyone in a five-mile radius know where he was," Logan finishes clapping his mate on the back. "Seriously, you could hear it all over. To say he failed is an understatement."

"Alright, smartass!" Calvin sighs, pushing Logan's hand from his shoulder and returning to the laptop in front of him.

"Oh, I get it now! Pippin knocked the skeleton into the well, letting all the Orcs know where they were!" I exclaim as the reference finally clicks into place. Logan and Drew both laugh as Calvin nods with a sigh.

"That name has stuck with me for ten years."

"Probably a dumb question. But what does SEALs stand for? I know it's like an advanced Marine, right?" I ask. "I've grown up knowing the main forces in the UK. Navy, Marine, Air Force and Army, but we don't have SEALs like in the US," I add when Logan frowns at me.

"SEALs are like a mixture of all of them. Navy SEALs stands for Navy Sea, Air and Land. We were members of Special Operations Forces. We are trained to be involved with direct raids, hostage situations, terrorists and so on," Drew explains.

"The UK does have something similar to SEALs, which is the Special Boat Service or SBS," Logan adds. Now, he mentions it. I remember my dad once mentioned the SBS, but I didn't know what he was referring to and never really asked.

I look at the clock and see it's coming up to three in the morning. We still have at least forty cards to get through, but we should manage it in time.

I'm having more fun than I thought I would with the guys. We've laughed and ate a ton of Chinese, which the other security guys joined us for. There is still plenty to last us the rest of the night, and we plan on having it for breakfast to celebrate our achievement.

I don't know what it is with these guys, but it's so easy to relax around them. They are obviously close, and I have heard so many amusing stories from their time in the SEALs. There are times I can see they are remembering difficult moments, so I change the subject as I don't want to bring them down. I like to think one day, I will get to listen to more of their stories and adventures, if that's the right word to use.

I'm sitting next to Logan, who is passing me the cards when they have been programmed, and I'm putting them in the right envelope and then into the correct department stack. He is the least chatty of the three and is more likely to withdraw from the conversation than the others. He never talks about anything personal and will sometimes give one-word answers. Occasionally, he joins in with the guys as two of them will gang up on the other, but it's like he will remember I'm there and withdraw again.

"Chels, I need to ask," Calvin says from the other side of Logan. "Why is a lovely lady like you on Tinder and not snatched up already?"

"Wow, straight to the point," I laugh as my cheeks warm again. I had hoped this topic wouldn't come up. I've already decided I could never go on a date with one of them, now I know them all a little better. Don't get me wrong, I could easily date them all, even Logan. But I don't think I would be able to choose which one I wanted more than the others. Plus, there is that worry that they would end up arguing because of it. Not that I think I'm anything special, but it would still feel wrong like I would be playing them against each other. They have such a close bond I would never want to come between them.

"Well, we are all wondering, so might as well ask," he chuckles, passing Logan a new card. I shrug as I take a card from Logan and write the name on the envelope.

"Truth is, I was drunk when I signed up for it. Seemed like a good idea at the time."

"Until you not only matched with three friends but had to spend a whole night with them all afterwards," Drew chuckles from the other side of me.

"Something like that," I laugh, handing him the envelope so he can file it in the right box.

"That only answers half the question," Calvin points out. "Why did you feel you had to go on there in the first place?"

"Why did you go on there? Any of you?" I ask, looking around. The three share a look, but it's Logan who answers.

"I only went on there because we need dates for these stupid events and dinners. I'm not looking for a romantic relationship, but if I could find a friend to go with me, that would do."

"I guess that's why we all went on there," Calvin answers. "With work, we don't have time to go out and find people to date, but we need someone to attend parties and networking events with us. We just needed someone who is…"

"Arm candy?" I offer. All three instantly protest.

"No, not arm candy. I want to be able to enjoy her company as well. These events can be boring as fuck, and I want to know at least there's one person there who can make them a little more fun and less like work," Calvin offers. I look to Drew, who's nodding in agreement.

"What about you? What did you hope to get from it?" Calvin asks. I shrug as I write the next name on the envelope.

"Same kind of thing, I guess. It's just been me and my daughter for so long that I've forgotten what it's like to have fun. Yeah, Penny comes round occasionally, and my friend Rochelle, but it's not the same," I admit, shrugging my shoulders. I don't want to tell them I'm lonely most of the time, but looking at the three of them now, I think they feel the same way.

"Do you want to date then? Or have a bit of fun now and again?" Drew asks. I shrug again as I don't know how to answer.

"I want to have fun, but that doesn't mean sexually; I'm not looking for one-night stands. I'm not looking for relationships, either. I want to be me now and again and not 'work Chelsea' or Mum." I sigh, leaning back in my chair and rubbing my face. "I'm sorry, I'm tired. I'm starting to lag, and I've been up twenty-one hours. You don't need to listen to me whining about my life. It's nothing compared to what you guys have been through."

"Hey, don't say that; you can moan as much as you want. We will listen," Drew says, touching my arm.

"It's just a thought, but hear me out," Calvin says as he leans around Logan to look at me. "You are looking just to have a bit of fun now and again, and we are looking for someone to make these boring events more tolerable. Why don't we come together and help each other out?"

"What?" I ask, laughing, staring at him in shock. "Absolutely not!"

"Why not? I see it as a win-win. As far as people will be aware at these events, we are just a normal couple having a good time."

"Until someone attends another function and sees me with someone else. They will think I'm a slut!" I protest.

"No, they won't. They will think we are in a polyamorous relationship."

I turn to Drew and frown.

"Are they really a thing? You name one person you know who shares multiple men, and everyone is okay with it."

"I used to work for four brothers who shared a fiancée."

"That's illegal for one!" I point out, but he shakes his head, smiling.

"The four guys are in a relationship with her. She is only legally marrying one of them; the others are having their relationship blessed. But to them, they will be married to her; they are all very happy and so in love, it's almost sickly," he smirks. I shake my head as I can't believe what I'm hearing. It's just madness. How can one woman be with multiple men and them all be happy with that?

"Anyway, it's not like you would be sleeping with us all; you don't have to sleep with any of us; we will just enjoy each other's company and share a few drinks," Calvin says as he shrugs and goes back to the task at hand, the ID cards.

"Just think about it; it could be fun," Drew says beside me as he takes an envelope from me. I look from him to Calvin and know I could have a laugh with them. But then I look at Logan and frown.

"What do you think?"

He shrugs his shoulders whilst tapping away on his keyboard.

"Doesn't make any difference to me. Like I said, I'm not looking for a relationship, just someone who can help me break the ice at the meetings and events."

We all go back to our little tasks, working silently as my mind tries to process everything they just offered me. I look around at the three guys and know any girl would be begging to stand beside them. They are funny and intelligent and could protect Luna and me if needed. They are not bad to look at, but am I really considering pretending to be their date? I think I need to sleep on it because right now, I'm struggling to find a reason not to.

Chapter Eleven

LOGAN

"Houdini, wake the fuck up!"

"I swear to God, Bambi. I will kick your ass, I'm sleeping!" I growl as I turn onto my stomach and hug my pillow to my head.

"I wish I were too, but this is an emergency!" Drew shouts through the door whilst banging on it. I curse loudly as I climb out of bed and storm to the door bollock naked. I throw it open and am ready to punch Drew in the face when he holds up his phone and shows me the screen.

"That's not a fucking emergency, Bambi. Now fuck off!" I turn to slam the door, but he puts his foot in the way.

"Yes, it is! Pippin's out with Jason O'Reilly trying to find out what's been going on in that basement, and I have to train the recruits, which leaves you to go and see Young and go through how many people had been given access to areas they shouldn't have been in."

"I will do it tomorrow. One day isn't going to make a difference. Or I will email it to him when I get up," I groan, climbing back into bed.

"He doesn't want an email. He wants to speak to you in person." Drew grabs the bottom of the bed covers and pulls them off me.

"Bambi, back off now. I'm about to lose my mother fucking shit!"

Drew backs away with his hands up.

"Fine, but if you lose us the biggest contract we have to date, you'll have to find us another one!" He snaps slamming the door as he leaves.

"Fucking bastard, asshat of a prick!" I yell, climbing out of bed, grabbing my towel, and charging towards my bathroom. "You better at least have the coffee brewing!" I shout, knowing full well he will hear me.

———————

I storm from my room ten minutes later, showered and in clean clothes. My mood is no fucking better, though. I'm exhausted and can't deal with people right now. Why can't he accept an email like ordinary people? Who likes to have face-to-face conversations these days? No fucker, that's who! But, of course, I have to be up after three hours of sleep to sort shit out.

I look around for Drew and see a note next to the coffee pot, which is full.

Gone to HQ.
Try not to kill anyone or get us fired.

How the hell are Calvin and him still going? They mustn't have even been to bed yet. They have always been able to go days without sleep, whereas I turn into the definition of asshat if I'm tired. I hit my limit of twenty-eight hours last night and came home to die for twenty-four peaceful hours.

Pouring myself a large coffee, I check my emails to find the one Calvin has forwarded to me.

Calvin
Thank you again for all the work you and your team did last night.
Everyone got their passes without any glitches this AM, and the few that were not done will be done later today.
Please ask Logan to call me to arrange a meeting ASAP, as I need to speak to him face to face. I know he will be sleeping, as I'm sure you all are, but it is important.
Thanks again,
Geralt Young

I down my first mug of coffee before pouring a second and dialling the number at the bottom of the email. It is answered after three rings.

"Mr Young's office."

"Chels? Is that you? Why the hell aren't you at home in bed?" I snap.

"Logan? I couldn't sleep, so I came in. I'm going home in a bit to try again."

What the fuck is wrong with these people? Who doesn't need bloody sleep?

"Make sure you do. What did Young want with me?" I ask, taking a sip of my coffee. I hear Chels telling me she is patching me through now. He answers on the first ring.

"Young speaking."

"It's Logan. What's so important you had to have me woken up?" I demand drinking the rest of my coffee.

"Sorry, Logan. I didn't mean for them to wake you; I figured you would all receive the message later in the day,"

Young stutters down the line. I roll my eyes whilst taking another sip of my coffee, hoping it will wake me up a bit.

"Well, I'm awake now, what's up?" I ask, reminding myself that I need to be nice to the guy. Drew's right; we can't afford to lose this contract. Especially with all the extras I'm charging him for.

"I need to speak to you in person about what I think was happening in that basement. Can you come in, please?"

I want to say no, but instead, I tell him I will be there in fifteen minutes and hang up. Grabbing my keys, I head for the door, wishing I was going to bed instead of to work. But something about that basement has been bugging me, and I think whatever Taylor was doing down there was dodgy shit, and we need to get to the bottom of it.

"There in the far corner, do you not see it?"

I look closer and see what looks like a wet patch.

"It's a bit of damp, or the concrete was a slightly different colour when relayed a couple of years ago," I answer with a shrug.

"But I never authorised any work to be done in here. I was sure he had done something down here, so I came to look myself. When I saw the marks on the floor, I figured there had been some kind of leak. I asked Chelsea to pull all the reports to do with this room and saw my signature on a job form for new flooring to be put down. The problem is I was on a two week cruise when it was signed, so it couldn't have been me."

I pinch the bridge of my nose, hoping to chase off the headache brewing from lack of sleep.

"So, what are you saying? That Taylor had some work done down here that you didn't authorise?"

"That's exactly what I'm saying. But the question is, why would he have it done? I know what he used to use this place for when he owned it, and I can't help."

"Wow! Back up a minute!" I interrupt, holding up my hands to stop Young from saying more. "Are you saying Taylor used to own this building?"

"That's exactly what I'm saying. He sold it to me at a great price, stating he was downgrading to smaller premises as he didn't want to work as hard as he was forever."

"And you are only telling me this now? Because of some new flooring?" I ask, confused. "Mr Young, I'm exhausted, and my brain is not firing on all cylinders. So just this once, tell me exactly what Taylor used to do down here when it was his building."

Young walks to the door and opens it as if checking for anyone listening outside before closing it again, looking more nervous than he was a moment ago.

"Taylor had a nasty streak."

"I figured that when I heard what he allowed to happen to the O'Reillys' woman," I point out. Young nods and takes a deep breath.

"When we were a little younger, Taylor considered himself the next Godfather. He ran this place until he couldn't keep the staff. Everyone kept leaving or disappearing. At first, I thought they were sick of his bullshit, but then I met his henchman, who he saw as a son, Hudson. I'm sure you have heard of his role in poor Jasmine's kidnapping?"

I nod because I have, and I know that if that prick were alive today, I would kill him myself for what he put her through.

"You will know that Hudson was a psychopath who

never felt anything for anyone." Again, I nod as this is all old news to me. But I know something is coming that will be new.

"It turns out Taylor used Hudson's lack of emotions to become one of the biggest drug trafficking and human trafficking organisations in the UK. They would kidnap people and get them to smuggle the drugs wherever they were sent."

"And you just fucking let them?" I roar at him.

"God, no! I had no idea until after he died, and they found a few men and women Hudson had hidden away to make the product," Taylor declares with his hands up defensively.

"What's that got to do with this room? Was he mixing them here?" I ask, frowning and looking around. Young shakes his head.

"No, but when Taylor owned this building, this was his personal storage area. No one knew what he kept here, as only his most trusted guys were given access. He admitted once when he was drunk, there were things hidden in a way no one would find them."

I look back to the miscoloured floor.

"Like burying them under the concrete," I whisper as it clicks into place. "You think before he died, he hid drugs and information on customers under there?"

Young looks around and lets out a deep breath. I guess it's hard enough finding out your so-called friend is a kidnapping, drug smuggling bastard who is possibly using your building to hide the evidence, framing you at the same time.

Are there people who worked alongside Taylor who have taken over what he started? Are they still hiding things in here?

I look to the floor and take a deep breath.

"We need to know more before we start digging. The last thing we need is for the police to get involved until we have solid evidence that it was Taylor burying secrets, not you."

I tell Young to lead us to his office, and if anyone asks, we are checking on the camera situation. The fewer people that know there is a problem, the better.

As we reach Young's floor, I look through to the reception desk and see Chelsea asleep, her head on the desk. I let out a sigh. Why couldn't she have stayed home and slept like a normal person instead of being Superwoman? I can't leave her there. I consider telling her to go home, but she is far too tired to drive safely.

"Do you have somewhere we can make her more comfortable?" I ask Young, who nods and points towards a small room to the side of his.

"There is a sofa in there; she won't be disturbed."

"Get the door for me," I whisper before walking over to the sleeping Chelsea and gently shake her shoulder. When she hardly stirs, I carefully lift her into my arms.

"What are you doing?" she mumbles as she opens her eyes slightly.

"Moving you to a more comfortable sleeping place," I whisper as I follow Young towards the room where I see a comfortable looking sofa. For a moment, I consider climbing onto it too and getting some sleep, but there is too much that needs to be done.

"I'll go home," Chelsea starts to protest as I lie her down on the sofa. She tries to sit up, but I push her shoulders back down. She's too tired to fight against me, which proves she's too exhausted to drive.

"Sleep first, then we will get you home."

As soon as her head lands on the arm of the sofa, her eyes close again.

"Just five minutes, then I will go," she whispers before falling back asleep. Young hands me a long coat, and I place it over her as she sleeps soundly.

"Five minutes, my ass," I mutter to myself whilst walking out of the room and closing the door, leaving Chelsea to catch up on some much-needed sleep.

Chapter Twelve

CHELSEA

I walk into my lounge and fall onto the sofa, not having the energy to even take my shoes off. Luna lands beside me and lays her head on my lap. Running my hand over her soft blonde hair, I let out a deep sigh. I'm exhausted, beyond exhausted. What was I thinking going back to work this morning? It's no surprise I fell asleep on my desk. I can't believe I did that and for Logan to find me, of all people. I vaguely remember him carrying me into the staff room and placing me on the sofa. I was too tired to fight him when he pushed me back down, telling me to sleep. I don't think it took me more than a few seconds to drift back off into a dreamless slumber.

I'd been woken up by Drew an hour ago, telling me the time and that I needed to pick up my daughter. I was down in the car park and rushing towards the school before I was even fully awake. Luckily for me and Luna, Drew had actually woken me a little earlier than I needed to be there, so Luna wasn't waiting around for me.

I would have never forgiven myself if I had missed her pick-up time. It's one thing I always make sure I am there for.

"Mummy, what's for dinner?" Luna asks from my lap.

"I don't know, sweetheart. I'll have a look in a bit," I reply, closing my burning eyes as I absent-mindedly continue to stroke her hair.

"Mummy, someone's at the door."

"What?" I wake with a jump.

Shit, did I fall asleep?

I look around, dazed, realising it's darker than when I got home.

"I said there's someone at the door," Luna says again as a knocking sound comes from the hallway. I jump to my feet and rush for the door, throwing it open before looking through the peephole. There, standing in front of me is a pizza delivery man.

"I have a delivery for ..." he looks at the paper in his hand, "Chelsea Hughes."

"I haven't ordered any pizza; there must be some mistake," I argue, but he shakes his head and hands me the slip.

"There's a message on the bottom," he says, pointing to a square at the bottom of the paper.

Chelsea, we know you will be too tired to cook, so we supplied dinner. Thanks for all your hard work. Rest tonight. Calvin, Drew and Logan.

"There's two pizzas, garlic bread, wedges and a bottle of pop," the delivery guy announces as he hands me a pile of boxes. He passes the pop to Luna, who is now beside me. "There are also a few cookies in there too, which I am sure you will enjoy," he adds as he hands a smaller box to her.

"Thank you," I reply, still clutching the receipt, unable to believe they thought to send dinner.

"You're welcome. Enjoy your meal," he smiles, turning around and heading back towards his car. I see that Luna has already rushed off, no doubt getting a drink of pop, as she's usually only allowed it on special occasions.

I walk into the kitchen carrying the pizzas and garlic bread and place them on the table. There is more than enough to feed us both tonight and tomorrow. Looking down at the receipt again, I smile whilst grabbing my phone and opening up Tinder to message them.

First, I open Calvin's profile and send a quick message.

CHughes18: Thank you so much for the food. I can't thank you enough.

I stop momentarily before adding my mobile number and sending the text. I send an identical message to Logan and Drew, making sure to add my number to see if they will message me directly.

It takes less than a minute for a message to come through on WhatsApp.

UNKNOWN: You are more than welcome. I hope it means you can relax a bit tonight. Calvin x

Two more come through with almost identical replies from Logan and Drew. I try to work out what to say to them, but I can't decide, so I close the app and place my phone on the table.

Luna has already grabbed two plates and loaded hers with food before sitting down and filling her face.

"This pizza is amazing! When did you order it?" she asks with her mouth full. I shake my head as I chew. Luna isn't wrong. The meat feast is possibly the best thing I have ever eaten.

"It's from the guys I was helping out at work last night," I answer once my mouth's empty. Luna smiles before going back to her food.

We continue to eat as Luna tells me about her day, which has thankfully been better than yesterday. The whole time I listen to her, my mind keeps wandering back to the offer the guys made in the early hours of this morning.

Could I do it? Would I be able to spend time with them and not develop feelings for any of them? I look at the food around us and know that no one else has ever done anything this considerate for me before. Even though I know it could be a way for them to persuade me to give them a chance, I don't think it is. We spent ten hours together in that room last night, and they never gave me the impression that they were faking the way they were with me or each other. There again, I've thought that about people in the past, and look how that turned out. I don't know why this feels so different from the apprehension I have felt about people since all that. I can't explain it, but my gut and heart are saying to trust them.

"Mummy, I've had enough. Can we eat the cookies in bed with a film?" Luna asks from across the table.

"Just this once. But you need to have a shower first," I only just finished saying before she jumps from the table, shouting that I need to turn it on for her.

We take turns to shower before curling up in my bed to watch a film. As I lay there watching *Barbie: The Nutcracker* for the hundredth time, I start looking through some of the messages I have received on Tinder. They range from reasonably polite to downright rude. Yes, people are offering just sex or to *"show me a good time"*. I shudder at the thought of it. Does this actually work for people? Because all it does is creep me the hell out. I know one thing for sure: I'm coming off this app. There is no appeal in it for me, and the slime balls on it need to do one.

As I close my account, I decide that I'm going to give in and go with the guys to these events. It might not be ideal, but as the four of us all said last night, we don't have time for the commitment of a relationship, and going to events with them could be fun. It's not like they are hard to get along with and are certainly nice to look at. I could see myself having a lot of fun with them.

I take a deep breath and type out a message to all three.

Chelsea: Okay, I'm in. I'll come to events and dinners with you when I can.

It doesn't take long for the replies to start coming through.

Drew: That's great, looking forward to it. x

Logan: Thanks.

Calvin: Thank you. I will message you tomorrow with a list of dates and see if you are available for any of them. I'm sure we will all have a great time. Xx

I place my phone on charge and lie in my bed as Luna dozes beside me. I think about moving her, but I'm too tired. One night in my bed won't do any harm. I close my eyes and realise I feel good after making the decision to help the guys. This could be the change in my life that I need right now. Time to help me find myself without the pressure of being what someone else wants me to be.

Chapter Thirteen

CALVIN

"Any luck?"

I turn to see Drew walking into the special Ops hub. Shaking my head, I look back at the whiteboard before me. We have spent the last week trying to track down all of Taylor and Hudson's drug smugglers. We plan on exhuming whatever's buried under that flooring but have to be careful about it as we don't know who has been continuing what Taylor started. The last thing we need is for people they were working with to realise we are on to them. From what we can gather, Taylor had his fingers in many big pies, and we could take down over half of the drug factories and distributors in the UK and possibly other countries by what's buried under that floor.

We reviewed the camera footage from the days Hudson went down to the room, but we quickly realised that the route he would take was unwatchable due to all the dirty or broken cameras. That's why so many were compromised, to hide who went in and out of the room. If I hadn't known Hudson myself, I would have never recognised him through the cameras. He was careful to avoid anything that would have given him away. He was smart, that's for sure.

"So far, we think we know who nine of their drug mules were, but there is no way of knowing for sure without either finding them or checking the files. We can only guess who they are because they were all last seen in Taylor's bars regularly, walking into the back offices."

"How didn't the police make that connection with Taylor and drug dealers?" Drew asks, standing beside me with his arms crossed. I point to the whiteboard, where there is a map of the city.

"The red pins are where those nine people were last seen. If you were looking at this, would you put the connection together?"

Drew shakes his head. All of them look like random locations; they aren't even all in Taylor's name, so there's no way the police could have linked them to him or Hudson.

"Who owns them all now?"

"The O'Reillys claimed them all when he died. Most were sold or knocked down. I think there were five that they transferred into their name. Two of which were gutted and turned into gyms and fight clubs."

"They made a tidy sum out of it then," Drew sighs, as I nod. The O'Reillys didn't need the extra money, but there are certain rules when it comes to the darker side of the business world. Sides that very few know about. The O'Reillys may do some illegal shit, but they always stay as clean as possible and ensure people benefit from what they do.

"Who do you think funded the equipment for this room?" I ask him, pointing out the high-tech hacking equipment and all that goes with it. Jason O'Reilly is the only one of the brothers in the know about this side of our company.

After everything they went through trying to find Jasmine when she was abducted, he was willing to do anything to ensure others were kept safe. When I informed him of all that we were learning about Hudson, he started to blame himself.

Hudson and Jason had a history in which Jason should have taken out Hudson years ago. But he failed to because he always hoped there was a chance Hudson would turn his life around. We all know he didn't, and, in the end, it was Jason who put a bullet through his head.

"What time are you going to the hotel where this function is tonight?" Drew asks. I look at my watch and sigh.

"I need to leave soon. I promised Chelsea we would have a drink beforehand to help calm her nerves and so I could fill her in on a few things."

Drew nods as he glances at the board again. The two of us have both been messaging Chelsea a lot over the last week. We have formed a good friendship with her, making this whole 'fake dating' thing a lot easier.

A week ago, I took her out for dinner and a few drinks, and we had a great time. Conversation flowed easily, as did the drinks, and before long, we were both singing at the karaoke at the top of our lungs. I can't remember the last time I let my hair down like that and just enjoyed the moment. But with Chelsea, it's easy to do as she brings out the playfulness in me.

"How was your dinner the other night?" I ask Drew as he picks up a newspaper clipping and reads it.

"We had a great time. She's a blast, isn't she?" he smiles as he flicks through some papers on his hand. "Did you get any info on her ex from her?"

I frown whilst shaking my head.

"Other than they are divorced, nothing," I answer

before walking over to the kettle and turning it on, needing a mug of coffee before I go. "Why do you ask?"

Drew shrugs as he leans back against a table.

"I'm not sure; I just wonder where he is. I mean, considering they have had a kid together, she never mentions him, even in passing comments. Just seems odd."

I nod and reach for my phone and wallet on the side while making my coffee to go.

"Why don't you look into him? See if you can find out anything that may help."

"Yeah, I might," he sighs, pulling a laptop towards him. I finish making the coffee and place his mug in front of him before heading towards the door, my travel mug in my hand.

"Let me know if anything turns up with him or anything else. I'll have my phone on me at all times."

"Have a good time, say hi to Chels for me!" he calls before I close the door behind me.

Chapter Fourteen

CHELSEA

"Where is it you are going tonight, Mummy?" Luna asks as I pack her shoes into her overnight bag.

"I'm going to stay at a hotel in York to help out a friend," I answer, rummaging through her drawers looking for matching socks. Why can I never find a matching pair in this house?

"Which friend? Do I know them?" she asks, bouncing on the side of the bed where she's sitting.

"No honey, you haven't met them," I answer as I give up on the socks and start looking for half-decent pyjamas for her. "Remind me to take you shopping next week. Your clothes are all getting too small for you," I sigh, grabbing a nightie and placing it in the bag.

"Is it a man you are going with? Kylie said you are going to spend the night with a man and go on a date."

I turn my attention to Luna and frown.

"Why did she say that?"

Luna shrugs, smiling at me.

"I think it's good if you're going on a date. You should get to have fun like other mums."

I sit on the bed beside her and take her hand in mine.

"I don't need to date; I have you," I say, smiling at my sweet girl, who smiles back at me.

"I know, Mummy. But you must miss dating a little. Not all men are like Daddy. Some could make you happier than you already are." As always, mentioning her father causes my breath to catch in my chest and my stomach to tighten.

"I know, honey, but I'm not sure I will ever date again, and I'm okay with that." I don't want her to ever think I am unhappy with our lives because I've never been happier than I am right now.

"Okay, as long as you are happy." She leans in and hugs me around the neck. "But just so you know, I would be happy if you had a boyfriend." She kisses my cheek and jumps off the bed before rushing out of the room. "I'm going to get my loom bands! We are making bracelets for all our friends," she calls as I hear her bounding down the stairs like a herd of elephants.

"Are you sure you don't mind having her all night?" I ask Penny for the tenth time since I arrived five minutes ago. She rolls her eyes, grips my shoulders, and pushes me towards the door.

"Stop looking for a reason to cancel. You had a great time with him when you went out the other night. Tonight won't be any different." We come to a stop at the front door, and Penny opens it. "Luna! Come and say goodnight to Mummy!"

Luna comes running down the stairs, closely followed by Kylie and runs straight into my arms.

"Have a great time, Mummy! Don't forget to take a photo of your dress!" she kisses my cheek before rushing back up the stairs with Kylie, not giving me a chance to kiss her back.

"Bye, honey! Be good, okay!" I call up after her. She turns and waves before disappearing out of view.

"See, she'll be fine. She's always as good as gold when she's here. Go and have a good time with the sexy American, and if you can, get some action afterwards!" Penny winks at me.

"I am not sleeping with him!" I hiss through my teeth, quickly looking up the stairs to ensure Luna didn't hear anything.

"If you say so." Penny opens her front door further and starts guiding me out of it. "Just go and let your hair down. You deserve it. I hear there's a spa in the hotel. See if you can get a massage off a hot guy if the Marine isn't willing to put out," Penny laughs before slamming the front door closed so I can't shout at her. I can still hear her laughing from inside the house.

"Bitch!" I call through the letterbox before walking down towards the car. I turn to look at the house to find her looking at me through the window, still laughing and waving like a lunatic. I quickly flip her off before jumping in the car and pulling away from her house.

It's an hour drive to the hotel where the function is being held tonight, so we are staying over. Calvin had offered to drive us, but I told him I wanted to drive myself. I guess part of me is still worried tonight will be a disaster, and I want to be sure I can make a quick getaway if I need to.

I turn on the radio and increase the volume. I don't get to drive long distances very often as I'm usually working or busy with Luna, so I decide to make the most of it and take my time. I'm child-free until tomorrow, which also doesn't happen very often. Sure, Luna will go to Penny's occasionally, but most of the time, I will stay as well.

As I drive, my conversation with Luna plays over in my mind. Would she really be okay if I started dating? I keep saying I don't want to date, but I enjoyed going to a meal with the guys, and they made me feel good about myself. They are funny and intelligent, and we laughed until I cried. When was the last time I got home feeling as I did those nights? Sure, Penny and I always have fun when we go out, whether just the two of us or with friends, but this was different. Both times, Calvin and Drew made me feel like they weren't there because they felt sorry for me. It was as if they didn't want to be away from me.

The only one who seems to keep me at arm's length is Logan. As well as we worked together that night, I think there is something about me that he doesn't like. He's always pleasant enough and says "hi" when he comes in to see Mr Young. But I don't think he would choose to speak to me if he didn't have to. Which is a little awkward, in all honesty, as I know there will be a time I will be asked to help him out like I'm helping Calvin tonight, and I don't know how I feel about it.

The thought of spending time with Calvin and Drew is appealing, but spending time with Logan is not. Maybe things will be different when we have to spend time with just the two of us. It was okay that night in the office, and he did carry me into the staff room the following day to make sure I got decent rest. Surely, that shows that he doesn't hate me completely. Maybe I should speak to Calvin about it tonight and get his take on the situation. Maybe I should stop worrying and concentrate on getting through tonight in one piece.

I continue to drive, my mind and nerves racing until I reach the hotel. When I look up at the impressive building, I start to worry that I must have the wrong address. I recheck the SatNav and see that it's the correct postcode. Maybe Calvin gave me the wrong one. He has given me the code to get into the car park, so I pull up alongside the barrier and type it in. The bar lifts, allowing me access, confirming it's the right hotel.

I find a parking space and park up before climbing out of the car and getting my overnight and dress bag out of the back seat where I placed it in the hope of avoiding any creases. You wouldn't believe how many hours of sleep I have lost over the fear of something going wrong, such as forgetting my shoes or dress. I have even had nightmares that I made a mess of my makeup, and everyone laughed at me. Stupid, I know, but it's a real fear that I'll make a mess of everything.

I walk up to the main entrance, and a bellboy holds the doors open for me.

"Afternoon, ma'am," he says with a smile and small bow.

"Good afternoon. Thank you," I reply, smiling. Ma'am, I don't think I have ever been called ma'am before. It makes me feel like royalty.

I'm still smiling when I reach the front desk, where I can see a few others with suitcases and suit bags over their arms. I smile and say a few polite afternoons, feeling completely out of place. Everything is marble, black and white. The place is pristine, and I don't think I have ever seen a floor shine as brightly as this one.

I move to the front of the queue and smile at the receptionist.

"Good afternoon, ma'am. Can I take your name, please?"

"Afternoon, it's Chelsea Hughes." I hold my breath, hoping she doesn't turn me away and tell me I'm in the wrong place.

"Ahh, yes, I have you here."

I feel myself relax for the first time since I pulled up.

"You are in room 382, and everything is ready for you. Mr Anderson called ahead to request that we let you know he will be running a little late, but he has booked you for a full body massage in one hour, which is all paid for."

I stare at her as she pulls out a key card and a few leaflets.

"Here are your room keys and some information you may need. The spa is open, and you can use anything that is in there. Your robe and slippers have already been left in your room, as well as your time slot for the massage, which is located in the spa." She gives me a big smile and hands me all the leaflets. "Would you like any help with your bags today?"

"Oh, um, no. Thank you, though," I stutter as I take all the leaflets from her. She smiles at me and directs me to the lifts, telling me which floor my room is before wishing me a pleasant stay. I thank her again and head off in the direction she gave me.

Luckily, I find my room easily and let myself in. I come to a stop when I see the room for the first time; it is beautiful and so luxurious. The bed's enormous, with pure white bedding, the comfiest looking duvet and pillows I have ever seen and pressed to perfection. The room is so big it also has a seat by a large window, which I realise is a door leading to a balcony. I quickly hang up my dress bag and open the door to let the chilled autumn air fill the warm space. Stepping onto the balcony, I look at the view and smile. It's beautiful up here; there's so much to see. I bet it's even better at night seeing everything lit up below.

Walking back into the bedroom, I retrieve my handbag and pull out my phone, planning on messaging Calvin to thank him, but I find he has beaten me to it.

Calvin: I'm so sorry I'm running late. I hope they have let you know at reception, I have booked you in for a massage to make it up to you. Enjoy it and relax a little; you deserve it. I will knock for you at about 19:30 to go down for the function. Enjoy your break. I look forward to seeing you xx.

I quickly type out a message thanking him and place my phone on the side before reading the information about the spa and what I can expect to find there. Smiling, I grab the robe and slippers and praise myself for having the sense to pack a bikini. As soon as I've changed and pulled my hair up into a bun, I leave my room eager to relax and make the most of this wonderful place.

Chapter Fifteen

CHELSEA

I'm putting the finishing touches to my lipstick when I hear a knock at the door.

"Two seconds," I call, doing a last check of my hair and makeup in the full-length mirror before walking over to the door and opening it.

"I am so sorry I wasn't here when you arrived. I-" Calvin stops mid-sentence when his eyes fall on me. His jaw drops open for a second before he closes it quickly and gives his head a quick shake. "You look amazing."

"Thank you. You don't look too bad yourself," I smile, taking in his black tuxedo. Calvin grins and holds up a bottle of champagne in one hand and two flute glasses in another. "I thought we could have a quick drink before going down."

I step back, holding the door open for him to enter. He heads to the balcony doors I have open to let the cool air in and places the glasses on the table. I follow him out, unable to wipe the smile from my face, which is still flushed from his compliments. He grins at me as he unwraps the cork and opens the bottle like a pro, not spilling a single drop.

"You've done that before," I tease. Calvin winks as he pours a little into the glass before letting the bubbles settle and filling it a little more. He hands it to me, looking very pleased with himself.

"I may have done it a few times, but hardly ever to drink myself," he says as his eyes find mine. "And certainly, never to enjoy with someone as beautiful as you."

"Stop it, you tease," I giggle as I look away, feeling myself blushing again. Calvin hooks a finger under my chin and applies pressure until I look back at him.

"It's not teasing when it's the truth."

For a moment, our eyes lock, and I remember how he held my hand as we sang on the stage the other night and how I caught him looking at me a few times with an adoring look. Nobody has looked at me in that way for years.

"Thank you," I whisper, taking the glass from his hand. He gives me another sexy wink before pouring his own drink. He holds it up, grinning at me.

"Here's to a lovely night with a beautiful lady."

I click my glass against his.

"And a very handsome man," I add before taking a sip of my drink.

"Why thank you, I do look rather dashing, don't I," he tries to say in his poshest voice, but the American accent is so thick that it doesn't work. I burst out laughing, nearly choking on my champagne. "Well, I didn't think I looked quite that bad," Calvin laughs as he tries to look disappointed. But as soon as our eyes meet, a smirk spreads across his face, and we start giggling again.

I don't know what it is with this man, but he makes me feel like a teenager. All adult responsibilities go out of the window, and we just laugh and joke with each other. I have a feeling tonight could end up being fun, and all the worrying I've been doing will be for nothing.

***

Tonight has gone without a hitch. I've stood by Calvin's side as he spoke to people. He has taken my hand or placed an arm around my back a few times, and I've let him. In truth, I've enjoyed the attention. Calvin has encouraged me to speak and put my two pence in, as if he wanted to know my opinion on things, making me feel appreciated and valued. It's not a feeling I'm used to.

"Calvin!"

I turn around as a beautiful young woman with long brown hair steps forward and throws her arms around Calvin, who smiles and hugs her back. A knot forms in my stomach as I realise I haven't thought about any exes. Is this one of his?

"I didn't know you would be here tonight," she says, stepping back from him. I realise I'm staring and standing around awkwardly, but as I turn to leave and give them space, Calvin takes my hand and pulls me back beside him as if realising I'm uncomfortable.

"Christian got me the invites, didn't he tell you?" he asks as he puts his arm around my waist, keeping me close. He looks at me, smiling. "Chelsea, this is Jasmine Connors, soon to be O'Reilly."

"Oh, you mean the O'Reillys you worked for," I exclaim, looking back at the young woman before me and smiling. "I've heard so much about you all. It's lovely to meet you." I hold out my hand, and she shakes it happily.

"It's lovely to meet you too. I hope he has been telling you all good things," she says, giving Calvin a playful look.

"I wouldn't dare say a bad word; Christian would have my neck."

"I don't know, it would probably be true."

I look to see a tall gentleman with short dark brown hair and tattoos that show under the collar of his shirt. "It's good to see you, Calvin." He holds out his hand, which Calvin shakes, smiling.

"It's good to see you too, Christian." Calvin places a hand on the base of my back and looks at me. "Christian, please meet Chelsea Hughes. Chelsea, this is Christian O'Reilly."

Christian smiles as he shakes my hand.

"It's a pleasure to meet you," I say, knowing that the man before me is richer than anyone I have met before, including Geralt Young.

"The pleasure is all ours, Ms Hughes. I'm glad to see Calvin has found someone to keep him in line," he says, grinning playfully at me.

"I wouldn't go that far," I reply, smiling. "He still hasn't mastered the art of keeping a woman's glass full," I reply, holding up my empty glass.

"I had planned on getting you a refill as soon as someone passed," Calvin chuckles beside me as I wink at him.

"At least he hasn't put a limit on how much you can drink," Jasmine sighs as she leans against Christian, who places an arm around her, looking with an arched brow.

"That's because you have a habit of forgetting what your limit is," he says firmly. It reminds me a little of how someone used to speak to me, and I freeze, not knowing what to do.

"No, it's because you're the strict one and like it that way," Jasmine replies, and I notice a little bit of a tease in her tone.

"Jasmine," Christian warns, but it goes unheard as Jasmine winks at me, lifts onto her tiptoes, and kisses his cheek.

"I know, behave myself. I'm only teasing," she grins before looking back at Calvin.

"I'm glad to see you here and that you took my advice. Hopefully, we will be able to catch up soon, and you can fill me in on any updates from when we last spoke," Christian says to Calvin, whose arm tightens around me.

"A catch-up would be great. I'll give you a shout in the week," Calvin replies.

"Great, I look forward to it," Christian says before looking at me. "It was lovely to meet you, Ms Hughes. Please excuse us; my fiancée will continue to bug me until I find someone she is looking forward to seeing," Christian says as Jasmine threads her arm through his, and he looks down at her, grinning.

"I like to keep you on your toes. Wouldn't want you getting bored now, would I?" Jasmine says, smiling up at her man.

"Sweetheart, there hasn't been a boring moment since you danced your way into our lives."

Jasmine once again lifts and presses a kiss to his lips.

"Good answer, Daddy," she winks before turning her attention back to me. "It was lovely to meet you, Chelsea. I hope we see you both again soon," she adds with a smile before Christian leads her away, and I can see them both grinning at each other, especially when Christian grabs a glass of champagne from a passing waiter and hands it to her.

"Did she call him Daddy? Or was that my imagination?" I ask Calvin, who laughs beside me.

"Yeah, I'm so used to it that I forget it's not normal for most people."

"So, is he her father or her fiancée? Because I don't know what just happened."

Calvin laughs again as he leads us away from the crowds and towards the table we have been sitting at for part of the night.

"Both, but let me explain," he says as I turn to face him with my mouth open. I was about to say that's illegal, but then I wait to see what he says.

"Do you remember me saying that the four brothers are with the same woman, Jasmine?" I nod. "Well, that was the O'Reillys, and they are also her doms; daddy doms, to be precise."

"I've heard of that before, but I thought it was just in the bedroom," I reply quietly, looking around nervously. This feels like the type of conversation that should happen in private.

"For most people, it is, but it's a lifestyle choice for some. The O'Reillys take care of Jasmine in a way no one else has. She had a tough upbringing, and the only people who had her back were taken from her at a young age. The O'Reillys look after her in the way she has always wanted. She doesn't have to worry about anything. I'm not just talking financially, as they make decisions for her and encourage her in a way that helps her stay on track.

"They may come across as strict at times, like when he said she couldn't have another drink. But for Jasmine, that's what she wants and needs. As you saw, he gave her another one anyway, but he would have only done so once he knew she wasn't close to getting drunk."

"So, she likes being told what to do?" I ask. Calvin tips his head from side to side as if trying to work out how to phrase it.

"Yes and no. She likes that they stop her from making bad choices. When I first met Jasmine properly, she was in a very bad place, physically and mentally. She had fled her home, as her mother was an abusive drug addict. She was in a lot of debt and lived in a rundown apartment because it was all she could afford. Jasmine was also close to being kicked out of her dance school, where she is a ballerina and a good one at that. She was stick thin as she couldn't afford to eat and a shell of the woman she is today.

"But the brothers changed that. They took her in and gave her everything she could possibly need. They made sure she started eating three meals a day, stopped drinking as much, and had everything she needed for school. She was in love with them for years before they took her in. They had loved her too and waited for years for her to become twenty-one. There is absolutely nothing that they wouldn't do for that woman; they may be her daddies, but she has them wrapped around her little finger, really."

I look around the room until my eyes fall on Jasmine and Christian. Jasmine is talking to someone excitedly as Christian watches her lovingly, with one hand on the bottom of her back, keeping close but letting her do her own thing at the same time. It's kind of the same way Calvin has been with me tonight.

I turn my attention back to Calvin, who is watching me with a slight smile on his face.

"They look happy," I say, looking back towards them to see Jasmine leaning against Christian, who lovingly kisses the top of her head.

"I've known that man for five years, and I can honestly

say she is the best thing that ever happened to him, to happen to all of them. She brought so much light into their lives when they needed it the most," he answers, watching the two himself. He looks around the room before grinning at me.

"Do you think we have done enough networking for one night?"

"I think you have certainly spread the word about your company," I answer, frowning. Calvin stands and holds out his hand for mine.

"Come with me."

I look at the grin on his face. Placing my hand in his, he helps me to my feet before leading me to the side of the room, keeping hold of my hand the whole way.

"Where are we going?" I laugh, rushing alongside him. He glances at me with a devious smile, making me laugh.

"One good thing about all the years I was security at these events is that I made friends in the right places." He stops by the kitchen door and winks before leading us inside.

The kitchen is spotless as if they hadn't just produced a five-course meal for hundreds of people mere hours ago. Calvin leads me past a few people who smile and say hi as he passes.

"You know you're not allowed back here, Anderson."

A man around my age steps forward with his arms crossed over his large belly. He is dressed in chef's whites, almost as spotless as the kitchen.

"Now, Hector, you know you would miss me if I didn't pop in to complain about the pitiful portion sizes," Calvin beams at him. The guy rolls his eyes before turning his back to us.

"The usual, Anderson?" he asks, shaking his head.

"You know it, but this time for two, if possible," Calvin

answers, stepping forward and sliding a bundle of notes into the chef's hand. "Room 382." The chef nods and waves us off as if bored of us already. "Thanks, Hector, you know I'm worth it," Calvin calls as he leads us past the chef and to the staff exit. Before we leave the kitchen entirely, Calvin stops, looks around and grabs two bottles of champagne from a side covered in open bottles.

"I'm taking these whilst I'm at it," he calls. Hector doesn't turn to look at him; he just waves his hands dismissively. Calvin winks at me before pulling me out of the staff exit and towards the lift.

"That's stealing!" I point out, looking around nervously.

"They would have just been tipped away anyway. It's fine; I know what I'm doing."

I start laughing as his face lights up again, and he leads me to the elevators. As soon as we are inside one and the doors close, I turn to see him smiling from ear to ear.

"Want to tell me what just happened?"

"I think it's time we let our hair down a little."

Chapter Sixteen

CALVIN

The elevator opens onto the third floor, and I lead a giggling Chelsea towards her room.

"My room is next to yours, so pick one."

"You just told the chef my number, so I guess there," she replies as her room comes into view. Grinning, we stop outside her door, and she pulls her keycard from her clutch. As soon as it's open, we rush inside before anyone can spot us with the bottles.

I head straight for the balcony where our two glasses from earlier are waiting. Chelsea follows my lead, sits in one of the chairs, and looks out at the nightlife before us.

Loosening my bow tie, I undo my top button before shrugging off my jacket.

"That feels so much better," I sigh before pouring us both a glass of champagne. I don't mind wearing suits. I'm used to them as the O'Reillys made us wear them as uniform most of the time, but when you are stuck in a packed room, which makes you feel claustrophobic anyway, they just add to your discomfort.

"If you can lose the tie, I can lose the shoes."

I watch Chelsea lift her dress from around her feet and start to unstrap her stiletto heels.

"How the hell did you stand in them all night? They're huge!" I exclaim, picking up the shoe she has just removed and looking at the heel. "These must be at least five inches!"

"Six. I thought it was best with you being so much taller than me," she shrugs before letting out a sigh of relief as the other shoe is removed as well. I turn my chair a little and pat my thighs.

"Put them up here."

Chelsea frowns at me, and I can see she's not going to, so I reach down, grab her feet and place them on my lap. I hand her a filled glass and hold out my own to her, and we toast before taking a small sip each.

"Thank you for all your help down there. You made the whole thing so much easier," I tell her as I sip my drink.

"I didn't do anything other than stand beside you and smile," she laughs.

"You did so much more than that. Having you beside me helped keep me calm and level-headed. I think I would have bolted early on if I hadn't had you there." I watch her face turn a slight shade of pink as she looks anywhere but at me. She always avoids eye contact when she is embarrassed or flattered. It's as if she isn't used to people being nice to her.

"Glad I could help. I had fun," she says as our eyes meet briefly, and my stomach knots as it has done numerous times through the evening. "So, are you going to tell me what the chef is making for you?" she asks, sitting back in her chair a little. A small laugh slips past my lips as I relax back into my own.

"After an event like tonight, when I'm always on high

alert for any threats, I need to unwind and clear my head. I found the most effective way to do that is to get out of the formal clothes, watch a movie and eat a load of junk food."

Chelsea's whole face changes from a content smile to a look of pure excitement.

"Do you mean I can get out of this dress and into something more comfortable?" she asks, almost bouncing in her chair. I laugh whilst nodding.

"Why don't you go and get into whatever you are sleeping in, and I'll pop to my room to do the same. I'll come back in ten minutes as the food should be here then."

Chelsea jumps to her feet, almost tripping over her dress, before rushing into the room, giggling.

I stand up from my seat and finish the champagne in my glass whilst pulling my jacket from the back of the chair.

"Take the keycard and walk straight in when you are ready," Chelsea calls, grabbing some clothes from her bag and heading into the bathroom.

"Will do," I call back as I walk through the room, finding myself looking forward to the next part of the evening more than the function downstairs.

I sit back on the bed and let out a content sigh. I look to my right, where Chelsea is looking just as relaxed and content.

It had taken me a total of six minutes to get to my room and into my sweatpants and t-shirt before walking back into Chelsea's room. I entered to find her already sitting on the bed, her back against the headboard, with a fresh flute of champagne in her hand. As beautiful as she had looked downstairs in her cocktail dress and her hair up, it was nothing to how she looked in a pair of shorts and a vest top, with her hair flowing in loose waves to just below her shoulders.

"I figured you would want another glass," she says, taking a flute from the cabinet beside her and handing it to me. I take it with a smile before walking over to the chair by the balcony door. I am just about to take a seat when there is a knock at the door.

"I'll get it." I place the glass on the side table and open the door to find a hotel porter with a trolley. After instructing him to put it all on the table, I see him out, handing him a couple of twenty-pound notes as he leaves.

When I close the door, I find Chelsea already looking under the plate covers.

"Time to have some real food," I declare happily as Chelsea grins.

It takes us a whole fifteen minutes to demolish the burgers, fries and milkshakes. I love it when functions are here as Hector spent some time in America and makes the best-tasting burgers this side of the pond.

"That was amazing, but I'm going to need a full two-hour workout in the morning, at least, to work off all those calories," Chelsea sighs with her hand on her stomach.

"Whatever, nothing wrong with ya," I chuckle.

Chelsea turns her head, frowning at me before reaching for the remote that's beside her.

"What do you want to watch?" she asks, turning the TV on.

"I don't mind you choose. I'm just glad to be able to relax finally," I sigh, putting my arms behind my head. "It can be so exhausting being alert at all times."

"Why were you on alert tonight? You were off duty?" Chelsea asks, turning to look at me. I can't stop myself from reaching out and brushing away some of her hair that's fallen over her face.

"Because the last thing I want is for something to happen to you."

Chelsea looks at me for a moment, unable to hide the look of shock and then confusion on her face. I can see her trying to process everything and know it's the last conversation I want to have tonight. Instead, I point at the TV.

"Choose a film."

Chelsea watches me momentarily before sitting back and flicking through the available films.

The film is almost over, and I look at the sleeping Chelsea, who's resting her head on my chest. I'm not even sure how it happened, but during the film, Chelsea had leant into me, and I'd put my arm around her shoulders. Soon, she was asleep with her head and one hand on my chest, and I couldn't bring myself to move her.

I know I shouldn't be letting us get this close. I was the one who initially said she was out of bounds. Yet here I am, the first to cuddle up to her and not want to let go. Not only that, but I know how Drew feels about her. As much as we are willing to share her whilst faking a relationship in front of others, are we willing to do it for real?

I look down at her sleeping so peacefully, and my head is telling me to leave and go to my own room, but my heart is saying stay.

I let out a deep breath and know I need to do the right thing.

Slowly, I go to remove my arm to go to my room. Chelsea moans slightly, stopping me in my tracks.

"Stay," she whispers, not even opening her eyes.

"Are you sure?" I ask, knowing I shouldn't encourage it.

We've both had a lot to drink. Even if we're not drunk, it's enough to cloud our judgment. But when Chelsea nods against my chest and her hand tightens its hold on my t-shirt, I know I've lost.

"Please."

Chelsea looks up at me with those bright blue eyes, and I know I'm in trouble. I can't fight it any longer as I cup her cheek in my hand and lean down to brush my lips against hers. When she doesn't pull away, I do it again, this time allowing my lips to touch hers for a moment longer. Her arm goes around my waist, holding me against her, and I deepen the kiss. In seconds, we're further down the bed and making out as I hold her close, my fingers threaded into the hair at the base of her head. I start kissing along her jaw whilst tightening the grip on her hair, tugging slightly to give me better access to her neck.

"Calvin," she gasps.

"Yes?" I whisper against her skin, silently begging her not to say stop.

"Stay."

I lift my head from her neck, look into her eyes, and see longing in them as her cheeks flush with arousal.

"What do you want, darling?" I ask, needing her to say it.

"Stay with me, just tonight."

"Tell me what you need." I feel her hand resting on my back as she applies a little pressure, pressing herself against me.

"All of you." She rolls on her back, tugging me with her. I press a knee between her legs, and she opens them, making room for me to lie on top of her.

"Are you sure?" I need to know this isn't the drink talking, but I'm terrified she will turn me away now. But with one nod, all my fears are pushed aside, and I kiss her like I've wanted to kiss her all night.

Since I walked into this room before going down to the function, I have been desperate to take her in my arms and hold her, kiss her, until she begs for more.

It takes all my self-control not to rip her clothes off and rush through the whole experience, as I desperately need her like I need air to breathe, but she deserves more.

As I kiss her neck this time, I place my hands on her hips and start pushing up her vest top. I already noticed earlier that she was braless, and now I thank the gods for the easy access to these perfect breasts.

Taking one in my hand, I squeeze gently as I take her pink nipple between my teeth, sucking it into my mouth. Chelsea gasps underneath me as her fingers thread through my hair, and her back arches up, pushing her breasts closer to me. As she moans again, all blood rushes to my aching cock, which is throbbing in my pants. I thrust my hips forward and let her feel how hard I am. I rub against her again and notice how fucking warm she is between her legs. I need to taste and feel that hot pussy around my fingers, tongue, and cock.

Cheslea takes hold of the bottom of my t-shirt and pulls it over my head as I sit up slightly. She looks at my bare chest, and I can see her following the tattoos and the moment her eyes land on my scars. Not giving her a chance to ask questions, I lower myself back over her and take her breast back in my mouth.

I savour them, teasing her with my mouth and hands until she is moving underneath me, trying to brush her warm, no doubt soaking wet pussy against my restrained cock. This gorgeous woman needs to find her release, and I have no problem at all helping her.

I slowly slide down the bed, kissing her stomach and hips until I am almost falling off the bottom. I stand at the end of the bed and drag her down towards me, causing a shocked and excited squeal to leave her perfect lips.

"Lift your hips, darling."

She does as she's told, and I pull down her shorts and underwear to reveal the most beautiful pussy I have ever seen. She has shaved and left only the smallest little runway of hair. Her thick lips are plump and begging to be kissed.

As I stand in front of her, I take one finger and run it between her pink pussy lips, from her entrance to her clit, almost coming from the sound that escapes her as she arches from the bed.

"When was the last time you were touched by a man, darling?"

She looks up at me, and I can tell from her eyes that it's been too long.

"Then lay back and let me remind you how good it can be," I command as I run my finger between her lips again, this time rubbing small circles around her clit.

"Fuck," she gasps as her back arches from the bed. I smile at her whilst lowering myself to my knees and pulling her closer so I can place her legs on either side of my head. Unable to hold back any further, I press a kiss to her pussy before forcing my tongue between her lips and tasting her for the first time.

I swear we both curse at the same time as her juices explode on my tongue, and I taste the sweetness that is the closest thing I can imagine heaven tasting like. I have never tasted anything like her, and I need more.

I start to devour her, slipping my tongue into her

entrance and around her clit. The more I consume of her, the needier I get. Chelsea struggles to stay still, so I place a hand on her lower stomach, holding her in place and applying pressure to the right area to make her even more sensitive than she already is.

"Calvin! Fuck!" I hear her gasp over and over again, making the ache I feel to fuck her intensify. I want to feel her clamped around my aching, throbbing cock as I fuck her in every position I can think of, and some we will invent just to hear that noise again.

I slide one finger into her and know I was right; it's been a while. When I add a second whilst I lap at her clit with my tongue, I can tell she'll cum soon, and I want her to flood my hand. The thought of collecting her juices in the palm of my hand so I can drink them makes me give her everything I have as I nearly suffocate between her legs.

Her whole body clenches as her hips lift from the bed, and her pussy clamps my finger inside of her tightly; and she explodes in a series of curse word gasps as she squirts into my hand, just as I had intended.

"Fuck," she curses one more time as I lick her oversensitive clit, making her orgasm last that moment too long, and she can't take anymore. I look at the small puddle in my hand as I slowly pull my fingers out of her, not wanting to lose a drop.

"Did I just?" Her question stops mid-sentence as she watches me lift my hand to my mouth and lick her cum from it. I can't work out if she is mortified or even more aroused than she was a moment ago.

"Squirt into my hand? You sure did, and it was fucking beautiful," I respond before standing up and looking down at the beautiful woman spread out before me. "Move up to the top of the bed, darling."

As she slides herself up the bed, I walk around to the side and help her climb under the duvet before sliding in next to her. Pulling her into my arms, I kiss her and brush some hair from her damp face.

"Not fucking you is one of the hardest things I have ever had to do. But I don't want you to have any regrets. So instead, I want to hold you for tonight, and next time we spend any time alone like this, I will make sure I have condoms on me," I smile at her, hoping she can see how gutted I am and that this won't be the last time for me. Now that I have tasted her, I know she will be my new addiction.

"Will the others be annoyed about tonight?" she asks. I smile, shaking my head. Logan won't be, but I need to talk to Drew. I owe him that much.

"After discussing the option with you, we discussed it together. We agreed that whatever happens, happens, and we will not hold it against one another."

Chelsea nods, but I can still see there is a worry in her eye.

"Does it bother you?" I ask, cupping her cheek. Chelsea shrugs her shoulders as she lies with her head against my chest.

"I'm confused, I guess. I don't know what to make of all of this," she admits. I press a kiss to the top of her head.

"What we have going on is not a relationship; it's more of a companionship, right?"

She nods and looks back up at me.

"Well, in that case, then, you would not be cheating on anyone if you were to do things with the others as well as me."

Chelsea lets out a deep breath and goes back to leaning against my chest.

She runs her fingers over my tattoo, and I can feel when she touches three small scars.

"Were you shot?" she asks quietly. I shake my head.

"No, it was shrapnel from a homemade bomb. My body took a lot from the explosion. It caused the most damage to my right leg." I explain, still hearing the explosion in my mind. "I was only meant to be doing a surveillance check. We had been doing them every few hours for days with no issues. We got lazy. I walked into a house with Douglas; he stood on the trigger, and I woke up in the medical tent."

"What happened to Douglas?" Chelsea asks beside me. I tighten my arms around her and bury my head into her hair, needing the emotional anchor.

"He was killed instantly," I whisper as I feel her body tense. "He was a good man and an amazing SEAL. He always said he wanted to die on the field, and he did."

"I'm sorry," Chelsea whispers into my chest. I kiss the top of her hair and force myself to remember my old friend smiling. It's a trick I learnt to help remember fallen comrades positively as they would like, rather than how they died.

"Will you still stay tonight?" she asks as her fingertips rub lightly over my skin.

"Absolutely, I would rather be here with you than missing you in the other room."

I hear her chuckling before she relaxes back in my arms.

"Sleep tight, darling," I whisper, listening to her breathing slowing and feeling her body relaxing further as she drifts off in my arms.

Not for the first time tonight, I realise I have done the one thing I swore I wouldn't. I have fallen for this beautiful older woman faster than I have ever fallen for anyone, and I'm in the shit.

Chapter Seventeen

CHELSEA

"So let me get this straight. You didn't have sex with him, but he gave you a mind-blowing orgasm and didn't ask for anything in return?"

"That's pretty much it," I reply, sitting back on Penny's sofa as I sip my wine.

"And he was still there this morning?" she asks, her eyebrows disappearing into her hairline.

"Yep, where he gave me another orgasm and then treated me to a spa morning followed by a cream tea lunch before we parted ways."

"And not once did he ask for a wank or blow job?"

Again, I shake my head, and Penny almost collapses into her seat.

"Then I want one of them. If his colleagues are anything like him, send them my way. I need a man like that, like yesterday!"

I chuckle as I sip my wine and take a deep breath.

Everything about the last twenty-four hours was terrific, from the function, to how Calvin treated me and showered me affectionately to the mind-blowing orgasms. I don't think I would have changed a thing.

"Is it stupid that I feel guilty?" I ask, looking over to Penny.

"What do you mean?" she replies, frowning.

"Well, I know we're not really dating, that I just attend functions with them with the occasional odd night out. But it still kind of feels like I cheated on the other two. Maybe not so much Logan, as there's nothing even remotely going on there. However, Drew is lovely, and I don't want to upset him in any way, and I certainly don't want to get between him and Calvin," I explain. I can see Penny thinking about it and wait to see her take on it.

"What did Calvin say about it all?"

"That I'm not to worry; the others will be fine. He said he would make sure of it." But it hasn't stopped the worry in my gut. The one thing I don't feel is regret.

I told myself from the start that I wasn't going to sleep with any of them and that it would be completely platonic, as they promised. But last night, I got caught up in being in a man's arms for the first time in years and knew I wanted to try for more.

Does that mean I want a relationship with any of them? No, I still don't think I am ready for any commitment, especially as I don't think I could choose one over the others. Even with Logan, there is something that keeps me from pushing him away completely.

Calvin told me this morning in the spa that Logan is sometimes difficult to read and not to take it personally. But I still feel like he's pushing me away, keeping me at arm's length, and I can't help wondering if there is something I have done to cause that.

"If I were you, I would be eating up all the attention. I

can't remember the last time I got laid, and I need a good orgasm or six," Penny sighs. We both look towards the lounge door as two excited girls run down the stairs sounds from the hallway.

"Mummy! Are we going soon? Or are we staying for dinner as well?" Luna asks as she jumps onto the sofa beside me, nearly spilling my wine.

"We are leaving in five minutes, so go and get all your things together and double-check you haven't forgotten to pack anything," I tell her, pointing towards the door. Luna rolls her eyes at me and climbs off the sofa before grabbing Kylie and dragging her out of the room.

Penny's older daughter, Ayva, walks into the lounge as I drink the last of my wine.

"Hey, Auntie Chels, you need a babysitter any time soon?" she asks as she sits on the other end of the sofa.

"Still saving for a new car?" I ask, smiling. She nods and lets out a deep sigh.

"They are so expensive. How do they expect nineteen-year-olds to save so much?" she sighs.

"Wait until you have to save for a house. That's even harder," Penny laughs as she places her glass on the coffee table.

"Don't!" Ayva sighs.

"Well, I could do with a sitter Thursday night if you are free?" I ask, checking my phone. Drew had messaged yesterday morning asking if I could accompany him to a dinner to try and complete on a big contract.

"I'm off Thursday, so it's fine. What time?" she asks.

"Be at mine for seven, and I'll order pizza and stuff for you."

"Thanks, Auntie Chels, you're the best!" Ayva smiles,

kissing me on the cheek before leaving the room. "Luna! I'm looking after you Thursday night! You better be good; otherwise, I'll lock you in the shed with all the spiders!" she calls as she leaves the lounge. Penny and I burst out laughing as we hear Luna protesting and shouting back at Ayva.

"Well, that's her terrified of the shed," I laugh as I stand and head towards the door, hoping to hurry Luna up and get home so I can get everything ready before the week ahead.

My phone pings around eight at night, just as Luna is going off to bed. I open it to see a message from Calvin.

Calvin: I just wanted to say thanks for a lovely weekend; I enjoyed myself. As promised, I've spoken to the guys about everything. As I told you, they were fine, and there is no expectation on you for anything else to happen with me or them. We are all happy for this to stay as it is, or if you want more when with one of us, then what happens, happens. So please don't worry about anything. See you during the week, darling. Night. Xx

I read through the message a few times before letting out a deep breath and opening the message from Drew. When I got home, I messaged him to say I had sorted out a babysitter for Thursday and could attend the meal with him.

Drew: Thanks, Chels. Let me know how much they charge, and I will pay it. I'll pick you up at seven fifteen; it's only at a restaurant in town. Looking forward to seeing you. Good-night. Xx

Looking at the time stamps, Drew's message came after Calvin's, so he would have already spoken to him at that point. There doesn't seem to be any signs that he is unhappy with me in the message, so maybe Calvin's right and all is okay.

I have no idea what will happen with these guys, but I think I need to stop worrying; otherwise, I will make myself ill and not enjoy the time I get with three hot men.

Chapter Eighteen

DREW

I sit in the car and take a deep breath. I don't know what I'm more nervous about, meeting with possible new clients for a huge contract? Or spending time with Chelsea? Part of me has been highly jealous of Calvin since he told me what happened between them the night of the function. Does this mean she likes him more than me? Is there no chance of her and I having our moment together? This woman has consumed my every dream, day and night, yet she chose my friend over me.

Calvin is convinced that she feels something for each of us. He told me what she said about not knowing what she wanted, and now I'm hoping she will give me a chance to show her how good we could be because I know we could be amazing together.

I take one last breath and climb out of the car. I said I would drive tonight because we're going to a restaurant. It's best if we turn up together. Chelsea agreed to let me pick her up from her house. I understand why she is reluctant for us to come here; she has a child and is very protective of her daughter, which I can only respect.

I straighten my suit jacket before pressing the doorbell. In seconds, the door opens, and I see a mini version of Chelsea looking up at me.

"Are you Drew?"

For a second, I'm speechless as the last thing I expected was for her daughter to answer the door.

"Luna Louise, your mother is going to kill you," I hear another voice call before the little girl looks up at the tall newcomer. "Get inside, out of the way," they say to Chelsea's daughter, gently pushing her away from the door before looking at me. "Sorry about that; Chels told Luna not to answer the door unless she knows who it is," the young woman explains.

"It's no bother. Is Chels ready?" I ask, smiling.

"I'm here!" I hear Chelsea call from inside, and my heart nearly stops when she comes into view.

Over the last couple of weeks, I've seen Chelsea at work a few times wearing trousers or pencil skirt suits. But tonight, she is wearing a beautiful black fitted dress that stops above her knees. The full-length sleeves and black stiletto shoes complete the look. She looks beautiful and professional, and I personally would sign my soul to the devil himself to please her.

"Is this okay? Do you want me to change?"

I realise I'm staring with my mouth hanging open and close it quickly.

"You look perfect, don't change a thing." I hold out my arm, and she steps out of the door and hooks her arm through mine. "Are you ready?" I ask, unable to wipe the smile from my face. She nods once before looking over her shoulder to where the young woman is standing, grinning at the two of us.

"I won't be late. Make sure she's in bed within the hour and keep the doors locked," Chelsea orders. The girl salutes with a smile before closing the door; I listen to be sure that she has locked it as ordered. Within seconds, the tell-tale sound of a locking mechanism sounds out. I lead Chelsea to the car and open the passenger door for her. As she climbs in, I feel like I'm being watched and turn to see mini-Chelsea watching us through the window. I give her a small wave, and she waves back enthusiastically.

"I think we have an audience," I chuckle to Chelsea, who looks to the window just as her daughter disappears from view.

"I should have known she would be nosey," Chelsea sighs as I close the door and walk around to the driver's side.

"Who can blame her? She sees Mom dressing up and wants to know why," I reply, climbing behind the wheel.

"Luna does what she wants; no one can tell her otherwise."

I laugh as I pull away from the house and head toward the restaurant.

"And I suppose you were as good as gold at her age?" I tease.

"Well, maybe she gets some of it from me," Chelsea chuckles. "So, who are these people you are trying to impress tonight?" she asks.

"The guy is someone who Calvin knows through a friend. He is a contractor but the high end. He is looking for a new security firm to watch his sites. So, night watch men kind of thing. He's had issues with thieves recently and vandalism. One of his guys was shot last week, so now he wants more experienced people."

I hear Chelsea gasp beside me.

"Shot? And you want to send your guys there?" she demands. I shrug whilst continuing to drive.

"Our people are all ex-forces; they have been trained to be on high alert at all times. They know how to handle any situation they could find themselves in. That's what makes our company so different from others."

"So, you only hire ex-SEALs?"

"No, not just SEALs," I reply, shaking my head. "We have ex-Navy, Army, RAF, Marines, Police and Firearms officers. All must have had hands-on experience with dangerous situations. For example, Pippin and I specialised in hostage situations. Houdini was explosives and fieldwork. We can all handle a number of different weapons; we know how to disarm someone and negotiate. There's very little we haven't experienced."

I stop at a set of traffic lights and turn to a quiet Chelsea.

"You've gone very quiet."

When Chelsea turns to look at me, I have no idea what's going through that head of hers. Did I scare her with how well we are trained?

"Will you ever be in danger like your guys?" she asks softly.

"There will be times. We would never ask our people to do something we wouldn't do ourselves. We might be the company's owners, but we will still get our hands dirty if necessary." I look back at the lights and curse quietly as they change to green. I glance at Chelsea to see her deep in thought.

"What are you thinking, Chels?"

For a moment or two, she remains quiet, and when I glance at her, I find her staring out of the window.

"I never thought of the fact you would ever be in danger. I don't like the thought of any of you getting hurt," she replies softly as I feel her eyes land on me. We stop at another set of lights, and I take advantage of the moment. I turn to look at her as I lift her hand to my mouth and press a kiss to her knuckles.

"We have faced many dangers in the past and made it through with only a handful of injuries between us. You don't have to worry about us; we are good at what we do," I tell her with a wink, hoping to lighten the mood a bit.

"I can't help but worry; I care about you all."

I kiss her knuckles before letting go of her hand and continuing the drive to the restaurant.

"We care about you too, Chels," I tell her as I glance to the side quickly. "A lot."

"I find it hard to believe that someone as young as you has any real experience in security. I hear you were a former SEAL like Anderson, but did you actually see any real action? Or are you training your employees from stuff you learnt from a handbook?"

I stare at Mr Godfrey in front of me, amazed by the man's audacity.

"With all due respect, sir. Would you have any doubt of Calvin's ability to train our employees if you were meeting him for the first time?" I ask, using every tool I was taught in my training to keep calm and not lose my shit.

"Well, I'm guessing he has quite a bit more experience than you."

"Actually, I am seven months older than Calvin, and I joined two years before him. I already had three successful hostage situations under my belt before he had finished his training.

"In fact, the day Calvin Anderson completed his training, I was on the other side of the world dealing with a situation where thirty-three girls were being held at gunpoint in a building filled with explosives. I helped with the safe release of twenty-six of those girls. So please tell me how Calvin has more experience than me." My palms are sweating from the anger that is rushing through me. How dare he question my experience.

"What happened to the other seven girls?" The guy next to Godfrey asks. I take a deep breath and feel my leg shake under the table as the sounds of them screaming ring in my ears.

"They didn't make it. There were three men in the room with them, all armed. They started arguing among themselves, and one shot the other. Unfortunately, the bullet went straight through him and hit a canister which contained mustard gas. We got them out of the room they were being held in, but all died within days of their injuries."

I feel something touch my shaking leg and look down to see Chelsea's hand on my thigh. She squeezes it, letting me know she's there, before letting go and holding my hand under the table. I am so grateful for her support in that moment.

"You may see that failure as proof that I shouldn't be in charge of a security firm, but I have saved more lives than you've had hot showers. I remember the names of every single person we lost and will still remember them until the day I die. Every death has left its own scar on me, and I have taken their loss and turned it into a learning experience. I am trained to hunt, protect and kill; don't underestimate me because of my appearance. If you were to sign the contract, this baby face would not think twice before stepping between you and a speeding bullet." I feel Chelsea stiffen slightly and give her hand a soft squeeze.

"Do you wish to continue telling me I don't have enough experience? Or shall we discuss the terms of our contract?"

Chapter Nineteen

CHELSEA

Drew's been quiet since we left the restaurant. After he shared some of his experiences in the SEALs, the bastard Godfrey signed the contract and showed a whole new level of respect to him.

I spent the evening watching him out of the corner of my eye. He remained the professional, outgoing man you would expect to see at a business dinner, one I've seen several times when he has visited Mr Young. But under the table, his leg shook, and his hand clenched into a fist.

When I could get away with it, I would place my hand on his thigh or hold his hand to try and give him the support I was sure he needed. If anyone had noticed, they would have thought I was just a girlfriend or wife wanting to show their partner some affection. But it was just a concerned friend, showing someone they care very much about, that they are not alone in their moment of need.

We pull up outside my house, and Drew lets out a sigh before turning to look at me. I think this is the first time I have ever seen the sparkle that always seems to shine bright in his dark eyes has gone. I don't like it.

"Thank you for everything tonight, Chels. I don't know what I would have done without you being there."

I reach across and take his hand; he looks down as I thread my fingers with his. As he did earlier, he lifts it and softly kisses my knuckles.

"Do you want to come in for a chat and a coffee?" I ask, watching his sad eyes as they find my own.

"I don't think I will be the best company tonight," he says with a small smile.

"That's why I'm asking." I lift my other hand and place it on his cheek. "Come inside, and I'll crack open the whiskey," I offer with a wink.

"Well, if there's whiskey," he replies, his smile more genuine. I roll my eyes and let go of his hand.

"Should have known the whiskey would win you over," I chuckle, opening the passenger door.

"Hey! I'm a man. There are only three things a real man needs," he announces as he climbs out of the car and heads towards me. I wait for him at the bottom of my driveway.

"Let me guess, whiskey, bacon and sex."

"Nope." He grins as he offers me his arm like a true gentleman. "Strong coffee, good whiskey." I slip my arm into his, and his smile widens further. "And an intelligent, beautiful woman on his arm."

I burst out laughing as he gives me a playful wink.

"Well, look at that. I will have had all three tonight." The playfulness I have learnt to expect from Drew is thankfully back in his voice, and I know inviting him in was the right choice.

I unlock the door and hold it open for him before

closing it quietly and heading towards the lounge, where I know Ayva will be watching TV.

"Hey, I'm back."

Ayva looks up from the TV and smiles, which brightens further when she sees Drew behind me.

"So, I see. Auntie Chels, you've brought home a stray."

"Ayva!" I gasp as Drew laughs behind me.

"Don't worry, I've been treated for fleas and ticks," Drew answers behind me. "Sorry, Chels. Can I use your bathroom?" he asks quietly.

"Sure, there's a downstairs one just through the kitchen," I point him in the right direction. He says a quick thanks and heads off as I look to Ayva, who grins like the cat who got the cream.

"Stop it," I warn, shrugging off my coat and placing it over the arm of the sofa.

"I'm not saying a single word," she teases, locking her lips and throwing away the key. "Although I can't promise Mum will be as quiet," Ayva laughs as she picks up her phone and handbag.

I pull my purse out of my bag and am just about to give Ayva her money when Drew walks back in.

"Put your purse away, woman. I told you I was paying for the babysitter tonight." He turns his attention to Ayva and smiles. "How much does Chels pay you?"

"Fifty for tonight," she answers, looking at me with arched brows. Drew pulls his wallet out of his jacket pocket and hands Ayva a pile of notes, who looks down at it, frowning. "There's too much here?"

Drew shrugs as he walks past her.

"Chels said you are saving for a car, put it towards that."

Ayva stares at me momentarily before kissing my cheek and smiling.

"Call me any time you need a sitter, especially if he is funding it," she winks before waving to Drew. "Thank you!" she calls, rushing towards the front door and shutting it behind her quietly.

"Do I even want to ask how much you gave her?" I ask, heading over to the cabinet where I keep my drinks.

"Twice what you were going to," he answers, shrugs off his jacket and places it near mine. "The guys and I decided that if you have to pay for childcare whilst accompanying us, we will cover the cost. I figured if I paid her well, she would be more likely to agree to do it more often," he says, smiling as I turn my attention back to the drinks I'm pouring.

"It's your money," I chuckle, turning around to find him rolling up the sleeves of his white shirt. Why is it a simple thing like that is enough to cause my pussy to throb? There is something about seeing a man rolling up his shirt sleeves, which hits the spot nearly every time.

I swallow the lump in my throat and walk over to the sofa. I sit down on one side as Drew sits on the other. It's not a large sofa; there is no need for it to be with only me and Luna here, but that means there isn't much room between Drew and me now.

I pass him his glass and hold up my own.

"To a new contract for your blooming business," I grin as Drew clinks his glass against mine.

"Cheers," he replies before taking a sip of the whiskey. "Damn, that's nice. What is it?"

"Macallan's," I reply, taking a sip of my own. "It's even smoother on the rocks, but I don't have any ice, sorry," I add, watching Drew swirl the liquor around his glass and smell it again.

"I need to get Houdini some of this; he would love it."

"Does that man love anything?" I ask, only partially joking. Drew laughs, nodding his head.

"Whiskey, computers and explosives, I think that's about it." With the mention of the explosives, Drew's smile drops slightly again before he forces it back on his face.

"When were you diagnosed with PTSD?" I ask, watching his face change, expressing his shock.

"Is it that obvious?" he asks, his head tipping to one side as I shake mine. "Then how did you know?"

I take a sip of my drink to hide the deep breath I take to compose myself.

"Let's just say I recognise the signs and know how they feel." I don't look directly at him, but I can feel Drew's eyes watching me carefully. Because I don't want tonight to be about me, I don't give him time to ask questions.

"If you ever want to talk, I want you to know I am a good listener. I'm also amazing at giving advice, but not so great following it myself."

I hear Drew chuckle and allow myself to look at him.

"Who is good at taking their own advice? I know I'm not." Drew looks into his glass and lets out a deep sigh.

"My last mission was a complete failure. We were sent to rescue an orphanage from a terrorist group. The kids had already lost their parents and grandparents in the fighting; they didn't need to lose their lives as well." Drew takes a deep breath as his hands start to shake again. I place a hand on his bouncing thigh, which instantly calms under my touch.

"The children were all dead. They had been tortured before we even got there. There was no need for the bastards to have done it, no fucking need at all." Drew lifts his glass and downs the rest of his drink.

"Something in me snapped that day, and I had a full

mental breakdown. I don't remember much. Pippin had already been discharged after the explosion; Houdini was on the mission with me and was the one who kept me alive. They say I calmly lifted my handgun and held it to my head. I don't remember doing it.

"Houdini managed to move the gun enough, so the bullet only skimmed me." He runs his finger over the back of his head where the hair is shorter, and a small scar shines through a long, thin, bold patch.

"My first memory after walking into the orphanage is Pippin walking into my suite at the hospital. It was like something clicked in my mind and told me I was safe. I'm told until that moment, I hadn't shown any emotion or said a word. My body and mind had shut down, and I was just on autopilot. But when Pip walked in, my mind clicked back in, and I broke down. I'm not ashamed to admit I cried harder than I ever have, and Pippin held me whilst I crumbled.

"Pippin was already living here then but stayed for two weeks. He came to every therapy session with me and let me talk and cry to him whenever I needed to. Even when he returned, he would phone the hospital and listen in to sessions with me until I told him I was okay to do them on my own." Drew looks up at me and forces a smile.

"When the psych board said they didn't think I would ever be able to return to the team, I didn't feel the dread I thought I would. I felt relief. I knew I couldn't do it anymore; I knew I would end up back in a hospital. But I was also terrified because being a SEAL was all I ever wanted to do.

"But once again, Pippin came to the rescue and, on one of his trips to visit me, he explained his plans for over here. I jumped at the chance to join him. So here I am, working alongside the two men who saved my life and are my brothers in every sense of the word."

Drew reaches over and wipes the tear from my cheek as I lean into his touch.

"I'm okay now. I still have episodes like tonight, but the guys are amazing and understand when I need to take a mental health break." He smiles at me again before running his knuckles down my cheek as he moves his hands away from my face.

"I'm a good listener too if you ever need to talk," he adds. I nod as he takes my hand. For a moment, I look down and let myself relax. I like him holding my hand. He'd done it a few times tonight before we took our seats at the restaurant, and it had felt real and natural. I guess the same can be said about when he would do little things like place an arm on the back of my chair or ask my opinion on something as if it mattered. He made me feel like I mattered tonight, even though it was a business meeting, and I was just meant to be the arm candy.

"I know what happened between you and Pippin."

I look into Drew's eyes as he smiles, reaching out and cupping my cheek again.

"I want you to know that I don't expect you to do the same with me. It wasn't part of the agreement we made. We don't want you to think it's expected of you by any of us."

"I know," I answer truthfully. "No one made me feel like you expect me to accept any of you physically. But…" I look away, not knowing how to put it without sounding desperate.

"But?" Drew asks as he places a finger under my chin and lifts my head to look into my eyes. "Tell me, sweetheart." The way he looks deep into my eyes has me blurting out the truth before I can stop myself.

"Even though me and Calvin did … stuff. I still want you to kiss me."

Silence surrounds us for a moment, but I feel Drew's thumb run across the skin on my cheek. He takes the glass from my hand and places it on the table in front of us with his, not breaking eye contact once as he leans in closer until he is mere inches from my lips.

"I want to kiss you too."

He closes the gap between us a little further. I can feel his lips brush ever so lightly against mine as he adds, "But I want to be sure it's what you really want, sweetheart." The smell of the whiskey on his breath is intoxicating. I close my eyes as my heart pumps hard in my chest.

"Kiss me, please," I beg.

Drew's lips are on mine before I finish saying the last word. He kisses me gently, testing the waters, but it's not what I want. A need fills me, making me more confident than I have ever been.

I grab his shirt and pull him closer, brushing his lips with my tongue. It's all the confirmation he needs, and he pounces, pinning me underneath him as the kiss deepens, and we both lose control. He wraps his arms around my waist and lifts me as he sits up and positions me so I'm straddling his lap. His hands move to my thighs and push up my dress, giving me the ability to sit, meaning our bodies are pressed against each other.

Threading my fingers into his hair at the top of his head, I sit back, smiling as a huge playful smirk spreads across his face. I lean forward and take his bottom lip between my teeth. Drew's eyes close as they roll to the back of his head, his hands gripping my hips as I grind against the large bulge in his trousers.

Without a single word leaving his lips, Drew places a

hand on the back of my head and kisses me hard on the mouth as another hand squeezes my hip, holding me in place so he can press himself against my aching pussy, coaxing a moan which I feel deep in my stomach. A groan leaves Drew as he rubs against me again. This time, I meet his thrust, making the sensation harder and deeper. We both moan at the same time, and I know I am soaking wet down there.

Drew's hand slides between us and cups my throbbing, aching sex. My head falls back, separating our lips as my breath catches.

"You're so wet, I can feel you through my trousers," Drew whispers against my neck as he kisses it, and his fingers start rubbing me through my soaking thong. He rubs my clit, and I know it won't take long for me to climax like this.

"More," I beg, grinding against his hand. Drew chuckles as he moves the fabric to one side and touches me, skin to skin.

"Do you want to know what Calvin told me about this soaking wet heaven?" Drew teases as his lips brush against my neck and his fingers circle my clit. Did they talk about me? I should be angry or humiliated, but the thought of the two of them discussing me in that way is a huge turn-on. I can feel myself getting wetter, and Drew notices.

"Do you like the idea of us discussing this pussy?" he cups and squeezes me applying enough pressure to heighten my arousal.

"Yes," I gasp as he squeezes me again.

"Do you want to know what he said?" Drew asks as his fingers start circling my entrance but not penetrating me.

"Drew!"

He chuckles whilst moving his fingers away as I try to push them inside me.

"He told me this was the sweetest little honey pot he has ever tasted," he teases as he starts rubbing around my entrance again. "That it had to be a portal to hell because the taste was too sweet and addictive for heaven." His finger enters me by a centimetre, and I cry out in frustration. "He knew that it was the perfect size for his cock, and that only finger fucking you near enough destroyed him." His finger enters me the slightest bit more, and I know my juices are flowing down his hand as I get closer to coming.

"He told me after he made you cum in the morning, he went for a shower, and the second the water sprayed his rock-hard cock, he exploded." Drew grips the hair at the back of my head and brings my head forward to make me look him in the eye. "That's the effect you had on him. He didn't even have to touch himself."

A wave of pleasure curses through me at the thought of Calvin coming in the shower without even having to touch himself.

That's what I did to him.

"Are you going to let me see if he was lying to me? Can I feel how tight you are and how sweet you taste?"

"Yes!" I gasp as his fingertip rubs the inside of my entrance.

"Here or your room?" he asks, kissing my neck lightly whilst massaging my entrance.

"My room."

"Wrap your legs around me," Drew demands, removing his finger and placing both hands on my ass as he stands from the sofa. I instantly wrap my arms and legs around him as he walks towards the stairs.

"Luna?" he asks quietly. I glance up the stairs and smile.

"Sleeping, her door will be open though," I whisper. A playful smile spreads across his face as he carries me towards my room.

"You better be quiet then," he teases before his lips find mine. We continue to kiss as Drew carries me up the stairs. I point to the door of my room, and he holds me with one hand as he opens the door and takes me inside.

"Lock it," I whisper against his lips as he closes the door. He feels the key in the lock, and I hear the mechanism click into place. I reach behind him and switch on the light, needing to see him.

Drew carries me to the bed before placing me on my feet.

"Turn around; I need to do what I've wanted to do all night and get you out of this dress."

I turn my back to him and move my hair out of the way so he can get to the zipper.

Drew unfastens the long zipper before he starts to push the fabric over my shoulders as his fingertips lightly brush over my now bare skin. His lips follow his fingers, placing featherlight kisses over my shoulders.

"You are so beautiful. I've wanted to tell you that since the moment I laid eyes on you," he whispers in my ear before kissing my shoulder again.

The dress falls to the floor, and Drew's hands land on my hips.

"As soon as I saw this dress, I knew you would be braless underneath." He turns me around and lifts me so I can wrap my legs around his waist. Placing me on the bed, I unhook my legs so he can pull away from me. Drew kneels and admires me lying on the bed, ready for him.

"This is exactly what I have been trying my hardest not to imagine all night." He reaches down and runs a hand between my breasts and down my stomach. His fingers take hold of the seam of my thong, and every muscle in my body tightens with anticipation. Everything this man does is slow and deliberate. As he slides my underwear from my hips, I swear my body aches and screams for him to hurry up. The longer he takes, the harder I have to bite my tongue from begging him to take me.

By the time he finally removes them from my body, I'm a mess, and he knows it from the look on his face.

"Fucking perfection," he says before his head falls between my legs, and his tongue is on me in seconds.

"Fuck!" I gasp, slamming my hand over my mouth as every nerve ending between my legs gets stimulated at the same time.

Drew starts to lick every part of me as if cleaning me of my own juices. I swear he is bringing parts of me alive that I never knew existed. I feel his finger massaging my entrance again before slowly working its way inside me, rubbing every sweet spot on the way. By this point, I know I'm getting louder, and I try my hardest to bite my tongue, but every now and again, I have to slam my hand over my mouth in an attempt to muffle my moans at least enough so as not to wake Luna.

But as Drew inserts a second finger, I know my hand isn't enough, and I only just manage to grab the pillow and hold it over my face as I scream through my orgasm. Drew continues to suck and lick me through it until I beg him to stop because it's become too much.

The pillow is removed from my face, and a grinning Drew appears above me.

"Remind me to take you somewhere you can be as loud as you want," he teases before pressing his lips to mine as I wrap my shaking legs around his waist.

"If you promise to do that again, then I will go anywhere you ask," I gasp as I feel his hard cock at my entrance. I lift my hips, desperate to feel him inside me.

"Let me get a condom," he whispers into my neck as he scraps his teeth over my skin, coaxing another moan from me.

"I have the implant," I gasp as he bites my shoulder slightly.

"You want me bare?" he asks, kissing me again.

"I need you now." I tighten my legs around him as his cock enters me the smallest amount. Drew lifts his head and looks me deep in the eyes, grinning as he places his hands on my hips, pinning me to the bed.

"You got me."

With one hard thrust, Drew buries himself so deep within me I swear he hits my cervix.

"Fuck!" we gasp together as my eyes roll to the back of my head. He holds himself still for a moment before grinding his hips into mine, rubbing against every spot within me.

"You were made to take my cock," he growls as he coaxes another gasp from me.

"Don't stop," I cry out before burying my face in his shoulder to stifle my cries of pleasure.

"Oh, sweetheart. I have no intentions of stopping any time soon," he teases, somehow pushing himself deeper within me again. "We've got all night, and I plan on taking full advantage."

As he hits every sensitive spot inside me, I bury my head into his shoulder as I cry out through another explosive orgasm and realise these men are going to ruin me.

Chapter Twenty

CALVIN

"You seen Bambi today?" I call as I enter the garage we've converted into a gym. Logan is lying on the bench, pressing at least three hundred pounds as he does every other day. He has always been the most disciplined of the three of us regarding his fitness. He never misses a day of training. Even when he was injured, he would work out the other parts of his body until he decided he was fit enough to train whichever part was healing. Medics and physios gave up trying to tell him what he should and shouldn't do as they knew he'd never listen.

I lean against the treadmill to the side and wait for him to finish his set, knowing better than to interrupt when he's in the zone. I watch him complete twenty-four more lifts before placing the bar back on the stand behind him and sitting up.

"What?" he asks, grabbing his towel from the floor beside the bench and wiping his face.

"Have you seen Bambi? I don't think he came home last night."

Logan sighs and gives me the side eye.

"In other words, you are worried you aren't Chelsea's favourite anymore, and he got more action than you did."

"No, I'm worried something has happened," I argue a little too loudly.

"Yeah, between him and Chelsea. You wouldn't give a shit if he had taken someone else with him last night." Logan stands from the bench and wraps the towel around his neck before walking to the treadmill I'm leaning against. "If you are going to throw a tantrum every time he takes her out, then this is going to get complicated fast," he adds whilst picking the settings he wants.

"Whatever, you know you are just as interested in what happened between them last night as I am. You just refuse to acknowledge it," I snap, walking over to the small fridge we have in here and grabbing a bottle of water.

"I don't give a shit if they slept together or not," Logan argues as he starts the machine. "At the end of the day, all I care about is if he got that contract or not. It would bring in a hell of a lot of money, which means more funds to be spent on the other stuff."

Just as I go to argue, I hear the door shutting and turn to see Drew in last night's clothes walking in, looking very smug.

"Guess who sealed the deal," he announces proudly.

"With Chelsea or Godfrey?" Logan asks with one arched brow. Doesn't care, my ass. He wants to know as much as I do what happened between the two of them. It's not because I'm jealous; for some reason, it doesn't occur to me that Drew is competition when it comes to Chelsea. It's hard to explain, but the thought of him and her hitting it off in that way feels right.

"Godfrey was a prick who managed to push all my

buttons, and if it weren't for Chelsea, I would have blown my lid."

"What happened?" Logan asks, stopping the treadmill to give Drew his full attention. I walk towards them and lean against the machine next to him.

Drew quickly fills us in on the conversation and how it triggered his PTSD. Out of all of us, Drew is the only one who suffers from the lasting emotional effects of the missions we took on over the years. We have always joked that he is the most sensitive out of the three of us, but we never mean it in a nasty manner. He is our brother and watching him have a breakdown a few years back was hard as fuck. I flew back and forth to make sure he knew I was there. It was one reason we chose to set up home here rather than in the States.

Drew is just telling us about getting to Chelsea's when Logan stops him.

"Hang on, what did she say about the PTSD?" he asks, frowning.

"That she understood the signs and how it feels," Drew replies, rubbing his neck.

"She has PTSD? What the fuck from?" Logan demands, looking furious.

"I don't know, she didn't want to discuss it further. Then we kind of got distracted. But this morning, I noticed she has three different locks on her bedroom door, two on the bathroom, three on her daughter's room and four on the front door."

"What the fuck?" Logan and I shout out together, both standing tall.

"I know. I couldn't ask about it as I was hiding from her daughter this morning. I didn't leave her bathroom until they had gone to work and school. But when I saw how many locks Chels had on her door, I checked the rest of the house. It's like Fort Knox, with cameras on the inside as well. I didn't want to check around too much in case she was watching, but I wouldn't be surprised if they were in hiding or something."

The three of us stay quiet momentarily as we all try to work out what they could be hiding from or, more importantly, whom.

"Surely if it were that bad, she wouldn't have signed up to a dating app, of all things?" Logan says, picking up his water from the floor where he had placed it with his towel and taking a sip.

"Maybe they were there from when she moved in and hasn't taken them down yet?" I suggest. The other two shrug but don't look convinced.

"So other than all that, I take it the night ended well?" I ask, which causes a grin to reappear on Drew's face.

"Very well, you weren't wrong; I could eat that sweet pussy all night."

"If you two are going to compare notes like horny teenagers, fuck off so I can train in peace." Logan points to the door before restarting the treadmill. Drew and I both know there is no point continuing to talk in there. He will make it his mission to be as loud as possible until we leave.

We exit the garage, which leads to the utility room and kitchen. I head straight for the coffee pot and hold up a mug to Drew, who nods while sitting at the table. The house isn't big, it's a three-bedroom detached house in a standard neighbourhood. But it's enough for the three of us. Sure, we get the odd, strange look, and I think people around here assume we are all in a relationship together, but it doesn't bother us.

I hand Drew his mug and lean against the counter opposite him.

"You fucked off with me?" Drew asks, leaning back in his seat and crossing his ankles in front of him. I shake my head whilst taking a sip of my coffee.

"We said we wouldn't get jealous of each other, and I stand by that. I know I probably should be, but for some reason, it feels," I stop as I try and work out the best way to phrase it.

"Natural?" Drew offers, and I nod. "She likes that we talked about her. When I mentioned it to her and repeated what you said about in the shower, she near enough came in my hand before I even touched her."

I reposition myself as my cock hardens at the thought of her hearing how I exploded like a fucking kid as soon as the water touched me. Drew looks at me knowingly and smirks.

"I made love to that woman for an hour last night and, at one point, asked if she thought she could handle the two of us at the same time. Her pussy clamped around me so hard I thought she was going to break it off," Drew adds, repositioning his own cock.

"Fuck, this is not what I need to hear when I have to be at Young's in half an hour for a meeting. How the fuck am I going to face her and not fuck her over that goddamn desk!" I snap, banging my half-full coffee mug on the side and storming towards the door.

"Where are you going?" Drew calls after me, laughing.

"Where do you think? To have a fucking wank!"

Chapter Twenty-One

CHELSEA

My heart is racing as I know Calvin and Logan are due to arrive shortly for a meeting with Mr Young, and I don't know if they know what happened between Drew and me last night. Because, boy, did a lot happen.

After he left me gasping for breath and questioning every life choice I had made to this point, we had the most mind blowing sex. The things that man can do with his tongue, fingers and cock are enough to send me rushing to the toilet to dry the constant wetness between my legs.

What shocked me the most was that whenever he mentioned getting Calvin to join us, I swear I came even harder. I have never thought of myself as experimental in the bedroom. In fact, I would say my sex life up to now has been beyond boring. But the thought of the three of us getting hot and steamy together near enough blew my goddamn mind. I swear there were even times I thought about how it would be if Logan, Calvin and Drew were all in the bed with me and ... fuck I'm throbbing again.

"Morning Chelsea, how are we feeling this morning?"

Calvin calls as he exits the elevator, with Logan walking behind him, rolling his eyes.

"You should know you got all the details from Bambi this morning," Logan says, his eyes finding mine. He looks at me so intensely that if I'd been on my feet, my knees would have buckled underneath me.

"Oh my god," I gasp as he looks away and Calvin's face comes into view. He walks behind the desk and takes my hand before pressing a kiss to it.

"Don't worry, we are just teasing you," he winks before leaning on the desk, his arms and legs crossed in front of him. "Did you manage to hide from Luna that he was there?" Calvin asks, smiling.

"I thought we had got away with it until I went to get her in the car. She noticed his was parked outside," I sigh, placing my face in my hands as Calvin laughs beside me. When I look up, I find Logan looking at the tablet in his hand. I thought I saw him watching me for a moment, but I'm sure I'm mistaken.

"So, she thinks you two are dating?" Calvin asks. I don't miss the real meaning of the question. He seems a little relieved when I shake my head.

"I told her his car was playing up, and you picked him up. Don't think she believed me as she had apparently seen his jacket in the lounge and the two glasses from our whiskey."

"Smart girl," Logan says from his seat, not bothering to look up from the screen in front of him.

"She takes after her mum," I reply, finally earning a look from the miserable bastard. Okay, it's a questionable one, but it's a look, nevertheless.

"Any heads up what this is about?" Calvin asks, nodding his head towards Young's door.

"Your guys not been in touch?" I ask, surprised. Both guys look at me and shake their heads. Before I get a chance to tell them what I know, the office door opens, and Mr Young walks out, looking at the three of us.

"If you have finished flirting with my PA, I need to speak to you both," he demands before walking back into the room, leaving the three of us frowning at each other. Calvin gives me a wink before walking into Mr Young's office. Logan gets as far as the desk and stops to look at me.

"I have to go to a business dinner in two nights, is there any chance you could accompany me? I'm not great with these things, but the other two have to work an event, and…" he rubs the back of his neck nervously. "I could do with a friendly face there."

I nod as I turn my chair around to look at him properly.

"Sure thing. Send me the details, and we can organise it."

Logan nods once as he goes to say something but obviously changes his mind and mutters a "thanks" before heading into the office after the other two, closing the door behind them.

Logan

I walk into the office and can see straight away that Young's on edge. I look to Calvin, who shrugs as we watch him pacing behind his desk.

"What's going on?" I ask, placing my tablet on the desk before me as I sit down.

"I could ask you the same thing. How the hell has someone been able to get past your new system and get access to the basement?" he demands, leaning on his desk and glaring at the two of us.

"What's happened in the basement?" Calvin asks, frowning. I pull up the feed on my phone, and it hasn't logged anyone entering or leaving the room until this morning when Young went in himself.

"You tell me! You are the security guys!" he yells, pushing himself away from the desk and pacing again.

"You will need to tell us exactly what happened because, as you know, the new cameras haven't been fitted yet and more than half the entrance sensors are still to be fitted. I warned you there would be a time frame to this, and you said it was fine!" I snap. If there's anything I hate more than being lied to, it's people accusing me of not staying true to my word.

Young stares at me for a moment before almost falling into his chair. He types on this keyboard and turns the screen to show us.

"I received this email last night but didn't see it until this morning."

Geralt,
Looks like you have bought more than just the building from Taylor. Be aware Taylor was into more than you will ever know. His death has caused a stir, and now people are looking for things he took.
Watch your back and who has access to certain areas of your building, as they may unearth much more than you would ever suspect.
An old friend.

There is no email address or contact details. The email isn't even in the inbox. It's in the drafts. I lean forward and take control of the keyboard and mouse before doing what I do best: getting into a system which is meant to be hackproof.

"When you received this, what did you do?" I ask, making a mental note of the time stamp and opening the cameras at that time. The only people I can see on any cameras are our two employees who were on the night shift. They are together as they are meant to be, and they look around for any issues. There is no one in the basement or this office.

"Like I said, this morning. As soon as I read it, I knew they were referring to the basement. I went down and found that a section of the room had been cleared of boxes. I haven't authorised anything to be done since I filled it and sealed the room as you suggested."

When we learnt something was possibly buried under the floor, I suggested turning the room into storage. That way, it would appear we were none the wiser about what was in there. What was the point in moving things around there besides digging the floor up?

I look to Young, still amazed someone got past my system.

"Show me."

We walk into the room, and there is no mistaking that someone has been down here moving things around. I notice the floor is covered in thick dust, so I move a couple of boxes to discover that there are signs someone has tried to dig a hole in the ground.

I look at the floor around the site and can't see anything

that indicates what they had used to try and break through the concrete.

"Who was on last night?" Calvin asks behind me.

"Jefferys and Haycock," I answer. I look up to Calvin, who gives me a knowing look. "I know," I mutter before climbing back to my feet. We've been having issues with Jefferys for a while and have already been discussing whether he will pass his probation period.

I walk to the door and look outside to see there is no evidence that anything has occurred in there. I look up at the camera that's meant to be facing the door, but instead, it's facing the wall. I growl under my breath and look back around. There are no footprints, scuff marks, or tracks from wheels, and there is nothing at all that would signal that something was amiss down here.

"It's too clean," I mutter, walking back into the room. I walk along the walls, tapping and pressing anything that looks out of place, but the walls are all intact. I look up at the ceiling, and it's all one solid mass. No vents, nothing.

"What are you thinking, Houdini?"

I turn to look at him and shake my head.

"There are too many missing pieces. There's no evidence of anyone being here besides the dust, moved boxes and damaged flooring. No footprints, nothing. What does that tell you?" I ask him.

"They knew how to get in here without being seen or heard," he answers. I nod and look back to Young.

"I'm going to spend the day here again, going through each person's access cards and where they can go. Someone is messing with you, and I don't like it one bit."

I walk from the room and head straight back up to the top floor, where we find Chelsea sitting at her desk.

"Is everything okay?" she asks as soon as she looks at us. I shake my head, not stopping to answer as I head into Young's office. I grab my tablet whilst holding the phone to my ear.

"Get to Young's now. Call up Jefferys and Haycock and get them here as well."

"What's going on? Weren't they working at Young's last night?" Drew asks.

"That's why I want them here ASAP. I don't care if you have to drag them out of bed. Get them here now!"

I hang up, not waiting to hear his reply. I grab a pen and paper from Young's desk and start scribbling ideas going around in my head, as well as a to-do list.

"What do you need?"

I look up to see Chelsea standing in front of me, her notebook ready to take notes.

"I want a fresh copy of the list we made up the other night of who can go where and why. I need everyone to stay the fuck out of the basement and a notice going out that no one is to work past their allotted times. That includes you," I warn her with a knowing look. I know she works late most nights, and it needs to stop.

"Anything else?" she asks. I frown at her, wondering what else I could possibly need. "Coffee? Lunch? Conference room to work from?" she asks.

"All of the above," I reply, looking back down at the paper in front of me. I hear her stepping away and take a deep breath. "Thank you, Chels." I look up to see her looking over her shoulder.

"You're welcome," she replies before leaving the office, leaving me to crack on with it.

Chapter Twenty-Two

CHELSEA

It's been two days since all hell broke loose at work, and I have never been more grateful for the weekend. Two days without dealing with Logan's constant mood swings will be bliss. I know he has every right to be pissed off, as things could not be much worse at work; I just wish he would stop taking it out on me.

I spoke to Calvin and Drew about his attitude, and they both answered with the same advice.

"He is like that when stressed. He will calm down once he works out what's going on." I was so relieved when he told me the dinner had been cancelled. At least I didn't have to spend that evening with someone who would rather fuck a barbed fence than be pleasant towards me.

It's Saturday afternoon, and I promised Luna we would go to the cinema in the morning, followed by a trip to the park. Luna loves being outside, but the weather has been crap the last few weeks. Winter is well and truly on its way, which means cosy nights in, which is great, but my outdoorsy girl hates it.

Luna looks up at me and smiles when she sees the play area coming into view as we walk through town. It's packed, so I decide to kill some time and get us both a warm drink while we wait for the area to clear slightly.

"Can I have marshmallows in my hot chocolate, please, Mummy?" Luna asks as we join the queue in Costa.

"Can you even have hot chocolate without marshmallows?" a voice asks behind us. I turn to find Drew and Logan smiling. I have to blink a couple of times to check that Logan is actually smiling.

"Afternoon, ladies. Are you having a good day?" he asks, smiling at Luna and me, as Luna grins at Drew.

"Oh, you're the one who stayed the other night," she exclaims excitedly.

"Luna!" I hiss as Drew's smile drops and Logan roars, laughing. I look up at him, surprised. I don't think I have ever heard him laugh like that before.

"I told you he didn't stay; he had to leave the car outside because it was making a strange noise," I lie, giving Logan a warning look when Luna isn't looking. But he's too busy smirking to pay any notice to me.

"If you say so, but I know you told him to hide when I knocked on your door that morning. Plus, your door was locked. You never lock the door in case I have to come in," she continues, not caring who's around and listening.

"Oh my god, someone kill me now," I groan, placing my hand on my face as Drew and Logan laugh and Luna giggles. "Fine, okay, he stayed, you happy now?" I hiss through gritted teeth. Luna smirks at me proudly.

"Very."

I turn around and give the barista our order, but before I get a chance to pay, Logan taps his card against the machine. I turn around, ready to point out I can afford a coffee and a hot chocolate, but he is busy asking Luna what she has been doing so far today, not even looking in my direction. Drew smiles next to him and shrugs.

"He's in a good mood this morning; make the most of it." Drew gives Logan and his order to the barista and adds four large cookies.

"Mind if we join you, ladies? There aren't many tables," Drew asks as Logan hands a cookie to Luna.

"Mummy, can they join us? Please?"

"Of course they can," I answer, looking at the two guys, wondering how they have won my daughter around so quickly.

I go to pick up our tray of drinks, but Logan takes it and tells me to go and grab a table. I thank him as Luna rushes off to the one he pointed at.

Once we are all sat down with our drinks, I watch Luna talk to Logan like she has known him for years.

"What are your plans with Mom today?" he asks, handing her half his cookie.

"Well," she starts dramatically. "We have been to the cinema, and then to pick out some new clothes for me. Mummy says I'm growing too fast, but I think I'm growing just right."

I roll my eyes as Drew and Logan both laugh.

"Now we are going to wait here until the park is quieter, and I can play. Although I can't go on the swings," she sighs, scooping out her marshmallows with a spoon.

"Why can't you go on the swings?" Logan asks her whilst handing her a napkin for the cream on her chin.

"Because I can't swing on my own, and Mummy can't push me because of her shoulder."

Logan's eyes snap to me so fast I almost fall from my chair.

"What's wrong with your shoulder?" he demands.

"Nothing, it's just an old injury that hurts when it's cold," I answer as he and Drew watch me. I look at Luna, who is lost in her own little world, eating the cookie she is dunking in her hot chocolate.

"When was it last looked at?" Drew asks as Logan looks at my shoulders as if he can x-ray them with his eyes.

"It's fine, stop worrying about it," I sigh, picking up my coffee and taking a sip, hoping they will drop it.

"How about I take you to the park in a minute, and then you can go on the swings?" Logan asks Luna.

"You don't have to do that," I protest instantly. Logan looks at me, and I realise he thinks I don't want him around Luna. Do I want him around her? I trust the guys more than anyone else with her. Otherwise, we would not be sitting here now.

"What I mean is, I don't want you to change your plans just to help her out," I add quickly, hoping to make him see I didn't mean that how it sounded.

"It's fine, we have time," he answers before looking at Luna, smiling up at him happily. "Let me know when you are ready, and we can go."

Luna grabs her mug and drinks it so quickly I'm sure she will throw up.

"You could have come back and finished it after the park," I point out as she wipes her face on the napkin Drew hands her.

"I didn't think of that. Oh well," she shrugs, jumping to her feet and grabbing Logan's hand. "Come on, I want you to push me on the swings before it rains."

Logan doesn't argue as he's dragged out of the warm coffee shop and towards the cold park.

"I hope he doesn't feel he has to do this," I mutter as I watch them rush into the park.

"Houdini doesn't do anything he doesn't want to," Drew chuckles as he watches his friend. "He has always been good with kids. Whenever we were dealing with young children, usually scared orphans, they seemed to attach themselves to him. There were a few times we would save babies, and they would cry and cry for their parents. One hug of the BFG there, and they would fall asleep on his chest. You would find him in a chair, fast asleep with a baby resting on him."

I watch Logan push Luna on the swing, and she squeals happily. The smile on his face is like none I have seen on him before. Maybe the miserable bastard isn't so bad after all. I think I sometimes forget what he and the guys have been through, that they haven't always been their own bosses. They have witnessed things I would never recover from, and it's no wonder they react the way they do at times. Watching him now playing happily with my daughter gives me a warm feeling I never expected when it came to Logan.

Chapter Twenty-Three

CALVIN

"There you are. I was starting to think you had both gotten lost."

Logan throws the bag of coffee onto my desk and walks over to the computer without saying a word.

"What's eating him?" I ask Drew, who's frowning, watching Logan typing away on the keyboard. The computer he is sitting at is the one we have linked to the UK forces. We are able to search anyone and see anything from their police records to where they took their first steps. I had been on there all morning looking through the employees at Young's to see if anyone raised any flags.

"I have no idea. He was in a great mood until twenty minutes ago. We bumped into Chelsea and her daughter in a coffee shop. Grumpy ass there even bought their drinks, then took Luna into the park for half an hour."

"Did the six-year-old wear you out? Do you need hot milk, cookies and a nap, old man?" I laugh out loud, expecting some reaction from Logan, but instead, he scribbles something on a piece of paper and jumps up from the computer.

"I'm going for a run," he snaps, shoving the paper into his pocket and storming out of the room. I stand up from my chair and walk over to the computer he was working on. He's closed whichever program he was using, and there is no way to know which one as the memory wipes on this thing instantly to ensure nothing can be used other than what we need it for.

"Somethings happened to rattle his cage; any idea what?" I ask Drew, who shakes his head.

"He was fine the whole time we were with Chels and Luna. He brought her back from the park and told Chels he would contact her later about a possible dinner he might need her for, and we left. The second he left the café it was like he was taken over by the usual stressed Houdini."

"He didn't look at his phone or receive a call?" I ask, trying to work it all out.

"Not that I saw. I mean, he could have whilst in the park, as I wasn't watching him and Luna constantly. I was chatting with Chels most of the time. But he was fine when he brought her back to her mom."

I rub my hand over my face and let out a deep sigh. I need to speak to him, but I know that if he is going for a run, he needs some time and space to process whatever is happening in his head.

"Any luck with the staff at Young's?" Drew asks. I shake my head and stand up from the chair.

"Nothing. We are missing something, and I don't know what. I was hoping to run a couple of ideas past him when you got back, but I can't see that happening until later tonight, at least."

We both make our way out of the secure unit and head back up to the main part of the building. As we walk through the building, we listen out for the sound of Logan moving about, but he's long gone. I try his locker on the off chance he's left that piece of paper in there, but it's locked, and I have too much respect for the guy to pick the lock. One, he will know; two, if it is important, he will tell us when he is ready.

Logan

As my feet pound the pavement, I tell myself I don't need to run this way, that I could go another route, and the heat gel in my pocket can be given to Chelsea another time. But I need an excuse to be out and away from the building and the guys. Chelsea's shoulder pain was the first thing I thought of when I saw the heat gel in my locker. I changed into my running gear in record time, and here I am, five miles away from the office, running up her street.

I'm still in shock from what I read on the screen, and I know I have to tell the guys, but I need time to do further digging. It's a sensitive subject I will need to approach gently and carefully with those involved. I might not be known for my softer side; it's something I have learnt is better off hidden away, especially in our line of work. Most people think of me as a heartless bastard who never thinks of anyone's feelings but my own, and in some ways, they are right. I've seen and done too much to wear my heart on my sleeve.

The human race can be a parasite that needs to have the dark and evil people wiped from the face of the earth so those pure at heart can live in peace safely. I know I'm not one of them; I don't deserve peace or happiness after some of the things I have done. I came to terms with that many years ago. But if I can give those who still have a chance of peace and happiness in their lives a real fighting start, then I will.

I rub my face as I feel the first few drops of rain hit me, dragging me from the dark place I was heading. I need to get this delivered to Chelsea and then head home for a shower. I have a bottle of whiskey with my name on it, and I think I will drink the lot tonight whilst planning the weekly training programme for our staff.

Turning onto Chelsea's street, I search for her number, coming to a stop outside a house with very little on the outside. The garden looks a little overgrown, and the house needs a fresh coat of paint. Considering how much she works, I'm not surprised she doesn't have time to do the little things like this. I'm sure one of the guys will do it if she asks. I don't have time, but they like doing things for her.

I walk up the gravel drive and knock on the door, wiping the sweat from my brow. I hear a commotion inside and frown as I try to hear what's happening. I can hear Chelsea's voice, and it sounds like she's shouting, but I can't work out why. I quickly knock again, a little louder, hoping to get her attention, when I hear a bang and her calling out. I grab the handle and push open the front door, which is thankfully unlocked.

"Chelsea!" I call out, looking around. I can hear running water coming from all angles and Chelsea's frustrated shout. "CHELS!" I call out again, heading for the stairs, where I notice water running down them.

"Logan?" I hear her call as she appears at the top of the stairs, looking close to tears. "Oh, thank God. Help me!" she cries as I rush up the stairs two at a time.

"What the fuck?" I curse as I reach the landing to see water flowing under the bathroom door.

"I was running a bath, and the door closed and somehow locked from the inside. I can't get it open, and the taps are still on."

"Where's Luna?" I ask, rushing for the bathroom.

"Here," a small sob comes from a doorway.

"Okay, princess, stay back. I'll kick it down." I look to make sure both of them are out of the way and quickly note the type of door and handle it is. I step back and kick out as hard as I can. The door groans loudly but doesn't budge. I kick it again, and the sound of the wood splintering sounds out.

"Come on, you prick," I growl through gritted teeth before kicking it again, and the door flies open.

"Oh, thank you," Chelsea calls as she rushes past me and straight for the bath, which is overflowing. She slips and slides across the bath and only just gets to it without falling over completely. She turns the taps off, then rushes towards me and throws her arms around my neck.

"Thank you so much. I don't know what I would have done," she cries at the same time as a sob sounds from the bedroom. We both turn to see Luna crying with her hands over her ears. Chelsea lets go of me and rushes towards her daughter, pulling her into her arms and holding her as she cries. I walk away from them, head into the bathroom to give them space, and start cleaning up.

It takes a while, but we slowly start to make progress as we clean up the water. It's, of course, dripping through the ceiling and into the lounge and dining room downstairs. I sent Calvin a message and asked if he knew someone who could come and check the electrics and that everything was safe. When he asked why I was here, I didn't bother replying. When I return, he will ask me again, and I'm not repeating myself.

I'm checking the ceiling in the lounge when I hear someone enter the room. I turn to see Luna looking up at me nervously. She has been avoiding me since I kicked the door down, obviously scaring her in the process. I climb off the chair I'm standing on and hold out my hand for her whilst squatting down so I'm at her level.

"I'm sorry if I scared you, princess. I didn't mean to," I say softly as she steps forward and places her hand in mine.

"I didn't mean for it to happen. I just closed the door, and it locked," she explains as tears roll down her cheeks. I reach up and wipe them away gently.

"I believe you; I saw the lock. It was old and loose. It could have happened to anyone."

Luna steps forward, wraps her arms around my neck, and hugs me, taking me by surprise. I quickly hug her back and place a kiss on her cheek affectionately.

"Thank you for not shouting at me," she whispers as she steps back and smiles.

"I would never shout at you, princess. If I ever do, you have my permission to punch me in the face," I wink, and a small laugh escapes her.

"Thank you," she whispers before pressing a kiss to my cheek and rushing off. I close my eyes for a moment and let out a deep sigh before climbing back to my feet.

That little girl is a sweetheart who won this old man's heart.

"Thank you for being so good with her."

I open my eyes to see Chelsea leaning against the door-frame. Her hair's up in a messy bun, her feet and the bottom of her trousers are wet, and she looks exhausted.

"She's a good kid," I reply, turning around and climbing back onto the chair to continue checking the ceiling.

"Yeah, she is. I must have done something right, at least, to deserve her." I can feel her sadness as I sigh, climb off the chair, and approach Chelsea. She looks up at me as I look around to check for Luna.

"I know why your shoulder bothers you. She told me about a few things in the park." I can see the panic on her face and shake my head.

"I've not said anything to the others, but you need to at some point. They know something is going on, and from the number of locks I've noticed on doors, I know it's more than just a precaution."

Chelsea looks around and sighs. I can see she is conflicted between telling me more and running away, so I make the option for her.

"Pippin has phoned a guy he knows and trusts to come out and check the electrics. If they aren't safe, I want you to call your insurance and stay in a hotel until they are." I step back and give her half a smile.

"If you need anything, call one of the guys. They can be here in minutes. If you can get a babysitter for Tuesday night, I would appreciate it if you could come with me for the meal." I watch as Chelsea nods again, and I make my way to the front door.

"You never said why you came round?" she calls out behind me.

"I brought over some heat gel for your shoulder. It's on the side in the kitchen. Pippin swears by it in the winter, so I thought it might help," I reply before walking out of the door and closing it behind me, not giving her a chance to respond or persuade me to stay.

There is a reason I'm keeping her at arm's length, and today just proved I was right. Chelsea Hughes and I would make a terrible pair. My temper is too short fused for someone as delicate as her. I would ruin things for the guys and the company.

Chapter Twenty-Four

CHELSEA

"Mummy, how much longer are you going to be?"

I look up from my computer and see a bored-looking Luna.

"I'm sorry, honey. I'll be as quick as I can, I promise. I will make it up to you when we leave here."

Luna sighs and heads back into the conference room, where all her things are set up. Looking back at my work computer, I let out a sigh. Of all the days for the school to have a teacher training day, today is not a good day for me.

Why do schools even have to have teacher training days? Can't they do their training during the school holidays when we are already forking out a small fortune in childcare? No, they have to have it when all the childminders are full, and I have no choice but to bring Luna to work with me. I know it's not her fault, but she's bored silly, so she's bugging me every five minutes, slowing down how much work I'm getting through.

I hear the elevator ping just before the door opens, and I don't miss the butterflies that explode in my stomach as

Chapter Twenty-Five

CALVIN

I watch Logan put the latest recruits and Jefferys through their paces. He is a far better trainer than me or Drew. Logan's dedication to fitness is one of the reasons I begged him to join me when I decided to set up this company.

I've been in a great mood since spending time with Luna three days ago. She told me all about a school show she is participating in today, and I've picked up my phone so many times to see if Chelsea would mind me watching it. But as I keep reminding myself, Chelsea isn't looking for a real relationship.

I probably shouldn't have watched Luna for her the other day, but it just seemed like the right thing to do. Plus, I want to help Chelsea in any way I can. She is such a lovely lady and deserves someone to be there for her for a change. Why shouldn't I be one of the people to help her?

"Why the fuck have I got to be here? I've done all this already."

That annoying voice that's pushing every one of Logan's buttons calls out, bringing me back to the training hall. Thomas Jefferys was possibly the worst mistake we ever made.

The guy is thick as shit, lazy, and downright pathetic. On paper, he is the perfect example of a dedicated firearms officer who will happily put their life on the line to protect others. He has had awards to celebrate his bravery during attacks in the UK. But in real life, he is happy for someone else to do the hard work now, and he will reap the rewards.

"Because you have obviously forgotten everything as you let someone not only get past you when you were on duty. But you also failed to notice when they hacked into the system and caused all kinds of shit. Now stop backchatting and do sixty burpees!" Logan snaps.

"Sixty? But they only have to do thirty!"

I push myself away from the wall I'm leaning against as Logan spins on the spot and storms towards Jefferys, who instantly looks ready for a fight.

"Did you get away with backchatting your superiors like this in the forces? I doubt it very much. If you did, I'm sure you would have had more than one disciplinary during your time with them," Logan snaps as he looks Jefferys straight in the eye. "Every time you open your mouth and argue, I will double your exercise. One hundred and twenty. Go."

"You do one hundred and twenty!" Jefferys snaps back. Drew curses under his breath as we watch the others stop what they are doing and stare at the showdown that's happening between Logan and the idiot.

"Two hundred and forty! Last warning." Logan stands over Jefferys, who just isn't going to back down any time soon.

"Fucking idiot is about to sign his own death warrant," Drew whispers next to me. I nod as I wait to see what the dickhead will do next.

"Fuck you."

Drew and I pounce at the same time and grab Logan before he punches the stupid ass prick. Drew keeps hold of a steaming Logan, who is bulked up and ready to fight. He's near enough snarling as he glares at Jefferys, who may have finally twigged. He fucked up.

"You want to work for us, you show your superiors some fucking respect!" I demand, standing in front of him. "You want to fuck around; you get the hell out of this building while you can still walk," I add, pointing towards the door. I turn around and ensure I have everyone's full attention.

"You can all listen to this. You want an easy ride? Well, there's the fucking door! We don't want jackasses who don't want to put in the work. We want individuals willing to put in the hours and give everything they have. You want in on the special ops, you have to fucking earn it!" I yell, looking around the room. The other fifteen people are now all watching the showdown, and I turn my attention back to Jefferys.

"You have two choices left. Pick up your bag, walk out of that door and don't bother coming back. Or get in that ring with one of us, and you beat us, you keep your job, lose, and your fate depends on how well we think you fought."

I don't need to guess which option he will pick. He's not the first to test our patience and try their luck. We always give them this option because it will never go how they think it will. We make an example of them in front of the others and show them why we are more than capable of running this company and taking out any threat that comes our way.

"I'll take the pretty boy in the ring," Jeffreys calls, looking at his choice, and I hear Logan laugh behind me before muttering, "Fucking idiot," under his breath as I point towards the ring.

"Get in there," I snap before turning my back to him and heading to Drew, who is already losing the t-shirt and heading towards the ring.

"Do you think he has any idea what he just did calling Bambi pretty boy?" I ask Logan quietly. He turns to me with a grin and shakes his head. They always underestimate the damage Drew can do. You get them to pick one of the three of us, and they pick him as he's smaller and looks less threatening. They don't know that we used to use that to our advantage and send the "small, innocent" one in first. Who would take them out from the inside, and they never saw it coming.

Logan holds the ropes, and Drew climbs in, already loosening up. Jefferys climbs in as others gather around ringside.

"How about we make this more fun and take bets?" Jefferys calls out smugly, as he pisses about, not taking it seriously in the slightest.

"Fight!" I call out at the same time as the smile on his face drops.

"What?" he yells just as Drew takes out his legs, punches him in the face and has his concealed weapon to Jefferys' head before he's even taken a breath.

"I wasn't fucking ready!" Jefferys calls out as his hands come up defensively.

"What's our number one rule?" I shout.

"Be prepared for anything," the others all call out.

"Do you think someone is going to let you get ready before attacking when out there?" I call out, pointing towards the door. I hear a chorus of 'no' called out. I glance at Logan standing with his arms crossed over his chest, that evil grin he gets sitting smugly on his face.

"Let him up," I call out, and Drew lets go of the pathetic prick and climbs to his feet. Jefferys climbs to his feet. This time, looking a little more aware of his surroundings.

"Fight."

This time, Jefferys is straight on the attack and screams whilst rushing towards Drew, who again takes out his legs, slams him into the floor and points the gun to his head again.

"Rule number two?" I call out.

"Never let them know you're ready," they call out.

"Give away that you are prepared; they can react quickly, probably ending your life before you've hit the ground!" I look at those around the ring and see they are paying attention; they don't want someone who is cocky and predictable on their team. They need to trust each other with their life, and right now, they can't do that with Jefferys.

"Let him up!"

Drew stands and walks to the other side of the ring as his opponent clumsily climbs to his feet.

"Last chance, Jefferys. You think you deserve a place on this team; you need to prove it to not only us but your teammates," I call, looking at him. He's lost it, and he knows, but in true dickhead style, he is going to see how far he can push his luck.

"Drew, go easy on him this time."

Drew walks towards him with his hand out.

"No hard feelings."

Jefferys looks down at Drew's hand and stupidly goes to shake it. Drew tightens his grip, tugs Jefferys forward, and headbutts him before spinning him around as he curses and cuffs his hands behind his back before kicking his knees from underneath him and slamming him back into the floor.

"Rules number three and four?"

"Never trust your opponent. If you can't trust your teammates, you can trust no one!"

Logan and I climb into the ring, where Drew is pulling Jefferys up onto his feet. His hands are cuffed behind his back, blood streaming from his broken nose.

"Do you trust Jefferys to have your back?" I ask as every single person in that room answers a firm "NO!" I turn my attention to Jefferys and shrug.

"Looks like you have your answer. You are no longer a member of the team, and all licences will be evoked. You are lucky I didn't let him beat the shit out of you." I turn back to the rest of the room.

"This is just a taster of what will happen if you try and disobey us. We give you an order; you follow it through to the best of your ability, and there will be no second chances. Work hard, and you will get rewarded. Now get back to training!"

Everyone disperses, leaving the three of us and a cuffed, bleeding Jefferys in the ring. Logan squats down in front of him, smirking as Drew grabs a fist full of hair and tips his head back.

"Well, that didn't go as you thought it would, did it?" Logan gloats. "I, for one, am glad you are gone. You have been nothing but a disgrace to the company since we made the mistake of hiring you. Time for you to fuck off and stop wasting our time."

I hear the office phone ringing from the other room and turn my attention to the others.

"You get him removed and check all passes and weapons are handed in. I'll deal with that." I don't wait for an answer before jumping out of the ring and running to the phone. I manage to pick it up before they ended the call.

"Multi-force security," I answer, leaning against the desk.

"Calvin?" as soon as I hear her voice, I stand tall, frowning.

"Chels? Is everything okay?"

"Shit, sorry, I didn't mean to call you guys. Your number is under the schools. They have phoned to say Luna is upset again and I wanted to check on her before her play in an hour." I can hear how flustered she is, which isn't like Chelsea. No matter what is going on, she keeps a straight head.

"What's the matter with Luna?"

"She has this class play, and the kids who give her a hard time are teasing her about her only having me watch. I wish I could say it's just kids being kids, but the parents can also give me a hard time at these things." I hear Chelsea curse under her breath before turning her attention back to the call. "I got to go; they are calling again. I'll message you later." She hangs up, leaving me looking at the receiver. She sounded so stressed and upset it was hard to hear. I hang up the phone and wonder if there is anything I can do to make it a little easier on them both.

An idea formulates in my head, and I rush off towards the area I know the others are in to start putting things into place.

Chapter Twenty-Six

CHELSEA

I brush some hair from Luna's face and give her a reassuring smile. I hate seeing her so upset. Time and time again, I have been to the school to discuss the way certain classmates treat Luna. But how are the schools meant to teach the kids to respect all family units when their parents are just as bad at home? Luna wraps her arms around my waist, and I hold her tight.

"Can I not just go home?" I hear her ask quietly.

I look around at the parents, who are starting to turn up to watch the rest of the class and consider leaving with her. But she has been practising her lines repeatedly for this part. I know them as well as she does because of how many times I've listened to her practice.

"I just want to go home, Mummy," she says again, looking up at me.

"If you go home, how am I meant to see the amazing dance you have been practising?"

We both turn to see Calvin walking towards us. Luna's whole face changes as she stares at him.

"Pippin! You are here!" she exclaims, wiping at her face. He stops before her, holding out a single white rose while squatting down. Something I've noticed they all do when speaking to her.

"I wanted to come and cheer you on. You told me how much you've been practising and how hard you have been working on your speech and dance. Drew and Logan wanted to be here too, but something came up at work, so I'm here and will record it to show the others when they finish later. The flower's from Logan."

Luna stares at the rose in his hand for a moment before throwing her arms around his neck. He chuckles as he hugs her back and kisses her cheek.

"Thank you," she whispers as she steps back and takes the flower from him. I hear someone clearing their throat and look up to see her teacher smiling at us.

"Are you coming back in now, Luna?" she asks, holding out her hand. Luna looks at Calvin and me and smiles before nodding to her teacher and taking her hand.

"See you in a bit, honey," I call as she skips off with her teacher, a completely different child than was in my arms asking to go home just moments ago. I turn around to see Calvin smiling to himself as he watches her.

"I can't believe you came. I don't know how to thank you for what you just did," I whisper as he turns his attention to me. He wraps an arm around my waist and tugs me against him before pressing a kiss to my lips.

"You don't have to thank me. If you can pretend to date us, then we can do the same for you," he whispers in my ear before smiling down at me. "The others wanted to come, but they are dealing with an incident." He looks up behind me and smirks. "I think we have an audience."

I look behind us to see a few of the mums staring at us

and the dads frowning. I look back to Calvin and press a kiss to his lips.

"At least it will give them something different to talk about," I wink before leading him to the queue to enter the building.

Calvin sits with his arm around me the whole way through the production. He cheers and whistles for Luna whenever she's on stage and records her as he promised to show the guys. As soon as we collect her after the show's finished, he sweeps her off her feet and makes a huge fuss of her. Luna is beaming from ear to ear and looking so proud of herself.

"You were amazing, Luna Bug. I think you even made Mommy cry," Calvin grins as he places her back on the ground.

"That's not hard. Mummy cries all the time," she sighs as she grins at me. I'm just about to answer when my mobile vibrates in my handbag. I dig it out quickly and see Mr Young's name on the screen.

"Hello?"

"Sorry if I'm interrupting the performance. I wasn't sure if it would be finished by now or not." Mr Young apologises.

"It's okay, sir, the show's over. We are just leaving the school," I answer. I look to my right, where Calvin and Luna are watching me.

"I'm sorry to ask, but is there any way you could pop back to the office? Something has come up, and I need your help. You can bring your daughter with you; I'm sure we could find a way to keep her entertained."

I look to Luna as guilt crashes into me. She gets so bored when she has to come to work with me. Would it be fair to her to take her?

"What's the matter?" Calvin asks. I hold up a finger and turn my attention back to the call.

"Let me see if I can get her into the after-school club. If I can't, I'll have to bring her in with me. Either way, I will be back there as soon as possible."

Mr Young thanks me, and I hang up to see a sad-looking Luna and a curious Calvin.

"Something's happened at work, and I need to go back in," I sigh as Luna's bottom lip starts to quiver.

"But you said we could go for ice cream after the show," she points out, and my heart breaks.

"I know, honey. But I can't afford to lose my job. I don't want to go in, but something is going on." I run a hand over her head and pull her into my arms. "Let's go and see if we can at least get you into the after-school club," I start as I take her hand.

"Why doesn't she come with me?"

Luna and I both turn to look at Calvin, who shrugs.

"I'm free for the evening now, and I can take her for ice cream, and then we could go and see the guys. Luna could show them her video herself."

"Please, Mummy! Please can I go with Pippin? It will be much better than going to your work, and I don't want to go to the after-school club."

I look back to Calvin and frown.

"Are you sure you don't mind? You don't have to have her if you are busy; I can work something out."

He steps forward and cups my cheek with his hand as he looks into my eyes.

"I want to have her. It will be no problem at all, I promise. As long as you don't mind me watching her?" he asks. I shake my head, and he smiles back at me. "Then go to work; she is fine with me. If I can keep Bambi and Houdini alive, I think I can handle Luna Bug," he says, looking down at her and winking. Luna squeals excitedly and jumps up and down before hugging me around the waist.

"I will be good, I promise, and do what Pippin says."

I laugh as I kiss her on the top of the head before digging my house keys out of my handbag and handing them to Calvin.

"You better because if I hear you have been naughty, I will make you do the dishes for a month!"

"A month!" Luna and Calvin exclaim dramatically.

"That seems a little extreme. In fact, it sounds like child cruelty to me," Calvin gasps. "Come on, Luna Bug, I won't let the evil mommy do such a thing."

Luna takes his hand, and they turn around and stick out their tongue at me before heading off together happily.

I shake my head and walk to where I parked the car. I'm about to climb behind the wheel when Calvin drives past, beeping the horn and waving with a beaming Luna in the front seat. I wave back, laughing as they disappear out of sight, and I sit in the car.

I start the short journey to work and wait for the anxiety to kick in as it does whenever I leave Luna with someone, but nothing happens. At first, I thought it must be because I was leaving her with someone whose job was literally to keep people safe, but it's not that. It's the fact that she will be with Calvin and possibly the other two.

In the short time I have gotten to know them, I realise I have also come to rely on them and trust them, possibly more than I have trusted anyone in a very long time. Even with Penny and her kids, there is an element of fear whenever I leave Luna with them. However, today, I feel nothing but relief that no matter what was to happen, she would be as safe, if not safer, than she is with me.

After a short drive to work, I pull into my allocated parking space and head into the building, waving to the main receptionist.

"Heads up, he's in a foul mood, and so is the arsehole of a security guy," she announces, rolling her eyes. I shake my head as I laugh, knowing she means Logan. This means he must be here, and they must know more about what's happening in the basement.

I haven't seen Logan since he turned up at mine the other day and helped me with the bathroom disaster. Do I believe he just turned up to give me some heat gel? I'm not sure. What I do know is that I dread to think what would have happened if he hadn't turned up and saved the day, not only by kicking down the door but by helping me to clean up and get someone out to check the electrics and bring an industrial dehumidifier to help get the water out of everything. I messaged him to say thank you, and all I got was a "no problem" in return. I don't know why I expected more from him. It's not like he has ever been mister chatty with me. We get along fine, but there is no real friendship like with the other two.

The elevator opens onto my floor, and I walk out to see Mr Young talking to someone by my desk. As soon as his eyes land on me, he visibly relaxes.

"I am so sorry to call you in like this, Chelsea. I know you had plans this afternoon."

"It's okay; someone is watching Luna and taking her for

ice cream, so she's still happy," I reply with a smile. "Where do you want me?" I ask, looking around.

"In my office, please. Logan is already in there. He will explain more."

I nod and leave him talking to the guy as I head into his office, hoping there is at least a coffee waiting for me.

But instead, I find a sour-faced Logan waiting for me.

"Afternoon," I say politely as I place my bag by the side of the desk and turn to give him my attention.

"How was Luna's production?" he asks, not looking up from his tablet.

"Really good. Calvin turning up gave her a real boost, and she loved the flower he gave her from you. He recorded her whole dance and promised to show it to you later."

Logan doesn't answer. He nods once and continues to tap on his tablet.

"So, what's happened?" I ask.

"We fired Jefferys today. I need you to check his log-ins to see if anything stands out to you. Then can you go through these staff profiles and pick out a replacement?" I nod and head out of the office to grab a pen and paper from my desk as well as a coffee since no one thought to get one ready for me, even though I would have made sure they had one, but hey, we can't all be perfect like Logan, can we?

I feel my jaw clench as I go about getting everything I need, as well as the new laptop Mr Young got for me so I could work from home if I ever needed to. It also makes it easier for me to work from his office at times like this.

Walking back into the office, I place a mug in front of Logan and one on the desk for Mr Young before heading back out for my own.

"I didn't ask for a coffee."

I spin around on my heels and stare at him.

"I'll drink it then," I snap before walking over and picking it up.

"You won't like it," he mutters under his breath.

"How, in the thirty-odd times you have seen me drinking coffee, have you not noticed that we take coffee the same way? Black, no sugar. Or are you that far up your own arse that you don't notice the simplest things about others?" I snap as I go to storm past him, but he stands in my way, dropping his tablet on the table.

"Up my own ass, am I?"

"Yes! A simple thank you would have been sufficient, but you have to make it sound like I forced you to drink poison. You could have thanked me for coming in on the afternoon I had booked off to spend with my daughter. Or even better, you could have allowed me the time off and done what was needed, considering you insisted you had access to everything everywhere!" I snap.

"Have you quite finished?" he snaps. "Or would you like to tell me another way I haven't noticed the simplest thing about you. Like how you smell the ends of your hair when you are tired. Or how about whenever a male you don't know walks into the same room as you, you instantly step away from them, putting as much distance between you as possible? Or when we talked about your shoulder the other day, you rubbed your right shoulder as if it was hurting. Maybe I was so far up my own ass I didn't notice how Luna eyes up every male that comes near her, yet with me and Drew, she visibly relaxed and stepped closer, just as you do. But please, tell me how I haven't noticed the simplest things about you." He grabs his tablet from the table and storms towards the door.

"I will send you the list of what I need. If you need me,

I will be in the security hub. If not, I will see you in two nights as organised."

With that, he storms out of the room, leaving me feeling like the biggest bitch, and even more confused by his behaviour than I was before. When the hell did my life get so fucking complicated?

Chapter Twenty-Seven

CHELSEA

As much as I wanted to spend the rest of the day avoiding Logan, the universe had other ideas.

Logan asked me to check Thomas Jefferys' whereabouts during his shifts. By complete fluke, I realised nothing was matching up, so I begrudgingly went down to the security hub to show him what I found.

After a few hours of digging and going through hours of CCTV footage, comparing it to his card logins, we realised Jefferys was purposely turning off cameras and leaving his security card for someone to come into the building and access places they shouldn't have been in. Logan disappeared for an hour and came back with a slightly roughed-up Jefferys.

"Are those completely necessary?" I ask, pointing to Jefferys hands, which are cuffed behind his back.

Logan grunts something about not trusting the prick not to try and do a runner. I opt to keep my mouth shut and let him do what he wants. The sooner we get the information we need, the sooner I can get home. Poor Calvin has had

Luna for five hours now, and I'm sure he's regretting offering to help, even if he is too nice to admit it.

Between the two of us, Logan and I managed to get Jefferys to tell us all, and boy, did he spill the beans. All it took was me showing him the evidence that he was seen on one side of the building when his card was being used on the other. He claimed he had no idea who they were, but they were scary enough to make him fear for his life if he didn't do as they asked.

He wasn't even that clever about it. It was as if he had wanted to get caught. But when I suggested that to Logan, he just huffed and muttered about Jefferys just being too big-headed for his own good.

I looked through all the camera footage with and without Logan to try and see something, somewhere, but whoever's accessing areas with the card might as well have been Harry Potter in an invisibility cloak as there's nothing.

This put Logan into a fouler mood than he was already in, as he took it personally. They had gotten past his security on a number of occasions. I don't even want to think what he did to Jefferys when he dragged him from the building. I can't imagine he just dropped him off at that was the end of it. Not without some sort of beating going on anyway.

By eight o'clock, I'm exhausted and ready to collapse into bed for the rest of the night. But I need to double-check everyone's cards to make sure it was just Jefferys leaving his card lying around or gaining access to areas they shouldn't have been in.

"Chelsea, go home. I can do this," Logan says from the other side of the room.

"I'm fine," I mutter, rocking my head from side to side to ease my aching neck.

"That wasn't a request. Go home, you're exhausted."

I turn to look at him with wide eyes.

"Who died and made you the boss of me?" I demand, crossing my arms over my chest. The prick doesn't even look up from the laptop he is working on.

"Someone needs to make sure you look after yourself since you seem determined to run yourself into the ground."

I continue to stare at him, amazed.

"You almost sound like you care," I sigh as I turn back to the computer and log myself out, not wanting to admit out loud that he's right.

"I never claimed I didn't," he mutters under his breath. I freeze, convinced I must have misheard him.

I quickly gather my stuff and stand up to head home.

"Thank you for all your help today, Chels. I'm sorry if I ruined your plans."

I turn to find Logan watching me with a look that makes me wonder if there is something else he wants to say.

"You're welcome. Goodnight, Logan." I am almost out of the door when I hear his reply.

"Goodnight, Chelsea."

I walk out of the building and head to the parking lot, determined to put some much-needed space between me and the guy with more mood swings than a teenage girl.

I pull up outside my house and let out a relaxing breath. I can't believe how late it is. I truly am exhausted, and all I can think about doing is eating some cereal and going to bed. But instead, I'm hit by the aroma of lasagna when I walk in through the front door.

"He let you finally leave then?" Calvin smirks as I walk

into the lounge and drop onto the sofa beside him, exhausted. I look at the clock on the wall and see it's gone nine o'clock.

"Is he always so busy?" I groan, leaning my head back and closing my eyes whilst Cavin chuckles beside me.

"We try to refer to it as '*passionate about his job*'. But yeah, he's a bossy bastard. He always has been." He places an arm around my shoulders and pulls me against him so I'm leaning my cheek on his broad chest. I allow myself to relax in his arms as I really need to be held right now—something I have always missed.

"Did Luna behave herself?" I ask, looking up. Calvin nods whilst running a hand over my head.

"She was as good as gold. She helped make dinner and fell asleep watching a film."

"Thank you for watching her. I'm sorry it all took so long."

Calvin cups my cheek in his hand and gives me a warm smile.

"If you ever need anything like a babysitter or even someone to do the shopping for you because you are too busy, I want you to phone me, okay? I want to help you, especially as you don't seem to look after yourself as well as you do others."

"Logan said the same kind of thing today," I sigh, rolling my eyes, as Calvin chuckles. "Can I ask you something?"

"Sure."

"Is Logan always so … confusing?" I jump slightly as Calvin bursts out laughing.

"The only person who knows what goes on in that head of his is him," Calvin answers as he kisses the top of my head. "What's he done now?"

"He was just being an asshole when I got there earlier. So, I called him out on it and told him he never paid a bit of notice to anyone around him, so he kindly listed things he had noticed about me. Things I hadn't even realised I do," I admit nervously. I'm in another man's arms, yet I like that another man pays such close attention to what I do.

Calvin laughs as he shakes his head. I sit up to see him without straining my sore neck.

"Ever heard of the saying, 'thou doth protest too much'? Well, that's our Houdini. He likes to pretend that he cares about nothing or nobody. You're more likely to work out the meaning of life than what goes on in that head of his. But if he does care about you, you can guarantee there is nothing he wouldn't do for you. The fact that he has even taken the time to notice things about you shows that he does care in his own way." Calvin reaches up and threads his fingers into the hair at the back of my head, locking me in place as he moves so his lips are barely touching mine.

"Now go get some food and then rest before I end up taking you to bed and showing you all the things I've noticed about you." He kisses my lips softly before looking deep into my eyes. "Like how your eyes roll back ever so slightly when I do this," his hand tightens in my hair, and I know I prove him right. "Or how your body shudders as you flood my hand and mouth with that sweet cum." His lips crash into mine, and I melt into his touch.

I wrap my arms around his neck, holding him as close as possible. I'm desperate for his touch, for him to relieve the pressure that is suddenly building within me. I need him like I need air, and this time, I want all of him. I lean back slightly, and Calvin takes the hint because, in seconds, I am on my back, and he is between my legs. Why, of all days, did I decide to wear trousers today?

"Tell me to leave, and I will. But ask me to stay, and I don't think you will be getting much sleep tonight," he teases as his hand runs up my thigh and cups my butt cheek. He squeezes slightly, and my mind's made up.

"Stay."

Calvin grins down at me before things start moving at a hundred miles an hour. I unfasten his jeans and reveal his gorgeous cock, which springs into view as soon as it's no long restricted. Is it wrong that it turns me on seeing the effect I have on this man?

I take him in my hand as I sit up and stroke him.

"Fuck," Calvin hisses through his teeth as he sits back, giving me better access. I kiss his lips and grin before bending down and running my tongue across the slit of his large cock. I hear him curse through his teeth again, which encourages me to do it again before taking him in my mouth.

Calvin sits back further as I tease him with my tongue and lick him from base to tip. Before I met my ex, I loved sucking cock. I could cum just from the salty taste of their release alone. I always preferred a man fucking my mouth over my pussy; there's something so dominating and yet degrading in its own safe way. The second Calvin threads his fingers into my hair and tightens his grip, tugging it slightly, I moan around his cock.

"Fuck," Calvin groans as he tugs again to coax another moan from me. He thrusts his hips up, causing his cock to hit the back of my throat. "Your mouth feels so good," he groans as I look up through my lashes to find him with his head back against the sofa, his eyes closed tight. It's a powerful feeling when you realise you can bring a grown man who has killed for his country to putty in my hands.

Calvin's hand tightens in my hair as he pulls it back,

forcing me to release his cock from my mouth. He meets me in the middle so he can kiss me.

"If you carry on, I will not last long enough to fuck you like I've been dreaming of since that night in the hotel." He kisses me again before sitting back, grinning. "Stand up, let me see my new favourite place."

As soon as I'm on my feet in front of him, he unfastens my trousers and pushes them down with my thong. We moan simultaneously as his finger slides between my wet pussy lips.

"Always so wet and ready for me," he grins before placing his hands on my hips and pulling me forward as he drops to his knees, making him the perfect height to lick me in the perfect way he did in the hotel.

As soon as his tongue finds my clit, I'm grateful that he thought to keep hold of my hips as my knees nearly buckle underneath me. Calvin chuckles, and I understand exactly how he felt when I moan with his cock in my mouth. The vibration from his mouth sends shockwaves through my body, and I swear I nearly cum from the feel of it alone. He continues to lick and suck on my clit as he slides one finger and then two inside me.

"That's it darling, cum for me so I can feel how perfect your pussy will be when wrapped around my cock," he growls, looking up at me as he fucks me with his fingers. I look down at him and, for a moment, get lost in his hazel eyes until he rubs that special spot inside me, and I cry out a little. He takes advantage of me being close and pushes me over the edge with his tongue and fingers working together in perfect harmony.

"Fuck," I curse out loud as my legs finally go from underneath me, as I have the most amazing orgasm. Calvin laughs proudly as he only just catches me in time and sits on the sofa, pulling me onto his lap, instantly impaling me with his large cock, causing us both to curse as he fills me and stretches me.

"Fuck, Bambi was right. You're fucking perfect," he growls through gritted teeth as I rock my hips needing him to give me more as I continue to feel the effects of the amazing orgasm. I want him to tell me what Drew said. I want to hear how much he enjoyed it.

"He thinks you would like it if we both gave you pleasure at the same time," Calvin continues as he lifts his hand and places two fingers into my mouth. I suck on them as he thrusts up into me. "What do you think, darling? One of us in your mouth whilst one fucks you." He removes his fingers from my mouth, and I instantly feel one against my back entrance. "Or one fucking your pussy as the other fucks your ass?" he slides one finger slowly into my ass, and I can't believe how good it feels.

"That's it, darling. Take what you need from my cock and finger because as soon as you cum again, this time around, my cock, I'm going to change positions and fuck you from behind."

"Yes!" I call out, grabbing his shoulders for stability as I bounce on his lap, selfishly chasing my own release. I can hear Calvin telling me things Drew told him, which only adds to the pleasure coursing through me.

Fuck. I never saw myself having group sex before these men, but I need to experience it at least once. The images that flood my mind send me crashing through another orgasm as I bury my face in Calvin's neck to muffle the moans that come from within me.

He removes his fingers and holds me tight as I come down from the most amazing high. Not giving me much time to recover, he stands, holding on to me, placing me on the sofa, giving me the instructions to turn around. I quickly do as he asks, desperate for more. He doesn't leave me wanting for long because as soon as I have my back to him, he grips my hips and pulls me back towards him.

"Hold on to the back of the sofa, darling and don't let go." He gives me a second to do as he asks before sliding into me. Both of us cursing at the same time. It feels so good as he goes deeper than he did before. Calvin pounds into me over and over again, quickly chasing my orgasm with another. When he reaches around and plays with my sensitive clit, I lose it and have to bury my face into the back of the sofa; knowing I am being so loud, I'm sure to wake Luna.

Calvin doesn't let up, though, as he continues to fuck me hard and fast.

"Fuck, you are perfect," he growls as his grip tightens, and he thrusts into me three times hard before finally filling me with all he has.

We fall onto the sofa, both gasping for breath and sweating from the intensity of the last half an hour.

"As much as I know I should let you sleep, I'm seriously not done with you yet," Calvin whispers in my ear. I can feel he's still hard inside me, and I moan when he pulls out of me. He rolls me onto my back as he positions himself on top of me between my legs, and his cock gently slides into my overstimulated pussy.

"This time, I want to watch you as you cum on my cock and my release fills you."

Chapter Twenty-Eight

CHELSEA

I haven't seen Logan in two days. He's been working in the security hub at work or from his office. We have exchanged a few text messages with information for tonight and the dinner I'm accompanying him to. Whenever I have had to speak to him on the phone for Mr Young, he has been short and to the point. Calvin has offered to speak to him if he is making me uncomfortable, but I told him not to. I don't want to cause any issues between the friends, and let's face it: things are getting complicated enough with me now, having slept with Calvin and Drew. Although I'm sure the guys are conspiring for me to sleep with them at the same time, which I have no problem with at all.

A knock at the front door snaps me away from the delicious daydream I was about to have. I groan as I leave the kitchen and open the door to find Logan looking very dapper in his cream suit and white shirt. Hopefully, his mood will be as light as his attire.

"You ready?"

Or not. Typical Logan, short and to the point. Great.

I roll my eyes as I grab my coat that's hanging up on the stand. I go to shrug it on, but Logan takes it from me and holds it up to help me.

"Thank you," I say, turning around and fastening it. He looks at my outfit and nods once, whether, in approval or recognition of my thanks, I don't know.

"Where's Luna tonight?" he asks as I lock the front door.

"Staying with a friend, my usual babysitter was working the closing shift."

Again, he nods once, and we silently head to the car.

As with any time I spend with Logan, the journey is in near silence but not completely unpleasant. He checks I'm warm enough and gives me a brief run down of the people we are meeting tonight. He reminds me he hates meeting new people, and I offer to help where I can.

As soon as we arrive at the restaurant, Logan notices the people we're meeting are also just arriving. They turn and see us approaching and almost glare at Logan before flashing me a large smile, instantly putting me on edge. Logan must notice as he moves closer to me and places a hand on the bottom of my back.

"Mr Wilson, it's good to see you again," the guy says, holding his hand out. Logan removes his hand from my back and shakes it. I notice Logan seems more tense than he was a moment ago. I hadn't realised his mood could get any tenser, but here we are. "And who is this beautiful thing beside you?" The gentleman asks, turning his full attention to me. Logan wraps an arm around my waist and pulls me against him.

"This is Ms Hughes. Ms Hughes, this is Mr Fallon."

I lift my hand to shake his, but he takes it and places a kiss on my knuckles. I instinctively pull my hand away, not wanting this man's lips anywhere near me.

"Forgive me, Ms Hughes, I'm a sucker for a beautiful woman." I feel Logan's hand on my waist tighten as his body stiffens. He's fighting to control his temper, and I step in quickly.

"That's okay, Mr Fallon. I just respectfully ask that you don't do it again," I request, smiling. He nods once and turns to Logan.

"Shall we head inside? I've been informed this place does the best steak in the area."

Logan nods once and holds his left hand out, signalling for Mr Fallon to go on ahead, and his right stays tightly around me.

"Are you okay?" I ask quietly.

"I don't like the way he was eyeing you up," Logan replies through gritted teeth.

"He's been told, so be good," I warn. Logan looks at me with an arched brow, which causes a small smile to appear on my face. "We won't stay for pudding, gotcha." I watch as one side of Logan's lips lift slightly as I wink. The waiter starts to lead us through the restaurant, and Logan stays close the whole time, not taking his eyes off Fallon, who looks over his shoulder at me and winks as if to flatter me.

"If we make it through dinner and you make sure I don't batter him, I will consider taking you elsewhere for pudding," Logan mutters as his body tenses again.

"Can I hit him?" I ask quietly before flashing the waiter a grin as he signals for us to take our seats. Logan grabs a chair and holds it out for me to sit, ensuring that Fallon is not directly next to me. As he pushes my seat back under the table, he leans his mouth down by my ear.

"I'll let you know."

Dinner progressed as I expected. Fallon is trying to come across as the perfect gentleman. Still, he keeps winking at me or asking my opinion on things I probably know nothing about, like he's trying to talk down to me. How Logan keeps his cool when Fallon's friend suggests that SEALs are just 'glorified Navy officers' or that the prices his company charges seem steep. But they are careful not to push Logan too far. They try to remain as businesslike as possible.

Halfway through dinner, I excuse myself, needing a moment to calm down after Fallon, who is quickly heading towards drunk, refers to me as beautiful again. Logan looks at me, questioning if I'm okay. I nod once and give his arm a quick squeeze to reassure him before heading off to the bathroom.

I take my time there washing my hands and checking my makeup, just needing a second and praying that nothing happens while I'm gone. I'm just opening the bathroom door to head back into the restaurant when Logan grabs my hand and pulls me toward the exit.

"We're leaving," he snaps, not allowing me to ask what I missed. He storms out of the restaurant and into the cold night air.

"My jacket!" I point out, but Logan holds it up in his other hand. He looks absolutely furious, and I know better than to push a man this close to the edge. He opens the passenger door of his car and holds it whilst I climb in, slamming it closed as soon as I'm safely inside.

I watch, shaking a little, as he marches around the car,

jumps in behind the wheel and speeds out of the parking lot without even putting on his seatbelt.

"Logan, what-"

"Don't. Just don't right now, Chelsea. I need to concentrate," he snaps, and I quickly sit back in my seat and keep my mouth shut as I start to shake.

Chapter Twenty-Nine

CHELSEA

The second the car stops in front of my house, I jump out and rush towards the front door, desperate to put some distance between me and the obviously angry Logan. As I get to the door, my hands are shaking too much to get the keys in the lock. I jump back with a startled yelp as Logan appears next to me and takes the keys to unlock the door.

"I need you to breathe, Chelsea. I'm so sorry I triggered you."

I spin around to look at him and can see how sorry he is through my tears, but my head's in flight mode, and all I want to do is lock myself behind the door. A sob leaves my chest, and I hear him curse, which makes me jump again.

Logan holds open the door and closes it between us as I walk inside.

"I'm staying here on the other side of the door until you let me explain and I know you are okay. I can't leave you like this. Fuck I screwed up, and I'm so sorry, baby."

I lean against the door as every sob catches in my throat, and I can't breathe. I can't see anything through the tears.

My heart's beating in my ringing ears, and I know I need to calm down before I make myself sick.

"Can you hear me, Chels? Listen to my voice, okay, baby? I need you to breathe in slowly to the count of five. Can you do that with me? Knock against the door when you can begin, and I will count with you."

I stare at it, desperate for him to leave and hold me at the same time. I knock on the door once, and he starts to count.

"Breath in with me, Chels. One. Two. Three. Four. Five. Hold it for five and breathe out for five. Knock, and we will start again."

Logan talks me through six cycles before I feel in enough control to open the door.

When I open it, I find him leaning against the door-frame, one hand on either side as he looks at me with so much sadness in his amber eyes.

"I am so sorry. Are you okay?" he asks as he stands up and cups my cheek. I shake my head and step back inside, leaving the door open for him to come in. The second he is inside, he closes the door and turns to look at me.

"I'm so sorry I lost control. I wasn't mad at you. The last thing I wanted to do was trigger you like that. Fuck, I handled it so badly, I just-" he stops mid-sentence and walks around with his hands on his head.

I walk past him and into the lounge, still clinging to my jacket like it's a life buoy. I throw it onto the sofa and walk over to the bar, where I proceed to try and pour two drinks, but I'm shaking so hard I can't get the bottle open.

"Let me," Logan says softly, walking over to me. I hand him the bottle, whisper a 'thank you', and place two glasses on the top. He pours two fingers into each and hands one to me as I sit on the sofa. He sits on the coffee table in front of me, and we both take a sip of our drinks and try to catch our breath and calm the tension between us.

After a few moments of silence, I look up to find Logan watching my every move. I take a deep breath and finally feel in control enough to speak.

"What happened?"

Logan leans forward so his elbows are resting on his thighs as he takes a deep breath.

"I lost my shit, that's what happened. From the moment we arrived, I struggled to stay calm. Every time that prick looked at you, I wanted to reach across and punch him in his fat face."

"Suppose it didn't help the way his little sidekick was bad-mouthing the SEALs," I offer with a small smile. Logan looks at me for a moment before shaking his head.

"I didn't give a shit about that, Chels. I didn't give a shit what he said about me and the guys. We are big enough and ugly enough to take it all and not bat a fucking eyelid. But when he said- Fuck." Logan jumps to his feet, causing me to jump back into the sofa before he starts pacing around the room again.

"What did he say?" I ask, no longer scared or worried by him. Now that the panic has settled, I can think logically. Logan has had plenty of opportunities to hurt me, and he has never so much as raised his voice. Even tonight, he didn't shout at me; it was just the feeling around him, as I knew he was on the verge of losing it, and I thought I was in the firing line.

Logan stops and stares at me.

"He wanted you and was willing to do anything to get you. He watched every little thing you did, and I hated it. I despised the way his eyes watched your chest as you breathed, the way he would wink at you as if it was meant to impress you. When you went to the toilet, I could see how uncomfortable you were, so I was about to tell him he needed to pack it in, or we were leaving. But instead, he looked me straight in the eye and asked if I would consider 'throwing you in as part of the deal'."

I gasp as Logan stares at me, and I know that if I asked him to, he would hunt Fallon down and beat the shit out of him, if not kill him.

I stand up and walk until I'm in front of him.

"Thank you," I whisper. Logan surprises me when he reaches up and runs his knuckles over my cheek.

"I am so sorry I scared you like that. You must know I would never hurt you. I know I've been a prick at times, but it's only because I feel like I'm losing my goddamn mind," Logan whispers as he leans his forehead against mine.

"Talk to me," I whisper, closing my eyes and listening to him, taking deep, calming breaths.

"I've tried so hard to keep you at arm's length, to ignore everything I've been feeling since the first day I met you. But I can't keep doing it. I listen to Drew and Calvin when they talk about how they have fun with you, not just in the bedroom but out of it as well. And I want to experience that with you, too. I want to taste you and feel you around me. I want to kiss every part of you. I've never been jealous of the guys until you came into our lives.

"So tonight, when Fallon spoke about you the way he did, I lost it. I stood up, somehow managed to stop myself from punching him and walked out."

Logan looks deep into my eyes before spinning us around and backing me up so my back is against the wall.

"He thought he could have you, but you are ours. No one fucking else is touching you whilst we're still breathing."

Logan cups my cheek again and looks into my eyes.

"I'm done fighting this. Tell me I'm not the only one who feels this between us." He leans forward until his lips are less than an inch from mine as if refusing to close the distance until I tell him to.

"You're not," I whisper before kissing him.

It is all the go-ahead he needs, and his arm wraps around my waist, pinning me to him as his other hand holds the back of my head so I can't escape him. Not that I want to. Not now this man is finally kissing me. I never want him to stop.

One moment, we're kissing as Logan keeps me stuck between the wall and him. The next, he picks me up and carries me up the stairs, looking deep into my eyes.

He doesn't say anything until we are in my room and places me back on my feet. From there, everything moves a hundred miles an hour as we frantically kiss and help each other out of our clothes until we are both completely naked. Logan grabs me and pulls me down onto his lap as he sits on the edge of the bed. I can feel his cock right there, where I need it so badly, but Logan has no plans on rushing this. He threads his fingers into the hair at the back of my head and tugs so my head rolls back, and he has access to my neck, which he kisses as his hand slides between us, and I feel his fingers brush against my throbbing swollen clit.

"Fuck," I gasp as his finger rubs over it again.

"You are so wet, baby. You're dripping on my cock, and it feels amazing." Logan's teeth graze my throat at the same time as I feel two fingers enter me.

"Logan," I cry out as he rubs that spot inside of me, nearly sending me hurtling over the edge instantly. He keeps doing it as the pleasure builds further and faster than I ever knew possible.

"Come in my hand like you did, Calvin, baby. I want

you to fill my hand with your juices so I can drink your sweet wine before tasting it straight from the glass."

My body acts at his command, and I cry out as I feel myself burst with pleasure.

"Fuck," Logan moans as his hand stills underneath me. His teeth graze my throat again before his fingers slide from my still-tightening pussy. He carefully lifts his hand, and I see a tiny puddle in it, like what happened with Calvin. I'm left speechless as he smirks before drinking from his hand, licking his palm and fingers clean of my juices.

"Fuck, they weren't wrong. You have the sweetest taste," he groans before wrapping his arms around me and lying back. His cock is pointing straight up, and I know if I move just right, it will be right at my entrance. I press my lips to his, tasting myself on his tongue as I shift my bottom half slightly and feel him right where I want him. I start to lower myself as I feel him glide inside of me, but Logan slaps my bare ass and pulls out of me.

"I'm not ready to fuck you yet, baby. We've got all night for that," he teases as he lifts his hips slightly, and I feel him right there again. "What do you want?" he asks as he kisses me whilst rocking his hips so his cock enters me ever so slightly.

"Your cock," I moan as he enters me a little further.

In one move, he pulls me down onto his cock as he thrusts up, filling and stretching me in the most amazing way.

"Like this?" he asks through gritted teeth.

"Yes!" I cry out as he does it again, and I swear I feel him hit my cervix.

"Tough," he chuckles as he jumps to his feet, lifting me as he stays inside of me. He lies down with me underneath him and rotates his hips, grinning at me as he hits every spot.

"Oh fuck, yes! Don't stop!" I beg as my head rolls back into the mattress. Logan's hands land on my hips as he pins them in place and continues to grind into me.

"You have twenty seconds to cum before I stop," he warns. My eyes fly open to see his amber eyes more alight than I have ever seen before.

"Twenty," he counts as he goes deeper still.

Oh fuck, he feels so good, but will I cum in twenty seconds?

"Fifteen." He lets go of one of my hips and presses his thumb to my clit before rubbing it in time to his cock.

"Ten."

Fuck I don't need ten.

"Holy shit," I cry out as I grab the sheet underneath me and my back arches from the bed.

"Five," Logan teases and I explode.

I cry out as I cum so hard I swear I see stars. All blood rushes from my head to my pussy as I feel it clamping tight around Logan's dick.

"Fucking hell, baby!" he groans as he stays still within me as I ride through an intense orgasm. I swear him calling me baby sets me off on another wave, and I cry out as the pleasure sends me completely over the edge. Logan pulls out of me, leaving me empty and wanting more.

"That may be my new favourite place to be," he whispers against my lips before kissing me. "The feeling of you clamping around my cock as you come apart like that. I would have blown my load if I hadn't pulled out when you did."

"I have the implant. I'm covered," I gasp, still feeling out of breath. Logan chuckles as he starts kissing my neck.

"I know, Drew told us," he whispers against my skin.

"Do you three talk about me often?" I ask, partially out of curiosity and partly because I remember how turned on I was when Drew whispered in my ear about him and Calvin talking about me.

"Drew and Calvin always talk about you, sharing notes to improve your orgasms." Logan takes my earlobe between his teeth. "What they don't know is I sit in the next room listening to everything they have to say, saving it all up so when I go for a shower, I can jerk one off thinking of you and ways I want to make you scream my name." His hand lands between my legs again, and he starts to rub my clit, which is still sensitive, but it feels so good.

"Now be a good girl and lie just like that whilst I drink from your cup and then fuck you in every position I can before filling you with my cum and making you mine." Logan grins at me for a second before taking my nipple between his teeth and sliding two fingers into me again.

"Fuck."

Chapter Thirty

CHELSEA

"Holy shit!" I cry out as Logan thrusts into me hard one last time and finally, after hours of holding himself back, cums deep within me.

"Fuck!" he growls out loud, thrusting into me again before collapsing to the side, pulling me with him so as not to pull out of me yet.

We both lie together, me pressed to his chest as he holds me in his arms. I try desperately to catch my breath, but he has taken me to so many highs tonight I don't know how to breathe normally anymore.

"I think you have ruined me for all other men," I chuckle into his sweaty chest.

"I can't wait to tell the guys that. They will be storming around here to prove you wrong," he chuckles into my hair before pressing a kiss to my head. "There again, I think we could truly ruin you if the three of us gave you our best efforts," he teases. I lean back a little so I can look at him wide-eyed.

"Ruin me? The three of you would break me if you

were all together!" I exclaim as Logan bursts out laughing before leaning in to kiss my lips.

"Challenge accepted," he replies with a wink before tightening his arms around me as I gasp with surprise. I can hear his laugh deep in his chest, and it instantly makes me smile. He seems happier, lighter somehow. I'm sure it is just the after-sex glow, but right now, it is a wonderful feeling.

"I'm sorry I've been a jerk to you at times."

I tip my head back and look at him, frowning.

"There's been times I thought you hated me," I admit. Logan's eyes widen as his smile slips.

"Fuck, baby. I never hated you. I think I hated myself for wanting you."

I cock one brow at him like he has done to me so many times.

"I think that may actually be worse."

Logan rolls his eyes before pulling me, moving slightly so I can look straight into his eyes rather than his chest. He lifts his hand, brushes some of the hair from my face, and tucks it behind my ear.

"Have the guys told you anything about my fiancée?"

My eyes widen as I shake my head.

"You're engaged?" I demand, pulling away from him.

"Shit no! Not now. Fuck, let me explain," he panics, and I nod whilst my heart races, scared he's going to say I just had mind-blowing sex with another woman's man.

"Seven years ago, I was engaged to an amazing woman who I met on an operation. Angie was a year younger than me and a credited Army Officer. We worked together and fell in love. Everyone told us it would never work, but we made it. Every chance we had, we met up, sometimes for only twenty-four hours and made every minute together count. Within six months, we were engaged and trying everything to make it work between us." Logan rubs at his face, and I see the spark that was just in his eyes go out.

"I was meant to meet her one night as we were both stationed in the same country. We worked out a way we could spend forty-eight hours together. But she told me her flight was delayed, and I went out drinking with the lads, thinking she wouldn't get there for a few hours. I woke up the next morning to the news a small plane had crashed, and there were three US Army officers inside."

I gasp as a small tear escapes my eye. Logan is focused on my shoulder, where he is rubbing the skin with his thumb.

"The last message I had sent her was how gutted I was that she wouldn't make it. She and two others had enlisted a local plane to fly them. The plane was unsafe, but the owner wanted the money they were offering, so he risked it. They all died instantly, which is a blessing, I guess, but the guilt never left me. If I hadn't been drunk and laid on the guilt trip, she might have never boarded that plane."

I reach across and cup Logan's cheek. He takes a deep breath before looking into my eyes.

"There is no way you could have known. You would have never expected her to commission a flight like that."

"I think I have known that deep down. But I have let it consume me for six years, and I haven't let myself feel anything for anyone." He takes my hand from his cheek and presses a kiss to the palm.

"Until you." He presses another kiss to my palm before kissing my lips. "When I realised that I was falling for you, I tried to ignore it; I tried to tell myself I was cheating on Angie. But the more time I spent around you, the harder it was to think of Angie at all, as you were in the forefront of my mind all the time.

"Then tonight was the final push I needed to show you I'm not the prick I've been acting. I care about you, baby. When Fallon said what he did, I honestly think the only reason I didn't punch him was because all I could think about was getting you as far away from him as possible. I had to protect you like I hadn't been able to protect her."

Logan leans in and kisses me on the lips again.

"I will do better, baby. I will if you will give me a chance to. I'm not asking for a full-on relationship. I think you feel something for all three of us for a reason, and it's something we all need to discuss together, but I don't think I can go back to hiding how I feel about you. Not now, but I finally feel like I have something worth fighting for."

I lean against his chest and let out a deep sigh.

"We all need to talk about this together, as I don't think I could choose one of you over the others. And then there's Luna to think about. It would be a lot for her to take in." I lean back and look into his eyes, offering a small smile.

"Can we just enjoy tonight? Then tomorrow, we will see what everyone thinks, and slowly, we can all work out what we want and don't want."

Logan presses a kiss to my lips, smiling.

"I think that sounds like a great idea," he whispers into my hair as I stay curled up against his chest and start to doze off to sleep, breathing in his calming scent as he holds me in his arms.

Chapter Thirty-One

LOGAN

"Oh, look who decided to finally show up!" Drew laughs as I walk into the kitchen, my suit jacket over my arm and my shirt sleeves rolled up. I look at the clock and see it's one in the afternoon.

"So, did someone finally accept they have fallen for a certain older lady and do something about it?" Calvin smirks as he sits in one of the chairs by the table.

"Something like that," I reply, unable to wipe the smile from my face.

Leaving Chelsea's bed this morning was so freaking hard. Whilst I was there, we could pretend that it was just the two of us and that we had no other worries in the world. But reality has to return at some point, and I know the four of us are going to need to have a long chat about things.

"How did the business deal go?" Drew asks, and my good mood slips.

"Yeah, let's just say we won't be hearing from them again unless it is to demand payment towards the bill I left them with."

"What the fuck did you do?" Drew demands. I turn and stare at him wide-eyed. "I worked my ass off to get them to give us a chance," he adds, and I slam the mug I just filled on the counter, spilling the content.

"Oh, they wanted to give us a chance as long as I offered Chelsea up as a bonus!" I snap. Drew and Calvin both curse and yell at the same time; I have no idea who says what. "That's right, he was checking her out from the moment we arrived. He was watching her chest and being a real sleaze to the point she left the table for a moment to escape. It was then he asked me to make her part of the deal, so I told him where he could shove it. No fucker talks about her like she is a piece of meat." I grab the mug and refill it with coffee from the pot before grabbing a cloth and cleaning up the mess I made.

I continue to fill them in on getting Chelsea home and triggering her PTSD that they both gave me shit for, and then, keeping all of the very dirty details out explained how I had spent the rest of the night and most of the morning making it up to her.

"So, what happens now?" Calvin asks as he looks around the kitchen.

"How do you mean?" Drew asks, taking a sip of his coffee.

"He means, where do we go from here? Chels and I spoke about it briefly last night and this morning, and she basically told me there was no way she could choose between us. We all mean the world to her. I personally don't think I could walk away from her and Luna now. Just in the short time I have known them both, I have cared about them greatly, and I can't imagine not seeing them."

Drew and Calvin both agree, and we all look at each other.

"I thought I would hate the idea of ever being with someone and sharing them with someone else. But the idea of the five of us living together feels natural," Drew says from his seat. I nod in agreement. It is basically the same as I said to Chelsea this morning.

We both look to Calvin, who has stayed the most silent.

"What are you thinking, Pippin?" Drew asks as Calvin looks around at us both.

"My only concern is Luna. She has had it rough in school because of bullies, and I know the last thing she wants is to stand out any more than she already does. If they realise her mum is with three guys, wouldn't that put her on the firing line even more?"

"Or the fact that she knows she has us behind her to support her may make her stronger," Drew suggests.

"Either way, I think Chelsea would have to approach the topic with her. But if we show her that we're there for her and don't want to make things difficult, we can maybe work together to come up with a plan of action," I suggest. The other two nod, and I see a smile spread across Calvin's face as he grabs his phone.

"I may just have the perfect plan to show her we are there for her as well as her mom. Give me ten minutes," he declares before rushing out of the room with his phone to his ear.

Chelsea

"Do you really have no idea where they are taking us?" Luna asks for the hundredth time this afternoon.

"Sweetheart, if I did, I would tell you. Pippin just said

we were to have an early dinner, and they would pick us up at six. That is all he would tell me."

"But he also said we had to look pretty?" she asks, looking down at her favourite red dress, which she's chosen to wear with white tights and black shoes. Her hair is hanging down in loose curls pinned half up just the way she likes it. She spins around, causing the dress to flare out around her knees.

"Yes, he did, and you look very pretty," I chuckle as she spins around again. Lights shine through the lounge window.

"They are here!" Luna exclaims excitedly, rushing to the window. She stops and stares before turning to look at me, confused.

"That car is huge!"

"What car?" I ask. But before I can get to the window to look, she drops the curtain and races towards the front door, where there is a knock.

"I've seen it's them!" she calls out, throwing open the door as I grab our coats and bags.

"Luna Bug, you are meant to wait for Mommy to answer the door," I hear Calvin chuckle as I reach the door and look through to see the three guys all standing on the doorstep in navy and black suits, each holding two roses, one white, one red.

"Who are the flowers for?" Luna asks, grinning as she can already guess.

"The white ones are for you, princess," Logan says, passing her his white flower and placing a kiss on her cheek before standing back up and looking straight at me over her head. "And the red ones are for Mommy," he adds, stepping around her to place a kiss on my cheek as I take the flower from him.

I feel my face warming as the guys take turns to give us each a flower and a kiss on the cheek. As Calvin steps back, Luna looks at me, beaming, holding her three flowers.

"How about I take Luna Bug to the car, and you can put the flowers in water real quick?" Calvin offers as I nod and take the flowers from her hand. She takes hold of Calvin's and Drew's hands and heads to the …

"Is that a limo?" I exclaim, staring at the long black car parked on the street at the bottom of my drive.

"This way, we only need one car, and we can all travel together," Calvin winks over his shoulder as Logan walks towards the kitchen and beckons me to follow. By the time I get in there, he has a glass from the cupboard and is filling it with water. He takes the flowers from my hand and places them in the water before pulling me into his arms and kissing me. As he pulls away, I smile and wipe my lipstick from his lips.

"So, they know about last night?" I ask. Logan nods, smiling and takes my hand.

"They do, and we plan on talking to you about it after this evening. First, we want to enjoy some time just the five of us. We want to test the water with Luna," he answers. I nod, letting him lead me from the kitchen to the front door.

I grab our coats and bags back off the peg, and we lock up before joining the others in the back of the limo, where a driver is holding a door open for us.

Once we are sat inside, I see Luna sitting between Calvin and Drew, looking around in awe.

"Are you going to tell us where we are going?" I ask, looking between the three men, who all share a very smug look.

"A little birdy told me that a certain little bug loves *Barbie: The Nutcracker*," Calvin answers, smiling at Luna, who nods excitedly. "Well, one of the owners of this big car is a very talented ballerina. Can you guess what she is performing tonight?" he asks her.

" *Barbie: The Nutcracker*?" she exclaims as we all laugh at her excitement.

"Close, it's just *The Nutcracker*, no Barbies, sorry," Calvin laughs.

"You really got her tickets to watch *The Nutcracker*?" I ask, amazed. Calvin nods before turning his attention back to Luna.

"And afterwards, we are going to meet a couple of the dancers," he adds. We all watch as Luna stares at him for a moment before throwing her arms around his neck.

"Thank you, thank you, thank you," she screams, no doubt deafening him. Calvin laughs as he hugs her back.

"It wasn't just me who organised it. It was all three of us," he says, winking at me over Luna's shoulder. Luna makes a point of jumping at each of the guys before sitting between Drew and Calvin excitedly.

"Mummy, we are seeing a real ballerina!" she exclaims, her feet dangling from the edge of the seat.

"I know honey, you are so lucky," I chuckle as I feel Logan take my hand in his and realise she isn't the only lucky one.

Chapter Thirty-Two

CALVIN

Everything about tonight has gone to plan. Luna and Chelsea loved that we were in a top box, and Luna could see the whole production from up high. Jason and Maximus O'Reilly were both in the box as well. They had requested ice cream and popcorn for Luna, and when she started dancing along to the music, the whole box cheered for not only the dancers but her as well.

By the end of the performance, the only thing keeping Luna awake was that she would be meeting three real-life ballerinas. She rushes off ahead, dragging Logan and Drew with her as I stay a few steps behind with Jason, Chelsea and Maximus. Chelsea is beside me, and I can't stop myself from placing an arm around her shoulders, keeping her close.

"She is going to crash the second she is in the car," Chelsea laughs, watching her daughter being swung between the two guys, laughing at the top of her lungs. I turn to Jason to see him watching her with a glint in his eyes.

"That will probably be your lot soon, bringing your child along to watch Mommy dance."

"If it were up to Christian, she'd be pregnant already," Maximus laughs. Jason turns his attention to me and rolls his eyes.

"Jazzy has told him not until after the next production has been cast. She's hoping to have one lead under her belt before she has to take a short break. That way, when she gets back into it, she will have proved she can do it."

"That makes sense. It's not fun coming back from pregnancy, but with her being young, it will be a little easier, hopefully." I look to Chelsea, grinning as Luna screeches. We all turn to see her bouncing on the balls of her feet.

"Mummy, look!" she exclaims as she rushes back to us, takes her mum's hand and starts dragging her away.

"Come on, Luna. Let me introduce you to Shorty and her friends," Maximus says, walking beside her. Chelsea continues to get dragged along by her daughter.

"I'll be there now; just give us a sec."

Chelsea nods and hurries along to keep up with Luna.

"I think it's safe to say I have never seen you happier," Jason says beside me as he leans against the wall. Jasmine looks over towards us and blows him a kiss before making a fuss of Luna.

"That's because I haven't been, mate. I just hope it works out." I watch as Luna spins around like a ballerina, and the three girls clap and join in.

"I get it's harder for you; it's happened suddenly, and there is a child involved, but the only advice I can truly give you is just accept it. There will be times you are jealous of the others if they are getting more attention than you. Like after Jazzy was rescued, she clung to Christian more than the rest of us. It was hard, but eventually, she came back to us all. She always will."

"Was there any point it felt wrong?" I ask. Jason smiles, watching his future wife and shakes his head.

"Not once. From the moment I realised my brothers loved her the same way as I did, it was like all my worries about it disappeared, and all that mattered was getting her to accept us all and not pick just one."

I turn to him and nod as that's exactly how I would describe my feelings about it all and judging from the way the guys were talking about it this morning, they feel the same way.

"Come on, Pippin, hurry up!" Luna calls as she waves me over.

"Coming, Luna Bug," I call back as I head over to what I hope will soon be my own little family.

"She's fast asleep. You unlock the door, and I'll carry her in and put her to bed," I whisper to the others. Chelsea nods and hands the keys to Logan, who walks on ahead and has the door unlocked and open by the time I'm halfway up the drive. Luna's still fast asleep in my arms.

I walk into the house, and Logan says he will pour the drinks whilst Chelsea and I put her to bed. Drew and he both place a kiss on the top of her head as we pass them, and I don't miss the way Chelsea's face lights up as she watches them with her daughter. She has smiled more tonight than I have ever seen.

I follow Chelsea into the bedroom and place Luna on the bed. Chelsea makes short work of unfastening her shoes and making her a little more comfortable. Luna only stirs slightly, but Chelsea runs a hand over her head, and she starts to settle back down.

"Mummy?" she whispers softly as she opens her eyes and looks at her mother.

"Yes, honey?" Chelsea whispers as she kneels down by the bed.

"Jasmine called Jason and Maximus daddy. If she can have two daddies does that mean I can have three?"

Chelsea stares at the daughter for a moment as my heart pounds in my chest.

"Who would be your daddies?" Chelsea asks as if needing to hear her confirm our suspicions.

"Houdini, Pippin and Bambi, of course. Who else, silly," Luna says, yawning before rolling onto her other side. "I love them," she adds as she settles back to sleep. I walk over to her bed and place a kiss on her head as her breathing slows down, and she quickly drifts off to sleep.

"We love you too, Luna Bug," I whisper in her ear before standing up and seeing Chelsea wiping a tear from her face.

I take her hand and pull her out of the room quickly before wrapping her in my arms.

"What's the matter, darling?" I ask, wiping a tear from her cheek.

"She's so happy, and I'm terrified," Chelsea admits, looking me in the eye. "If you guys are going to end up leaving in a month or two, do it now. Don't break her heart as well as mine."

"Come on, we had planned on talking to you after tonight anyway. We want to show you that you have nothing to worry about," I reassure her as I press a kiss to her lips and lead her down the stairs to where I know the others are waiting in the lounge as planned.

As we walk into the room, the other two turn their attention to us as they see that Chelsea is upset.

"What's happened?" Drew demands, taking a step forward.

"Everything's okay. Luna just gave us a bit of a shock," I explain as I put my hand out to stop him.

"Is she okay?" Logan asks, holding out a drink to Chelsea, who nods as she takes it and sits on the sofa. Drew sits to her right as Logan perches on the arm of the sofa to her left. I sit on the coffee table in front of her and watch as she takes a sip of her drink.

"You tell them," she whispers, looking at me. I nod once and turn my attention back to the guys, who are both watching me with a look of worry on their faces.

"When we were putting Luna to bed, she woke up slightly and pointed out that Jasmine called Jason and Maximus daddy."

"Oh shit, I think I'd be scared too after being asked about that," Drew sighs leaning back in his seat, which manages to coax a small giggle out of Chelsea at least.

"Thankful that wasn't why she was questioning it," she chuckles. She looks at Drew and Logan and sighed. "She asked if Jasmine could have two daddies, does that mean she could have three?"

Logan and Drew stare at Chelsea momentarily, and I know exactly how they feel.

"But did she mean?" Drew asks, looking at me, and I nod.

"When Chelsea asked, her words were 'Houdini, Pippin and Bambi, of course'." There is no missing the smile that spreads across Drew's face. It's as if all his dreams are coming true. But Logan isn't looking as happy.

"Why did that scare you, baby?" he asks, placing a hand on Chelsea's back as she looks up at him.

"I'm scared you are all going to leave in a month or two. I don't want to see her getting her heart broken." She turns her head to Drew, who is watching her intently. "I can't cope with getting my heart broken either. You all need to decide what you want."

"We all want you, both of you," Drew says as he places his and her glass on the table next to me and takes her hands in his.

"We have spent the best part of the day going over what we want and how we can make this work with all of us together. You name a scenario, and we have discussed it, from Luna rejecting us to her being bullied, how other mums will treat you at the school, and Geralt at work. There is nothing we haven't thought of." He lifts her hands and presses a kiss to her knuckles.

"The one thing we kept coming back to is that this feels so right to all of us. Not once have any of us felt this is wrong or we shouldn't be getting close to you," I add.

"Baby, we care about you and that little girl so much. There is nothing we wouldn't do for either of you. Whatever you need from us to make this as easy as possible for you both, then just ask us, and we will do it. You want to keep this place, and one of us will stay at a time you got it. If you want a big house where we can all live together, say the word, and we will start house hunting. Nothing is too much when it comes to both of your happiness," Logan explains as he runs a hand over Chelsea's hair and kisses her head.

I reach over and place a hand on her leg.

"The most important thing in all of this is that you and Luna are happy with us. This can go as fast or as slow as you want it to go. But please consider giving us a chance to give you both all the love you deserve."

Chelsea looks between us all, and I can see this is becoming a lot for her to take in. It's time for us to leave her in peace and give her time to process everything. I look at Logan and see that he realises it, too.

"Why don't we head home and leave you to unwind, and you can sleep on it," he says, looking at Chelsea, who nods in agreement.

The four of us stand together, and I gather up three of the glasses, knowing Chelsea will want another drink after we go. I walk into the kitchen and place them in the sink before heading back to the front door, where Logan and Drew are both talking quietly to Chelsea.

Logan pulls her into his arms, and she leans her head against his chest.

"If you need to discuss anything at any time, call or message one or all of us. We don't care what time of day or night it is, okay baby?" He hooks a finger under her chin and tips her head back to press a kiss to her lips. He steps back and smiles at her before stepping further back so Drew can get to her.

"Hug our girl for us in the morning. Get some rest, and I will message you tomorrow to see how you are feeling." He leans in and kisses her before stepping back and opening the door to give me room to get to our woman.

I thread my fingers into her hair at the bottom of her head and press a long, hard kiss to her mouth, purposefully leaving her wanting more.

"Go to bed, darling. We are just a message away. Sweet dreams."

"Good night," she whispers as we all head out of the

door. "Thank you all for the perfect night," she adds quickly as we all turn, smiling at her.

"You are both more than welcome, baby. Now go inside and lock the door," Logan says as Chelsea smiles and moves back inside. We watch the door together until we hear the sound of the deadbolt sliding into place.

"What do we do now?" Drew asks as we all head towards the car, which is still parked up. Logan holds the door as we all spare one last glance at the house. The downstairs light goes off, and we know our woman is moving up to her bedroom.

"We wait and hope she gives us all a chance."

———

I'm just walking into the house when my phone signals a message simultaneously with the others. We all share a look before retrieving our phones and looking at the screens.

Chelsea has created a group chat on WhatsApp with the four of us. I open the message and see that she is typing. We all wait impatiently for her to send her message.

"Please, for the love of all that is holy, don't reject us," Drew mutters. I reach over and squeeze his shoulder.

"If she does, we just make it our mission to prove that she made the wrong choice," Logan says as he hands out three glasses, all containing whiskey. Our phones ping in unison, and again, we all share a look before reading the message.

Chelsea: It seemed like this is the easiest way to message you all at the same time. I think I had made my decision before we even went out tonight but seeing you with Luna and how happy she was confirmed my instinct is right.

I want us to try this relationship with the four of us. But if I think Luna is better off without it at any point, I will put her before the rest of us. We will have to make some kind of arrangement when it comes to what people do and don't know, as I will not have her bulled or told her mother is a slut or a whore.

As for the long term, I don't know what to say. I want to believe this will last forever, but I learned many years ago that love isn't always enough to make something last.

I need to go to sleep as the extra-large whiskey I just downed is kicking in, and I need to sleep it off. Thank you for the perfect night. I really hope we can have more like it as a family of five.

Good night. XXX

I slump back in the chair and rub my face as I fully relax for the first time all day.

"Well, there we have it. We are all in a relationship with the same woman," Logan chuckles as he slumps into his own chair.

"Yep, and stepdads to one cheeky six-year-old who has us wrapped around her little finger," I chuckle as it all starts to sink in.

"Anyone else not feeling as scared as they thought they would?" Drew asks next to me. I look at him, smiling.

"I'm not worried in the slightest, you?" I ask, turning to Logan, who is grinning from ear to ear like the two of us.

"Not at all. I think this may be the best decision we have ever made," he declares as Drew and I nod in agreement because although this may have been the last thing on our minds when we agreed to all move to the UK, it is by far the best thing to happen to us, ever.

Chapter Thirty-Three

DREW

"So, you happy with everything you need to do whilst here?" I watch as the new recruit looks around the security hub and nods.

"All seems standard enough. What about the staff? Anyone in particular I need to keep a close eye on?" I nod, pulling out the file we put together of people associated with Taylor.

"You are aware of the situation of people gaining access to areas they are not meant to be in. These people are not to be permitted into the building without a constant guard. As far as we are aware, there is no reason for them to arrive, but if by chance they do, you search them and follow them everywhere. Letting them know that you are armed and have no problem using it."

Roger takes the file from me and starts to flick through it.

"That file doesn't leave here, but you can look at it any time you need to be sure. The best thing to do is if you think someone looks familiar, bring them in here and place them in the interview room. That gives you time to check the file and compare pictures. If they are not on the list but you are still feeling uncomfortable, then follow your gut. From what I have read in your file, you have a good instincts, so we trust you to use your intuition."

Roger nods again and places the file on the table next to us.

"Use the next few days to shadow your teammates and get used to the layout of the building. There are a lot of floors and rooms to learn the locations of and the exit procedures for each of them." I hear Chelsea's voice as she talks to Hugo outside of the room we are talking in.

I haven't had a chance to see her properly since we all went out the other night, as I've been pricing up a security job in another part of the country. It's killed me not seeing her, and I know Calvin stayed at hers last night, but we have spoken on the phone every night and morning and messaged constantly.

A knock sounds at our door, and Rogers opens it as he's closer. There in the doorway is my woman, looking stunning in a dark grey pencil skirt suit with a black blouse.

"Hi, I'm Chelsea. I've brought your passes and terms and conditions." She holds out her hand, which Roger takes and shakes.

"You asked if there was anyone to watch out for, then you need to pay particular attention to this one," I say, walking up to Chelsea, who grins at me playfully.

"Are you implying that I am a troublemaker, Mr Cambell?" she asks, placing her hand on her chest in mock surprise. I grin as I wrap an arm around her waist and pull her against me.

"No, I'm implying that if any harm comes to you on anyone's shift, they will have the three of us to deal with," I answer before looking at Rogers. "And by all three, I mean me, Logan and Calvin, so take that as your one and only warning."

Chelsea rolls her eyes, places a hand on my chest, and looks at Rogers.

"Ignore him. You are not my personal bodyguard and will not be held accountable for anything that happens to me." She looks back at me with an arched brow. "Will he," she says in a tone that dares me to argue with her.

"Actually, ma'am, no offence, but as scary as I'm sure you can be, I'm fully aware that my employers know several ways to kill me and make it look like an accident or get rid of my body so no one would ever find me. I think I will stick to what he said."

"Right answer, Roger," I answer, not taking my eyes from a smirking Chelsea. "Why don't you go and get your lunch? I expect you back here in an hour to start shadowing," I order, turning my attention to him. He nods once and places his Llanyard around his neck.

"Yes, sir." He turns and nods his head to Chelsea. "A pleasure to meet you, ma'am."

"The pleasure was all mine," she mutters under her breath as she watches him leave.

"Excuse me, are the three of us not enough for you?" I ask as the door closes. Chelsea laughs out loud, grinning at me.

"I was only teasing you," she laughs, putting her arms around my neck. I hum deep in my chest, looking down into her beautiful blue eyes.

"I've missed you," I whisper, kissing her lips.

"I've missed you too. Are you coming round for dinner tonight? Luna's been asking where you were."

I smile at the thought of that special little girl.

"I can do that. Want me to stay?" I ask, wiggling my eyebrows at her, which causes another bout of laughter. She nods before kissing me in a way that leaves no doubt in my mind that she knows exactly what I plan on doing to her tonight.

"Want me to cook-" she stops mid-sentence as her phone starts to ring. She pulls it from her jacket pocket and curses.

"Hi," she answers as she steps out of my arms. I watch as her shoulders slump and her eyes close. "Okay, thanks for letting me know. I'll get there as soon as I can ... Okay, thanks, bye." She hangs up the phone and curses under her breath.

"What's happened? Everything okay?" I ask, placing a reassuring hand on her back. She shakes her head and looks up at the clock on the wall.

"That was the school, Luna's been sick. I'll have to go and get her, but I'm meant to be going to a meeting with Mr Young and recording the minutes," she mutters as I can see her starting to panic. I take her hand and pull her into my arms.

"Let me call the guys. Between the three of us, we can collect her and take her home to rest. In fact," I quickly look at my calendar on my phone and see that I don't have anything other than paperwork planned for the rest of the day. "I can pick her up and get done what I need to do at yours whilst she rests on the sofa."

"You don't have to do that? I can-"

I place a finger over her lips, stopping her, before taking her chin between my thumb and forefinger and tilting her head back so she is forced to look into my eyes.

"When we asked you to be in a relationship with us, that meant us taking on the responsibility of looking after Luna as well. Let us help you to take some of the pressure off. I know it's a lot to ask, but it's what we want to do." I look into Chelsea's eyes and see the moment she realises I mean it. She nods before lifting up onto her tiptoes and pressing a kiss to my lips.

"Thank you. I will inform the school that you are collecting her and make sure your name is on the list of approved people she can leave with."

I run my knuckles down her cheek, smiling at her.

"Add the guys too. That way, one of us can always pick her up, and you can stop using the after-school club that costs a fortune." I lean in and kiss her hard on the lips whilst threading my fingers into her hair. "What's the point in her having three stepdads if they can't make sure there is always someone to pick her up from school?"

"I want to discuss it with her and then you all first. But I will add your names for now."

I know I can't ask for more than that. She is putting a lot of faith into us as it is when it comes to our relationship with her and her daughter.

"Okay, sweetheart. You call the school and let me know if I need to take any ID or anything with me. I'll just let security know I'm leaving." I kiss her again as she smiles at me.

"Thank you."

"Thank you for trusting me to care for you both," I whisper against her lips before walking from the room as she lifts her phone to her ear to call the school.

An hour later, I pull up outside of our office building and turn to find Luna looking a little green.

"Come on, baby girl, let's get my stuff as quickly as possible, then we can get you home."

She turns to look at me and nods slowly. I climb out of the car and walk around to the passenger seat, where I help her out and lift her so I can carry her on my hip. She leans her head on my shoulder while wrapping her arms around my neck.

"Are Houdini and Pippin here?" she asks quietly.

"Their cars are here, so they should be," I answer, pressing a kiss to her warm forehead. We walk into the building and head straight for our joint office.

As soon as I walk through the door, I see Logan sitting behind his desk. His face drops as he looks up and sees Luna on my hip.

"Princess, what's the matter?" he asks, standing up and walking around to us. He places a hand on her head.

"I was sick in school. Bambi picked me up," she answers, looking at him.

"Why didn't he take you home?" Logan asks, frowning at me.

"I have to get my laptop and stuff so I can get the accounts sorted. I tried to call you both, but you were unreachable," I answer as Luna leans out of my arms towards Logan, who takes her and holds her tight.

"Oh, princess, you are burning up. Have you had any medicine?" Logan asks as he walks to his desk chair and sits with her on his lap.

"She had liquid paracetamol two hours ago. I need to go to the shop and get her ibuprofen as well as more paracetamol," I answer, grabbing my laptop case from under my desk and placing my laptop and paperwork into it.

"Hey. Is Rogers settled in at-" Calvin stops short as he

walks into the office and spots Luna. "Luna Bug, why are you not in school?"

"She's ill," Logan answers, pressing a kiss to her head.

"Bambi is taking me home once he has his work stuff," Luna says as Calvin reaches her. She leaves Logan's lap to wrap her arms around Calvin's neck. He lifts her and carries her to his own desk chair.

I listen to Calvin talking to her quietly as I throw the last few bits I need in the case before walking over to the two of them and holding out my hands for Luna. She climbs into my arms and leans her head on my shoulder.

"Get her home. I will go to the shops and get what she needs. I'll bring it around within the hour," Logan says as he stands from his desk and retrieves his wallet and car keys from the drawer.

"I have a meeting with some potential clients, but I will be around as soon as I've finished with them," Calvin adds, walking over and pressing a kiss to Luna's head.

"Will you all be coming around?" she asks, looking at us.

"Do you want us all there?" Logan asks. Luna nods as she closes her eyes.

"I always want you all with me," she answers quietly. The three of us share a look, each of our hearts bursting wide open at this little girl.

"Then we will be there as soon as we can, princess," Logan says, running his hand over her head.

"Come on, let's get you home, baby girl," I whisper into her hair before leaving the office as the guys tell us they will be there as soon as they possibly can.

As I pull away from the office and look over to see Luna almost asleep in the passenger seat, I realise she never favours one of us over the others. Today, she went to each of us without even thinking about it. She needed to be cared for and felt safe enough to come to us all for the care she needed. To me, that speaks volumes of the trust she is putting in the three of us, and I know we will all do whatever she needs us to do to ensure we never do anything to lose that trust.

In the short time we have known this amazing little girl, we have fallen in love with her mom and her. She has three men who want nothing more than to be her daddies and give her all the love her own father never showed her.

Chapter Thirty-Four

CHELSEA

Why the hell did the meeting have to run late today of all days? I couldn't even get a few minutes to message Drew to check in on Luna. It's so unlike her to be poorly, and I know she hates being sick. I hope she is okay with him being there and not me.

I pull onto my street and almost slam on my breaks when I spot not one but three cars parked outside my house.

Is something wrong? Is that why they are all there? I park onto the drive and jump out of my car, not grabbing my phone or anything as I race for the house.

I throw open the door and nearly hit Logan as he was about to open it for me.

"Where is she? Is she okay?" I demand. Logan places his hands on the top of my arms and smiles softly.

"She's fine. Take a deep breath and calm down. She's in the lounge watching TV with the other two. She has only been sick once since getting home, and her temperature is slowly coming down." He presses a kiss to my lips before turning me towards the lounge.

I walk in to see Luna lying on the sofa, her head on Drew's lap and her feet on Calvin's. She's covered in her favourite blanket and watching a film on the TV. Drew is the first to notice me, and a smile spreads across his face.

"Look who's home, Luna?" he says softly as he runs his hand over her head. She looks up and smiles when she finally notices me walking towards her.

"Hey honey, how are you feeling?" I ask quietly as I go to kneel down in front of her, but she sits up and wraps her arms around my neck. I pull her into my arms as Calvin moves the blanket, and I sit between the two men with my girl on my lap.

"I'm so sorry I wasn't here, honey," I whisper into her hair. She looks up at me with her flushed cheeks and smiles.

"It's okay, Mummy. Bambi looked after me until the others got here." She leans her cheek against my chest as I hold her tight. Drew places an arm around my shoulders, and I lean against him. I'm so grateful for these men walking into our lives. I close my eyes and bury my nose into Luna's hair, which smells sweeter thanks to the medication. The two of us cuddle up to Drew as we sit quietly.

I feel someone lift Luna out of my arms and wake with a jump.

"Shush, Chels. Houdini's just putting her to bed," Drew whispers into my hair. I look up to see Luna asleep in Logan's arms.

"I'll come with you," I whisper as I blink back the sleep and go to stand up. Drew instantly jumps to his feet and helps me to mine. I thank him before following Logan out of the lounge and up the stairs to Luna's room. Pulling back

239

the covers, Logan places her gently on the bed, and she instantly curls up, holding a teddy to her chest.

"I don't recognise that," I frown at the brown fluffy bear.

"It's new. I saw it in the pharmacy and couldn't resist getting it for her," he says as he steps behind me and wraps his arms around me so I can lean back against him as I watch my poor baby sleep.

"I feel so bad for not being here with her. It's been eating at me all day."

"I promise she's been fine. She's slept on and off most of the time, and she has had the three of us wrapped around her little finger," he whispers into my ear before kissing my cheek lovingly.

"There is nothing we wouldn't do for that little girl. We want you to believe us and see how much she means to us."

"It's hard," I sigh, turning in his arms and placing my arms around his neck. He's the only one who knows a little about my past.

"I know, baby. Trust me, we all do. But we will do whatever it takes for you to see we are not changing our minds or leaving you both." He runs his knuckles gently down my cheek. "After Angie, I never thought I would love anyone ever again. But here I am, falling headfirst for you and that little girl. There is nothing I wouldn't do for the two of you, and I hope you realise how much I love you both."

I stare at him, unsure how to answer. He smiles as he leans in and kisses me on the lips.

"I don't expect you to say it back. I just want you to know that no matter what the future brings for us all, I, for one, am never willingly leaving either of your sides." He kisses me once more before leading me from the bedroom and back downstairs, where the other two are in the kitchen setting the table. I realise the pans on the cooker and the smell of the food coming from the oven.

"Have you cooked?" I ask, amazed, looking around at the three of them.

"Houdini is a mean chef and wanted to show off," Calvin chuckles as he winks at Logan, who shakes his head whilst walking over to the cooker.

"It's nothing special. I just figured the last thing you would want to do after a busy day is cook." He turns to look at me, and I can't help grinning.

"He also nearly had a heart attack when he saw all the frozen meals in your freezer," Drew laughs.

"Hey, at least I'm eating something. Sometimes I really cannot be bothered to eat when it's just me at mealtimes," I argue. Drew pulls me into his arms and kisses the top of my head as I wrap my arms around his waist.

"Well, in that case, we will try our very hardest to make sure you are never alone at dinner time from now on."

"Except for the next five nights," Logan adds with raised eyebrows.

"What? Where are you all going?" I ask, looking around at them all.

"We are providing security for a huge festival, and we know it will look better if we show our faces and they see that we are ensuring everything is running smoothly," Logan explains as he turns back to the stove and pulls something out of the oven that smells amazing.

"It was booked nearly a year ago and will be our biggest payout yet. We have to go, sorry, darling."

I turn to Calvin and frown.

"I wasn't moaning. I would never expect you to put us before your business, especially with how it's still early days for you all."

"We know you wouldn't, baby. But we would put you two over the business if you ever needed us to. That's the great thing about this relationship. Even if you needed two of us, there is still one to keep things running," he points out.

"Plus, we don't actually have to work in the office most of the time. We can work from home, too. So, if there is ever an issue like today, one of us will always be available to pick up Luna and bring her home," Calvin adds as he pulls out my seat so I can sit down as Logan places a plate of pasta bake in front of me.

"I didn't expect you all to drop everything for Luna like that. I know it would have meant the world to her," I say, smiling at them all.

"She's our girl, who was poorly; of course, we were all going to do what we could to make her feel better," Calvin says beside me. "We know that usually kids have two parents who share responsibility for the child, but she is lucky enough to have four of us who can work together to ensure she has everything she needs," he continues.

"Whether that's being picked up from school or taken to a friend's party. We are here for all of it," Drew adds. I look around at the three men all now sitting around my little table, making the place feel like a home and showering me and my baby with nothing but love.

"Thank you, all of you." I look around at their three faces and wish I could tell them how much they have already done for us. "It will take a bit of getting used to, but we will get there," I add, picking up my fork.

"And we will be here showing you both all the care and affection you deserve until you realise how much you truly mean to us," Calvin says, placing a hand on my arm.

I smile at him before I hear Logan clear his throat.

"In the meantime, eat your dinner. I want to know you have eaten at least one decent meal whilst we are away," Logan orders as he picks up his fork.

"You do remember I'm older than you, right?" I argue playfully. Logan gives me that raised eyebrow look, and I can't stop the smirk that spreads across my face.

"Does that mean you're too old to go over my knee?"

I feel the smile disappear from my face as Drew chokes next to me.

"Yes!" I argue, shocked he would even suggest such a thing.

"We'll see. Now be a good girl and eat your dinner," he replies as he starts to eat his food, unable to wipe the smirk from his face.

I look to Calvin, who shrugs as he stabs some pasta on his own plate.

"You never know, you might enjoy it," he chuckles as Drew roars, laughing.

"I can't believe we are having this conversation at the dinner table," I point out, shaking my head.

"Finish eating, and we can move it to the bedroom," I hear Calvin whisper beside me. I pretend I don't hear him, but I'm sure the fact that my cheeks are bright red gives me away.

Fuck, I had planned on asking Drew to stay tonight, but I might have to consider if I have enough room for more than one ... Damn it, I need a bigger bed.

Chapter Thirty-Five

CHELSEA

"How is Luna now? Has she recovered from the bug?" Calvin asks as I move the phone from one shoulder to the other.

"Yeah, she's fine. She hasn't been sick since that first day and is eating normally again. Thankfully, it means she could go back to school today," I answer, rubbing the night cream into my face as I get ready for bed. "How has the festival gone? Any major issues?"

"Don't ask. I swear all I've done is deal with drugged-up pricks," Logan groans down the phone. "I can't wait to crawl into bed tomorrow after a long shower."

The guys have been gone for five nights, but they have made a point of calling every day together to check in on us. They have also messaged me individually to check we are okay. You would think I couldn't handle life without them here, the way they act at times. They seem to forget that it's just been Luna and me for the past six years, and we survived just fine then. We will be fine for five days at least.

"Take it you were never the festival type?" I chuckle as I

activate the loudspeaker before placing the phone on the bed while I get changed.

"Never understood the appeal. I spent enough time living in a tent when deployed. I certainly didn't wish to sleep on a roll mat if I didn't have to," he answers.

"He moaned like a bitch when deployed, no one ever wanted to bunk in with him. We used to pull straws to see who the poor unfortunate soul would be," Calvin laughs as I hear a radio static in the background. One of the lads curses, and I know that's the end of the phone call.

"Sorry, Chels, we have to go. We will see you tomorrow, though," Calvin calls, as I hear them all moving about. I'm torn between wanting to know what they are being called out for and not wanting to know what danger they are in at the same time.

"Be careful, all of you!" I call out as I hear all three calling goodbye.

"Give Luna Bug a hug from us all. Love you both." Calvin calls as the phone goes dead, and I stare at the screen for a moment, gobsmacked. Did he really just say he loves us? I know Logan has already said it, but I think part of that is because he is scared something will happen again after what he went through with his fiancée.

I pull on my pyjamas as I ask myself the one question I need to work out.

Do I love the guys?

I know Luna does. She even referred to them as her daddies the other night. I haven't told the guys yet, as I think it is something we really need to discuss. They all say they want to be stepfathers to her, but how will that work on paper? Are the two of us always going to have a different surname to them? I know Jasmine is marrying the older of the O'Reillys and having a blessing with the other three, but it's different from our situation. The guys are all O'Reillys, so Jasmine will be changing her name to all of theirs. However, I would have to choose one of their surnames, and I don't think I could do that. I wouldn't want them ever to think I favour one over the others. They are all so important to me, and I know I need to know the outcome before I allow my daughter to love the men she wants to call Dad.

I look into my mirror as I brush my hair and stop. Am I really thinking of marriage and name changes? I swore I would never marry again. When I changed our surname to my maiden name, I promised myself I would never change it to anything else ever again. Yet, here I am, wondering what my name would sound like with each of theirs. Chelsea Wilson. Chelsea Anderson. Chelsea Cambell. I think I could use any of their names. There may be so many questions and things to consider, but if my train of thought has told me anything in the last five minutes, it's that I love them.

I love all three of my men.

Shit. I love them.

I need to stop reevaluating everything and just come clean to them. I love them, and I want a future with them. They say they want one with us, too, and promise to show me that daily. I need to stop fighting my feelings and just let myself feel the love they are showing us.

I climb into bed and check my phone is on charge, hoping secretly that one of them has messaged, but they haven't. But as I slide down under the covers and reach over to turn the bedside lamp off, I try to ignore my racing thoughts and all the worries about the guys and get some sleep.

But sleep doesn't come to me naturally tonight as, for some reason, I'm a little on edge and can't help feeling like

I'm missing something big. That something is happening or going to happen shortly. I just have no idea what. I repeatedly try to tell myself that the guys are okay and aren't in any danger, but if that's the case, why can't I shake this feeling?

I finally manage to relax enough to close my eyes as sleep starts to drag me under until something hits my window, causing me to wake with a start.

I jump from my bed and head to the window, sure there will be something or someone out there. It sounded like a rock or stone hit the window, and I want to prove that it was just a strange dream starting to take hold. When I see nothing in the garden or down the street, it confirms I was dreaming, and I reclose the curtains before returning to bed.

I take a few deep breaths to calm myself enough to drop back off to sleep and am about to succeed when a piercing scream sounds through the house.

"MUMMY!"

I jump from the bed and rush to Luna's room as she screams again. I switch on the light and find her curled up in the corner of her bed underneath her duvet.

"What happened?" I demand as I pull the covers from her. She's crying uncontrollably as she throws herself into my arms and buries her face against me.

"Someone was at my window!" she sobs loudly. I look up at her window as my heart races. Her curtains are closed, but with the moon shining so bright tonight, I can see the shadows from outside. I pull myself out of her arms and stand to head to the window.

"Mummy, no! They will get you!" she cries out as she grabs my hand. I shake my head and reluctantly pull my hand free.

"No one can get in, honey; I'm just going to look." I walk over to the window, throw open the curtains and look into our small garden. I can't see anyone or any sign that someone was there at all.

Behind the fence is an alleyway at the bottom of the garden. I guess there could be someone in there, but there is no way of knowing. But for now, the area seems empty.

"There's no one there, Luna. I promise there is no one trying to get in." I tell her in an attempt to reassure her. She shakes her head and looks at me with her tear-soaked face.

"There was, Mummy. They woke me up by knocking on the window."

Is that what I heard before? Was it someone at Luna's window and not my own? It's possible, I guess.

I walk over to the bed and pull Luna into my arms.

"Can I sleep with you tonight? I don't want to be on my own."

I nod my head as I lift her onto my hip.

"Of course you can, honey." I start walking towards the door when she yells for me to stop. "What's the matter?"

"I forgot my Loggie bear!"

I frown at her for a moment as she wiggles in my arms, and I place her feet on the floor. She rushes back to the bed and grabs her bear from Logan. I smile as she grabs my hand and pulls me from the room. She has been inseparable from that bear since he gave it to her, and I know he will love the name she gave it.

As soon as we are in my room, she jumps on the bed and wiggles under the duvet.

"Lock the door, please, Mummy. I won't sleep if it's not locked." I look to the bed and see her hugging the bear for dear life to her chest as she rests her chin on its head. She looks so scared, and I quickly do as she asks, hoping it will help her relax.

I climb into bed next to her, and she instantly rolls onto her side to look at me.

"Do you think someone was trying to get in?" she asks. I brush some hair from her forehead and offer her a smile.

"No honey, I think you were dreaming, and something woke you, but that's okay. You felt scared, and you did the right thing by calling me. I will always do what I can to make sure you feel safe and happy in our home." I press a kiss on her head and smile at her. "Get some rest. You have school in the morning."

Luna nods before closing her eyes.

"Goodnight, Mummy."

"Goodnight," I whisper as I close my eyes and try to get back off to sleep, but nothing works. Instead, I lie with my eyes closed and listen out to the garden and for sounds around the house.

What are the odds that Luna and I would hear something at our windows the same night? Something isn't right. Neither of us should have heard any noise. There are no trees close by for the branches to knock across the windows, and we are too high up for it to be a creature unless it was a bird or a bat. Neither idea makes me feel any better.

I roll onto my side and see my phone. I consider messaging the guys and asking what they think, but I decide against it. They will only panic, and what could they possibly do to help when they are hundreds of miles away? No, I need to leave them to deal with whatever is happening there and tell them when they are home tomorrow because no matter what I said to Luna, I believe someone did try to get in her window, and I don't think I like the idea of who it could be.

Chapter Thirty-Six

LOGAN

I drop my large kit bag on the floor next to my favourite chair and fall into it. I'm exhausted, stinking, and ready for a decent meal. The food carts may have been amazing, but there was very little healthy food on the menu, so now all I want to eat is a salad.

"Can we make a deal never to do one of those ever again? Seriously, festivals are not my scene," Calvin moans as he drops down into his chair. I nod whilst resting my head back.

"I don't know. I kinda enjoyed myself. The people were crazy, and the music was amazing. I want to go again," Drew laughs as he walks into the room, already stuffing his face with a sandwich.

"That's decided then; Bambi is managing all festivals from now on," I call out, closing my eyes.

"Fine by me. You boring bastards just don't know how to have fun," he laughs.

We sit quietly for a moment, enjoying the sound of absolute silence for the first time since we left the house on

Thursday. It's now Tuesday, and I can't think of any better way to spend it than silently cuddled up with our woman. Shame she's at work.

Actually, I don't remember her sending us a message letting us know she got there like she did each morning we were away. I pick up my phone and check it. I haven't even received a good morning text, which isn't like her. For the last two weeks, we have messaged each other every morning as soon as we wake up. But this morning, there's been nothing.

"Have any of you heard from Chels?" I ask, looking at the others, who are both shaking their heads. Something isn't right, and I don't like it.

I pick up my phone and call her mobile, which goes straight to voicemail. Chelsea never has her phone off. She refuses to turn it off in case the school needs to contact her. I dial her office number and wait for her to pick up.

"Good morning, Geralt Young's office."

"Who's that?" I ask, not recognising the voice.

"My name's Sandy. I'm covering for Mr Young's PA. Who is this, please?"

"Where's Chelsea?" I demand as I climb to my feet. Both Drew and Calvin are watching me as I start to pace around the room. I knew something wasn't right.

"She called in sick this morning. Is there anything I can help you with?" the woman asks.

"No, it's fine, thanks," I answer before hanging up. I walk over to the cabinet where we keep our keys, having used Calvin's car this weekend.

"I'm going to check on them as you both have things on this morning. I'll keep you posted," I call as I close the door, not waiting for them to respond.

I jump in my car and start the ten minute drive to their

home. The whole time, I'm trying desperately to work out why she hasn't gone to work. Has she become ill with Luna's stomach bug? Has she had an accident? No, she called in sick, so surely she's safe, at least. So many different scenarios start racing through my mind as to why she hasn't been in touch and has needed to take time off work, each getting progressively darker the longer I think about it. When I pull up outside her house, I'm picturing her lying on the floor in a pool of blood.

I jump out of my car and race to the door before knocking. I wait impatiently for any noise to come from within, but there's nothing. I look to the drive where her car is sitting and know she must be in unless she or Luna were so ill they had to call an ambulance. Shit, my fucking imagination is running away with me here.

I knock again, a little louder this time, and press my ear to the door, hoping to hear anything that might be going on inside. I'm about to go around the back to check the back door when I hear someone moving about inside.

"Chels? Are you in there?" I call out. I hear the sound of the locks being opened and realise she has used all four, which I've never noticed her using before. When the door finally opens, I know I made the right decision in coming straight here.

Chelsea stands before me in a pair of jogging bottoms, an old t-shirt and her hair in a messy bun. I've never seen her look less like herself. She looks like she hasn't slept or has only just woken up, and I know that can't be right. Chelsea is an early riser and hates running late for anything.

"Why aren't you in work? Are you okay?" I ask, stepping into the house as she steps straight into my arms. "Baby? What's happened? Where's Luna?" I ask, holding her tight against me as I kick the door closed.

"She's asleep upstairs," she whispers into my chest as I plant a kiss on the top of her head. I lead her onto the lounge, where I can close the door and talk to her without waking Luna.

Sitting on the sofa, Chelsea instantly sits on my lap and curls up small against my chest. For the strong, independent woman who usually gives me hell for wanting to do stuff for her, she is acting the complete opposite now, and it worries me.

"Talk to me, baby. What's the matter?" I ask, running my hand up and down her back as I kiss the top of her head.

"We had a bit of a scary night. I thought I heard a noise like something banging against my window. Then Luna woke up screaming, saying someone was trying to get in through hers."

"What? Did you see anyone?" I ask, leaning to the side so I can look at her. Chelsea shakes her head and closes her eyes.

"Nothing, but after those two incidents, I couldn't settle. I was awake until the sun came up, so I called us both in sick, and we have slept on and off all morning," she explains, and I kiss the top of her head.

"Were there any more noises after Luna thought someone had tried to enter her window?"

Chelsea shakes her head and lets out a deep sigh.

"Maybe I'm just being paranoid. It wouldn't be the first time."

I hold her tighter for a moment, letting her know I'm here now and she isn't alone anymore.

"Why didn't you call one of us?" I ask, running a hand up and down her thigh.

"You were hundreds of miles away. I didn't see the point

in worrying you, especially when you couldn't do anything about it."

I let out a deep breath whilst shaking my head.

"Baby, we own a huge security business. We have people on standby at all hours of the day and night in case our clients are concerned about someone being outside their homes. We could have gotten someone here in less than ten minutes checking the area out to put you at ease," I explain.

"I didn't want to be a nuisance. Plus, I was probably just being paranoid. Luna probably dreamt it and-"

I stop her with a look.

"I don't care. If you or Luna are scared, call us. Your safety matters to us more than anyone else. If we can't be here ourselves, we will get one of our people here; nothing matters as much as you two."

I lift Chelsea's head so I can press a kiss to her lips.

"Where is Luna now?"

"In my bed. She wanted us to lock ourselves in last night, so I did. I wouldn't have left the room when you knocked if I hadn't seen your car."

"Then go and get some more sleep with Luna. I will look around and then call the guys to ask them to bring me an overnight bag. I desperately need a shower, as I probably stink."

"You are a little ripe," Chelsea teases before squealing as I tickle her.

"So would you if you had to live the way I have for the last five days," I chuckle as she wiggles on my lap.

"You can use the main bathroom; that way, you won't wake Luna," she smiles up at me. "She will be happy to see you. She's missed you all."

I kiss her on the lips again as my heart skips a beat.

"We've missed her too. We picked her up a few things

we thought she would like. I know the guys want to give them to her tonight when they are free."

"Big family dinner tonight, then?" Chelsea asks as I grin happily.

"Sounds perfect." I press a kiss to her lips one last time before helping her to her feet.

"Go and lie down. I'll have a look around and then take a shower before making lunch for you both. The guys will also want to know you are okay, so I will call them whilst outside."

"Sorry for worrying you," Chelsea whispers as I guide her towards the stairs.

"Don't apologise, just let us help you. You aren't on your own anymore. Okay?"

She nods, offering me a small smile before walking up the stairs.

"Thank you, Logan."

"Anything for you two, baby. You know that." I continue to watch her as she walks up the stairs and into her room before turning to the front door, opening it, and grabbing her keys from where they hang by the door so I can close it behind me.

I walk out into the front garden and look around for anything that stands out as being out of place. Everything seems to be as I last saw it. I head over to underneath Chelsea's window, half expecting to find a dead bird or bat that may have hit her window in the night. But what I find is that one of the bushes seems a little trampled. I can't make out any footprints, so I can't say it was a person for sure. This area is known for its wildlife, such as badgers and foxes; either of them could have made this mess.

I continue to look around and spot one or two other areas where the long grass seems to be trampled down, but again, there is no way of knowing for sure what made the marks. But as I start to examine the area under Luna's window, I find two unmissable footprints—both identical boot prints. I look up the side of the house and realise someone has tried to climb the wooden trellis that stops underneath her window.

"Shit."

I pull my phone out of my pocket and call Calvin.

"Hey, you found them? Are they okay?" he asks as soon as the call connects.

"Someone tried to break into the house last night through Luna's window."

"What the fuck! Who, I'll fucking kill them!" he yells. I can hear Drew asking questions in the background and Calvin filling him in.

"We are on our way. We want to check in on them and make sure they are alright," Calvin snaps through gritted teeth.

"Wait up. I've sent Chelsea back to bed, and Luna is sleeping in with her mom. They haven't slept much, so don't rush. I need you to do me a favour, though, as I promised I would stay until they woke up."

"What do you need?" Calvin asks. I give him a list of things to chuck in an overnight bag for me and let them know I'm staying tonight. Calvin asks if I think we should make sure one of us is there every night, and I agree. We don't know who it was who tried to get in, and they might not try again, but with everything that's been going on at Young's, I can't help wondering if it's all connected somehow.

"Before you come round, go into the storage at work and get some surveillance cameras. I want to fit them around the outside so we can keep an eye on things when we can't be here. I'm also going to ask Chels about the locks on her doors. I think it's a conversation we should all be present for." The other two agree and tell me they will be here in an hour to make a start on getting the cameras installed before it gets dark.

As I walk back into the house, I have no idea how Chelsea is going to react when I confirm her fears last night were not her being paranoid. Somebody tried to climb through Luna's window, and I, for one, will not rest until I find out who scared my girls when they should have felt their safest tucked up in their beds.

Whoever it was will pay.

Chapter Thirty-Seven

CHELSEA

Luna and I leave my room as Logan walks out of the bathroom with a towel around his waist, drying his hair with another one.

"Houdini!" Luna squeals as she rushes towards him and jumps into his arms. He catches her with ease and holds her close whilst kissing her cheek.

"Hey, princess! Did you miss me?" he chuckles as he places her back on her feet.

"Of course I did. Where are Bambi and Pippin?" she asks, looking around.

"They're in the garden. Why don't you go and see them?" he says, smiling as she rushes down the stairs. "Don't run in case you fall!" he calls after her, but even I know she won't listen.

I walk up to him and wrap my arms around his waist as he kisses me on the lips.

"Do I want to ask why they are in the garden?" I ask nervously. Logan looks down the stairs before nodding towards the bedroom. He leads me in, and I sit on the edge of the bed as he kneels in front of me and takes my hands.

"You weren't being paranoid, and Luna wasn't mistaken. Someone climbed up the trellis to get to her window last night."

I gasp as I place a hand over my mouth, suddenly feeling sick. Someone nearly got into my baby's room!

"If she hadn't woken up," I start but can't bring myself to finish.

"But she did, Chels, and she raised the alarm. No one will get that close to getting in here again. The guys are installing new cameras outside, and we are going to be checking all entrance points around the house. But I need you to do something for me, and I know you aren't going to like it, but we need to know everything about who it may be. We also need to know where your ex is."

I look to the window, where I can hear Luna laughing happily, knowing she will be with two men she loves.

"As far as I'm aware, he's still locked up, but I will call my lawyer and ask her to double-check for me."

Logan lifts my hands and presses a kiss to my knuckles.

"There is always another option, and that's you come and stay with us. It will be cramped, but I don't mind giving up my room for Luna to sleep in it, and I know the guys won't mind sharing with you," I can see the smirk on his face and know he is trying to put my mind at ease, but it's not working.

"I'd rather not move Luna unless I have to," I whisper as I lean my forehead against his. "But having one of you here would make us feel safer until we know that last night was a one-off."

"Whatever you need, baby. We are here for you, okay."

He kisses my forehead and stands. "I'm going to go and get the clothes I left in the bathroom. Why don't you make that phone call whilst I get dressed and Luna is distracted. Then we will go and see the guys."

I nod as he gives me another small smile and heads out of the room, leaving me to ask the question I think I already know the answer to.

"Luna is fast asleep in her room. She was scared that someone will try and get in her window again, so I promised to sleep on her bedroom floor," Drew announces as he walks back into the lounge.

"You can't sleep like that; you will kill your back!" I point out as I lean against Calvin whilst Logan sits beside us, working on his laptop. He is trying to link the cameras from outside to the ones he's also placed inside.

"I have my roll mat and sleeping bag in the car. It will be fine. I've slept in worst places," he points out. Calvin's arm tights around me as he kisses the top of my head.

"I'm going to go in a bit as I can get you all some clean clothes and stuff for the morning," Calvin whispers into my hair.

"I feel bad you are leaving on your own," I sigh, looking up at him.

"Don't, darling, it's fine," he smiles at me before pressing a kiss to my lips. My phone signals an email, and Logan passes it to me without looking up from his screen. He has been glued to it for the last half an hour, and I know better than to ask what he's doing.

I look at the notification, and my heart drops.

"Chels?"

260

I can hear the worry in Calvin's voice and feel all three sets of eyes land on me as I pull my legs from Calvin's lap and stand up, clicking the call button.

My solicitor answers in three rings.

"Evening, Chels. Sorry to request a call so late, but I figured you would rather hear this now than in the morning," she says as I walk behind the sofa and wrap an arm around myself, feeling sick.

"It's what I feared, then?" I reply, not trusting myself to ask the question out loud without being sick.

"It is. He was released two weeks ago. I have spent the best part of the day trying to get answers, and tomorrow, I will demand to know why you weren't informed as promised."

"But there's still three years left of his sentence," I point out, and I hear her sigh.

"I know Chels. So far, I can tell you that he went up against a parole board and won them over. He is back in the local area, and that's all I know for now."

"They promised I would be warned," I gasp, trying to speak through the lump burning in my throat. "They promised I would have time to put safety procedures in place to protect my daughter. Someone tried to get into her room last night, Sharon!" I snap as Calvin jumps up and wraps his arms around me, letting me lean against him.

"Shit, Chels, you know I would have told you if I had been informed. Have you got the police involved?"

"No, I know some people who work in security. They have been out and fitted security cameras and stuff today," I sigh into Calvin's chest as he runs a hand over my head.

"Good. If you are worried at any time, call the police. I will get on to the hostel where he is staying and his probation officer tomorrow to ensure they are aware that he is not to contact or approach you. Do you need anything for school or work?"

"I don't think so. I will let you know. Thanks for doing all that for me, Sharon. Keep me posted on what you hear, and I'll do the same." We end the call, and I lean into Calvin as he guides me back to the sofa. Logan gets up, pours me a drink, and passes it to me. I thank him before taking a sip and closing my eyes, desperate for this to all be a bad dream.

"Speak to us, darling. We can't help you if you keep hiding things," Calvin says, running a hand over my head.

"I know, but it's a lot," I admit, taking a deep breath and looking at the guys around me. Drew is now sitting on the coffee table in front of me, Calvin and Logan to the side. I take another sip of my drink and decide to just go for it.

"My ex was an abusive piece of shit and tried to kill us."

"What the fuck?" Drew and Calvin gasp behind me as Logan takes my hand. Drew looks from me to Logan and curses.

"You knew?" he demands. Logan nods.

"I don't know the ins and outs. But that day in the park, I noticed Luna was cautious of any men that came too close. I know I shouldn't have, but I asked her about Chelsea's shoulder, and she said, 'Daddy hurt it'. So, I went on the computer as soon as we got back and did a little digging." He turns his attention to me and cups my face. "All I know is that he hurt you badly, and you had him arrested for it. I didn't feel right looking any deeper without your consent."

I nod and look back to the others.

"Everything was fine until we married. I knew he partook in the odd smoking session, as in weed and never thought anything of it. But a year after we were married, I knew he was on the harder stuff and addicted.

He would disappear for days and come back looking like shit. He hardly ate, was paranoid and constantly accused me of cheating on him. If I wasn't cheating, I was leaving him. He would be so out of it that he would hit and rape me, but the next day he would be so remorseful I didn't leave. I told myself that if I could just help him get clean, everything would return to how it was, but he could never stay clean.

"When I told him I was pregnant, he promised to clean up his act and even booked himself into rehab. He came out saying he was clean and wanted to start afresh."

"So, you did; you gave the marriage another go?" Drew asked, placing a hand on my knee. I nod and wipe at the tear that had slid down my cheek. Logan reaches to the side of him and passes me the box of tissues I keep there. I thank him as I wipe my face with one.

"I had to try, at least. His parents begged me to for the sake of their grandchild, so I agreed. But I warned them all that it would be his last chance; I would not have my child around drugs.

"By the time he came out of rehab, I was eight months pregnant, and he stayed sober for the first two months of her life. Then, I noticed little changes in him. He would snap at me or refuse to eat whatever I put in front of him. Other than the moods, there were no signs of drug use. I thought maybe it was the pressure of a new baby so close to getting clean. But then, one night, I caught him standing over her crib and staring at her. When I asked him what was wrong, he looked at me with such hate in his eyes and told me everything was mine and her fault. He only did it to give us everything we needed. I had no idea what he meant, but he refused to talk about it and acted like everything was fine the next day."

I go to take a sip of my drink as my hand starts to shake, and I realise it's empty. Drew passes me his, which he hasn't touched, and I thank him. I hate reliving that part of my life. I was so stupid to believe he had changed.

"If you want to leave the rest for another time," Calvin starts, but I shake my head, cutting him off.

"I need to do this now. Otherwise, there is a real chance I won't tell you everything."

He runs his hand up and down my back as Drew squeezes my hand, and I feel Logan place his hand on my leg. All of them supporting me when I need it the most. I take a deep breath and carry on.

"Three weeks after I found him in Luna's room, he went missing for two days. When he returned, he had a black eye and scuffed knuckles. He told me he had been jumped and hadn't wanted to worry me, scared I would think he was using again. But I knew he was lying; I could feel it in my gut. I watched him carefully for a few days and noticed small signs that he was using. I called his parents and told them, and they confronted him. He said he wasn't, but even they knew he was lying. The second they left, he flipped and beat me. I could hear Luna screaming upstairs. She was nearly one at this point, and I knew then I had to get her away from him.

"But something changed that night in him. He became so paranoid that he locked me in the house and destroyed all forms of contacting others. He had his phone, and that's it. He changed all the locks and would lock me in whenever he went out. I tried to escape a few times, but somehow, he always knew.

"After a month, I noticed a pattern of him going out

and coming back, and I knew if I was going to disappear with Luna, I had to do it when he would be gone for a few days. I waited, and sure enough, the next week, he told me he was going out and would be back later and left. I grabbed Luna and a bag I had packed and ran. I couldn't take the car as he had buried the car keys so I wouldn't get to them. I had to leave on foot and pray he didn't see me."

"But he did?" Logan asks. I shake my head and take a sip of my drink.

"Not at first. I got to his parents and begged them to help me escape, and they did. They had been putting money to one side, knowing that something was wrong, and they had planned on getting me and Luna out. They gave me one of their cars and five thousand pounds. I thanked them and ran. That was the last time I ever saw them alive. They were run off the road a week later. The money they left for me and Luna in their will was how I bought this house."

"Did your husband kill them?" Calvin asks. I shrug before looking at him.

"He said he didn't, and because he was only a town away from me at the time, the courts and police said there was no way to confirm their suspicions. But I think he paid someone to do it. He was too far gone by that point to know the difference between right and wrong."

"So, you managed to get away for a week?" Drew asks. I nod and down the last of my drink. The alcohol is kicking in now and giving me the courage to continue talking.

"He found us in a hotel. I was in the bathroom drying Luna off after a bath at the time, and I hid her in there and placed myself between her and him. He beat me and told me I had cost him everything. He said that he did it all for us and that I had ruined it. He left me bleeding on the floor and grabbed the fire extinguisher to break down the bathroom door. I threw myself in the way, and he smashed my collarbone. Even through the pain, I couldn't move away from that door. I would not let him touch my baby.

"Finally, security turned up and pulled him from me as he was choking me against the door. The look in his eyes still haunts me to this day, and it's something I will never forget. I'm just glad Luna never saw him that night."

I look at Logan and can see anger and pain in his eyes.

"What did you read about my injuries?"

Logan takes the hand Drew isn't holding and lifts it to his lips.

"I'll never forget the list. Shattered collar bone, broken cheekbone and nose." He runs his fingers over my head as he continues. "Missing chunks of hair, a broken ankle and four broken fingers on your left hand. As well as internal bleeding. They had to remove your spleen and gallbladder as well as repair a rib and kidney."

"Jesus, no wonder you disappeared like you did that afternoon," Drew says, shaking his head at Logan. "How the fuck did you keep your cool?"

"I didn't. I ran all the way here. I needed to remind myself that she was okay and safe now. I had to see with my own eyes that she wasn't hurting physically anymore."

"Instead, you found me drowning in my flooded house," I chuckle as Logan smiles at me.

"Yeah, I think that helped me to calm down, actually," he says, cupping my cheek again. "Why wasn't he charged with attempted murder?" he asks. I shrug as I shake my head.

"I don't know; Sharon has always believed the jury had been compromised as he somehow had a top-level lawyer, and they played on his mental health. Sharon was sure we would get him sent down for a long time. Instead, he got eight years. He's served five."

The room is silent for a moment as the guys watch me, and I wait to see what they will say. Very few people know about my past, and that's the way I like it. I hate it when they look at me with pity in their eyes and start watching what they say around me.

But most of all, I hate when they tell me how brave I've been; I don't tell people to hear that. I wasn't always brave enough, but that night, there wasn't anything I wasn't willing to do to protect my baby girl, and looking at the guys now, that's the part they have focused on.

"Want a job working for us?" Calvin jokes beside me. "Cause damn, no one would dare go up against you if you can have all those injuries and still stand between him and your daughter."

"No one hurts my baby," I answer with a shrug.

"No, they don't, and no one will ever hurt you again. Neither of you are on your own. You have three trained men that are more than happy to kill the fucker if he comes anywhere near this house," Logan exclaims as if he already has a burial plot picked out for him.

"Do you think it was him last night?" I ask, looking around. The three guys share a look, and I can tell they aren't sure.

"If it was, he will be back, and we will catch him on camera if not in person," Logan answers.

"But if he sees the cameras, he might not come too close," I point out. Logan shakes his head as Drew grins.

"He won't see the cameras. They are too small and fitted into the walls. So even if he saw us fitting them, which he didn't, he won't know which way they are pointing."

"After hearing that, I think we should all stay here

tonight, just to be on the safe side. I will take the sofa and Houdini in with you. Bambi can stay on Bug's floor. I'll pop home and get supplies in the morning before everyone gets up," Calvin says, holding my hand. "We will protect you, darling. Don't doubt that."

"I don't," I whisper, kissing his lips before looking at the other two and realising I have never felt as safe as I do now.

Chapter Thirty-Eight

DREW

"Hey, how did the meeting go?" I ask as I walk into the high-tech surveillance hub. Logan looks up from the computer and shrugs.

"They are hiring us; it was an easy sell, to be honest."

"But it was a big sell; working for that family will pay out big!" I clap him on the back and sit in the chair beside him. I look at the screen and see Leon Prince's mug shot. "Any sightings of the bastard?"

Logan shakes his head and pulls up the list of the guy's visitors from the prison records. Sometimes, the amount of access we have to confidential information can work in our favour.

"Chelsea had a nightmare last night. It took me and Pippin to calm her down," I sign, rubbing the bridge of my nose.

"He said, I fucking hate that I couldn't be there." Logan was called away in the early hours of the evening to a system failure at Young's. He's convinced whoever was trying to access the basement caused it. We think people are starting to realise we know there's something down there and want to get their hands on whatever it is before we do.

"She understands, buddy. Chels would never expect any of us to put her over our work."

"But that's what I was doing," Logan exclaims. "Every little thing that goes wrong in that place puts her in more danger. I want to know what the fuck I'm missing and why I think her ex is linked to it somehow!" Logan growls under his breath before jumping to his feet.

"Every time I think I've managed to block them from the basement, they somehow find another way to access it. I'm at my fucking wits end with it. I can't sleep because all I can see is ways they could hurt Chelsea in their hunt for whatever they think is in there."

I can't remember the last time I saw him this highly strung. He's taking the issues at Young's as his own personal failures and beating himself up about them constantly. He's making himself ill, and I think we all need a break of some kind.

"Bambi, you in here?"

"Yeah!" I call over my shoulder as Calvin walks into view.

"Makes sense, as Chelsea's been trying to call you."

"Everything okay?" Logan demands, spinning around to face Calvin.

"They are both fine. It's just Bambi's turn to collect Luna, but she's going to a friend's after school for a sleep-over. Chels is picking her up from there at two tomorrow."

"Which friends? Does Chels know their parents? Are they able to look after Luna properly if anything happens?"

"Wow! Houdini, calm the fuck down!" Calvin snaps, holding out a hand to stop him. "Chelsea would never put that girl in any danger. I get you care for her, we all do, but chill the fuck out. Shit."

I watch as Logan looks at Calvin for a moment before grabbing his water bottle and storming out of the hub.

"What the fuck is his problem?" Calvin sighs, running his fingers through his hair.

"He's not in control of the situation, and it's making him feel like he is failing not only with Chels but at work, too," I point out, taking a deep breath and looking back at the screen Logan had just been looking at.

This guy's rap sheet is enormous; not only is it for the assault on Chelsea, but the moving and handling of drugs, drug smuggling when he was younger, theft, breaking and entering. You name it, it's on there. How he is still walking around, I don't know.

"I think we all need a break and some time off. When was the last time any of us had a holiday? Or even a full night off?" Calvin sighs as he takes a seat. I'd just been thinking the same thing. We are all exhausted, not only because we are taking turns sleeping on Luna's floor, the couch, or Chelsea's bed, but also because we haven't switched off for so long.

"Did you say Luna's going to her friend's straight from school?" I ask, turning my chair to look at him properly.

"Yeah, why?"

"I think I may have a way for us all to have a night off and to just relax with our woman," I tease, jumping to my feet and heading back to the office. "Give me an hour and keep your schedule clear. I'll meet you in the office," I call out, not waiting for Calvin to reply.

Chelsea

I walk into the lounge to find all three guys looking smug. I stop in my tracks and look between them all.

"I knew giving you all keys was going to be a bad idea," I sigh, dropping my bag on the floor and kicking off my shoes before walking over to the sofa where Calvin and Drew are sitting. I attempt to sit between them, but Drew drags me onto his lap.

"I need a bigger sofa," I look over to Logan, who is leaning against the wall with his arms crossed over his chest. "And some extra seating," I add, smiling at him.

"I am more than happy to help you christen them," Logan replies with a cheeky wink.

"I can think of a few ways we can all help with that," Drew adds, nibbling on my earlobe.

"Bambi, not yet," Logan warns as Drew rolls his eyes and smiles at me.

"Why are you all here? I thought you would have taken advantage of Luna being out and sleeping in your own beds." I honestly thought I wouldn't see two of them tonight. It can't be fun for them to sleep on the couch and Luna's floor, but I haven't heard any of them moaning about it once.

"Actually, we will be sleeping in our house tonight, but we are taking you back there with us," Drew informs me.

"What?" I ask, looking around.

"Well, as you pointed out, it's not easy for us all to be comfortable here. We are all exhausted, physically and mentally, so we thought we would take advantage of Luna being out and take you home with us. That way, you don't have to worry about anyone finding you, and we can all chill out, have a few drinks and see how loud we can make you scream without worrying about waking Luna," Drew answers.

"It also gives us a chance to see how big a bed we need on the off chance all three of us want to sleep with you at the same time," Calvin answers as he leans in and kisses me sweetly.

"And how do you plan on working that out?" I tease.

"By all of us spending tonight in my bed as it's the biggest," Logan answers. I look at all three of them, amazed.

"I don't have to choose. I can sleep with all three of you tonight?" I start and realise that sounds a damn site dirtier than I meant for it to. "Shit, I didn't mean sleep as in sex, I meant."

"Oh, that's exactly what you meant. I think you would love to have all three of us at the same time," Logan declares, walking over to me and taking hold of my chin, forcing me to look into his amber eyes. "I certainly think that is something we would all thoroughly enjoy," he adds before his lips crash into mine.

"What was that about not yet?" I hear Drew ask as Calvin chuckles. Logan pulls away from me slightly and grins.

"Fair enough." He stands tall and points to a bag I hadn't noticed before. "I want you to take this bag and pick out anything you want to bring with you. Change of clothes for the morning. Toiletries. Your favourite comfy clothes and what you want to sleep in, if we let you put anything on, that is," he winks before walking back over to the wall.

"Go get packed, darling. We leave as soon as you are ready," Calvin explains as he helps me off Drew's lap. I grab

the bag and rush for the door, eager to get away from this
house for one night and spend some time with all three of
my men together for once.

Chapter Thirty-Nine

LOGAN

I open my eyes and instantly smile, remembering the way we all came together last night. The three of us pleasuring our woman together like that was the perfect way of confirming we had made the right choice. Chelsea is ours; no one will ever love or care for her like we do.

I listen to the sound of the shower running in my en suite and lift my head to see that Chelsea isn't in bed anymore. Drew and Calvin are both still fast asleep and don't show any signs of waking up soon. I smile as I climb out of bed, planning to spend a moment on my own with my woman.

I walk into the bathroom to find her naked in the shower, her back to me as she washes her hair. I lean against the wall and watch her for a moment as the water runs from the showerhead down her body, leaving it clean and ready for me to dirty all over again.

My cock is rock hard, and I know exactly where it wants to be right now. I wrap my hand around it and stroke it a couple of times whilst watching the amazing show in front of me. When Chelsea starts to wash her body and leans over to clean her legs, presenting that perfect ass and pussy to me, the last of my self-control snaps.

I stride over to the shower and throw open the door, startling Chelsea, who was oblivious to me being in here.

"Logan, when did you-" I cut her off as I slam my lips into hers and hold her tight against me. The water flows over the two of us as she wraps her arms around my neck and kisses me back, matching the intensity I feel.

I pull back from her and spin her around so her back is to me as I reach around and run my finger through her pussy lips.

"What have you been thinking about to get this wet, baby?" I ask as I nip at her earlobe and kiss her neck. I grind my cock between her ass cheeks and feel them tighten around me as she tenses.

"Last night," she gasps as her head rolls back. "It was perfect."

"You were perfect, baby. You always are." I circle her clit with my finger loving the noises coming from deep within her. "How are you feeling?" I ask, picking up the pace as she leans her head back against my shoulder. "Can you take more?" I slide a finger into her cautiously as she nods her head. "This poor pussy took a pounding last night. Do you want me to keep it soft and gentle? Or can I fuck you like I long to?" I insert a second finger and feel how she clamps around me.

"Fuck me, please!" she begs, her head back against my shoulder as she grinds her hips and fucks my hand, which makes her push up and down my aching cock as she goes.

"Thank fuck." I spin her around and lift her with ease so she can wrap her arms and legs around my neck and waist.

"Hold on to me, baby," I order as I press her back against the warm, wet tiles and position myself at her entrance. In one swift thrust, I pull her down onto my throbbing cock as we both cry out loudly. Instantly, she starts to clamp around me, and I know I'm not going to be able to last long.

"Logan," she moans as I thrust into her hard again, holding her against the wall. She takes everything I give to her and cries out as she gets closer to her release.

"That's it, baby, cum on my dick like a good fucking girl," I groan through gritted teeth as I feel her fingers nails digging into the skin on my shoulders as we both try not to slip apart from the water still cascading over our heads.

"Oh my god!" Chelsea cries out as she throws her head back and clamps around my dick. I cum so hard I swear I see stars. I hold her against me as we both gasp for breath and come down from an intense orgasm.

"Do you think you can stand?" I ask into her shoulder as I feel her arms tighten around my neck and her head shake into my shoulder where she has buried her face. "Did I hurt you?" I ask, worried I was too rough after last night. Again, Chelsea shakes her head and gasps.

"Ruined."

I laugh out loud as I wrap an arm around the bottom of her back and hold her against me whilst turning the water off and stepping out of the shower. Carefully, I walk over to where the sink is located and place her on the side next to it. I grab a towel from the pile I have in here and wrap it around her body and one around my waist before carrying her into the bedroom, where the other two are still asleep in my bed.

Placing her on the bed beside Calvin softly, I kiss her head and smile at her.

"Get some rest. I'm going to make us all some breakfast."

Chelsea smiles back up at me before closing her eyes and no doubt drifting off to sleep happily as I leave the room, grabbing my sweats from the floor on the way out.

On the landing, I make short work of drying my hair and getting dressed before heading down to the lounge and collecting all the glasses and plates that were left down there last night. I also collect the phones and plan on taking them all up with breakfast when I notice a notification on mine, which the other three all have as well. It's from the security cameras at Chelsea's.

I quickly check mine and see that the cameras were activated four times last night. Each time, the same person comes on the screen, walks around the house, looking in through the windows before walking away again. I manage to freeze frame the last time they walk up to the house, as they look straight at the camera. My blood starts to boil as my temper rapidly rises. There, looking straight at the camera, is Leon Prince, Chelsea's fucking ex!

───────

"You are out of your fucking mind if you think I'm going to let you go back to the house your crazy ex-husband is stalking, waiting for you! I will not put you or Luna in danger like that!" I snap as Chelsea sits on the sofa curled up next to Calvin.

"Stop! You are not helping the situation here. Step the fuck down!" Drew snaps back as he stands between me and Chelsea and holds a hand out towards me. "Can't you see you are scaring her!"

I look back at Chelsea and see the tears in her eyes.

Chapter Forty

CALVIN

"Are we really staying for the whole week?" Luna asks her mom excitedly as we lead her out of Penny's house and to my car, in which Chelsea has fitted a child booster seat in the back for Luna.

"Yep, we have spent today getting your new room ready for you," Chelsea smiles at her as she straps her into the car whilst I keep an eye out for any trouble.

We have already been to their house and packed them both bags for the week. Drew went out and picked up some new bedding for his room, which will now be Luna's.

"If I will be sleeping in Bambi's room, where will you and him be sleeping?" Luna asks innocently from her seat. I glance at Chelsea, who looks more nervous now than she did when we went to the house to help her pack up. I give her what I hope is a reassuring smile as she turns in her seat to look at Luna.

"I will be sharing with all three of them. Pippin and Houdini will sleep in their rooms, and I will go between

Fuck!

I spin on my heels and storm from the room, now more pissed off with myself than her for even suggesting she is going home after seeing the footage. As soon as the door is shut behind me, I grab my head in my hands and take a deep breath to calm myself.

Why the fuck can't she see I'm right, that going back there is a mistake. The last time he got his hands on her, he almost killed her. I can't forget what I read in that police report and the pictures they took; I won't let him hurt her again.

"He's going to go back to hating me," I hear Chelsea sob through the door. I know I should go back in there, but I need to calm down first.

"That man has never hated you, Chels. He loves you and that little girl so much," Calvin tells her, and I sit on the stairs by the door listening.

"Houdini has seen things that have messed with his head, a lot more than he is willing to admit. But never doubt the love he has for you two. He might not always show it in the right way, but there is nothing he wouldn't do to protect you both; he would kill for you," I hear Calvin say. I know I shouldn't be listening, but in its own strange way, it is helping me to calm down. I take a deep breath and walk back into the room.

All three turn to look at me from where they are sitting. Chelsea is still leaning into Calvin, and Drew's squatting down in front of her. As I walk over, Drew stands and blocks my way.

"I'm good," I say quietly as he nods once and steps to the side so I can get in front of Chelsea. I squat down and take her hands in mine.

"I'm sorry, baby. I didn't mean to shout. I'm just scared of something happening to either of you."

Chelsea moves out of Calvin's arms and takes my face in her hands.

"I know you don't understand why I need to do this, but I don't want to keep running from him. I love my home, and I want Luna to feel safe there; she never will if we run."

"I get that, I do, but please just reconsider staying here, just for a little while until we can try and catch the guy. We won't tell Luna why you are staying, just that we are trying to see what it would be like to live all together in a bigger house. It's the school holidays next week. We could make it a holiday for her; she would never know." I know I'm begging, but at this moment, I don't care. I need to make them as safe as possible, and I can't do that there.

"It's not the worst idea, Chels. She would never know the truth, and we could spend today turning a room into a place she would feel happy and safe in. Houdini is not the only one who doesn't want you to go home," Drew says behind me as he places a hand on my shoulder. Chelsea looks at the two of us for a moment before turning to Calvin.

"What do you think?" she asks. He reaches forward and brushes some hair from her face so he can look her in the eye.

"I would rather you both moved in here until we can make it safe to go home."

Chelsea closes her eyes and takes a deep breath before slowly nodding her head.

"Okay, we will do it your way, but I have no idea how this is going to work and who is going to sleep where," she sighs, rubbing her face. I smile as I lean forward and press a kiss to her lips.

"Leave that with us. We can have a plan in n When do you have to pick Luna up?"

She looks at the clock on the wall behind me and s

"She is staying longer, so at five. That gives us hours."

I look between the guys, who are both smiling and k they will support anything Chelsea wants to keep them b here and safe.

"Okay, let's get everything sorted, and we can have room ready in time for her to come home for the first time.

them. Bambi will be on the sofa or in whoever's room I'm sleeping in."

Glancing in the rearview mirror, I can see Luna trying to work it all out.

"But which one is your boyfriend?" Luna asks slowly. Chelsea turns in her seat further so she can see Luna better.

"They all are, honey. I love all three of them very much, and I could never pick a favourite. I know it probably doesn't make sense right now," she starts, and I check the mirror just in time to see Luna smile a little.

"It does make sense, as they love you too. I like that you are happy now."

I glance at Chelsea and see her eyes tearing up.

"I was happy, honey. I told you I only needed you," Chelsea smiles, tipping her head to the side. I glance in the rearview mirror again and see Luna smiling back at her mom.

"I know, Mummy. But Pippin, Bambi and Houdini make you smile more."

I reach over, take Chelsea's hand and place a kiss on her knuckles.

"Mommy makes us smile more, too; you both do," I say, grinning at Luna in the mirror. "Luna Bug, do you want to order pizza for dinner tonight, or shall we make something?" I ask.

"Pizza!" she yells, throwing her hands back up in the air as Chelsea laughs out loud.

"Pizza it is, then. You can tell the others now as we are here," I announce as I pull onto our street and see the house coming into view. Luna looks around excitedly before pointing in front of us.

"There's Bambi's car! Is that your house?"

"Sure is, and looks who's outside waiting for you," I

laugh as Logan walks out of the door, grinning from ear to ear. I bet the daft bastard has been watching for us since we left the house.

As I pull to a stop outside of the house, I see Logan instantly looking around for trouble before giving me a subtle nod, letting me know we're clear. By this point, Luna had already loosened her seatbelt and thrown open the door.

"Remind me to put the child locks on," I sigh, making Chelsea laugh as she opens her own door.

I climb out of the car just in time to see Luna launch herself at Logan, squealing happily.

"Hey princess, did you have a good time last night?" he chuckles, holding her tight.

"Yep. Pippin said we can order pizza tonight!" she exclaims excitedly. Logan looks at me with an arched brow.

"Oh, did he now? Well, I hope he's paying for it then."

Luna turns in his arms and grins at me. I roll my eyes dramatically as I walk up to her, and she instantly jumps into my arms.

"How about you go and ask Bambi if he will buy you pizza? He can never say no to you," I laugh, walking into the house as Logan puts a protective arm around Chelsea, walking in with her behind us. I hear Logan call that Drew is putting the finishing touches to Luna's room, and we all head up to see him.

As soon as we get to the top of the stairs, Luna wiggles in my arms to be let down and rushes towards the only room with the door open. I hear her giggling before Drew lets out a loud puff of air.

"Luna, have you gotten bigger since I last saw you?" he jokes as we all walk into the room and see Luna in his arms.

The room looks so different than it did this morning. Drew likes black bedding and an uncluttered space. But now the bedding is bright pink with ballerinas dancing on it. There are teddies and dolls clustered in the middle of the pillows of the king size bed, as well as in one of the corners of the room. I smile as I see her jewellery box and some ballerina figures Drew must have picked up when he went to buy the bedding. I should have known he would go over the top. None of us are very good at reeling it in when it comes to this little girl.

"Oh, Drew, it's beautiful. Thank you so much," Chelsea walks over to him and presses a kiss to his lips as he wraps an arm around her waist, smiling at her. "Do you like the room, honey?" she asks Luna, who laughs and kisses Drew on the cheek.

"Thank you, Bambi. Mummy, look, ballerinas!"

Drew takes Luna over to the chest of drawers to show her where he has put her things, and Logan leads Chelsea to his room to check if she wants to move anything.

It made sense that being her main room for now, as Logan rarely sleeps anyway; he works out at five, if not earlier, every morning. Plus, we found last night that it's the best room for us to share if more than one of us is sleeping with Chelsea.

I have no idea how this is going to work in the long run. Ideally, Chelsea needs her own space as well, and to be honest, I don't like the idea of her main room being one of the others. It feels like their relationship is superior to the others. I think the best way going forward may be a five-bedroom house, but I know we need to get through this whole stalking ex-husband mess before we think about anything like that.

"Pippin, I hear I'm to buy pizza tonight?"

I turn to see Drew holding Luna's hand as she giggles, grinning at me.

"You weren't meant to tell him I said that Luna Bug!" I laugh as I rush towards her, and she runs away, squealing. "You better run, Bug; 'cause when I get you, I'm going to tickle you!" I call out, chasing her around the room until she runs into Logan, who picks her up and hides her behind his back. She looks over his shoulder at me and sticks out her tongue, still giggling.

"Who's paying for dinner, princess?" Logan asks as Luna climbs across his back and jumps into her mom's arms.

"Pippin!" she calls as everyone else laughs around us. I roll my eyes and let out a dramatic sigh.

"Fine, I'll pay. Come on, Luna Bug, let's go order the food whilst the others finish sorting stuff up here. I hold out my hands, and she jumps into my arms, smiling. I place a kiss on Chelsea's cheek as we walk past, looking forward to our first night here as a family of five.

———————

A couple of hours later, we are all chilling out in the lounge, full and content. I may have gone a little overboard with the amount of food I ordered, but we still managed to eat it all. I look over to the sofa where Chelsea is leaning against Drew whilst Luna sits on Logan's lap in his chair. We are all watching *The Lorax*, which is another one of Luna Bug's favourite films. She has settled in quickly and made herself at home. I can see her refusing to leave when the time comes, and I already know I will be okay with that.

Since the guys and I moved into this place, it has always just been somewhere to sleep, eat and train when we're not working. But for the first time in seven months, it feels like a home and somewhere I want to be. Are we all moving too fast with this relationship? Probably, but it just feels so right and natural. The guys and I have been friends for so long; we have faced unimaginable things together and have a bond that runs deep. But Chelsea and Luna seem to have filled the gaps in our cracked armour and made us whole.

"Chels, I meant to ask. What did Young say about everything?" Logan asks from his seat. Chelsea turns her attention to him and smiles.

"He was great. He told me to work from home for as long as I needed to. He knows you guys will get everything sorted quickly," she replies, smiling at me.

"So, he knows about our relationship now?" Drew asks. Chelsea looks at me and smiles.

"Yeah, Calvin told him everything."

They all turn their attention to me, and I shrug.

"He apparently wasn't surprised and only seemed worried about Chelsea getting hurt, which I told him would never happen. He was quite protective over her, to be fair," I explain with a smile.

"If you are all Mummy's boyfriends, does that make you all my daddies?"

We all turn to Luna, who is happily brushing her doll's hair as if she hasn't just opened a bag of worms.

"Do you want us to be your daddies?" Logan asks, running a hand on her head.

"Well yeah, I love you all too, not just Mummy," she frowns up at him like he should have already figured that out for himself.

"We all love you too, Luna Bug. I know I, for one, would be proud to be your daddy," I tell her, sitting up in my chair as she climbs off Logan's lap and walks over to me. I help her to climb onto my lap and run my hand up and down her back as she looks at the other two, who are both smiling at her.

"All three of us would love to be your daddies," Drew adds as he presses a kiss on Chelsea's head. She looks like she is going to burst into happy tears.

"Yay! I have three daddies!" Luna exclaims happily while dancing on my lap, making us all laugh out loud. She turns to me with a big grin on her face.

"Daddy Pippin, will you read me my bedtime story tonight?"

My heart freezes as I take in my new name. I've always been proud of my nickname; it's always been a reminder of how far I've come from that first training fail. But hearing this little girl call me Daddy Pippin has just blown my heart wide open. I know from this moment that no matter what may happen with this relationship, I will always be this little girl's daddy.

"Of course I can, Luna Bug, anything you want."

Chapter Forty-One

CHELSEA

It's been three days since we moved in with the guys, and everything has been running smoothly. I don't think I have ever felt more at home than I do here. I was expecting there to be some adjustment period, but in fact, it just works perfectly.

I've been working from home since we moved in, and Mr Young has been so supportive. I hated having to walk into his office and tell him all about my ex and that he had been released early. I was sure he was going to tell me that if I couldn't do my job, then he would look for someone else. But instead, he gave me a big hug and told me to do whatever I needed to do to keep Luna and myself safe. What more could I expect from a boss?

I do miss going to work, though. I haven't seen Penny since I picked Luna up the other afternoon, nor have I seen any of my other friends I have coffee with at lunchtime. But I know it won't be long until I can get back to the office, as the guys have made it their mission to find Leon and make sure he stays away for good.

"You okay, sweetheart?" Drew asks as he wraps his arms around my waist from behind. I lean my head back against his shoulder and sigh contently.

"Never better," I reply honestly. He places a kiss on my cheek and holds me close.

"I'm glad to hear it," he whispers before turning me in his arms and kissing me. "I don't think I have ever been as happy as you two make me," he adds, smiling.

I place my arms over his shoulders, trying to keep the water and soap suds from the washing up off his clothes.

"Can I make you even happier tonight? Whether just the two of us or with one of the others?" he asks as he leans in and places feather-light kisses on my neck. "I need to feel you inside and out."

"Where's Luna?" I gasp as he runs his teeth across my skin, instantly making me wet and ready for him.

"Playing in the lounge. Do we have time for a quickie?"

"You can't do quickies," I chuckle.

Yesterday we tried to sneak off for ten minutes which ended up being an hour, as he couldn't stop licking my pussy, making me cum over and over again until I couldn't take any more.

"You taste too damn delicious. Eating your pussy is like eating."

A loud scream cuts him off, quickly followed by another ear-piercing one.

"Luna!"

We rush to the lounge, where Luna runs into Drew's arms.

"He's there! The man!" she cries, pointing towards the patio doors that lead to the back garden. Drew passes her to me and rushes for the door.

"Lock it behind me!" he shouts as he slams it closed and

disappears from sight. I only just manage to lock it as my hands shake whilst holding Luna, who is crying uncontrollably, her whole body shaking. I grab the phone from the side and dial the first number that comes into my head.

"Multi Force Sec-"

"He's here!" I cry out, interrupting Calvin.

"Chels? Where's Bambi?" he demands as I hear the sound of him rushing around.

"Gone after him, Luna saw him."

"He's at the house?!" Calvin calls out. I'm not sure if he's asking me or calling out to Logan as I hear him curse in the background. The sound of the phone changing hands sounds before Logan comes on the line.

"Baby, where is he now?" Logan demands.

"I don't know. Drew told me to lock the door behind him."

"I need you to look out of the window and see if you see anything. Can you do that?" he asks calmly, instantly having a calming effect on my own anxiety. I nervously head over to the window and look out, terrified of seeing Leon in person. It's one thing to see him through a screen but seeing him in the flesh makes my heart beat hard.

I look around the garden, which is basically just a patch of grass with a shed at the back. The guys haven't done anything other than cut the grass, and why would they? At the bottom of the garden is a waist-high wooden fence and a gate which leads to a woodland area.

"The back gate is open; other than that, I can't see anything," I tell Logan down the line as a loud bang causes me to scream out loud.

"Chels! What was that?" Logan yells down the phone, making me jump once again. My nerves are shot, and I want to get the hell away from here now.

"I don't know. There was a bang," I sob as the panic starts to take over. I can feel Luna still shaking in my arms, and it's usually enough for me to pull in my panic attack, but not today.

"Baby, I need you to breathe. You are safe. Drew would never let anything happen to either of you. Breathe with me." Logan continues to coach me through some deep breathing for a moment but stops when I hear the door connecting to the garage bang open.

"Daddy," Luna cries out as she rushes to Drew as he walks into the lounge. He picks her up and places a kiss on her cheek as he storms across the room and pulls me into his arms. I start crying whilst he somehow takes the phone from my hand and holds it to his ear.

"Pip?"

"No, he's driving. What's happened?" Logan asks.

"Meet me at the location. Get our best guys there, too. I'm on my way," Drew demands as I frown at him.

"You got him?" I hear Logan ask quietly.

"Yeah, see you in ten." Drew ends the call and holds Luna and me close to him. "You are safe now. The man's gone," I hear him reassuring Luna. He looks down at me before kissing the top of my head. "He won't be back." He steps back and hands Luna over to me.

"I have to go. I will call once I know when we will be back; keep your phone on you."

"Be careful," I whisper as he threads his fingers into my hair and presses a hard kiss to my lips.

"Don't worry about us; we know what we are doing," he winks before kissing the top of Luna's head.

"Love you, Daddy," she whispers as she does every time one of them leaves.

"Love you too, sweetheart," he replies with a smile as he

turns and rushes out of the room. I hold on to Luna as we hear a car door slamming before pulling away from the house.

Not knowing what to do with myself, I walk over to the sofa and sit with Luna on my lap as she cries quietly. I don't know what to say or do, as I'm terrified, but not for the reason I thought I would be.

Are we finally free? Is this the end of the nightmare that started all those years ago when I met Leon Prince? I'm too scared to believe that we are finally free from the psychological cage he has imprisoned us in. Even when he was in prison, we were never truly free of him, but now, I know the guys will make sure that he can never get near us again.

"You okay, honey?" I ask Luna quietly. She looks up at me and nods. Does she even realise that her biological father is the man she was terrified of? Or is this fear that she feels so deep inside us that she doesn't even understand where it comes from?

I look around and feel trapped. I need to get up and move, to do anything but sit here and wait for someone to tell me what's happening.

My phone starts ringing in my hand, causing us both to jump, fuck we need to do something to relax, if only for a little while. Mr Young's number comes up on the screen, and I let out a deep breath before answering.

"Yes, sir."

"Chelsea, is there any chance you can access my computer and try to sort out my files? I don't know what's happened, but they're all over the place, and I can't access anything."

As I place Luna on the sofa next to me before standing, I realise this might just be the distraction we need. There is no reason to stay hidden now, not if Leon is with the guys. I cover the phone speaker and look at Luna.

"Get your shoes on, honey; we are popping out." I watch as she climbs off the sofa, looking as eager as me to leave this house. "I'll be there in fifteen minutes, sir, and sort it myself."

Chapter Forty-Two

CALVIN

"Looks like we chose a good day to pop in," Christian O'Reilly says next to me as he opens up the warehouse.

"You have no idea. Thanks for letting us use the space," I reply as Terry and Logan walk past me to get things in order.

Christian and Jason had called into the office to discuss us purchasing a few weapons from them. These are usually only available to the forces when deployed at war. Christian has contacts which he uses to supply organisations like ours to keep up with the growing population of predators. The people he took over from would supply the worst possible people with weapons of mass destruction.

The O'Reillys, however, only sell them to people who will not use them against the public. They believe in keeping the country as safe as possible, and if that means supplying people like me with drones which have attached weapons, then so be it.

"What do you know about the guy?" Jason asks as we walk behind the others.

"He's an abusive piece of shit that beat and raped his own wife for years, tried to kill her and her baby, his own daughter. He was also deep into drugs, using and selling. Chelsea reckons he was working for someone big as he had a lot of help getting a shortened sentence."

Jason's and Christian's jaws clench as they share a look; if there is one thing they hate more than paedophiles, it's people who rape and beat others for their own personal pleasure.

"Well, no matter what you do to him here, no one will hear or know about it. I don't need to ask if you know how to dispose of a body. You have done it enough times for me," Jason smirks at me as I shake my head.

"You really are one of a kind, jackass," I sigh, earning a laugh from him and his brother.

A car pulling up outside catches my attention, and Jason claps me on the back.

"We will be in one of the back rooms. This guy did your woman and child wrong; do what you need to do to give them the peace they deserve."

I nod once before Christian and he walk out of sight.

"Houdini, he's here!" I call out. Logan jogs into view and heads straight to the car, not losing his stride until he gets to the trunk where Bambi is now standing.

"The fucker in there?" he demands. Bambi nods and opens it.

Inside is Leon Prince, hog-tied and gagged. There is an open wound to his head, and he has a black eye—no doubt from Drew taking him out.

"I knocked him out. Tied him up and gagged him before he even knew what had hit him. He was unconscious until about five minutes ago if the racket he was making is anything to go by," Drew explains. Logan stares down at the bastard and punches him hard in the face.

"Get him in there, I just need five fucking minutes with the prick!" he growls through gritted teeth. How he hasn't cracked one yet, I don't know. Logan has always been amazing at keeping his cool when it comes to interrogating prisoners, but something tells me he will lose all control with this one, and I'm not sure that's the best thing to do here.

Drew and I grab an arm each and pull Prince out of the trunk. At first, he tries to run but soon realises there is no way of getting loose, so he hangs whilst we drag him into the warehouse. I've been in here many times in the last five years. I have seen blood spilt and lives taken, each one more deserving than the last.

Usually, it's Christian who does the killing, but occasionally it would be one of the other brothers. Each time, I would help them clean up and dispose of the bodies. It's not a pleasant job, but as I said, each one was a deserving death and one that would ensure others were a bit safer.

We drop him on the floor in the middle of the warehouse as Terry and Gordon close the doors behind us. As soon as we have let go of him and cut the rope around his legs, Prince tries to climb to his feet as he mumbles through the gag. None of us pay a blind bit of notice of him as we purposely stand in front of him as we lose our tops, not wanting to get any blood on them. We're not stupid enough to leave a trail behind. The whole time, the bastard keeps mumbling through the gag.

"Shut the fuck up, and we will tell you how this is going to go," I snap, kicking out and hitting him in the chest, causing him to fall backwards. He quickly sits back up as I squat in front of him, pulling in as much of my temper as I can. Otherwise, there is a real possibility that I will break his neck. This prick doesn't deserve a fast death, and I want to make it as slow and painful as possible. Let him feel some of the pain he inflicted on Chelsea. I want him to understand what he did to her and how he made her feel. I don't plan on killing him until he has at least pissed himself with fear.

I grab a handful of his hair and hold it tight, forcing his head to lift higher than normal.

"Do you know who we are?" I ask. Leon shakes his head quickly, and I feel the strands being pulled from his scalp. "We are three men who were trained by the United States to dispose of any threat. We know how to track, interrogate, and kill, and no one would ever find out." I pull on his hair, forcing him to look up at me. "Do you know who Chelsea Hughes is to us?" I ask. This time, he nods, and I shake my head whilst tutting. "Then stalking her and our little girl was a foolish mistake. What do you think we would do to protect those we love?" I lean in closer, so my mouth is by his ear. "We kill them." Leon instantly starts fighting against his restraints and trying to yell through the gag.

"I think he has something he wants to say." I look over my shoulder to Logan and Drew and can see they do too. Logan walks over to me and takes Leon's hair as soon as I let it go. Logan pulls him to his feet, forcing him to stand. He is a good half a foot, if not more, shorter than Logan.

"I know everything you did to her in that hotel. I have read the police and hospital reports and seen the photographs. Did it make you feel big beating a woman so much shorter than you? A mother who was willing to be killed if it meant protecting her baby." Logan throws him back to the ground hard enough that the sound echoes around the room when his head hits the concrete flooring. Logan pulls out a knife from his belt and points it at Leon, whose eyes widen with fear.

"Give me one good reason why I shouldn't gut you like the pig you are," Logan growls through his teeth as he walks behind Leon, who is frantically trying to turn around to see him but stumbles forward, faceplanting the ground. Logan plants his foot on the middle of Leon's back and holds him in place as he squirms underneath his boot. Logan leans down as Leon yells through the gag and cuts the ties around his hands, freeing them. "I might think you are a fucking coward, but I'd never kill a man who was tied up." Stepping back from Leon's body, Logan walks back over to us as Leon pulls the rag from his mouth.

"You have it all wrong. I wasn't trying to hurt Chelsea or my daughter."

"She's not your fucking daughter!" Drew roars as he charges forward, his hands fisted by his side. "You lost all rights to her the moment you laid a hand on her mother!" he yells as Leon backs away from him with his hands up on the defence, but Drew doesn't stop until his fist collides with Leon's face, and I hear his nose break. He drops to the floor, clutching his face. Drew kicks forward, hitting his chest, so he rolls onto his back, gasping for breath.

"I know, and I regret it, but I'm clean now, and I need to show them how sorry I am."

"And you thought chasing them from the only safe place they have ever known was going to achieve that?" I scoff as I stand beside Drew.

"I had to scare them. I was looking out for them! Protecting them!"

"The only person they need protecting from is you, and we are going to make sure they never have to worry about you ever again," Drew growls as he grabs Leon's shirt to lift him onto his feet.

"Wait!"

We all spin around to see Christian and Jason rushing towards us.

"I know him," Christian declares as he comes to a stop beside me. "He worked for Taylor as a drug mule."

"What the fuck's that got to do with anything? We know he was a fucking drug mule," Drew snaps as I look at Logan and can see the cogs turning in his head. He turns around to face Leon, lifts him to his feet, slams him against the wall, and places his arm over his throat.

"What do you know about the shit going on in Young's basement?" he demands as he tightens his hold on Leon, reducing his air supply but not cutting it off completely.

"Everything, which is why I was watching over Chels. She's in danger; you need to protect her!"

"What's down there?" I yell as I come to a stop beside Logan.

"Nicholson's drugs."

"Fuck!" Jason and Christian both curse together.

"Who the fuck is Nicholson?" I demand, turning to look at them.

"He makes McIntire look like a goddamn saint!" Jason sighs, shaking his head.

"McIntire has a conscious and limits to how far he is willing to go to teach someone a lesson. Nicholson is a straight-up psychopath. He would kill his own mother if it meant getting what he wanted," Christian adds, rubbing his face. "What happened?" he asks Leon directly.

"Taylor stole three million pounds worth of cocaine off one of Nicholson's shipments and buried it, figuring that after a few years, he would give up looking for them, but he never did. As soon as Taylor was killed, he got wind of things being found in places only Taylor and a few of his men knew about, so he got hold of an old buddy of mine and tortured him until he told him about Taylor selling the building to Young on the cheap but making sure he kept constant access and surveillance on the place. They realised where the drugs were, but Young is under McIntire's protection, and even Nicholson knows better than to make an enemy out of him." Leon looks around at us all and must see how much we are all trying to make sense of it all.

"I was only trying to scare Chelsea enough that she would leave; if she gets caught up in all this mess with Nicholson and the drugs, they could kill her to get access to the area!"

My mind starts racing as I try and come up with a plan. A phone rings in the background, and I hear someone answering it.

"Boss! You want to take this!" one of our guys calls out.

"I'm a little fucking busy!" Logan growls through his teeth, adding pressure to the arm, which is still restricting Leon's airways.

"It's Hugo at Young's. There's been a security breach!"

"Fuck!" Logan growls as he throws Leon to Drew. "Tie that fucking prick to something!" he roars as he charges towards the guy holding out his phone. "What's happened?" he snaps as soon as the phone is to his ear. "Fuck! Get them back! You hacked things for the military fucking get the cameras back up." Logan spins to look at me. "Some fucker has taken down the cameras and is controlling the security system."

"Let me call Young and tell him personally to evacuate the building." I pull out my phone to call him when Young's name flashes up on the screen.

"I was just about to call you," I answer as Logan tells security to sound the evacuation alarm if they can.

"Somethings happening here!" I hear her voice before the siren-like alarm goes off in the background.

"Chelsea? What the fuck are you doing there?" I yell as my heart freezes.

"Mr Young called me about a computer issue, so we came in."

I turn to see Drew and Logan staring at me as the realisation hits me.

"Luna's there too?"

Chapter Forty-Three

CHELSEA

"I wasn't about to leave her at home!" I snap, pushing a finger into the ear the phone isn't against, hoping to drown out the sound of the alarm.

"Baby? You need to listen to me; get out of there now! Tell Young there's been a major security breach, and you need to."

The whole building shakes, causing me to drop the phone as I grab for Luna.

"What the fuck was that!" Mr Young yells beside me as he grabs his office phone from the floor. "It's Young. I think there's been an explosion. The whole place just shook!"

Over the sound of the fire alarm and Luna crying, I can't hear what's being said on the other end of the call, but I can see the colour draining from Mr Young's face as he turns to look at me and down at my daughter who is clinging to my leg.

"I'll get them to safety … I will tell them now. Get a message out to McIntire and tell him what's going on," Young snaps before hanging up the phone. He looks down at Luna. "Your daddies are on their way and will be here really soon. But Mummy and I need you to be very brave and come with us, okay?" he says to Luna gently, who nods her head and takes his hand when he holds it out for her. He looks up at me, and I see guilt all over his face. "I'm so sorry, Chels. We will get you both out of here."

I nod once and take Luna's other hand as we rush towards the stairwell, knowing better than to take the elevator.

We rush together down one flight of stairs, but as we get to the next, we come to a stop when we are greeted by a thick wall of smoke, which is quickly moving up towards us.

"Shit. I can't see through it, can you?" Young snaps. I shake my head and lift Luna into my arms. Thank God I'm wearing my casual clothes, jeans and trainers, and not my usual work attire. At least like this, I can carry her and run if I have to.

"Get back up; we will try the other exit."

We quickly rush up the stairs, but when we attempt to open the door to the other stairwell, we find it also filled with smoke. By this point, I can feel Luna shaking in my arms as she cries. Why the fuck did I come in today? I'm meant to be at home with her, safe and sound, not in the middle of a goddamn disaster movie!

I look to Young, who's looking as lost and worried as I feel. I hear my mobile ringing from the bag I had left behind and rush for it.

"Please tell me you are both out!" Calvin calls down the phone as soon as I answer.

"We can't get out. Both stairwells are full of smoke. I don't know what to do!" I cry out. I can hear cursing and the phone moving from one of the guys to the other.

"Baby, listen to me," Logan's voice comes over the

phone and my heart races. I know this is bad if he's in control. "I'm going to be honest and straight to the point. We think the building's being targeted due to a large amount of drugs buried in the basement. With the new locking system I put on the door, only you or Young can open it. You will probably be targeted. We have to hope that they think you are still working from home. I want you to lock yourself and Luna in a room and hide, okay? You need to stay hidden, and no matter what, do not leave that hiding space. We will get you out. But you have to stay safe until we do."

"Okay," I only just manage to reply.

"I know it's scary, baby, but you got this. Give the phone to Luna." I do as Logan asks and hold her close so I can hear what he is saying to her.

"I promise everything is going to be okay, princess. Do everything Mommy says, even if you don't want to, and I promise we will be there as soon as possible. Can you do that, princess?"

"Yes, Daddy." Luna's voice breaks, and I hold her close as I kiss the top of her head and blink back the tears.

"Good girl, we are coming to get you. You are so brave, Luna Bug," I hear Calvin say and realise they are all on the line, the phone on loudspeaker in the car.

"We love you," I whisper, knowing all three will hear.

"Not as much as we love you both. Now, go hide and hand the phone to Young," I hear Logan say, and I take a deep breath before handing the phone to Young, wanting to keep it with us.

As soon as he takes the phone, I hold Luna tightly to me and rush for the conference room, knowing there is a corner table with a cloth over it that I can at least hide Luna under. Whatever happens, I know the guys will be here as soon as they can to get to us but handing that phone over to Young was one of the hardest things I have ever done. I want to keep hold of it and listen to their voices, so I know how far away they are. I need to know they are close to getting my baby out of here. I close the door behind us and place Luna on the floor beside the table.

"Get under there, sweetheart and stay there. No matter what you hear, even if Mummy has to run, you stay and wait for your daddies. Can you do that?" I ask, running a hand over her head as she cries and clings to my arm.

"I want you to hide with me, Mummy. Don't leave me, please!" she begs, and I try everything to hold back the tears and force a smile on my face.

"I will only leave you if it is safer for you. Do you understand, sweetheart? I won't stay if it is putting you in danger. But I promise I will come back for you, okay. If your Daddies get here first, you go with them, and I will find you." I watch my brave girl wipe her eyes and nod. "I'm so proud of you, honey. Now hide in there and do not make a noise or come out no matter what you hear." She nods again as I lean in and plant a kiss on the top of her head. "No matter what, you stay quiet and in there, okay? I love you."

As soon as I lower the tablecloth back into place, I hear the sound of shouting outside of the room, where Mr Young is still on the phone with the guys.

"I'm here alone. It's me you need to open the door."

"Don't fucking lie to us, Young. We saw her coming in here with a kid, and I will search the whole fucking floor until I find them both."

"Even if she is here, you don't need her. You can get wherever you need to with me; it's my building, and I have access to every room and floor." The sound of flesh hitting flesh sounds out quickly, followed by Mr Young moaning. I crawl to the door and peek through the window.

There are three people, all in black, with their faces covered. Each is holding huge guns. The biggest of the guys has his gun aimed at Mr Young, who is on his knees with his hands behind his head. I can see where he has been hit, and it breaks my heart knowing he is hurt because he is trying to protect me and my baby.

"If we have her, we have more leverage. In fact, I only need your hand. So, unless you tell us where she is, I will send you back to your wife and kids in a fucking body bag."

"She's not here. They already left," Young continues to argue. The guy holding his gun lifts it higher, and I know he's taking aim.

"Then just your hand it is."

"I'm here," I call out as I throw open the door and stand with my hands up in the air. "Don't hurt him, I'll do whatever you want." I slowly step out of the room and pray that Luna stays quiet and hidden.

"Where's the girl?" One of them asks, looking behind me.

"I dropped her off at the crèche when I arrived. She will be with those kids." The lie flows smoothly from my lips, and I hope they believe me. The guy holding the gun to Mr Young's head looks to the others.

"It's possible boss. She was next to the crèche when we switched the cameras off."

I hold my breath as the leader seems to think about it before nodding to the door.

"Check the room."

I want to jump in front of the door and tell them no. I want to take one of their guns and shoot each of them for daring to try this shit with my daughter in the building. But

I can't. Instead, I have to wait and see how deep a search they will do.

The guy stands behind me and scans the room; he doesn't look for long. I hear the door close and feel something poke me in the middle of the back, causing my whole body to go ridged.

"It's clear, nowhere she could hide a girl that size either," the guy behind me announces before pushing me forward. We come to a stop beside Mr Young, and he hits the back of my knees, causing me to fall, only just catching myself before I face plant the floor.

"Don't hurt her; she is only my PA. Tell me what you're after, and I will get it for you," Young argues next to me. I know he means well, but now I know that Luna is in that room and safe for the time being. I want to get them as far away from her as possible. If the guys do turn up here, I don't want to risk her getting caught in the crossfire or seeing anyone getting hurt or killed. I need to protect her and lead them away.

"What do you want from me?" I ask, trying to act dumb. If I let them know about the drugs, they will know the guys are aware of what's going on. Or they could think I've been in on the whole thing and kill me.

"None of your fucking business," the one in charge snaps before stepping forward. "Get us into the room and stay beside us until we are free from the building; then maybe, just maybe, you will see your little girl again. Is that understood?"

I nod as tears fill my eyes. One of the guys grabs my arm and pulls me onto my feet. I don't fight it. I need to get them all off this floor. As he leads me away, I turn to look at Mr Young while the leader grins at him.

"I have a message from Mr Nicholson," the gun goes off, and I scream as Mr Young falls to the floor.

"You didn't need to kill him!" I cry out as I see the blood starting to soak his chest.

"He might survive, he might not. Depends if his old ticker can keep going," the guy laughs as he grabs my arms and pulls them behind my back. I feel something tighten around my wrists and can only guess it's a cable tie.

"Now, are you going to do as you're told?"

I nod twice before he leads me to the staircase, which is still filled with smoke but starting to clear.

As we descend towards the basement, I notice the building is quieter than usual. I hope everyone is outside or hidden away from danger. I look around and see all three guys are with me, which means there is no one left up there with Luna. At least my baby is safe until my men can get there.

My eyes fill with tears as I think of my baby up there alone. I don't bother trying to blink them away. I want these men to know I'm scared; let them see my vulnerable side because it may be the only thing that gets me out of this alive.

Chapter Forty-Four

CALVIN

I can't fucking handle this shit.

I've been in hundreds of situations where buildings have been swarmed and people held hostage, yet my family has never been on the wrong side of the barrier before.

I look around at the mayhem going on around us. There are eight or nine police cars, five police vans, four fire engines and a handful of ambulances. All the general public is being kept away by the police, and they have agreed to let us run the show. It took some persuading, especially when they realised our woman and child were in there. But they admitted they are out of the training grade here, and the trained departments are all deployed in a possible terrorist attack out of the area. They agree, and we have far better training and experience in these kinds of situations. Personally, I can't help thinking the other incident was to ensure fewer people were available to interact with this one.

I walk over to the van, one of our guys brought from the offices, where Logan has set up camp. He is currently trying to access the security cameras to see what's happening inside the building. We have had a number of people report a loud noise like an explosion, but no one could see any damage. We also have no idea how many people are still inside.

"Where do you need us?"

I turn around to find Terry, Layton and Gordon all standing behind me, dressed from head to toe in black.

"What are you doing here?" I ask, looking around and noticing a couple of other O'Reilly security guards behind them, as well as Jason and Christian.

"You put your ass on the line for me enough times. Time to return the favour," Jason replies as he looks at the building. "Are they in there?"

I nod, knowing he's referring to Chelsea and Luna. I hear Layton curse under his breath as he looks at the building. There is smoke coming from some of the windows, and we don't know if it's an actual fire or smoke bombs.

"Where was their last location?" he asks, looking around and taking it all in.

"The top floor, Young's personal office last I heard. We haven't had any contact since the call ended abruptly. We know better than to try and contact them again."

Nothing had prepared us for the line going dead the way it did. One second, we were giving Young directions on what to do if found before we could get there; next, there was a bang, and the call ended. As much as we have tried to tell ourselves that our girls had already gone into hiding, we can't ignore the growing anxiety and fear that they are hurt, being held at gunpoint, or worse.

"We will get them out," Terry declares, placing a hand on my shoulder and reassuringly squeezing it. I nod and turn back to the van, where I can see Logan and Drew talking over the blueprints of the building.

"I'll be right back," I mutter as I walk away from Terry and his gang and stop next to Drew. "Where we up to?" I ask as Logan points to what I think is the stairwell.

"Drew and three men are going to the ground floor to check for anyone left. The crèche had already been assisted out; they were out before the initial suspected explosion." Logan looks at the screens, which are all still blank. Whatever walls they put up when taking down the security feed, he can't penetrate it. It's driving him as mad as the rest of us, not knowing what's going on in that building.

He hands Drew an earpiece, and I watch as he picks up his gun. I want nothing more than to go in there with him, but we have to do this right, which means I'll be in charge of negotiating with the perpetrators when we find a way to communicate with them.

"Take Terry and a few of his men with you. I trust them to follow your lead and not take any unnecessary risks."

Drew looks over my shoulder and nods before looking back to Logan.

"I'll get into position and wait for your signal."

Logan nods at him once before they grasp hands.

"Keep safe and no heroics, Bambi. We will get to them."

Drew nods once before letting go of Logan's hand and turning to me. I grasp his hand in the same way.

"See you on the other side," Drew says with a deep breath before walking over to Terry. We watch as Terry, Layton, and one other join him, and they quickly pull their weapons and head to the side of the building where they will be entering, hoping to avoid anyone who could be a potential threat.

Logan and I stand in silence for a moment and wait for Drew's signal.

"We are in position; all seems quiet on the ground

floor," Drew says quietly over the radio, which is synchronised to his earpiece.

"Proceed with caution," Logan says as we now can't do anything but wait and see what's happening on the inside.

It's been half an hour since Drew and the guys first entered the building. They have managed to take out a handful of armed guys and helped numerous members of staff to safety. We have one more floor to go before we can get to the top floor, and my stress and anxiety levels are through the roof.

We found out that the explosion we heard, and Chelsea would have felt happened in the emergency staircase. It wasn't a big one, but it caused enough damage to stop people from making an immediate escape. It's as if the people orchestrating the whole thing want to scare as many people as possible. Whether it was their way of keeping people where they were so there was less chance of being seen, we don't know.

We can only assume that they didn't storm the place at night because they needed Chelsea or Young to open the basement door. The whole thing is just a complete nightmare and has either been planned down to the last detail, or they are making it up as they go along and have so far been lucky. Either way, I'm going to enjoy killing the bastards.

"How are you doing over here?"

I turn to see Terry approaching with two cups of coffee, which he hands me and Logan. He came out with the last batch of civilians and had been getting them all checked over.

"Not great. We had confirmation just after you went in

that the basement had been accessed. It was Chelsea, but that doesn't confirm where Luna is. Whether she is with her mom or on her own; we also have no idea if Chelsea is unharmed as she is with the fuckers who stormed this place." I rub my face with my free hand as I take a deep breath.

"They are going to be okay. That woman would never let anyone hurt her baby, and Luna is just as brave and stubborn as her mother. They will work out a way to let us know where they are," I hear Logan say, but I'm not sure who he's trying to convince more, me or himself.

"I found our guys who were on duty." Drew's voice grabs our attention instantly. Logan picks up the walkie-talkie, and we share a look before he connects to Drew.

"Alive?"

We wait a second before Drew's voice comes back over the radio.

"That's a negative for both. They had barricaded ten people into an office, and it looks like they went down fighting. All ten people alive and accounted for."

I send up a silent prayer and thanks to the two guys who gave their lives today. These are the first two bodies Drew and his team have found. I'm taking that as a positive. If they aren't killing on sight, then our girls stand a real chance of getting out of this alive.

"Wilson!"

We turn to see a policeman rushing towards us.

"A call came through from the switchboard. They called 999 and asked to be put through to the scene. They refuse to speak to anyone but Logan Wilson, Calvin Anderson or Drew Cambell. We think they are calling from inside."

Logan grabs the phone from the office.

"This is Logan Wilson."

"Daddy?"

My legs buckle from underneath me at the sound of her scared little voice. Terry grabs me before I fall completely.

"Luna, princess? Is that you?" Logan asks as he grabs the table for support.

"Daddy, I'm scared," Luna's voice breaks as she cries down the phone.

"I know, but you have been so brave so far. We're coming. Where are you, princess?" Logan asks as he throws the cup of coffee out of the way and pulls out the blueprints again.

"In the room I colour in, when I come to work with Mummy. She hid me under a table, but it's been so long, and I don't know where she is. Mummy told me to stay hidden, but when she didn't come back, I used the phone in here to call the police to ask for you." Luna starts to sob, and my heart breaks. I point to the room on the blueprint for Logan.

"It's the same one I sat in with her the first time I met her," I explain when he frowns.

"Is Daddy Pippin there?"

"I'm here, Luna Bug. I'm going to tell Daddy Bambi where you are now. One of us will be there soon, I promise." I grab our walkie-talkie and connect to Drew.

"Bug's on the line. She's safe and thinks she's alone," I tell him. "I'm going in. What's the best route?"

"No, you're not. You are going to negotiate with the ones in the basement. We need to get a way of communicating with them so we can get Chelsea out of there ASAP," Logan snaps.

"I'll go."

I turn to see Terry standing beside me. "Tell her I'm on my way. I know what route the others have taken and can get to her quicker and safer. You need to get her mum to safety."

Before I can reply, Terry pulls up his mask and rushes back to the building. I stand watching the guy who gave me a new path to follow when I felt lost. Now he is running to save my new reason to live. I look to Logan, who is watching Terry disappear out of sight before he picks up the phone, which Luna is still on the other end of.

"Princess, Daddy Pippin's old work friend is on his way. He's going to bring you to us. But I need you to go back to your hiding spot until he gets there, okay?"

"Okay, Daddy," is all I hear before the line goes dead, and once again, all we can do is wait.

Chapter Forty-Five

DREW

Since Calvin told me Luna was on the top floor alone, I've done everything possible to get up here. I'm just leaving the second from last floor when I run into Terry on the stairs.

"Luna's on the top floor. Calvin was going to charge in to get her, but I told him I would. They are going to try and speak to the guys in the basement now they know that's where Chels is," he explains. I notice he is a little out of breath, and to be fair, I'm not surprised. We have all inhaled quite a bit of smoke from what turned out to be smoke bombs set off in several places on each floor. I fucking hate those things and have always avoided them when I can. But right now, that's the least of my worries. I need to get to Luna.

We continue to head up the stairs, taking our time in case there is anyone still hanging around, but luckily, we are met by no one. We reach the door, but as I go to enter first, as I have on every floor, Terry holds out a hand and stops me.

"Let me go. The last thing your baby needs is to see you getting shot."

I nod once and force myself to step back; it's not a natural position for me in these situations. I have always gone in first as I'm quicker on the trigger than any of the other people I served with. But if it means my little girl is less traumatised than she already is, then I will do it.

Terry holds up three fingers and slowly counts down before barging through the door as I wait to hear if anyone is there.

"Clear, but Young's down," Terry whispers as he opens the door for me. I walk in and keep my gun at the ready as we head for the room Calvin said Luna is in. On the way, we search other rooms, which are all clear, before Terry heads to Young.

"Get Luna, I'll check him."

I nod once and walk slowly into the room.

At first sight, I can't see her anywhere. I check under the conference table and open the cabinet, but she's nowhere to be seen. I'm just about to contact Logan to say she's not here when I spot the tablecloth on the small table where Chelsea usually places jugs of water and pots of tea and coffee. I look at it and can see what looks like a silhouette through it; just as I think I'm seeing things, it moves slightly, and I rush to it, dropping down to my knees and pulling it off the table, forgetting all my training about not startling children who are hiding.

Luna looks at me and screams at the top of her lungs before backing away, her eyes wide and bloodshot from crying. I grab my mask and pull it down to reveal my face.

"It's me, baby girl. It's just me."

For a second, Luna stares at me before she bursts into

tears and throws her arms around my neck. I hold her tight as she cries into my shoulder.

"I want Mummy," she sobs hysterically into my armour.

"I know, baby girl, we will find her, I promise. But first, we need to get you out of here. Then I will come back and keep looking for Mommy." I pull away from her slightly and cup her little face in my hands. "You were so brave and so clever getting a call to us. I'm so proud of you; we all are."

Luna wipes her nose on her arm and tries to stop crying.

"Let's get you out of here and to your other daddies. They have been so worried about you." I lift her into my arms and hold her tight. I'm just about to open the door when I remember Young is outside on the ground, possibly dead. I place her on the floor for a second and grab my ear pods out of my pocket. I quickly pull out my phone and play the music from the Nutcracker she enjoys so much. I look at her and give her a small smile.

"I'm going to put these in your ears, and I need you to close your eyes for me. There are things out there that might scare you, and I don't want that. So, I need you to be brave for me for just a little longer. Can you do that, baby girl?"

Luna nods and wipes at her eyes before pushing her shoulders back. I can't help but smile as she looks just like her mother when she does that.

"Atta girl. Now, let's get you out of here, shall we?"

Luna nods, and I kiss her head before placing the earbuds into her small ears. I hold up my hand in an okay sign, and she repeats it.

Lifting her into my arms, I make sure her face is buried into my shoulder so she won't see anything when leaving the room.

As soon as we exit the room, Terry looks up at me and nods towards Luna.

"Is she okay?"

I nod and keep her face hidden.

"Young?"

"Alive, but just. I've called it in, and I'm going to carry him down. Layton is on his way to guide us and make sure the way is clear."

I nod once and turn to look at the door as Layton walks in, looking exhausted.

"Everyone on all other levels has been evacuated. The only floor we haven't been to now is the basement. But Calvin is heading down there as we speak with two others in the hope of making contact with them."

I take a deep breath and hold the back of Luna's head, reminding myself that I just need to get her out, and then we can work on saving Chelsea.

We make it down the first two flights of stairs without any issues, and I start to think we might get out without any hiccups, but then, out of nowhere, a guy comes running up the stairs.

"Stop!" Layton shouts as he aims his gun at the man, who I notice is dressed similarly to the others we have taken out already.

"I was coming to save the girl. I know her mother hid her, and I didn't want to see her hurt."

"You take one step closer to my daughter, and I swear I will kill you myself. Where's her mother?" I demand through gritted teeth as I prepare myself to shoot the fucking prick.

"Please, I didn't want to do any of this. I was forced into it. I want to help, not hurt you or your family. Your wife is safe at the moment, but if they don't find the drugs soon, I have no idea what they will do. They already plan on blowing-"

The sound of an explosion fills the air as the whole building shakes. I drop to my knees and use my body to shield Luna, who lets out an ear-piercing scream. Debris starts to fall from the ceiling. I realise we are in some real deep shit here.

"We need to get out, now!" I yell over the rumbling of the building. "GO!"

Layton grabs one of the guy's arms and points to Terry and Young's body.

"You want to help? Give him a hand. One attempt to distract us or cause us any harm and you are dead, understood?"

"Of course!"

We start moving down the stairs at a much faster pace, the rumbling has stopped, and there doesn't seem to be much damage to the structure, but we also know that means shit right now. I need to get Luna out and come back for Chels.

The second we are out of the building, I don't stop moving until I see Logan rushing towards me.

"Luna!"

I release her and turn her around just in time for Logan to pull her into his arms. I reach around and remove the earbuds so she will be able to hear him properly.

"Daddy," she cries as her arms tighten around his neck.

"I'm right here, princess. I'm so proud of you. You have been such a brave girl."

I have only ever seen this man cry once, and that was when I accidentally walked in on him, sitting alone in the middle of the night after Angie's funeral. But watching him now, I see the tears rolling down his cheeks.

"The explosion?" I ask when he finally looks at me.

"Distraction on the other side of the building. It shouldn't cause any structural damage, but we will have to wait and see. Pippin went down to speak to the people in the basement."

"Is that where Mummy is?" Luna asks as she looks up at Logan from his shoulder.

"We think so, but we will get her out as soon as possible. I promise."

Chapter Forty-Six

CHELSEA

Where the hell is my baby? Is she still hiding underneath the table? Have the guys found her yet, and is she safe? I hate not knowing what is happening outside of this room. I felt the explosion a moment ago, and I'm so scared that Luna will be hurt by it. Are the guys hurt? I know the ones in here have lost contact with a few of their men. Are they dead or arrested? The guy who searched the office has just snuck off, and I don't think the others have noticed yet.

I have watched the three of them, and there was no mistaking that the guy didn't want to be here and was afraid. I almost felt sorry for him, but then remembered my baby alone in the office, Mr Young lying dying on the floor, and God only knows how many others have been injured. No, I don't feel sorry for him. He has made his bed, and now he has to face the consequences of his actions.

I try to move slightly so I'm at least in a more comfortable position, but it's useless. They have sat me on a cold concrete floor after all. My wrists hurt from the cable ties, which I know have cut into the skin. They have also tied up my ankles. I don't know why, as I wasn't even attempting to escape. They have also stuck some duct tape over my mouth. Apparently, they don't want to risk me shouting out. Like anyone would hear me over the racket they are making anyway, these two really are morons. Is this the best their boss has?

I wiggle again, trying to get the feeling back in my ass cheeks, when I catch the attention of the leader, who turns, pointing at me.

"Don't be getting any stupid ideas, like running. I have no problem with putting a bullet in your brain," he snaps before turning back to his work. I'm not stupid enough to attempt to run. I plan on getting home to my daughter mostly unharmed. Even if there is only a slight chance of this happening, I have to try at least.

If anything was to happen to me, who would Luna end up with? The guys have no legal rights to her, and her waste of a space father is the last person she should be left with. There is no way I am letting that arsehole get his hands on my daughter. No, I have to survive this just to get home to her.

I look over to where the two morons are breaking up the concrete a few meters from me. If Logan was right and there is a huge supply of drugs under there, it must be worth millions as the patch they are breaking up is huge. The equipment they are using isn't particularly quiet, and even though they have ear protectors and goggles on, I do not. My head's pounding, and I have to keep shutting my eyes to avoid the flying chunks of concrete and dust.

One of the guys stops for a moment to wipe his brow and takes off his ear defenders before punching the other guy in the arm.

"Where's Joey gone?"

The other guy starts looking around and curses.

"Has the prick left? I'm going to fucking kill him!" the leader yells, throwing off his goggles in a temper tantrum. He spins around, and his eyes lock on to me. "Did you see him leave?" I quickly shake my head.

"How the fuck are we meant to get all this out with just two of us?" The leader grabs the radio off the side and lifts it to his mouth.

"Any of you fuckers still out there?" he calls into it. He's met with radio silence. I have to stop myself from smiling; if no one is answering them, then it really could just be the two of them, which means they have no way of getting this dug up and taken out on their own.

"I told you this was a stupid plan, Kian!"

The leader of the two, I now know, is Kian, curses as he turns around and stares at his accomplices.

"Don't use my real name, you arsehole!" he yells, pushing him.

"Shit, oh well, not like we are getting out of this alive. What's the big plan here? Do you even have one?" The other guy snaps.

"Yes, I fucking have one. But do you think I'm going to tell you, Frank? Fuck no, especially in front of that bitch. Now get back to work; we are running behind schedule!" Kian snaps before putting his goggles back on. He lifts his ear protectors and is about to place them on his head when the walkie-talkie makes a sound. He looks down at it and frowns before picking it up.

"Is this coming through?" Calvin's voice rings through the room, and my heart skips a beat.

He's here!

If he's here, that means the others are too. I start calling through the duct tape, but Kian grabs his gun and points it at me.

"One noise, and I will kill you. Understood?"

I nod quickly and watch as he lifts the walkie-talkie to his mouth.

"Who is this?"

"This is Calvin Anderson; I am here to negotiate the release of the woman you have taken hostage."

Calvin

My heart beats hard as I wait and listen for a response. This could go one of three ways.

One, they respond, and we can negotiate Chelsea's release.

Two, they could refuse all contact, and we have to do things the hard way, which could result in Chels getting hurt or, worse, killed.

Or three, they kill her to show us they are in charge.

"You will get her back when I'm ready to send her back," his voice comes back through the walkie-talkie I took from one of his guys Drew killed earlier. I force myself to take a calming breath. Fuck this is hard.

"Is there anything we can do to help speed that process up?" I ask, looking at Gordon, who has come down with me. We are squatting down just out of view from the door leading to the basement. We still don't have any eyes on what's going on down there. Logan has been fighting with the security feed, but it's down completely. He thinks they have cut through as many wires as possible, which could take hours to find and repair. Whilst he comes up with a new plan, I'm left with the job of speaking to the prick that has our woman.

"Unless you are offering to come down and help us dig, then no."

"Would you consider letting me swap places with the hostage?" I ask. I can feel Gordon's eyes on me, and I know Logan will have my ass for suggesting it. But I need to get her out of there and to Luna.

My phone vibrates in my pocket, and I pull it out to see a message from Logan.

Houdini: Bug is out, unharmed. We have one of their guys in custody who is feeding us information.

"Do you really think I am that stupid? Now fuck off."

Fucking asshole prick. The fucker still thinks he's in charge, but he will soon learn his boss has sent him to his death, as when he feels my wrath, he will pray for the devil to take him.

"Well, at least let us know she's okay," I reply, trying every technique I have ever learnt to keep my cool. My phone buzzes again, and I look down to another message.

Houdini: Bambi's going into the ceilings to try to get eyes inside the room.

If Drew is no longer looking for people, that must mean the building has been secured. Does this really only leave two people to get all that cocaine out of the room? Something doesn't add up here. There have to be more people somewhere to help them, or are they expecting more to turn up? I need to speak to Christian, but not until I have proof that Chels is still alive in there.

"I need proof of life of the hostage; otherwise, all negotiations will be off, and we will just come straight in. The choice is yours." The fact that they are no longer replying does not help my growing fears.

"She's a little tied up at the moment," the guy replies as my jaw clenches. I know Logan is listening in and wait to see if he has anything to add before I reply.

Houdini: Their guy says she has hands and ankles tied with cable ties, and her mouth is covered with duct tape. I believe him. Get back here and get as much info from him as you can.

I look back to the door and hate that I have to leave her in there. I want to kick it down and take them out, but right now, we have no idea what they have in there as a precaution. We have to take this slow and steady, which is the opposite of what I want to do now. I lift the walkie-talkie to my mouth and close my eyes as I say the one thing she will want to know.

"Fine but let her know we have Bug. I will be in touch soon."

Chapter Forty-Seven

CALVIN

I rush from the building and head straight for Logan's van.

"Where is she?"

"Over there with Penny," Logan points behind the barrier to another of our vans. I rush to it and throw open the door to see Luna sitting on Penny's lap.

"Luna Bug," I gasp, jumping into the van just in time to catch her as she throws herself in my arms. "I'm so sorry I didn't find you sooner," I sigh, holding her tight as I kiss the top of her head. "You were so brave and did such a good job at hiding."

Luna leans back in my arms, and I can see how red her eyes are and how tired she looks. This poor girl has been through so much today, first with the asshole Prince and now with all of this. I want to bundle her into the car, take her home and never let her leave again.

But first, I need to get her mom safely out of there.

"Is Mummy okay?" she asks. I force a small smile on my face as I try to figure out how to answer that.

"Luna knows that Mummy is stuck at the moment, but

you are trying to get to her," Penny says from where she is sitting. I look back at Luna and nod.

"Bambi has gone in to try to get a camera in the room so we can see what's happening and check on Mommy. We will know then the best way to go in and get her out." My throat and eyes burn as I desperately try to keep it together for my girl. The last thing she needs is to see one of the men she thinks will save her mommy crying like a baby. I swallow the lump in my throat and press a kiss to her head whilst holding her against me.

"We will get Mommy out, and then we can all go home," I whisper into her soft blonde hair. "I love you, Luna Bug," I add, needing her to know how much she means to me.

"I love you too, Daddy," she whispers back as I kiss her cheek.

Reluctantly, I walk over to Penny and whisper into Luna's hair.

"I need to get back out there, but we will keep checking on you. You be a good girl for Penny, okay."

Luna nods as I place her back on Penny's lap, who wraps her arms around Luna's waist.

"I've got her; she's safe with me. You focus on Chels."

I nod once before turning and walking out of the van. I look back at my girl as she curls up against Penny. She gives me a small wave before I close the doors on them.

I take a moment and lean against the doors, trying desperately to control my emotions.

I never thought I would be lucky enough to have a family; people who have done some of the things I have don't get happily ever afters, but when I left for work this morning, that's exactly what I thought I had. I had a beautiful woman and daughter waiting for me at home. I get to

Chapter Forty-Eight

CHELSEA

I glance to the vent, where I saw the tiniest of flashes. I don't know why, but I'm sure it had something to do with the guys. In case they found a way to see inside here, I started telling them what I could via Morse code. I have never been so grateful for my dad teaching it to me when I was younger.

Since I heard Calvin say Luna was safe and with them, I've relaxed enough to pay attention to everything around me, and I quickly realised these two morons have no idea what they are doing. If they think they will be able to walk out of here scot-free, then they are seriously mistaken.

Kian finally let Frank in on the master plan, which includes someone gaining entrance through the far wall and helping them load a truck which will be waiting at the end of the tunnel. At first, I thought they were mad, but then I remembered something Logan said when he was down here one day about the original building being an old bank. There would have been a tunnel leading from the basement, which was the safe so large sums of money could be

335

brought in easily. Apparently, they have been working their way through the tunnel for the last couple of weeks, ensuring it was safe to use and clearing out any blockages.

None of it makes any sense to me because if the tunnel is still usable, wouldn't it have been easier for them to do all this at night? But then I remember the one thing that probably spoiled their plan to do that. Logan put the new fingerprint lock on the door. One that only Mr. Young or I could open.

The thought of my mentor brings tears to my eyes. I hope that the guys got to him in time to save him. I would hate to think of what would happen to his family if he died.

I close my eyes, lean my head back against the wall and take a deep breath.

"How long have we got until we have to be ready to go?" Frank asks. I open my eyes and watch the two of them as they load up packages of what I'm guessing are drugs into a trolley I have seen the maintenance guy use to push around the large water barrels and boxes of paper.

"Ten minutes, so stop talking and hurry the fuck up!" Kian snaps as he goes back to lifting the packets out of the container they were buried in.

"What are we going to do with her?" Frank asks, nodding towards me. Kian turns and looks at me before shrugging.

"We can't leave her; she knows our names. She'll have to come with us, and the boss can decide where to put her." Kian grins, making my skin crawl, and my hands curl into fists. "He has a couple of whore houses around the country. I'm sure he will find a place she can start calling home."

Fear settles heavier in my stomach as I think of the kind of places he is talking about. If my mouth wasn't taped up, I think I'd be sick. Luckily, my mouth is so dry I want to cough, but I can't because of the duct tape. The longer it's over my mouth, the harder it is for me to breathe properly. I know it's probably all in my head, but it feels like I can't get a deep enough breath anymore. Is it possible to suffocate with just your mouth covered? Or am I just becoming paranoid?

A rumbling sound comes from the opposite side of the basement, causing all three of us to turn in that direction. Kian looks at his watch and grins.

"Looks like they will be a little early." He turns back to Frank. "Get a move on; we still have about twenty packets to upload!"

I watch the far wall and pray they make enough racket for the guys to realise what's going on. I start signing "Underground Passage" over and over again and am just giving up when the radio springs to life.

"This Is Logan Wilson," his voice calls. "I'm here to tell you that your time is running out, and you should consider all your options carefully." I can hear the authority in his voice, and the look on Frank's face tells me he hears it, too.

"Where's the other guy?" Kian asks, smirking. "Was he the good cop?" he laughs.

"No. He was the bad cop," Logan replies. I swear I would smile if I could.

"What does that make you then?" Kian asks, frowning.

"The one they call in when stupid mother fuckers like you haven't realised their time is up and the big boys are coming out to play."

I hear what sounds like drilling coming from the other side of the basement where we heard the rumbling before, but this time, it's louder, and I swear I can see the wall starting to shake.

"Well, good luck; we are the ones with the pretty lady

here. One move from you, and I kill her," Kian replies, not even picking up his gun.

"We will see. Final offer. Release Ms Hughes, or you will see how many torture skills I have picked up in my fifteen years with the Navy SEALs."

I watch the colour drain from Frank's face as the drilling stops, and he looks from me to the wall.

"Just let her go, Kian. It will be easier to get out of here without her anyway."

Kian looks at him and rolls his eyes.

"Please! He's not a SEAL; he's just your standard security guard. He's all mouth and no action," Kian groans and looks over at me. I slowly shake my head, and I watch as, for a moment, he starts to look worried. "He's really a SEAL?"

I nod my head once as I see the panic really set in. The drilling starts again, and I hear the radio spring to life.

"Last chance to do the right thing, release Ms Hughes and leave with your hands up, or face the wrath of the men whose fiancée you are holding hostage."

I feel my eyes bulge. *Fiancée?* Kian looks at me, and I quickly straighten my face and shrug. The drilling sound stops, and for a moment, there is a deadly silence. Kian looks from me to the wall and smirks as what sounds like a sledgehammer hits the wall, and a large crack appears.

"I choose a third option. Say goodbye to your fiancée," he smirks before grabbing and hurling the walkie-talkie at the wall which breaks as I hear a noise that sounds like Logan shouting. Another loud bang comes from the wall as Kian grabs a couple more packages and piles them into the trolley.

"Get the rest of that in there," he snaps at Frank, who looks like he's close to having a panic attack. Kian storms over and slices through the cable ties on my ankles before grabbing my arm and roughly pulling me to my feet.

"Hope you said goodbye to your daughter and fiancée this morning, 'cause you're never going to see them again," he laughs before pulling me towards the wall where there is a medium hole now. A couple more bangs, and the wall falls away, leaving a large dust cloud and a hole big enough for them to push the trolley through. Two men in black outfits, like Kian and Frank, walk through the dust with masks on their faces and helmets on their heads.

"Right on time, I see. Help Frank with the stuff whilst I take this little thing for a walk. I want to make sure her little friends can't find her." But as Kian goes to walk me past the guys, one of them stops in front of me, takes my chin in his hand, and tilts my head at angles as he checks me out. He's lucky I have tape on my mouth otherwise, I'd spit in his face. My eyes find his amber ones, and my heart stops when he winks and punches Kian in the face. In a flash, he has a gun to Kian's head as he grabs me and hides me behind his back.

In that second, all hell breaks loose. Three fully armed police officers charge into the room, screaming for everyone to get down. I feel someone grab me from behind and drag me away from Logan. I instantly start to fight and scream behind the tape. I kick out and catch them on the shin, and I hear them curse and stop as they wrap their arms around my waist.

"It's me, darling. I've got you."

I look into Calvin's eyes and burst into tears. He pulls a knife from his trousers and slices through the cable ties on my wrists. As soon as they are free, I bring them to the front of me and look at the deep bleeding cuts around them. I reach up and rip the duct tape from my mouth, which feels like it takes my lips off with it, causing me to scream out. Calvin goes to lead me away, but shouting sounds through the hole in the wall, and Calvin points to the door that leads to the building.

"Get up there now!" he yells before pulling his gun and keeping me behind him as I run for the stairs. He follows me backwards, watching my back the whole time until I'm out of the basement. I rush for the entrance, where I can see a couple of police officers waving me towards them. As soon as I am out of the building, they surround me and guide me quickly towards an ambulance behind the barricade.

"The guys will be out as soon as everyone's contained. You need to get checked over until they get here." One of the police officers says as they try and lead me into the ambulance.

Suddenly, a loud bang sounds from inside the building, and I feel the ground shake. As the bright entrance fills with dust, the windows and glass doors on the first two floors shatter, showering us with glass shards.

"No!" I scream as I turn to go back to the building, but the officers stop me. Everything turns into a blur as I fight and scream, trying desperately to get back to the guys. I see people running towards the building, pulling on protective gear as they go. Firemen, police officers, and people in gear like the guys were wearing, screaming out orders and pointing in all different directions.

"Miss, if you don't calm down, I will sedate you!" the paramedic calls behind me as I feel my legs go, and I fall to the ground as a sob like no other leaves my body. I feel it building in my chest as it explodes from me. I can't see, and I can't breathe; all I can do is look at the building and pray all three will make it out of there somehow alive.

The police officer drops beside me and holds me as I scream over and over again for them. I try to get to my feet again, but my body just won't work. At some point, I hear Luna scream my name as she rushes to me, falling onto my lap, and I cry harder, holding her close. We cry together as I watch for a sign there are survivors inside.

After what feels like hours, a police officer covered in dust comes out and screams for three stretchers. My heart freezes as I climb to my feet and watch six people carry out three bodies. They are all so covered in dust that I can't tell the uniforms apart. With Luna on my hip, I go to step forward, but the officers stop me. I realise then their radios are going crazy. I hear three injured and three dead, but there is no word of who.

"I need to know!" I beg, spinning around to face the office. "I need to know if any of them are hurt!" I can see on her face that she doesn't know what to do. I'm sure she wants to tell me everything is fine, but even I know it can't be, not after that. Something big has happened down there, and all three of the men I love are there, hurt or dead.

The police officer tells me to wait here, and she will find out what's going on. I turn to watch her walk away at the same time as a large group of people walk out of the building, clustered together. As they all start to step apart, I see them. Even covered head to toe in dust and debris, I know them anywhere.

All three look up, and I can see they are all walking unaided. My feet start moving on their own accord. I hold Luna to my hip as I run to the guys as they rush to us. Logan gets to me first, and I throw an arm around his neck, crying.

"You're okay, you're all okay," I repeat over and over again. I feel Luna leaning away from me and turn to see

Calvin taking her from my hip in time for me to throw myself at Drew.

"We are okay, sweetheart. The blast was in the tunnel; we just got knocked around a bit, but we are okay," he whispers into my hair.

"Have you been checked over, darling?" Calvin asks as I hug him, and Drew takes Luna from him.

"No, I was a bit busy thinking you were all dead!" I yell, hitting his chest. He laughs as he rubs it and pulls me back towards him.

"We are fine. Now, let's get you checked over whilst we leave the police to sort this mess out. I want to get everyone home together so I can lock you all in and never let anyone leave again." he jokes as he starts leading me back towards the ambulance.

"Sounds like a fucking amazing plan to me," Logan sighs as he falls into step beside us with Luna on his hip.

Chapter Forty-Nine

CHELSEA

I hiss through my teeth as Logan applies the cream to my wrists.

"I'm sorry, baby," he whispers as he starts to wrap the right one. The paramedics gave me a clean bill of health and allowed me to come home. I was asked to go down to the police station and provide a statement, but Calvin persuaded them to let me do it tomorrow. So, for now, the guys have me under strict orders to relax and let them take care of Luna and me.

Calvin is downstairs with Luna whilst Logan helps me shower and apply clean bandages to my wrists. Luckily, my ankles are nowhere near as sore from the cable ties. They were wrapped around my jeans, which protected the skin, but my jumper had ridden up when they placed the cable ties around my wrists, so they cut in deep.

Logan finished wrapping my left wrist before lifting my hands, palms facing up and placing a kiss on each of the bandages.

"How do they feel?" he asks gently.

"Better." I offer him a strained smile as my eyes start to feel heavy, and all I want to do is curl up and sleep.

Logan holds out his hand and helps me to stand before guiding me to the lounge, where we find Drew lying on the sofa with Luna fast asleep in his arms. I walk over and place a kiss on her head before sitting on Logan's lap sideways so I can curl up against his chest but still see Luna and Drew. I look around but can't spot Calvin anywhere. My anxiety instantly starts to rise as it has each time someone has gone out of my sight this evening.

"Where's Pip?" Logan asks as he wraps his arms around me and runs his hand up and down my thigh.

"He's calling the O'Reillys. They left a message for him to call when he was free."

I look at Logan and can see his mind has gone to the same place as mine. Mr Young.

Last we heard, he was in surgery. The bullet had become lodged and avoided anything major, but he had still lost a lot of blood and hadn't regained consciousness. Logan's arms tighten around me as I lean into his chest, listening to his heartbeat and reminding myself he is okay; we all are.

We all look up as Calvin comes into the room, rubbing his face. As soon as I see the sadness in his eyes, I know.

"Oh no!" I gasp as he walks towards me and takes my hand whilst squatting down in front of me and Logan.

"I'm sorry, darling. Geralt didn't make it. When the surgeons told them, Christian was at the hospital with Gethin, Abigail and Molly. His heart just couldn't take the added pressure to his body."

A sob burns my throat as I cover my mouth from crying

out and waking Luna. Logan holds me tighter as I grip his shirt and cry into his chest.

"He didn't deserve that; he didn't need to die. They did it just because they could," I gasp in a whisper. "It's all my fault. He was just trying to protect us. He kept saying we weren't there and that they didn't need me. I revealed myself when they threatened to shoot him and search for me and Luna. I thought if I went out there, I could lead them away from her and save him. But it was all for nothing as they shot him anyway." I gasp for breath as another wave of hysteria washes through me.

"Baby, it wasn't for nothing. You saved Luna's life by hiding her, and you did lead them away from her. I hate to think what would have happened if they had found her," Logan says into my hair.

"I knew Geralt a long time, and I know he would never have wanted you to feel guilty about this. He'd just be grateful that you both got out of there in one piece," Calvin says, taking my hand again. "He would be proud of how well you handled the whole situation, and how you tried to protect him."

All I can do is look at him and nod as deep down I know he's right, but it all still feels like this nightmare is never going to end.

I wake to the feeling of being moved.

"Shush baby, I'm just taking you to bed," Logan whispers as he continues to carry me through the house.

"Where's Luna?" I ask, looking around.

"In her bed with Pippin. She didn't want to be alone, so

he's sleeping there with her tonight. Drew has popped out and will be back soon.

"Where's he gone?" I ask as Logan walks us into his room and places me on the bed before squatting in front of me.

"He's gone to take your ex to the train station. We decided that even though he is a complete arsehole who broke his parole by being within fifty feet of you, he did give us a heads up of what was happening and because of the information he gave us, we were better prepared for when we reached the building."

"What will happen to him? If he's free, he will come back, and we will never be rid of him," I start, but Logan shakes his head as he cups my cheek, giving me the contact I need to calm my racing heart.

"He will never come near you again. He has signed over all parental rights to Luna and knows that if we ever see his face again, we will go down the illegal route to make sure you are rid of him for good." Logan leans in and rests his forehead against mine. "He knows what we are capable of and that we will do whatever it takes to protect you and Luna. Trust me, baby, you are finally free of him."

I close my eyes and let out a deep breath, feeling the weight of my history with my ex finally lifting. If Logan and the guys say I'm finally free, I believe them.

"I don't deserve you," I whisper as I start to feel over-whelmed.

"Baby, it's us that don't deserve you two," Logan replies before kissing me gently on the lips. He pulls me to my feet and helps me out of my leggings, leaving me in an oversized T-shirt he lets me use. I look at him with one arched brow, which earns me a smile.

"No, you need to sleep. Now get into bed and close your

eyes," he says softly as he holds lifts the duvet for me to climb in. He walks around to the other side of the huge bed and pulls me into his arms, so my head is against his now bare chest. "Sleep baby, I've got you," he whispers into my hair as I close my eyes and sleep drags me under again.

Chapter Fifty

LOGAN

I wake up to the sound of hushed talking out on the landing. I check Chelsea is still asleep before climbing out of bed and heading out to see what's going on.

"Are you trying to wake the whole house? Or just me," I moan, rubbing my face. Both turn around to face me as I approach.

"Sorry man, I was just checking how everything went with Prince," Calvin sighs, rubbing his neck. I turn to Drew, who shrugs.

"Nothing to tell. He's been warned what will happen if he ever comes near them again and signed the paperwork regarding Luna."

"No questions asked?"

Drew shakes his head, and I nod, feeling like something has finally gone right today.

"What's going on?"

We all turn to see Chelsea standing in the doorway in nothing by my t-shirt, looking gorgeous with her bed hair.

"Nothing, darling, we were just talking. We didn't mean

to wake you," Calvin says, walking up to her and placing a soft kiss on her lips.

"I wasn't in a deep sleep," she sighs before looking around at us. She looks us each up and down as if checking us out. I see a small smirk on Drew's face as he walks up to her and backs her against the door frame, pressing his body tightly against hers.

"Anything your men could do to help?" he asks before kissing her lightly against the lips. A smile appears as she looks directly at me as Drew kisses her neck. I feel myself getting rock hard; when I look at Calvin, I see he's watching just as intently as Drew kisses her on the lips and slides his hand between her legs, which open slightly, giving him better access. Drew lifts her t-shirt with one hand whilst moving her thong to the side and burying his fingers inside her.

"You are so wet. Is that for us?" he asks as he removes his fingers so they glisten in the light for us all to see.

"Fuck," I growl as I palm my cock. "Get her on the bed."

Drew grabs her ass and lifts her so she can wrap her legs around his waist and carries her into the room. He lays her on the bed and makes short work of stripping her bare. As Calvin and Drew both step back to strip out of their clothes, I drop to my knees between her legs, dragging her so her sweet pussy is in my face. I take one finger and rub it around her entrance. Fuck I have never seen anything as beautiful as this woman's pussy when she is aroused.

"So wet and fucking ready," I groan as I watch one, then two of my fingers slide into her entrance. She makes that sweet sound that escapes her the first time you insert a finger or cock into her. It's a noise I could listen to over and over again.

"How does she taste tonight?" Calvin asks over my shoulder. I move out of the way slightly without removing my fingers.

"As sweet as always, try it for yourself."

Calvin runs his tongue over her clit as I fuck her with my fingers. I hear him hum, causing Chelsea to moan again. He sucks on her clit and slowly lets it slip from his lips with a slight pop.

"Perfection," he sighs as he climbs onto the bed and kisses her on the lips while Drew comes in beside me and starts licking her pussy.

"Do you remember a discussion we had that night I fucked you from behind whilst you held on to the back of the sofa?" I hear Calvin whisper to her.

"Yes," she gasps as Drew sucks on her clit.

"We talked about two of us doing you simultaneously, but we never discussed all of us. Do you think we could combine the two options so all of us can be inside you at the same time?"

Drew and I both look at Chelsea and Calvin, but they are grinning at each other.

"We could try," Chelsea says nervously.

"Are you sure?" he asks her, and she nods whilst her smile turns into a grin. Her pussy tightens around my fingers, causing me to smile.

"I don't know what you have planned, but fuck I'm loving how much it's turning you on. Your pussy has just sucked my fingers deeper," I groan as I reposition my dick which is painfully hard. Calvin looks at us and smiles.

"Before Houdini decided to finally join the party, I asked Chels if she would ever consider sleeping with Bambi and me at the same time?" he explains, grinning at Chelsea. "I showed her two options. One where she sucked on one of our cocks whilst the other fucked her. Or, two where one of us fucked her sweet pussy as the other took her ass."

"Fuck," Drew and I both curse together, and Calvin grins at us smugly. I stand up and remove my fingers from between her legs as I lean over her and press a kiss to her lips.

"You don't have to do anything you don't want to. You never have to do more than you want, not with us." I look deep into her eyes, looking for any sign of apprehension, but there's none.

"I want you all in me at the same time. I've been thinking about it for a while." She brushes some hair from my face before looking at the others beside us.

"I belong to all of you, and I want us to try this."

I kiss her hard on the mouth, letting my lips and tongue devour her as she moans. I look behind me and see Drew's face buried between her legs as he eats her up, just the way she loves it. I continue to kiss her as he licks her until I can feel her body starting to shudder underneath me. She moans straight into my mouth, and fuck, it feels amazing. There's something about the way the four of us come together like this that feels so fucking right.

Listening and feeling the way Chelsea is reacting to another man giving her pleasure right underneath me, would it make me hard if it was anyone else? Hell no, I would straight up kill the fucker. But when it's Drew or Calvin, making her squirm and cry out with pleasure, fuck, it's hot as shit.

"Oh shit!" Chelsea cries out, instantly slamming a hand over her mouth in fear of waking Luna as Calvin and I chuckle at her.

"I'm going to buy us a huge house and make sure every room is soundproof because the sounds you make when you cum are fucking beautiful," I groan in her ear before kissing her neck.

"I need you," she groans as Drew removes himself from between her legs. "I need you all; you complete me."

I smile as I climb off her and stand at the bottom of the bed.

"Which of you wants her mouth and which her pussy? Her ass is mine."

Drew rolls his eyes as he climbs on the bed and kisses Chelsea, who licks his lips. I love how she reacts to the taste of herself in our mouths.

"I want to be up this end. I can't wait to see how you look as you take us all," he says, grinning. Chelsea smiles as she lifts up and kisses him again.

Calvin climbs between her legs, nudging his way up her body as he kisses her from her stomach up. Drew seems to know what's coming as he moves backwards just in time for Calvin to roll them so Chelsea is on top of him—her perfect peach of an ass in front of me. I can't stop myself from rubbing it before laying one slap on it. Chelsea cries out and looks over her shoulder at me.

"I told you one day I would spank you," I wink as she chuckles at me.

"And I told you, you might like it," Calvin adds from beneath her. I watch as he grabs her hips and lowers her hard and fast onto his hard cock.

"Fuck!" she cries out as her back arches and her head rolls back.

"Do it again," Calvin calls out as he thrusts into her, and I spank her in time with him impaling her.

"Oh my god, yes!" Chelsea cries out as Drew kneels in front of her.

"Wait a second, Bambi, I need to get her ready," I say,

grabbing hold of her perfect cheeks and rimming her back entrance with my tongue. Calvin holds himself still as Chelsea wiggles and squirms on top of him. I grin to myself as I spank her again. Her head shoots around to look at me over her shoulder.

"Stop moving; otherwise, you will get another one," I warn.

"And if I can't stay still?" she asks, frowning at me.

"Then I won't be able to do this." I rim her again and hear her crying out in pleasure, but this time she stays perfectly still. "That's what I thought," I point out as I wink at her and go back to licking her asshole, getting it nice and wet before sliding one finger into her tight hole.

"I don't know if you will be able to take me tonight, baby. I need some lube. You are far too tight."

"Bambi, my top drawer in the nightstand," Calvin calls and Drew winks before jumping off the bed.

"Do I want to ask why you have lube?" Chelsea asks, grinning down at him. Calvin shrugs as he smiles back.

"Wanking dry doesn't do it for me, and since I've met you, I've been as horny as a teenage boy," he smirks before Chelsea leans in and kisses him. Her ass is there right in front of me, begging for me to continue eating it, which I happily do whilst waiting for Drew, who comes rushing back into the room a few seconds later.

I make short work of lubing Chelsea's ass and my fingers before sliding one back into her. She is so perfect and tight. I can't help but wonder if we are still not going to be able to do this tonight. But Calvin continues to fuck her pussy, bringing her closer and closer to an orgasm that slowly she starts to open up and relax, and I can add a second finger as we work together, making our girl scream out with pleasure.

I look to Drew as she starts to come back down and give him a nod before positioning my hard cock at her entrance.

"If it gets too much, call red, baby," I instruct her as I massage her cheeks. I hear her agree, and slowly I start to push my cock into her tight hole. "Fuck, baby, you were made to take me," I growl as I slowly but surely start to get deeper until she has taken all of me.

For a moment, everything stops as she cries out through another orgasm, and we worry we are overstimulating her, but as always, our woman surprises us and gives us the go-ahead.

For the next ten minutes, we are all in heaven. All three of us fuck our woman together, it's not perfect, and I know we are going to have no problem working at it until we find the best way for this to work. But it's another way for us all to feel complete and together.

"Fuck baby, I can't hold out much more," I gasp as I watch Drew's face and see that he, too, is about to blow his load. He grips the hair on the back of her head and thrusts deep into her mouth as I push deeper into her ass, both of us filling her with our release at the same time as Calvin cries out from below.

We all fall into a sweaty, very happy pile. I hold on to my woman from behind as she rests her head on Calvin's chest, and Drew holds her hand from behind Calvin.

"Are you ever going to bring up the small matter of you calling me your fiancée today?" I hear Chelsea ask as Drew chuckles from beside Calvin.

"I thought you would reject the title of wife," I chuckle into her neck as I kiss her.

"You guessed right," she scorns before looking over her shoulder at me as Calvin and Drew both laugh. I lean forward and press a kiss to the tip of her nose before lying my head on the pillow beside her.

"That is a conversation for another day. For now, I just want to sleep with you in my arms," I whisper as Chelsea hums and lies down next to me.

"Fine," she sighs as I watch her eyes close. "But just so you know, I didn't hate the idea, just the fact I can only marry one of you," she whispers as sleep quickly takes her under. I find both Drew and Calvin watching me, and we share a look, knowing that one day, it is a serious conversation we plan on having with our woman. But now is not the time.

I look around at us all, and my heart feels fuller than it has ever. I nearly lost everyone in this bed today: my brothers, the love of my life, as well as my daughter sleeping peacefully in the room across the hall. But here we are, all safe and together, just where we are meant to be. It's a future I thought I had lost forever when I lost Angie. But now I know the best was still to come.

Chapter Fifty-One

CALVIN

Fuck, today's been harder than I anticipated. I tighten my arm around Chelsea, who is leaning against me as she talks to one of the girls from the office. I look around at the sea of black and white and hate to see so many people I know who usually seem happy and carefree, looking so sombre and hurting.

Today, it's Geralt Young's funeral. It's been one week to the day since the attack on the building, and things are still far from normal for any of us.

Yesterday, we attended Roger's funeral. Seeing his young children clinging to their mother, who was heartbroken, hit home for the three of us. We know there are some things we will need to discuss now we have Chelsea and Luna to think about. But that will have to wait, as tomorrow we have Hugo's funeral and the day after, we are attending another one for the armed forces guy who died in the tunnel collapse. He lost his life getting me back the love of mine; going to his funeral is the least that we can do.

I spot Jason and Sean O'Reilly across the room where

Jasmine is sitting with Abigail, Geralt's daughter. Not far from them, I spot Maximus and Christian talking to Gethin and Molly. Not far from the O'Reillys are three of their guards, Layton, Terry and Gordon.

"I'm going to speak to the old team. Will you be okay for a minute?" I ask Chelsea while pressing a kiss on her head. She looks up at me with her bloodshot eyes and nods.

"Want me to come with you?" she asks. I shake my head and give her a small smile.

"You're fine. I'll only be a moment anyway," I reply, kissing her on the lips before excusing myself and heading over to the guards I used to work with.

I shake each of their hands as we exchange various versions of pleasantries. Terry's team took over a couple of our jobs so we could mourn the loss of Rogers and Hugo as well as look after our family.

"How's Luna doing?" Layton asks as I shake his hand. I let out a deep breath and shrug.

"She has nightmares; bless her. She wants one of us to sleep in with her each night, or she sleeps between her mom and one of us."

"She went through a lot that day. It's no surprise she is struggling to be away from you all," Layton sighs. He has been around a couple of times to see Luna and bring her little gifts. Jasmine came with him a couple of days ago and sat with her for a while whilst we went to see Hugo's family. When we came back, Jasmine was teaching her to dance and told us to enroll her in a class as she has a real talent. I already plan on doing it as soon as possible. I want to give that amazing little girl the world. She deserves it and so much more.

"Are they both still staying with you all?" Gordon asks. I nod and look over to where Chelsea is still talking to the receptionist. Drew is standing nearby watching her as Logan looks like he would rather be anywhere but here.

"Yeah, I don't think anyone wants to go back to the two households, but the house is getting a little crowded now. We could do with a bigger one. I just have no idea where even to start looking."

"I could help with that."

I turn to see Jason smiling behind me. "I couldn't help overhearing. I own a house I bought before we decided to all share and wait for Jazzy. I could show you around and see what you think. It's big enough, for sure. It would be ideal for you guys."

I stare at him for a moment in disbelief. Of course, this man would have a huge house just sitting there empty; most of the O'Reillys have more money than sense.

"Would I be able to have a look at it before discussing it with the guys?"

Jason looks at his watch and then around the room.

"I have a spare hour if you are free now; we could have a look around and work out a price if you like it. So, you have some figures to tell the guys."

I tell him I will be right back, head over to the others, and tell them I'm going to meet them back at the house. We came in Logan's car, and they don't ask any questions when I say I'm going with Jason. I place a kiss on Chelsea's cheek and promise not to be long, looking forward to the possibility of finding us all a new home we can share together.

Chelsea

I lie on the sofa with Luna in my arms as I try to watch the film with her. My eyelids are heavy, and I feel physically and mentally drained.

"Sweetheart, why don't you both go to bed for an hour? You might feel better for it," Drew suggests, running his hand over Luna's head.

"I'm fine, Daddy," she yawns, making us both chuckle.

"Neither of you are fine. You have had a really tough week and need to rest," Logan declares as he walks into the room, stirring a cup of hot chocolate for Luna.

"You've had a tough week, too, and you don't need a nap every day," I point out as Luna sits up and takes her drink from him.

"I don't mean this as it sounds, but we have had much worse," he says as he presses a kiss to my head. I look up at him and feel even sillier for feeling like this when I've been through a lot less than they have in their time as SEALs. Logan, as always, quickly picks up on my change of mood and shakes his head.

"Please don't think what you two went through is any less important than what we did. We were paid professionals who went through years of training before we went out in any really dangerous situations. You were just going about a normal-ish day. You didn't ask to be taken hostage, and you certainly didn't ask to be separated from your daughter in the worst possible way." He lets out a sigh as he leans over and presses a kiss to the top of my head.

"Go and curl up in our bed with Luna, put a film on, and at least then, if you fall asleep, you will be in a comfier place."

I look up at him and see the concern in his warm, amber eyes.

"Okay, I need to do something first," I reply as I go to climb off the sofa. Logan holds out his hand and pulls me to my feet and straight into his arms.

"Want me to cook your favourite for dinner tonight?" he says, kissing my lips.

"Put a pin in that thought. I have something to show you all!" Calvin announces, stalking into the room, looking very smug. Luna jumps off the sofa and into his arms. "Hey, Luna Bug, want to go for a drive and see something cool?" he asks, grinning.

"What?" she asks excitedly.

"Pip, the girls were just going to rest," Logan starts, but I place a hand on his chest and smile.

"It's fine. We will probably feel better for getting out of the house, anyway."

Logan looks down at me, and I can see he's unconvinced, so I flash him a big smile, earning me an eye roll.

"Come on then, get your coats; we are leaving now."

Chapter Fifty-Two

CHELSEA

I look out the window at the passing scenery and love how beautiful and green this area is. It's not quite in the middle of nowhere, but there are only farms and manor houses around. Far from the busy town life we live in.

"You okay, darling? You've been quiet since we got in the car," Calvin asks as I turn to look at him whilst he drives.

"Just wondering what you are up to," I laugh. He's not stopped smirking since we left the house. He had insisted that Luna and I travel with him, with Logan and Drew following us in another car.

"We need a bigger car, Daddy." Luna points out as she waves over her shoulder at the others behind us. She has done this every few minutes, and yet they are still smiling and waving back every time.

"I know, Bug, I might have something in mind," Calvin answers, checking once again that the others are still behind us.

"Is that what you are up to? Have you got a new car?" I

ask. Calvin just grins further as he lifts my hand and presses a kiss to my knuckles.

"Stop trying to guess because you won't," he laughs, suddenly flicking on his indicator and taking a right so we are off the main road and going up a narrow one. I look around before noticing a large house coming into view.

Calvin drives up the driveway and parks outside the main building before turning to me, winking and getting out of the car. He opens Luna's door for her and holds it whilst she climbs out. I open my door and am just getting out when Logan and Drew climb out of their own car, which is now parked behind us.

"Whose house is this, Pippin?" Logan asks as Luna rushes around the car and towards a tree where there is an old tyre swing hanging from it.

"Princess, don't go on that; it looks too old to swing from!" Logan calls, causing Luna to stop in her tracks. Walking around the back of the car to where the three guys are standing, I look around, confused.

"At the moment, it belongs to Jason, but he has offered it to us at a very reasonable price if we want it," Calvin announces. All of us come to a standstill and stare at him.

"This is our house?" Luna asks excitedly as Calvin picks her up and puts her on his hip.

"Not yet," he answers before looking at the three of us. "I don't know about you guys, but I hate the thought of us all living in two separate households again. But neither of our houses is big enough for us all to live comfortably together. But this house is."

I turn from Calvin and look up at the house. It is beautiful and certainly looks big enough to house all of us. I look back at Logan and Drew and can see them both looking back at the house.

"Is that what you two want as well? For us to find a way to live all together?" I ask nervously. Both guys' heads snap to look at me.

"Of course!" they say in unison.

"I have been dreading you guys going back to your place," Drew answers. "I just didn't know how to approach the subject with you."

"Same here. I have loved having you both at home, and I never want to go back to only seeing you a couple of nights a week," Logan adds. "There is no way we could all stay at yours, and ours is getting a little cramped. Luna won't want us sleeping in with her for much longer." He holds out his hands, and Luna jumps straight into his arms from Calvin's. "To be honest, I don't sleep well in there as she's a fidget bum," he laughs as he tickles her, and she starts squirming and squealing with laughter. I look back up at the house as I blink back the tears.

"You do want to stay with us, don't you, darling?" Calvin asks, taking my hand.

"Of course I do! We both do. I was scared you would all have had enough of us," I admit. All three guys instantly start arguing, declaring their love for us.

"Come on then, let's look inside, and we can have a chat about it and sum up all our options," I say, smiling as I look back at the house.

"You are going to fall in love with this place," Calvin declares as he takes my hand and guides me to the front door, where he stops and pulls a set of keys from his pocket.

"What? He just gave you the keys to his mansion?" Logan asks with a cocked brow. Calvin shrugs as he unlocks the door and then rushes in to disable the alarm.

"I saved his life three times, helped rescue Jasmine and

took a knife for him once as well. Think he knows he can trust me."

"Fair enough," Logan laughs as we all walk into the entrance hall, which is huge! From the ceiling hangs the most beautiful chandelier.

"It's a palace!" Luna exclaims as Logan puts her down. "Mummy, look at those stairs!" she giggles, rushing over to the grand staircase that the three of us could easily walk up side by side.

"There are six large rooms on this floor, including a kitchen big enough for a hotel and a laundry room. There is a small apartment behind the three-car garage, which Jason said is usually for the staff to sleep in. We could use rooms as an office, lounge, dining room, and a large conservatory, which I'm sure Luna would love as a play-room. But come and look upstairs at the best bit!" he exclaims excitedly. He pulls me towards the stairs, and we rush up them.

At the top of the staircase is a hall full of doors.

"There are two big bathrooms and four bedrooms, two of which have en suites, as well as two bedrooms and a bathroom on the next level." Calvin turns around and grins at us as we all look around. Luna grabs my hand and drags me to the nearest door. Behind it is a beautiful bathroom with a walk-in shower, a large bathtub, two sinks to one side, and a door on the other, which no doubt leads to one of the bedrooms. This means the two separate bathrooms are the same as en suites anyway.

We spend the next half an hour exploring the whole house before heading into the grounds, where we all stand back and watch Luna run around the overgrown flower beds and to the back of the garden, where there is a paddock big enough for a horse.

"So, what do you all think?" Calvin asks as he steps behind me and wraps his arms around my waist.

"It's beautiful and certainly has enough space for us all," Drew says from the bench he is sitting on with Logan.

"How much is it?" Logan asks, being the sensible one, as always.

"It's a steal," Calvin starts, but Logan gives him a look.

"How much, Pippin?" he asks firmly.

"Jason has offered it at a reduced price of one million pounds."

"A MILLION!" all three of us yell together as we stare at Calvin.

"No bank is ever going to agree to give us a mortgage for a million pounds!" I point out as disappointment washes through me.

"We don't need a mortgage; Jason has offered us a payment plan," Calvin answers as I frown at him. Calvin is still grinning as he looks at the others. "We brought our house outright between us; if we sell it, then that cash is rightfully ours other than the legal fees. So, there is a little over two hundred and a half thousand pounds." Calvin then turns to me. "How much was yours?"

"One hundred and fifty," I answer. "It was everything left to us from Leon's parents," I add.

"Would you want to invest all of it into a house for all of us?" Logan asks. I look at him and shrug.

"I can't see why not. It would be nice to put some of it into savings for Luna to cover university costs, and she is still on about the dance school, so that won't be cheap."

"So, if you put half in savings, which we will start adding to, and make sure she has more than enough for when it's needed, we could potentially pay Jason three hundred thousand up front."

"And what about the rest? Surely, he wants the money as soon as possible?" Logan asks. But Calvin looks at him and shakes his head.

"No, he wants us to be happy. It's not like he needs the cash anyway, and he doesn't need the property, so he is offering us the house as a loan. We agree on how much we can afford to pay back, and he will legally sign the house over to us."

"And what happens if there is an issue and we can't make the payments?" Drew asks.

"Then we discuss it with him like adults, and he has already said that unless he thinks we are lying to him, then he is happy for us to pay what we can when we can. There will obviously be a section in the agreement that he can take it back if we don't make reasonable payments, but I can't see why we couldn't. Business is getting better and better each month, and with our savings and other investments, we can afford to own this place outright in ten years.

A silence fills the air around us as we all start thinking about it all. I look down at Luna, who is happily singing to herself whilst running around. I look back at the house and can see us living here happily.

"It's certainly big enough for us all," Logan says quietly from his place on the bench.

"Are we seriously considering this?" Drew starts. "I mean, I'm all up for it as it's everything we could wish for in a home. It's close enough for Luna to stay in her school, so it won't take her away from her friends. It's close enough to both our works, and there is plenty of space in the house and around it."

All three guys look at me as I chew on my fingernails. Logan steps forward and pulls my finger from my mouth.

"What's holding you back?" he asks, running his

knuckles down my cheek. I open my mouth to answer nothing, but he gives me that cocked brow, and I know I need to be honest.

"What happens if you three decide you don't want to be with us? Or if one of you meets someone else?" I sigh, looking over at Luna, who is sitting on the grass picking daisies. "I know this works for the O'Reillys, but Christian is marrying Jasmine to make her an O'Reilly so they will all share a surname. We can never do that." I look at each of the guys.

"I could never marry just one of you, and Luna and I could never take one of your surnames and not the others. It's not like we could have a four-barrel surname." I take a deep sigh as I look at all three of my men individually. "It's something that scares me. Where would we all fit in legally? If one or all of you leave us, will we even be able to get another house?"

"This has been playing on your mind for a while, hasn't it?" Drew asks as he comes to stand with the rest of us. I nod and go to chew on my fingernail again.

"What if I said we have all been thinking and talking about it as well?" Calvin says, smiling at me.

"You have?"

All three guys nod and smile at me. Logan takes my hand in his and lifts it to his mouth.

"We discussed the same things the day we decided to approach this relationship with you. We were all worried about how we would feel if one of us married you or if you took one of our names. We decided that there was only one acceptable option. That we would take yours."

"What?" I feel my eyes bulge as my jaw drops. The guys chuckle as they all share a look.

"Hughes is your maiden. It's the name you chose to go

by when you were feeling your most vulnerable because it made you feel safe. So, why would we ask you to change that?" Drew offers, taking the hand Logan isn't holding. Calvin wraps his arms around my waist again from behind, holding me against him.

"We figured this isn't the most traditional relationship, so why stick to traditional rules? What's stopping us from taking your name? Absolutely nothing. As for legally, well, not that I think we will ever need to worry about it, but we all agreed that everything would be split between the four of us equally."

I look over my shoulder at Calvin as my eyes start to burn. He leans in and presses a kiss to my lips.

"We love you both, darling; you know we do. There is absolutely nothing we wouldn't do for you both. So, what do you say? Do you want to buy this huge house with us?"

I look between them all, unable to stop the smile that spread across my face before replying.

"When can we move in?"

Epilogue

CALVIN

"You do realise it doesn't matter how you organise this place. She will just move everything again."

I turn around and see Logan and Drew standing behind me. I look at the kitchen cupboards and frown.

"What's wrong with the way I'm organising them? It all makes perfect sense having the plates and bowls there."

"Can you reach them easily?" Logan asks. I look at the cupboard and reach out to prove I can. "Now drop down a foot and see if you can reach them."

As soon as I squat down a little, I see the problem.

"Ahh."

"Yep, there is no way Chels could reach them," Logan laughs. He pats me on the shoulder, and they slump with defeat.

I thought I was doing a great job. I was sure she would be impressed with everything I had done in here. I sigh and start pulling the plates and bowls from the cupboard.

It's been three weeks since we decided to buy the house. Jason has agreed to let us decorate and start moving things in while our two houses are sold. In all fairness, he has been amazing.

All four of the O'Reillys and their security team have been here at some point, helping us decorate the bedrooms, lounges, dining room, kitchen, and everywhere in between. Terry and Logan spent three days in the garden, creating a play area for Luna and an area in the sun where we could all relax during the warmer months. I couldn't ask for more from my old work family.

Everything has been moving at a hundred miles an hour since the funeral. Geralt's son has taken over from his dad. McIntire and Christian O'Reilly have been helping him as much as possible while he learns the ropes. Abigail also wants to know more about the family business and is now Chelsea's assistant. Chelsea has been doing a fantastic job helping the family while they come to terms with Geralt's death, and I know they are so thankful for all she has done for them.

I hear a car pulling up outside, and we all share a smile before heading to the front door to welcome Luna and Chelsea home. Nothing compares to seeing our woman and daughter for the first time every evening. We try to be home as much as possible in the evening, and it has worked out well so far. We take turns to be on call to ensure two of us are always home to help Chelsea with Luna or just to be present. We missed the first six years of her life but plan on being here every day from now on. She is our daughter, and there is nothing we wouldn't do for her.

Logan gets to the door first, and Luna throws herself into his arms.

"Papa! Guess what happened in school today!"

Luna has given us all different names now, as all three of us, being Daddy, was getting a little confusing.

"What, princess?" he asks, kissing her cheek as she leans back in his arms.

"I got all my spelling right, and I moved up a reading stage!" she exclaims happily.

"That's amazing, Luna Bug! Well done!" I exclaim as she jumps from Logan's arms and into mine.

"I got four stars from the teacher and have the most in the class now, Pops!" she adds as I kiss her cheek.

"Does this mean we get to take you out to celebrate?" Drew asks as I hand the excited little girl to him.

"Can we go to the place that does the ice cream in a glass, Daddy?" she asks him, smiling.

"If that's where you want to go, I can't see why not," he kisses her cheek before placing her back on her feet. I look at Chelsea and notice her and Logan whispering to each other. Chelsea looks pale and close to tears.

"Luna, can you go and have a look at your new room and put the toys where you want them, please? I will be up in a minute to help," I say, realising that something is wrong with her mum, and the three of us need to check she is okay.

"Ok, Pops," she calls, rushing up the stairs, singing to herself as we watch her disappear from view.

I turn and look at Chelsea and know that something is seriously wrong.

"Is everything okay?" I ask, taking a step forward at the same time as Drew. Chelsea looks up with tears in her eyes as she shakes her head.

"Baby, we can't help you unless you tell us what's going on," Logan says softly, placing his hand on her cheek. She looks up at him and bursts into tears.

"You're going to hate me," she cries as he drags her into his arms.

"Baby, no matter what's going on, we could never hate you."

I watch as her whole body shakes as she cries into his chest. It breaks my heart to see her so upset. We have seen her cry many times over the last few weeks since the incident at her work, but it feels different this time.

"Come on, let's head into the kitchen, and you can tell us what's going on," I say, stepping back whilst nodding towards the door that leads to the kitchen and utility room.

The four of us walk into the kitchen together. Logan keeps his arm around Chelsea's shoulder as he guides her to the small table we have here and places her on a seat. Drew walks over with a glass of water and some kitchen roll for her. Chelsea thanks him as she dries her face.

"I'm so sorry," she whispers, refusing to look at us. I squat down in front of her and take her hands in mine.

"Why don't you tell us what's happened. We can't help you until you do," I explain. Chelsea takes a deep breath and starts fiddling with the tissue in her hands.

"I haven't been feeling too well recently. At first, I put it down to stress after everything, but when I wasn't feeling better as the weeks went on, I decided to have some blood tests done. I have a history of vitamin D and Iron deficiency, and sometimes I need infusions to help."

"Why didn't you tell us you were feeling so run down? We would have made sure you rested more," Drew points out.

"The blood tests showed something, didn't they?" Logan asks. The concern in his voice causes my heart to race when she nods.

"I didn't know the doctor was ordering this particular test until today when they phoned to tell me the results." Chelsea bursts into tears again, and I pull her into my arms.

I look up at my best friends and can see the terror I'm feeling mirrored on their faces. All the different illnesses go through my mind as I hold the crying, shaking Chelsea against my chest.

"I didn't know; I swear I had no idea," she cries. I know then that whatever she's been told she has will affect all of us.

"Whatever it is, darling, we will face it together," I reassure her as I lean back from her a little to look into her tear-filled eyes. Logan drops beside me and cups her cheek, forcing her to look at him.

"We are a family, and we will deal with whatever comes our way as one. But for us to do that, you have to be honest with us and tell us what the doctor said."

Chelsea looks at him for a second before nodding once.

"I'm pregnant."

"What?" the three of us exclaim together as Chelsea bursts into tears again.

"I thought I had another year of my implant, but I should have had it changed six months ago," she cries into her hands.

"Is that all?" I exclaim, sitting back on my heels.

"What do you mean, *is that all*? I'm fucking pregnant!" Chelsea exclaims, her eyes bulging. "You can't tell me you actually want a kid with me?"

"Why the fuck not?" Logan says from beside me.

"Because I don't even know which of you is the father?"

"Does it matter? We will all bring them up anyway," Drew points out behind us. Chelsea looks around at us as if she's speechless.

"Even if this were planned, we wouldn't have cared who the father was. Luna has three daddies, and so will any baby you have with us," I point out.

"You want a baby with me? You aren't mad?"

"Sweetheart, do you want to have a baby with us?" Drew asks. Chelsea looks around us all.

"I didn't think you would want one with me," she whispers as Logan laughs.

"I can't think of anything I want more than to have a baby with you. I was biding my time until I mentioned it." Logan looks from me to Drew, and I see the pure joy in his eyes.

Before Chelsea and Luna came into our lives, it was as if Logan was surviving from day to day. But now he smiles and laughs more than he has since losing Angie. I know the idea of Chelsea being pregnant is a dream come true for him.

"Sweetheart, now you know we are okay with you being pregnant; I want you to think about what you want. If you don't want another baby, you say the word, and we will do whatever you want. You are the one who has to do the hardest bits," Drew says as he moves beside Chelsea. "Whatever you decide, you have our complete support."

Chelsea looks around us all nervously.

"I always wished I could have another baby," she whispers nervously.

"Then it's a good job you are pregnant," I smile.

"Are we doing this then? Are we having a baby?" she asks, looking around at the three of us, who are all smiling back at her.

I reach up and place a hand on her stomach as Drew and Logan do the same. The three of us have been to hell and back together more times than we can count. We have faced terrorists, explosions, hostage-takers and death. We have supported and loved each other through our darkest days and fought to keep each other alive.

Now, we face a whole new challenge of fatherhood together. Nothing could prepare us for what is coming our way, but as always, we will face it together, side by side, this time with our daughter and the love of our lives beside us. I always saw these guys as my brothers, and now, there is no greater bond than being fathers together. They may have always been family, but now we have created a family unit I can't wait to grow.

I look up as Chelsea places her hands over ours to find her smiling at us. I lift and press my lips to hers before smiling at her.

"Looks like we are."

Bonus Scene

CALVIN

Looking around the lounge, I know we made the right decision to come back here tonight. Chelsea is looking more relaxed than she has in days. She's curled up in the corner of the sofa, her feet on my lap and her head on Logans. I picked her up a thick, super soft blanket, which she loves, and we fed her Chinese takeaway, whiskey and snacks. She now looks ready to sleep, and I think she would if it wasn't for the fact we are watching "The Lord of The Rings", which is apparently her favourite film as well as Logans. They have been comparing notes and taking the piss out of me all the way through, and I have no doubt they will be watching the second one at some point tomorrow before we head back to pick Luna up and take her home. If they do watch it, I know it will be the perfect time for me to go for a run or hit the gym, as I plan on being as far away from them as possible.

I watch the screen and realise we are getting to the part which influenced my nickname. I can see the smirk creeping onto Chelsea's face as she looks up at Logan and then me.

"Stop it," I warn playfully.

"What? I didn't say anything!" she protests as Logan laughs, running his hand up and down her arm. I wait as she continues to watch the film, but there's no missing the way her smile is getting bigger the closer we get to the moment. With perfect timing, Chelsea turns to me with a huge grin and snaps.

"Fool of a Took!"

"That's it!" I grab her calves and drag her closer to me as she squeals, laughing. As soon as she is close enough, I start to tickle her, but she's quick and rolls off the sofa before trying to get away. Only to tangle herself up in her blanket. I take that as my cue and pounce towards her as she scrambles away and towards Drew, who is laughing from his chair.

"Help!" she squeals, laughing, grabbing at his leg as she tries to climb onto his lap, but I pin her between him and me as I tickle her. Dragging her to the floor, Drew drops down with her to help me.

"Stop!" she laughs hysterically as we all laugh at her.

"Not until you admit you like me best!" I tease, knowing she never would.

"NO!" she yells as she continues trying to get away from me, but the more she wiggles, the more turned on I am becoming. Logan comes over and tries to save her, but I knock his hands away laughing.

"Say it!" I laugh as she squeals louder.

"No! I love you all the same!"

I stop tickling her as she looks at all three of us, staring back at her, shocked to hear her using the L word. I think we have all told her we love her, but after everything she has been through, we knew it would take longer for her to feel safe enough to allow herself to feel anything that strong back.

Chelsea is between Drew's legs, pressed against him by my body as Logan stands beside us.

"I love you," she whispers, looking at all of us before zoning her attention onto me. "*All* of you."

I grab the back of her head and kiss her, instantly demanding access to her mouth and tongue. The need to show her what those three words mean to us overwhelms me. She throws her arms around my neck and kisses me back with just as much passion. Drew leans in and kisses her neck as I feel his hand slide between us and rest on her stomach. Chelsea lets out a deep moan, and I know all her fantasies are about to come true. I will make sure of it.

I stop kissing her and smile before sliding her top up to find her braless. I look to Logan, who's standing over us, watching as Drew continues to kiss her neck as I take her nipple between my teeth. The second a gasp leaves her lips, Logan grabs the back of her head and kisses her, confirming the film is over and the fun is about to begin.

As I tease her nipple between my teeth and squeeze her other breast, I feel Drew's hand drift lower until he is grasping her sweet pussy. Chelsea lets out the most beautiful sound as she moves her head to kiss Drew on the lips. Logan stands to the side of us as he loosens his sweatpants and pulls his hard cock out to stroke it. He looks as hard as I feel; I sit back, pulling Chelsea up with me, freeing her from Drew's lips before pulling her top off.

"I think Logan needs a hand, Darling," I wink before leaning her back so she is still sandwiched between Drew and me. I watch as she looks at Logan as he kneels beside us and takes hold of his cock.

"Fuck, that's it," he moans as he steps forward, giving

her better access. I know we all plan on fucking her tonight, and I want to be the first to make her cum.

I move myself back a little and whisper for her to lift her hips as I take hold of her shorts and slide them down, removing the last items of her clothing, leaving her naked and open to us. Drews's hand cups her bare sex again, his finger circling her clit, causing her to gasp and moan. Fuck. Why is watching him giving her pleasure so much of a turn-on? I've never had a threesome before, let alone a four-way, but now I plan on having them as often as possible.

As Drew continues to circle her clit I slowly slide one finger into her and play with that special spot. Just as slowly, I insert a second finger and curse as she clamps around them. Fuck she is so perfect.

Removing my fingers, I take Drew's hand, move it down a little, and watch as he slides his fingers into her, the three of us letting out a moan at the same time. I sit and watch him finger fuck her for a moment, obsessed with how it looks, before leaning forward and running my tongue around the edge of her clit. Chelsea gasps loudly as I feel her hips lift as she grinds against my face and Drew's hand.

I look up in time for Logan to move even closer and run his dick over her lips. Fuck me; when he slides into her mouth, I grow even harder in my sweats. The sight of this woman sucking off another man is mesmerising, and I could cum from it alone.

As I continue to lick and suck on her clit, Drew gets rougher with her as she gags on Logan's cock. I can feel her getting closer and closer to her first climax of the night, and it's going to be beautiful.

"That's it, baby, suck on my cock as the others get you off," Logan growls as he starts thrusting his hips harder, and I watch, knowing how amazing her mouth feels.

Chelsea's moaning around his cock now and has to remove it from her mouth as she screams out through an orgasm that floods my mouth. When this amazing woman cums she shakes from head to toe, and it is a beautiful sight to behold. She loses all control, and her body pushes her past her limits naturally.

I continue to suck and lick up her juices, making her orgasm last as long as possible before she becomes overstimulated and begs me to stop whilst attempting to wiggle away from me. I chuckle, reluctantly moving away from her and watch as she gasps for breath, the three of us watching the fantastic woman we love shake with the pleasure we gave her.

"Bed," she gasps, looking at each of us. "Please, I need each of you."

I stand as Logan steps back, and Drew lifts her into his arms. As soon as I'm no longer touching her, I long for the feel of her skin under my fingertips, to taste that sweet pussy again, but more importantly, to bury my cock deep within her.

I follow the others up to Logan's room, which is at the far end of the house and the bigger of the three. He has a queen-sized bed, which is why we agreed that if we were all going to sleep together tonight, it would be in here.

Drew places Chelsea carefully on the bed as we all strip out of our clothes. As soon as he is naked, he crawls between her legs and kisses her on the mouth.

"Pick a safe word," he whispers against her lips. Chelsea's eyes widen.

"Do I need one?"

Logan sits on the bed beside her and brushes some hair from her face.

"We have never done anything like this before and want

to be sure we don't hurt you or make you do anything you don't like."

"If things become too intense, or you don't like something, all you have to do is say the safe word, and things will stop instantly," I add, sitting on the other side of her.

"Can't I just say stop?" she frowns. Smiling, I lean in and brush my lips against hers.

"Do you know how many times you tell us "Don't stop", it would easily become confusing," I explain. Chelsea nods as she realises we're right. "The last thing we want is for you to hate this and think it wouldn't work. So, for the first few times, at least, we will have a safe word which hopefully you never have to say."

Chelsea looks around at the three of us, and we see her visibly relax.

"Red."

"Sounds good to me, Sweetheart. Red it is," Drew says as he crawls down the bed, covering her body in kisses as he goes. Logan leans in to kiss her lips whilst cupping her face lovingly.

"I love how much you trust us," he whispers, sliding his hand down to her breast.

"You would never make me do anything I didn't want to," Chelsea replies, causing my heart to swell.

"No, we wouldn't, Darling," I whisper as I kiss her with Logan watching on.

"Oh shit!" Chelsea gasps, pulling away from me, her eyes rolling back with pleasure. I look down the bed to see Drew eating her sweet pussy, his hand moving between her legs as he fucks her with his fingers again.

"Fuck I love the noises you make when you are close to coming apart," Logan says from the other side of her.

"As well as the way she tastes as she cums," I add, licking my lips where I can still taste her sweet cum.

"Drew," Chelsea cries out as her back arches off the bed, and she grabs at the sheets for something to hold on to.

"That's it, baby, be as loud as you like tonight. No one will hear you," Logan grins before taking her nipple between his teeth.

"Yes," she screams. Drew and Logan give her everything. She rushes to that release she so desperately needs, but the look on Drew's face tells me he is planning on making her work for it. "More," she cries out, gasping for breath as Drew sits back on his heels and takes hold of her hips.

"Do you need more, Sweetheart? How much more?" he asks as she nods.

"All of you," she cries out with frustration as he runs one finger from her entrance to her clit. "Please, Drew. Fuck me."

"With pleasure," he growls through gritted teeth as he takes hold of her hips and drags her down the bed towards him as he kneels up, taking her hips with him as he thrusts into her.

"Fuck," the four of us moan at the same time.

"I never thought I would get so aroused by watching someone else fuck my woman, but shit," Logan gasps as he takes his dick in his hand.

"Right!" I hiss through gritted teeth as I start stroking my own cock.

For a few moments, the only sound in the room is Chelsea moaning as Drew fucks her hard and fast, his balls slapping against her ass as he pounds into her again and again.

"So fucking perfect," I moan as her eyes find mine. She

looks down at my hand around my cock and reaches out to take hold of it. "Don't forget Houdini, Darling," I sigh as she starts to stroke me. I close my eyes and feel her hand tightening around my cock as Drew and Logan both curse through gritted teeth. I open my eyes and watch the scene before me.

Drew continues to fuck her as she grips Logan and me. Her hands move up and down our cocks in time to Drew's pounding her pussy. It is a beautiful sight to behold, and I don't know how much longer I can take it all before I blow my load.

"Yes, oh god, yes," Chelsea cries out as she squeezes her eyes shut. "I'm gonna," Chelsea gasps before crying out as she cums all over Drews cock.

"Fuck," he curses through gritted teeth as he thrusts into her hard once more and moans through his own orgasm. Chelsea lets go of my cock as Drew drops down to kiss her hard as she throws her arms around his neck. Both of them gasping for breath from their orgasm.

"I fucking love you. So much. You are everything I ever wanted and more," I hear Drew gasp in her ear as she buries her face in his neck.

"I love you," she pants as he pulls away from her and places a small kiss on her lips whilst grinning before sitting back up and moving from between her legs.

Logan leans in and presses a kiss to her lips.

"How you doing, baby?"

I should have known he would be the most cautious of us tonight. He is so worried that she will decide all of us together is too much and run for the hills.

"Amazing," she answers as I let out a quiet sigh of relief. Chelsea reaches up to cup his cheek whilst kissing him. "I want you," I hear her whisper against his lips.

"Thank fuck, because I *need* you," he whispers back. He glances up at me, and I give him a nod to signal for him to go ahead.

Whilst Drew and Logan swap places, I lean in and kiss our woman on the lips as she smiles at me.

"Fancy having a little more fun?"

"More than we are already having?" she smirks at me. I don't let my eyes leave hers as I call out.

"Houdini, you up for taking her from behind?" I wink at her as I hear Logan quickly calling out in agreement. "On your hands and knees, Darling. I think I want to finish somewhere other than your pussy, for now."

Chelsea grins as she gets onto all four, so her ass is up in the air in front of Logan as I position myself at her mouth.

"Let's try one of the positions we discussed that evening," I whisper into her ear as she giggles and nods. Fuck, I love how this woman is up for anything. I don't think one lover would ever be enough for her. Thankfully, the three of us are all here for the long haul and eager to give our woman whatever she needs.

"What the?" Chelsea bucks in front of me as she looks over her shoulder at Logan, who is grinning with his hands on her ass.

"Trust me, baby, you will like it," he winks before he buries his head between her cheeks, and I realise he is rimming her.

"Fuck," Chelsea moans as her head rolls back and eyes close.

"Oh, I think she loves it," Drew chuckles from beside us as he stands beside the bed, watching our woman. "Have you done anal stuff before?" he asks.

"Only a finger," she gasps as she smirks at me, and I wink.

"Would you do more?"

Chelsea nods as her eyes close, and she moans as Logan chuckles.

"Maybe not tonight, but soon," I add as I place a finger under her chin and apply pressure so she is looking at me. I thread my fingers into the hair at the back of her head and kiss her hard as she moans with pleasure.

"Open wide, baby; I need to feel that naughty mouth around my dick." I look up and catch Logan's attention. He removes his tongue from her ass and positions himself at her entrance. With a subtle nod, we both enter her at the same time, and she moans around my cock.

"Fuck," Logan and I growl together as we stay still for a moment, both trying desperately to hold off on the orgasm that's building in us all. The hardest part is that whilst we are trying not to cum, Chelsea has fallen over the edge and moans with her own release. Her mouth and pussy clamp around our cocks as she shudders and tenses from the pleasure that's cursing through her.

"Fuck that's better than any porno."

I look at Drew, who is holding onto his cock, which is starting to harden again. I take hold of Chelsea's hair and hold her head in place as I begin to fuck her mouth. I start off slow and gentle, but as soon as she moans again around my cock I know I have lost all restraint, and I start fucking her throat. Thankfully, I have done this a number of times before, and I'm aware of her limits.

For the next five minutes, Logan and I fuck our woman through two more orgasms before I feel my balls tightening, and I know I'm not going to last much longer.

"Fuck, baby," Logan roars as pushing into her once more and cums, which causes Chelsea to orgasm as well.

She sucks on my cock so hard that I slide even further down her throat as I empty my release into it.

I swear this woman could suck the soul from my body through my cock, as she takes everything I give her and doesn't even gag.

The three of us slowly come back to reality as I release Chelsea's hair and pull my softening cock from her mouth.

"Come here, Sweetheart," Drew says as he helps Chelsea, who is looking thoroughly fucked and half asleep, to lie down comfortably on the bed as I collapse beside her. Drew holds her from behind as she rests her head on my chest.

"Open your legs, baby," Logan instructs as he cleans her below with what looks like a wet flannel before drying her with a towel. Chelsea whispers a small thank you as he disappears and comes back to the bed before lying beside me.

It should probably bother me that my best friend is completely naked behind me, his cock mere inches from my ass, but it doesn't. We have seen each other naked so many times over the years; it doesn't even phase us anymore.

"You okay, Darling?" I ask, running a hand over her head. Chelsea nods and looks up at me, smiling. "Was it as good as you thought it would be?"

"Better," she grins before resting her head back on my chest. I move her slightly so she is lying on top of me, so all three of us can see her. "Think you can take a little more? As I don't think I could ever get enough of you," I smile as I start hardening again.

"I'm more than willing to make you scream a few more times," Logan says beside me as he lifts his head and kisses our woman.

"You guys are going to ruin me. You know that right?"

she smirks at the three of us. We all look at one another and grin.

"That's the whole point, baby. We need to ensure you never want another man ever again," Logan answers as I lift my hips and slowly ease my cock into her warm wet pussy.

"That won't be a problem," she gasps as her eyes roll back, and we start pleasuring her all over again.

Three Stepbrothers Save Christmas: Chapter One

VERITY

"I'm glad to hear your father is *finally* coming home for a bit."

Looking up from my book, I find Danielle King taking a seat beside me.

"How do you know? I only found out this morning," I ask, picking up my mug and sipping my latte. I love this time of year; the coffee shop on the school grounds gets gingerbread flavouring, so I can drink gingerbread lattes whenever I want.

"Dad told me last night. He said Henry called to ask if he would be around as he wants to talk business or something."

Why did he tell someone else he was coming home before me? You would think that as his daughter, I would be the first person he told.

"I'm hoping that will mean he's home for a while, maybe even for Christmas. Otherwise, why would he be coming back next week?" I answer, trying to keep the hurt from my voice. I can't believe he spoke to Mr King before his own daughter. Then I remembered I texted him that I was exhausted, so he must have wanted me to rest. That makes more sense than him thinking of me last.

My father's work forces him to live in the States for most of the year. Which means he's away more than he's home. I've suggested several times that we move over there, but he doesn't seem to like the idea of me being out there. He's never let me travel with him; I've never been to the States, and I don't even know what he does other than make money through stocks and shares. Occasionally, he will invest the money he makes into businesses like Danielle's father's casino and racehorses. But otherwise, he spends everything he makes, ensuring that I have everything I could need.

"Wasn't he home last Christmas?" she asks, cutting up her baguette. I shake my head whilst picking at the fruit salad I picked up this morning. I will never understand how others can eat large meals hours before a performance. It makes me feel heavy and fat, distracting me from the dances, so I prefer something light with no carbs.

It's the first of December, so we're in the final month of our Christmas production. This year, we are performing *The Nutcracker*. Usually, we only perform in December, but with the rising costs of everything at the dance school I attend, we have been performing for the last two months, trying to sell as many tickets as possible to raise essential funds.

The whole company is physically and mentally exhausted and cannot wait to finish on Christmas Eve. We then have three weeks off to recover before returning in the new year to prepare for the summer production. We will also have our final exams for our degree in dance.

"Huh," Danielle mutters, catching my attention. "I'm

"sure he was at my parents' Christmas Eve party," she frowns.

"No, he was in the States as something came up at the last minute, and then he couldn't get a flight," I explain. She must be mistaken because he wouldn't lie about being away, especially at Christmas.

Danni starts eating her food as I sit quietly, contemplating what it will be like to have Dad home. I can't remember the last time he was here for Christmas. Being in the States makes it difficult to travel at the best of times, but the holiday season makes it near impossible.

"What's your plans if he doesn't stay for Christmas?" she asks next to me. I shrug and look into my almost empty glass cup.

"Nothing, I guess. I'll just be on my own."

"You can't spend it alone!"

I look up at my friend and see the concern on her face.

"It's fine. It won't be the first time," I smile, hoping she'll drop the subject because, in all honesty, it's far from fine. But I hate the idea of her worrying about me.

It's crazy to think that this woman was a bitch to Jasmine and me just eight months ago. I think it's fair to say she hated us. We stayed out of her way, and she made it her mission to make our lives hell. All that changed when Jasmine was attacked seven months ago. Danielle found her and raised the alarm. Since then, they put the past behind them, and I gradually warmed to her as well.

Six months ago, she proved how good a friend she could be when my drink was spiked during a night out for Jasmine's twenty-first birthday. The night had been amazing until that point. We later discovered my drink had been spiked to ensure Jasmine's bodyguards were preoccupied so she could be kidnapped. The whole experience has brought the three of us closer than ever. The drugs they gave me were strong, and it took me three days to recover completely. Danielle didn't leave my side for the first night until the eldest of my stepbrothers, Travis, turned up and took over my care. Even then, she called numerous times a day and kept me posted with all the updates whilst people searched for Jasmine until she was rescued a few days later.

Danielle and I spent some time with Jasmine afterwards, helping her to heal and come to terms with a few things she learnt during her time with the kidnappers. Since then, we have been inseparable. We do everything together, and it's hard to believe we were anything other than best friends.

"Has Jasmine been picked up?" I ask, looking for a way to change the subject.

Danielle nods whilst finishing her baguette.

"Yeah, Maximus picked her up twenty minutes ago. He is taking her to her therapy session and then bringing her back to get ready for the show."

Poor Jasmine has been having therapy every week for the last five months. The O'Reilly's, her four fiancés, insisted on it after she was taken, not only for the fact she was kidnapped but for the truths she discovered during that time as well. There is nothing those four guys wouldn't do for her, and they have done all they could to give her the safe environment she deserves while she heals.

Jasmine is so lucky to have not one but four men willing to give her everything she needs. There is nothing they wouldn't do for her, and I have to admit I'm jealous of her for that.

I look down at my phone as it vibrates on the table with a text from my boyfriend.

Marshall: I'm on break. Call me if you are free. Xxx

"I'm going to make a call before we get into costume. I'll see you in a bit," I say quickly, grabbing my bag. Danielle l looks up and smiles at me.

"Okay, save me a mirror if you get there first."

Promising I will, I pick up my phone and head towards the courtyard, hoping for some privacy.

As soon as I'm out in the cold winter air, I pull my jacket tighter around me whilst looking for a vacant bench. Sitting down, I pull up my boyfriend's number and look at it momentarily. I promised to call him, and I want to speak to him. But something is holding me back, and I have no idea what.

Marshall is a lovely guy; he's sweet and says he cares for me and all the romantic things a boyfriend should say, but I can't help wondering if he means it. It probably doesn't help that he can be incredibly immature and likes to tell his friends he is with a tall, blonde, skinny ballerina. Sometimes, I feel he is with me because of how I look on his arm rather than who I am. Not that I think I'm anything special because I know I'm not. Especially compared to the likes of Jasmine and Danielle. But I have the typical innocent girl look, which men seem to find attractive. Marshall loves to tell me how jealous his friends are that he is with someone like me. Yet, he never comes to any of my performances to support me or even seem remotely interested in my dancing. Maybe I'm looking too deep into this.

There again, my own father hasn't seen me dance in years, but he will boast to all his friends that I will be the "next big thing", and I know he loves the recordings I send him of the productions. I wish it were easier for him to come and watch them in person. Maybe when he comes back next week, he'll be able to watch one of the shows? Then he could finally watch me like I always wish he would.

My mum was the one who got me into dancing. It was always something we shared. I used to love watching her dance, and I hope I look as graceful as she did. Dad always said she looked like a goddess when she danced, and he was right. We used to watch her together in the makeshift studio she created. She loved it when I watched her practice whilst sitting on my Dad's lap. I loved those times, too. I think that's why my father doesn't watch me dance anymore, as it reminds him too much of my mum.

Miriam Stevenson was a loving and caring woman; everyone who met her instantly liked and loved having her around. There was nothing she wouldn't do for anyone, especially me. In every memory of her, she is smiling, laughing, dancing, or combining all three. My mum became ill and died quickly when I was seven years old. She had a brain tumour, and there was nothing the doctors could do to help her. There were only a few months between her getting diagnosed and dying. I know now that it was a blessing, as she could have suffered for years. But I still miss her daily, and I know my dad does, too.

Around that time, my father started working away more, and I saw less and less of him. It's not like he neglects me. He ensures I have the best of everything; I want for nothing, and I get to live in a big house without paying any bills. I attend the best dance school in the UK and have wonderful friends whom I would do anything for. But even though I have so much, I miss my parents. When Mum died, a part of Dad died with her, and I don't think he will ever get that part back. He was left heartbroken by her death, and I thought he would never recover. Then, five years ago, he announced he was getting married to a woman he met through work.

Linda Donavon is a widow whose husband was killed in

a car accident, leaving her with their three sons: Travis, Ryan and Ethan. They are all quite a bit older than me. Travis is ten years older at thirty-one. Ryan is seven years older, and Ethan is five. I only met them once before the wedding.

I get along with my stepmother; she seems like she loves my father, but they aren't home enough for me to build an actual relationship with her. I am probably closer to her sons than I will ever be with her. I don't hear from them all the time, and I can go weeks before Ryan or Ethan message. Travis has been checking up on me more since my drink was spiked, but I'm sure he only does that because my father would have asked him to keep an eye on me. The Donavon brothers spend the odd weekend here and there at my house, but even then, they seem to go about doing their own thing. I wish sometimes we were closer, and then maybe they would visit a bit more often. I like it when they are around. They are fun, and we always have a laugh. It's nice not being the only person in that big house. I never admit it out loud, but it can sometimes get lonely.

I take a deep breath and look at my phone again. I have ten minutes before I have to start getting ready for the show, so I might as well do something during that time. I tap on the screen and hold the phone to my ear. Hoping to still catch Marshall on his break.

Three Stepbrothers Save Christmas:
Chapter Two

VERITY

Exhausted and aching, I make the drive home. I am looking forward to having some company tonight, as Marshall messaged to say he is on his way around.

The performance went well, as it always does. No one would dare to mess up; otherwise, Mrs Florence would have us all back at the studio at the crack of dawn for extra rehearsals. No one wants that this late in the year; we are all exhausted as it is.

As I pull up in front of the house, I notice a car in the driveway and lights on inside the house. My body comes alive with excitement as I park next to the strange car and grab my keys before jumping out. Rushing to the front door, I unlock it with shaking hands, hopping from one foot to the other, desperate to get inside as quickly as possible. There's only one person it could be, and I can't believe he tricked me by saying he would be home next week.

"Dad!" I slam the door shut behind me. I listen out for any noise and hear something from the kitchen. Rushing forward, almost tripping over my own feet, I race to where I know he must be.

"Daddy, you're home!" I call excitedly, only to come to a screeching stop.

"Well, I can be your daddy if you want me to be, Baby girl." Ethan, the younger of my stepbrothers, grins at me as he stands at the counter, making himself a sandwich. I drop my bag on the floor as my heart breaks a little.

"I thought you were someone else," I murmur, trying to hide my disappointment but failing miserably as I grab a bottle of water from the fridge behind him.

"I'm sorry to disappoint," he replies, looking over his shoulder as I turn to face him. "Am I not even going to get a hello?" he asks with one arched brow. I smile slightly as I step beside him to kiss his cheek.

"Hello, Ethan."

"That's more like it," he winks before returning to his sandwich. "I filled the fridge for you, by the way. There was nothing in there." I can hear the accusation in his tone.

"Thanks, I've been eating out most of the time cause of the shows. I was going to go shopping tomorrow," I lie, trying to ignore how he's watching me. I wait for him to call me out but relax when he hums deep in his throat.

"How come you're here? Have I missed something?" I ask, walking around the other side of the counter he's standing over to build his chicken salad sandwich.

"Mum called last night saying they would be home next week and wanted to see us all. I have some potential clients in this area, so I thought I'd come early and kill two birds with one stone."

It's not the first time one of them has come to stay for business reasons. Ethan and Ryan are personal trainers with a high price tag, meaning all their clients are all super rich.

They do online sessions as well as one-to-one sessions. They are amazing at the job, and both helped me recover from a dancing injury a couple of years ago. They are both fully trained PTs and physios, specialising in sports injuries.

"So, the others aren't with you?" I ask, reaching over and grabbing a slice of the tomato he's cutting. He slaps my hand away and sighs before passing me the other slice as I smile sweetly at him. Ethan always gives me what I want, not that I ask for much. But if I ever do, he gives in quicker than I can blink.

"They'll be here in a couple of days; they are taking care of a few things first." He cuts into his sandwich while grinning at me. "So, sorry, you're stuck with just me for the time being."

I pick up my bag and sigh dramatically.

"Well, don't bug me, and I won't bug you," I say, walking out of the kitchen smiling.

"But, what if I want to bug you?"

"Tough!" I laugh. "I have someone coming over, don't tell anyone, especially our parents!" I call out nervously, rushing up the stairs to my room. I hear Ethan asking who's coming over, but don't bother answering. He will know soon enough as he should be here any minute.

I don't think any of the guys have met a boyfriend before, and now that I know Ethan is here, I'm not sure how I feel about him coming over. My love life is something I keep very quiet, and even the girls haven't met him. It's not that I'm ashamed of him or that he isn't attractive because he is. But my father has always told me to stay away from guys, and I find it easier to hide it from him if no one else knows either. I might be twenty-one, but I still want to ensure I don't upset my dad. He does so much for me; the least I can do is do as he asks, most of the time.

Dropping my bag at the bottom of my bed, I shrug off my jacket and place it on the chair. I'd been so excited when I thought Dad was home. As happy as I am to see Ethan, it's not the same. I miss my dad and having him around. When he's home, everything seems a little better with the world. Even if he is only back for a few days, those days mean the world to me.

I rush into my bathroom to brush my teeth and check my make-up. It's been a long day, and the performance tonight felt like it was dragging. I think we are all in desperate need of a break. Thankfully, I have tomorrow night off before the last three weeks of performances start. Marshall is staying tonight and tomorrow after we go out for a meal at his favourite restaurant. I know I should probably use the night off to rest, but it's Christmas, and it's not like I have anything else to do with my time.

Walking back into my room, I grab my phone from my bag and check the time stamp on Marshall's last message. I realise he should be here any moment as headlights light up my bedroom window. Throwing my phone onto the bed, I rush down the stairs, eager to get to the door before Ethan. I'm just getting to the bottom step when he comes out of the kitchen at the exact moment Marshall knocks on the door.

"Who's that?" he asks as I rush past him to open the door.

"Hi!" I call a little too loud as I throw my arms around Marshall. He chuckles to himself whilst hugging me back.

"Anyone would think you'd missed me," he says as I take his hand, leading him into the house.

"I have," I reply, smiling before turning to see Ethan at the bottom of the stairs, frowning at us. "Can we help you?" I ask as Marshall comes to an abrupt stop beside me.

"Oh, hi," he says nervously, looking at my stepbrother.

"Who's this?" Ethan asks, staring at him.

"Marshall. I told you not to bug me when I have company," I point out as I go to pull Marshall up the stairs, but Ethan blocks our way.

"Are you the boyfriend or gay best friend?" Ethan asks, staring at him.

"Boyfriend. And you are?" he asks, standing tall beside me. For crying out loud, are they going to get their cocks out and compare sizes too? There again, if it came to a fight, I know Ethan would win. He has a lot more muscle mass than Marshall, who is relatively thin in compassion.

"The one who will break your legs if you hurt my … stepsister."

"Okay, enough," I snap, stepping between them. "Ethan, move," I order, pushing him out of the way.

"Actually, Ver, I can't stay for long. I'm heading to Toms. Do you want to come?"

I turn to Marshall, frowning. He knows I don't like going to his friends.

"His parents are away, and we are going round in a bit for a gaming session."

Ethan snorts behind me before trying to disguise it with a cough. Man, I want to kick him right now. Going around to his mates while they all play on their game consoles is not how I want to spend my evening. He knows this and is probably only mentioning it now, knowing I will say no.

"It's fine; why don't you go, and I can see you tomorrow." I can feel Ethan's presence behind me; I can almost see the stupid smirk he has on his face.

"Are you sure? I promised we could chill out tonight," Marshall starts. I hear Ethan cough as he walks away from us and back into the kitchen.

"It's fine; you go and enjoy time with your mates," I smile as I lead him back towards the door. He turns around and wraps an arm around my waist. "I love you," I whisper, smiling up at him.

"You're the best," he smiles before kissing me and turning around to almost run to his car. I wave as he drives off and close the door, letting out a deep sigh.

"What? No, I love you?"

I spin and glare at Ethan.

"We did say it!" I snap. One side of Ethan's mouth lifts as he smirks at me.

"No, you did, he didn't. I was listening in from the kitchen."

I roll my eyes and head towards the stairs, planning on getting as far away from him as possible.

"F.Y.I, you could do better." He turns and walks into the lounge as I storm towards my room.

What does he know? "*You could do better*," please! Marshall is loving and caring, and he does love me; I know he does. Just because he didn't say it that one time doesn't mean he doesn't care about me.

I walk into my room and slam the door behind me. Well, there goes my plans for the evening. It looks like I won't be getting what I hoped for, which is why I was so eager to get Marshall upstairs to my room. The truth is I love the feeling you get after a good orgasm. It's something I crave to the point I could probably say I'm slightly addicted.

People would never believe me if I told them. They all see me as the shy, quiet woman who probably doesn't even have sex. But it's a side of me no one can ever know about. It can be an issue because I've noticed if I go too long without one, I can get moody, and then people start asking questions I don't want to answer. To prevent this, I need to orgasm almost daily; otherwise, I get cranky and irritable, making it a struggle to concentrate when dancing. I usually handle it by getting myself off in the shower most of the time. But tonight, I needed more and had hoped Marshall could relieve some of my built-up tension. Not that he's amazing at the actual sex part; I rarely get off unless I'm on top. But he is good at foreplay, and if I give him a little help, I can usually get off. But I guess that's not going to happen tonight.

I realised about a year ago, when I was with my ex, that my constant mood swings and concentration issues were always better after we had a good night of sex. He is the only person I ever talked to about this, and he left me because I was too high maintenance. Since then, I have dealt with the issue on my own, having not found anyone who makes me feel the way he did during sex. I figured all I could do was try to make the most of a bad situation.

Looking at my drawer where my selection of sex toys is hidden, including my favourite vibrator, I consider getting it out, only to remember I have a houseguest whose bedroom is next to mine.

I open my door quietly and listen, trying to gauge where Ethan is. I can hear the TV in the lounge in the distance and know if he has a film on, he'll be down there for a while. Closing my door with a smile, I head to my bed whilst stripping. I can feel the aching between my legs building as I climb under the covers and pull my toy and lube from the drawer. I won't need the lube, but it will add to the pleasure as it tingles, meaning I come quicker than I do without it. Not that it will take me long tonight. I have been on edge all day.

I get myself comfortable in bed; I squeeze a little lube onto my fingers and rub it over my clit, it takes a second to start working, but when it does, I feel my eyes rolling into the back of my head. I love this lube; it's cooling and feels the best of the many I have tried.

I lie back on my pillow and just enjoy the feeling of the lube and my fingers around my clit. It doesn't take long to have a small orgasm, but as I predicted, it isn't enough. I pull out my vibrator and listen out one last time for any sign that Ethan has come upstairs before turning it on to the lowest setting and teasing my entrance with it. I bite my lip as the vibrations course through me. I run it up and down between my lips from my entrance to my slightly sensitive clit and back again. Slowly, I push the vibrator inside and sigh as it fills me. This is what I needed, to be filled to the point it nearly hurts. I love the whole pain-with-pleasure element. I long to find someone who will grab my hair, slap my ass, and choke me. I want to be fucked hard by someone, as well as made love to. But it's hard to attract the kind of men I want when you are as quiet as me, and everyone expects you to be the good little ballerina.

I start moving the vibrator in and out of me, starting slow until I know I have to go harder. With one hand on the vibrator and the other rubbing my clit I pick up speed. It feels so good; why can't I find a guy to make me feel this way?

"Ahh god," I gasp loudly before quickly reminding myself I'm meant to be quiet. I stop for the briefest second, and when I don't hear anything, I carry on. I know I need to hurry up, so I concentrate purely on the sensation of the vibrator hitting every spot within me. As I start rubbing my clit, I feel myself heading quickly to that sensation I am so desperate to feel.

As my body tenses and the pleasure builds, nothing else matters but this feeling right here. God, I love sex, but when you can give yourself the most perfect orgasm, hitting just the right spots, who needs a man?

I cum loudly and have to slam my hand over my mouth as my release vibrates through my whole body. My pussy clamps around the vibrator, and I swear it nearly sucks it completely inside of me. I'm breathing heavily and know that if Ethan walks past my door right now, he will hear me, but I'm too relaxed to care.

Removing my vibrator, I lie still in the after-orgasm glow and enjoy the content and satisfied feeling that overcomes me. This is what I love, this feeling of being so satisfied I could curl up and sleep.

I reach for the tissues I keep in my top drawer and clean myself up before dropping them into the bin beside my bed to throw away in the morning.

With everything hidden away, I curl on my side and close my eyes, ready for a half-decent sleep. Pushing all my insecurities and worries to the back of my mind as I do every night. Tomorrow is another day, and I want to start it feeling refreshed.

Grab your copy...
vinci-books.com/Threestepbrothers

About the Author

D.E. Bartley lives in Wales, UK, with her husband, three feral boys, four cats, and a budgie.

To say her home is a madhouse would be an understatement, but she wouldn't have it any other way.

When she isn't running around after her tribe or driving her husband up the wall, she can be found reading and hoarding books like a dragon.

Nothing is as important to her as time with her family, and she loves her trips home to Cornwall with them more than anything in the world. What could possibly compare to sitting on a Cornish beach, with a glass of Cornish gin in one hand and an authentic Cornish pasty in the other, while the monsters, I mean children, play and bodyboard in the sea?

Absolutely nothing.

Acknowledgments

I was starting to think this book was never going to happen!

Over the last few months, life has gotten in the way, and I was devastated when I had to cancel the release. Nothing was going to plan, and I wasn't going to give only half of Chelsea, Luna and the guys' story. Chelsea and Luna deserved to have their happily ever after, and I was determined to give it to them.

Thank you to Karen, who once again helped me and encouraged me when I was struggling to write this book. I know I say it each and every time, but this book, like the others, wouldn't be here without you. I hate that you live in another country because I would give anything to thank you in person and give you the biggest hug.

Of course, I have to point out that my husband and kids have been amazing and have given me all the love and support I needed when working on this book. There were many tears, and each time they picked me up and reminded me that I do love writing and I do love my characters, even when they don't do what I want them to do. They were, of course, right, and I really do love this book and writing.

But most importantly, I want to thank you guys, the readers. None of this would be possible without you all, and I hope you know I mean that from the bottom of my heart. Because of the love you guys have shown the O'Reilly series, I have been able to cut down my night shifts at work and now only work three. This was something I never dreamt I would be able to do. Never in my wildest dreams did I think I would be able to make enough money from my writing to cut down my hours at work, but I have, and again it's all thanks to you guys.

Since the release of books one and two of this series, I have been sent so many wonderful messages from readers, and I try to reply to them all. You guys all rock, and I love hearing how much you love the O'Reillys. I just hope you love these SEALs just as much.

There really isn't much left to say other than thank you from the bottom of my heart, and I promise there is plenty more to come very soon!

Thank you all!!

xxx